The
Rediscovered
Annals
of
Sherlock
Holmes

The
Rediscovered
Annals
of
Sherlock
Holmes

Previously Uncollected Accounts of
The Heroes of Baker Street

Written by
Terry Golledge

Curated by
Niel Golledge

Edited by
David Marcum

978-1-80424-077-9   Hardcover
978-1-80424-078-6   Paperback
978-1-80424-079-3   AUK ePub
978-1-80424-080-9   AUK PDF

Published in the UK by
MX Publishing
335 Princess Park Manor, Royal Drive,
London, N11 3GX
www.mxpublishing.co.uk

Editor Foreword ©2022 by David Marcum
David Marcum can be reached at:
thepapersofsherlockholmes@gmail.com

Cover design by Brian Belanger
www.belangerbooks.com and *www.redbubble.com/people/zhahadun*

COVER PAINTING: *St. Pauls and Ludgate Hill, c.1887* - William Logsdail

CONTENTS

Foreword

Adventures

The following stories previously appeared
in these volumes of

The MX Book of New Sherlock Holmes Stories – 2022 Annual:

Part XXXI – (1875-1887)

"The Case of the Woman at Margate"
"The Grosvenor Square Furniture Van"

Part XXXII – (1888-1895)

"The Merton Fiends" (under the title "The Merton Friends")
"The Addleton Tragedy"

Part XXXIII – (1896-1919)

"The Crown of Light"
"The Adventure of the Silk Scarf"

Editor's Foreword:
Rediscovered Treasures
by David Marcum

As I've noted elsewhere, I discovered Sherlock Holmes in 1975, when I was ten years old. Of course, I was aware of this universally known figure before that, but I can be specific as to when I actually *discovered* Holmes – reading my first Holmes adventure, and owning my first Holmes book.

Not long after, I discovered those post-Canonical adventures known as *pastiches* – before I'd even found and read all of The Canon. Nicholas Meyer created the new Golden Age of Holmes with his 1974 novel, *The Seven-Per-Cent Solution*, and I was right there, enjoying every bit of it as it grew. The fire that Nick lit had more gasoline poured upon it the following year with his film version of his book, and that fire has only grown bigger in the nearly fifty years since.

After reading through the pitifully few sixty stories of the original Canon a few times, I realized that it simply wasn't enough. Those very few recollections of limited pieces of Holmes and Watson's lives only provided the barest hint of The Great Holmes Tapestry. I knew that there must be more.

Over the years, I could only find a few new Holmes adventures each year, usually by accident. There was no internet then, so I could only discover new Holmes adventures when I ran across one in a bookstore, or perhaps on a library shelf. But as I grew older, I was able to winkle out more and more – one seemed to lead to another, and eventually I've managed to collect almost every traditional Canonical pastiche that's been written. (My wife is an amazing and tolerant person, and I give thanks for her every day.)

I've collected, read, and chronologicized literally thousands of Canonical Holmes pastiches since the mid-1970's in the form of books, short stories, radio and television episodes, movies and scripts, comics, fan fiction, and unpublished manuscripts, but I'll never have all of them, because some are so rare that it just isn't worth the cost to obtain them, and others are hidden away, known only to a few people – or maybe even just one.

I've now personally written and published nearly one-hundred Holmes pastiche of my own, but when I wrote my first ones, back in 2008 while laid off from an engineering job, I never intended that they would be seen by anyone else. It was simply an exercise to see if I could do it,

1

and because I wanted to contribute in a small way to that bigger part of the Holmes world that I admired so much – *pastiches*. But gradually I had the itch to show them to someone, and then another person, and the feedback was positive, leading to the idea that maybe they should be published after all. It was a slippery sublime slope, and one of the best life-changing decisions that I ever made.

There are other people out there like I was – they started writing Holmes pastiches just to be a part of *The Great Holmes Tapestry* – even if nobody knew it but themselves. (Those are the pastiches that I don't know about and can't collect and read.) Some of these authors never intended to share their efforts, and they still haven't. Others eventually went ahead and cracked open the door and saw their stories published. It's an addiction, as they know, and writing one leads to writing more.

Terry Golledge wrote a number of Holmes adventures in the 1980's and 1990's before his death, and sadly they remained unknown for too long – until now, when they're finally being shared with the world.

In early 2022, I received an email from Niel Golledge, Terry's son, with a sample story, "The Addleton Tragedy". Terry had written it, along with nine others, before his death, but they were never published. Niel had recently approached another editor about them, but that chap felt that it would be too much work to convert and prepare the original typewritten manuscripts for modern publication. That was his massive mistake, for it was absolutely worth the extra editorial work, as Terry Golledge's stories are both wonderful and Watsonian.

Niel graciously agreed to let me edit the entire set, and then to initially include six of them in the Spring 2022 volumes of *The MX Book of New Sherlock Holmes Stories – 2022 Annual (Parts XXXI, XXXII, and XXXIII)*. The royalties from this series go to support the Undershaw school for special needs students at Undershaw, located in Hindhead, England, one of Sir Arthur Conan Doyle's former homes. The MX anthologies were created in 2015 to present traditional Canonical Holmes adventures set in the correct period, and with Holmes and Watson portrayed as the heroes they were, rather than how they were being shown more and more in various contemporary books and television programs.

Initially, the MX anthologies were supposed to be a one-time project, but they were so popular that they kept going, and we're now at 33 volumes – with more in preparation! They contain over 750 traditional Canonical pastiches from over 200 contributors worldwide. By June 2022, the books have raised over $100,000 for the school – that's *One-Hundred-Thousand Dollars!!!* – and I'm told by the school that of even more importance is how the books have made the world aware of the school.

Niel Golledge generously agreed to allow the royalties from the six stories included in the Spring 2022 MX Anthologies to be donated to Undershaw, and he's also doing the same with the royalties from this volume, containing all of his father's Holmes pastiches.

Terry Golledge (according to his son Niel) had a life-long love of all things Conan Doyle, and in particular Sherlock Holmes. This was obviously inspired by the fact that his mother worked as a governess for Sir Arthur Conan Doyle for several years in the early Twentieth Century when he lived in Windlesham, Crowborough in Sussex. She married Terry's father after leaving Sir Arthur's employment around 1918.

Terry was born in 1920 in the East End of London, and left school at fourteen, like so many back then. In 1939, he joined the army in the fight against the Germans in World War II. He left the Army in 1945 at the war's end, residing in Hastings. There he met his wife, and his life was a mish-mash of careers, including mining and bus and lorry driving. He owned a couple of book shops, selling them in the 1960's. He then worked for the Post office, (later to become British Telecom, equivalent to AT&T), ending his working life there as a training instructor before his retirement.

In the 1980's and 1990's, Terry Golledge wrote these Holmes stories as a retirement project and he passed away in 1996.

As mentioned above, I am always on the lookout for more Holmes pastiches. Being the editor of the MX Anthologies, as well as quite a few other Holmes anthologies, has allowed me to meet – in person and by email – hundreds of amazing Sherlockians and writers. It has also put me in the position where my love and support of Sherlockian pastiche is well known, and therefore I receive over two-hundred new pastiches every year. Occasionally I also receive additional unexpected treasures, such as the stories in this collection.

Terry Golledge's stories perfectly capture Watson's voice and Holmes's personality and methods. I am thrilled that Niel Golledge reached out to me, and then trusted me to edit them, and that he is generous enough to allow the book's royalties to be donated to Undershaw.

I know that there are other caches of unknown Holmes pastiches out there – perhaps by authors who passed away before sharing them, or written by living authors who just create for themselves – and I hope that by seeing these, other treasures will be nudged into the light.

In the meantime, we have these ten amazing stories, thanks to Terry Golledge who wrote them, and Niel Golledge who curated them and then sent them into an appreciative world. I know that you'll enjoy them as much as I have, with both joy and a tinge of sadness because there won't be any more from such a talented Sherlockian author.

David Marcum
July 20th, 2022

The
Rediscovered
Annals
of
Sherlock
Holmes

Terry Golledge
(1920-1996)

7

A Recollection . . . .

*A*s the film drew to its improbable conclusion, the elderly man pulled *himself from his chair to switch off the television set. For several seconds he stared at the blank screen with an expression of angry distaste before turning away impatiently.*

"Why in Heaven's name is Dr. Watson always portrayed as some kind of half-witted buffoon?" he muttered. "If only they had known him as he really was."

He paused irresolutely. Then, going through to the bedroom, he opened a wardrobe and from the floor took a worn and scuffed leather case which he laid reverently on the table. He stroked the scratched leather with affection and smiled as his eye lit on the tarnished brass plate with the initials V.H. *engraved thereon.*

Opening the case to reveal the neat bundles of paper within, he picked up the topmost envelope and tapped it against the palm of his hand, as if remembering. Presently he extracted the single sheet of paper it contained and allowed his eyes to scan it lovingly, although he knew it by heart. Dated July, 1956, it was brief and to the point:

My dear Henry,

As my only child, and indeed my only relative, you will naturally inherit what little I may leave on my death, but this old case and its contents may well prove to be the most valuable of my possessions, perhaps with the passing years even more so than either of us can envisage. I am bound not to make any of the material public during the lifetime of any of the protagonists, which virtually means also my own lifetime, as I know for a fact that the central figure still lives, although of a very great age. The letters enclosed with the other papers explain all and I leave you to make what you will of the matter.

Your affectionate father,
John H. Hunter

The man returned the sheet to the envelope, placing it back in the case and picking up another. This showed signs of much greater age, as indeed the stamp and postmark confirmed. It bore the date of May 12th,

9

1894 and was addressed in a tight angular hand to Miss Violet Hunter, Fiveways School, Walsall, Staffs. The letter inside gave evidence of being composed in circumstances of extreme agitation, this being borne out by the content.

My Dear Miss Hunter, *[it began]*

It is with a sense of shame and self-disgust that I pen these lines to you, not to excuse my conduct, but in the hope that you will understand how it was I came to act in such an indescribably caddish manner. It must appear that I callously abandoned you in a cold-blooded and cynical way, but I beg you to read on and find it in your heart to believe that I had no inkling of the shame and humiliation that I had inflicted on you.

After our brief but idyllic interlude fallowing the strange affair which I chronicled under the title of "The Copper Beeches", I returned to my lodgings in Baker Street and was willy-nilly swept up in a flurry of activity with my friend and colleague Mr. Sherlock Holmes. I wrote to you on three occasions, the first two eliciting no response, the third missive being returned to me marked *"Address Unknown"*. Assuming that your interest in me had waned, I made no further advances, and as time passed, the memory of our brief liaison became less painful to bear. It was not until the reappearance last month of my friend after his reputed death that I became aware of the wrong I had done you. When we were in Birmingham on the matter of Mr. Hall Pycroft some five years ago, Holmes inadvertently heard of your situation, but in view of my marriage shortly before, he decided to keep his own counsel. It was on his return from the grave last month that he saw fit to put me in possession of the fact that you had borne a child of whom I was the father,

It was a bolt from the blue and my first impulse was to come to you in order to right the terrible wrong I had wrought. Holmes, wise as he is, dissuaded me from this course which might cause you embarrassment, advising me to write to you first to discover you feelings in the matter.

Whatever you thought of my conduct, please accept that I did not desert you heartlessly. A word would have brought me to your side, and if I can now make amends by offering you marriage, I will be proud and honoured by your

10

acceptance. I am free of attachments, having been a widower for more than two years, and I offer you my complete and utter devotion. I remain,

Yours humbly,
John H. Watson

Shaking his head the man replaced this letter and taking out another, he read on.

My Dear Dr. Watson,

Thank you for your letter and the sentiments expressed therein. I knew through Mr. Holmes that you were ignorant of my condition and I hold no animosity towards you, as I bear at least as much responsibility as you do. I must decline your honourable offer of restitution, conscious as I am of the generous gesture that is typical of the gentleman that you are.

I feel it would not be in the boy's best interest to make him aware of the circumstances. However, if, when he attains a more mature age, should you wish to meet him, I will place no obstacle in your way. My solicitor is instructed to inform you in the event of my death, but otherwise I think it best if we have no future communication.

Yours Sincerely,
Violet Hunter

"That must have shaken the old boy," the man muttered to himself as he took the final letter from the battered case. It was dated July 1908 and ran:

My Dear John,

It is with deep sorrow that I learn of the death of your esteemed mother at such a tragically early age. To my dismay, I received no word of this unhappy event until the funeral had taken place, so please do not attribute my defection as indifference on my part. I have been on an extended visit to my old friend and colleague Mr. Sherlock Holmes who is now in retirement in Sussex.

11

In the seven years since you were made aware of our relationship, I like to think we have become firm friends, and it is a source of regret that your mother would never consent to meeting me. Should you at any time be in need of assistance, financial or whatever, please do not hesitate to approach me. Although I am by no means a wealthy man, what I have is at your disposal, but meanwhile I enclose something that has little value in itself, but may in time be an interesting addition to what is known of the greatest and wisest man it has been my privilege to call friend.

These are the accounts of several cases in which I was associated with Sherlock Holmes, and for obvious reasons there is an embargo on their publication for many years to come. Cherish them well, and if at any time you wish to bring a little cheer into the life of a sinful old man, you know where to find me.

I Remain,
Your Loving Father,
John H. Watson

Dr. Watson's grandson laid this last letter aside to pick up the remaining item in the case, a folder of manuscripts which he carried over to the chair in the living room. For several minutes he sat with it on his knee, a far-away look in his still-sharp eyes, reflecting that although the doctor's self-deprecatory style may have created an impression of naive obtuseness, it was unthinkable that Sherlock Holmes would have suffered for so many years the kind of dim-wit so often portrayed on film and television. Henry Hunter recalled that as a very young boy he had been taken on a visit to the old man, shortly before his death in 1929. Across the years, he could still remember the kindly eyes and slow firm voice of the man who, for almost fifty years, had been privy to the workings of one of the most brilliant minds of his age.

He opened the folder to look once more on the familiar handwriting of a century ago, again feeling a nostalgia for a world he had never known. A world of gas-light and horse-drawn carriages when the British Empire spread over a quarter of the earth's surface, and seemed likely to endure as long as time itself.

Henry Hunter began to read, and his mind became part of that bygone age as he immersed himself in the atmosphere evoked by the out-moded phrases and less abrupt manners of the England of Sherlock Holmes . . . .

The Pihdarus Papers

I took the stairs of our rooms in Baker Street two at a time and threw my Gladstone bag into a corner of the sitting room. Sherlock Holmes was sitting with the cold remains of a belated breakfast, the pages of the morning papers strewn in careless confusion beside his chair and a look of boredom on his hawk-like face. As I entered he gave me a sardonic look, accompanied by a twitch of the lips.

"Ah, the traveller returns!" he observed. "I trust your sojourn in the Midlands was a pleasant one?"

"Holmes!" I cried. "You have been spying on me!"

"Really, Watson, that is most unkind of you. I must confess to a certain concern when three weeks elapsed with no word from you, but you are not accountable to me for your actions."

"How did you know I had been in the Midlands?" I demanded.

"I had no idea where you were until you bounced – yes, positively bounced – into the room not two minutes ago. Look out of the window," he went on before I could speak. "The sun is shining, as is its duty in mid-April, and has done so unfailingly over most of the country these ten days past. Yet I read in the morning papers that on yesterday evening the counties of Warwickshire and Staffordshire suffered a freak storm of tropical intensity. The mud splashes on your boots and trouser-legs are from soil common to the Birmingham area, so I deduce that you travelled from that city by the early milk train, and from the ebullience of your entry, it follows that your absence was a source of pleasure and gratification to you. Ah, your face confirms my reasoning."

"As usual, you are quite correct, and as I made such an early start, I shall be obliged if you will have Mrs. Hudson prepare breakfast while I have a wash."

I picked up my bag, but before going up to my room, I thought to give Holmes another chance to exercise his deductive powers.

"Here, see what you make of this." I laid a charred and battered brier on the table. "I found it on our doorstep as I came in." When I rejoined him, Mrs. Hudson was tut-tutting as she set about reducing the chaos of the table and placing a large plate of ham and eggs out for me, the aroma of which served further to whet my already-sharp appetite. I fell to with alacrity, stealing the occasional glance at Holmes, who had retired to a chair by the window to examine the trophy with which I had presented him.

13

He peered at it closely through his lens, turning it this way and that before raising to his nose. Then he removed the stem to give it a separate scrutiny.

"You say this was lying on our doorstep?" he asked as I mopped the last vestiges from my plate with a piece of bread.

"Yes, as if it had been dropped by a caller or else some lounger who had chosen our doorway for his loitering. What do you make of it?"

"Very little," he replied, shrugging his thin shoulders, "It belonged to a young to middle-aged man in good health who in recent years has gained some affluence, but still holds to the tastes of his less-prosperous days."

He fell silent and, although I knew he was teasing me to prompt him, I ignored him. As I poured my second cup of tea, I looked up and found him eying me with amusement.

"Come, Holmes," I chaffed. "Surely you can say more than that. Was he right or left-handed, and what colour were his boots?"

"Oh, right-handed, of course, but not being clairvoyant, his boots must remain his secret."

"And the rest of it?" My curiosity got the better of me.

He smiled thinly and held up the subject of discussion.

"Observe, my dear Doctor, the bowl of the pipe is of some age and a cheap reject. See where the blemishes have been filled with some kind of putty? The thing would have cost coppers rather than shillings, yet the mounting is hall-marked silver and the stem of the finest amber and has been carefully machined to make it a perfect fit. It therefore follows that the pipe was originally purchased when he was in straitened circumstances, but is held in so much affection as to justify such expensive repairs. How often it was done I cannot say, but the last time was probably within seven days."

I nodded to indicate that I followed his reasoning and he continued:

"That he is young to middle-aged is likely, as the indentations already on the stem point to a strong jaw and a near-perfect set of teeth. The dottle is a Virginia shag similar to that favoured by myself, which leads me to suppose him faithful to the tastes of his youth."

He laid the pipe down as though dismissing the matter and gazed pensively out of the window.

"Of course," I put in, not to be outdone, "that he is right-handed is shown by the charring on the right of the bowl where he held a match to it, but how far your reading is correct we shall never know."

"You think not?" He was leaning forward to peer out of the window, his former attitude of lethargy gone. "We shall see."

The words had scarcely passed his lips before the jangle of the doorbell came faintly from below, followed by the sound of Mrs. Hudson's voice as she ascended the stairs.

"A gentleman to see Mr. Holmes," she announced on my answering her knock.

"Send him in," Holmes called from behind me.

I stood back to let the caller enter. He was a well-set individual of some thirty-five years, soberly attired, and with a frank open countenance. Holmes waved him to the basket chair and took his place facing him, his long legs stretched out across the rug.

"Now, sir," said Holmes encouragingly, "how may I be of assistance?"

"Perhaps you cannot, Mr. Holmes," our visitor replied. "But if not you, then to whom can I turn?"

My friend remained silent and began to fill his pipe which he drew from the pocket of the old blue dressing-gown he was still wearing, then offered the jar across.

"Are you a pipe smoker, Mr. – ?" He raised an eyebrow.

"I'm sorry, Mr. Holmes. Ellis is my name, Hubert Ellis, and yes, I do favour a pipe."

"Then if your taste runs to my particular brand please take some, or if you prefer Dr. Watson's Arcadia Mixture he will not begrudge you."

"I shall accept yours if I may. It looks very similar to my usual choice."

Ellis took out a shiny new brier which he looked at with no great pleasure as he reached out for the jar. Instead of handing it over, Holmes put out his hand and removed the pipe from the other's astonished grasp.

"Perhaps, Mr Ellis, you would rather have your old friend back. Ah, I see that you would. It lies on the table behind you, and you may thank the good Doctor for its retrieval."

"Good Heavens, sir!" cried our visitor as he twisted round, "I never thought to see my old faithful again!" He picked it up and caressed it lovingly. "It was given to me by my late wife in the early days of our courtship when I was struggling to find the wherewithal to marry. If she had but been spared to enjoy my present prosperity, how happy we would have been." He looked gratefully at me. "I owe you a great debt, Doctor. How came you to find it? How did Mr. Holmes know it to be mine?"

"I found it on our step when I came in about an hour ago," I said. "I assume you called earlier and dropped it then. As for Mr. Holmes knowing it to be yours – well, he has his methods."

We soon settled down to our pipes, and Holmes eyed our client sharply.

15

"Now, Mr. Ellis," he prompted, "pray lay your problem before me, for it cannot have been a missing pipe that sent you up our stairs, however attached you may be to it."

"Indeed, sir, it is of more moment than that," began Hubert Ellis. "I am a dealer in second-hand furniture. Not the rickety old stuff found in junk shops, but good quality period pieces that have survived the years and have received loving care and attention. Do not think I look down on the junk men, for I am not ashamed to admit that I started in that way myself, However, I have a love of beautiful things and took a deal of trouble to learn the basics of cabinet-making and joinery, and I have some small repute as a restorer of antique furniture.

"Last week, I attended an auction at Peckham where the only item to take my fancy was an exquisite Georgian bureau or writing desk. It was from the effects of a widow who was disposing of her furniture after the recent death of her husband, one Edwin Clarke, and it was so out of character with the other articles that it was hard to believe it part of the same menage. My first modest bid went unchallenged and I congratulated myself on acquiring such a fine specimen. Once it was in my workshop, I spent some time in inspecting the piece in order to determine what might be needed in the way of restoration. As is my wont, I took internal and external measurements and quickly found a discrepancy that hinted at the possibility of a concealed or secret compartment, a thing of which I have often read but never had the fortune to find.

"It took me about twenty minutes to locate a catch that released a small compartment, some six-inches-square and two-inches-deep, and in this hiding place was a small packet wrapped in American cloth. Imagine my elation, gentlemen, as I speculated on what mysteries were about to be revealed, but on opening the package I found it to contain nothing but a half-dozen letters which at first sight appeared to be of recent origin." Ellis paused to relight his pipe while I, sitting unobtrusively behind him, endeavoured to keep pace with his narrative, my pencil flying over the pages of my notebook.

"I had to look at them, of course," our visitor resumed, "I hoped I might obtain some clue as to the owner or, if not that, at least find if they were important." He looked at us with hot, angry eyes. "Gentlemen," he went on fiercely, "I like to think I am broad-minded and I am certainly no prude, but on reading those letters I felt physically sick that such obscenity could be written to a man by one of the so-called fair sex. Such they undoubtedly had been, although the phrasing clearly showed it to be a two-way traffic and each missive answered another obviously couched in a like vein."

He stopped to mop his forehead with a hand that trembled with indignation and outrage while we waited for him to recover.

"I rewrapped them," he continued, "determined to destroy them at the first opportunity, but other matters took precedence and I forgot them. Then, last Friday afternoon, I had a caller at my shop in New Cross, a man who exhibited signs of considerable agitation.

"'Mr. Ellis?' says he, to which I answered I was. 'I understand that on Wednesday you bought a desk at the sale of Edwin Clarke's effects.'

"'Why, yes,' I said. 'It stands in my workshop this very minute waiting attention.'

"Now I am not a devious man, Mr. Holmes, but I felt no urge to confide the results of my examination to this person, but he seemed immensely relieved at my answer and assumed a confidential manner. 'Well, Mr. Ellis,' he said, 'Ned Clarke was my brother-in-law and I'd like to have it for old times' sake. You'll not be against selling it to me as it is and making a handsome profit into the bargain? I'll give you half-again what you paid for it, and a bit more for your trouble, if I can have it right away.'

"This I considered, weighing the advantages of an immediate sale against the amount of work entailed before I could hope for a better price. As I hesitated, the man pulled out a purse and spilled some coins on to the counter. 'Come, sir, ten pounds and you'll never make a better deal. I'll make it guineas, then.'

"Even if I spent a whole week working on the thing I would not do better than that, so without more ado the deal was struck. I took him round to my workshop and helped him load the desk on to the cart he had optimistically brought with him, and that was the last I expected to hear of the thing."

"But it was not?" Holmes leaned forward, a gleam of interest in his eyes.

"Indeed not, for early on Saturday morning as I was taking down my shutters, I had a second visit from this same man. This time his agitation was replaced by truculence as he demanded to know what game I was playing. Taken aback, I asked his meaning, and accompanied by a torrent of abuse he said I had stolen a package from a secret drawer of the desk. Much incensed, I refused to discuss the matter, telling him he had bought and paid for a Georgian bureau which he had seen and taken. He adopted a threatening attitude and, as his manner became more menacing, I offered to send for the police. At that he retreated hurriedly, slamming the door with such violence that I feared for the glass."

"Does this person have a name?" Holmes asked.

17

"I insisted on giving him a bill of sale when he paid for the bureau and the name he gave me was Dibden, although from the hesitation in his manner, I would be surprised if it was the one he was used to.

"But that still not end the matter, for that night as I was closing the shop for the weekend I had a further inquiry about the wretched desk. Frankly, gentlemen, I was beginning to wish I had never clapped eyes on it, despite the profit I had made. This time the approach was from a shifty individual who barged in and asked if I had a packet of letters taken from a desk I had purchased last Wednesday. I retorted that it was none of his affair, but he set me back on my heels by saying he was a Scotland Yard man in pursuit of a gang of criminals."

At this Holmes straightened up and interrupted sharply. "Did he identify himself to you?"

"Only by saying he was Inspector Gregson. I asked him for proof, but he said he had come from Scotland Yard in a hurry and had left his warrant card on his desk. I have had little to do with the police, but although he seemed assured, I was not easy with him and played for time."

"One moment, Mr, Ellis – what manner of person was this inspector?"

"Oh, shorter than I am. Plump, with a dark oily skin and black hair. I noticed too that his teeth were in need of attention,"

"Good Lord!" I gasped, "That – " But Holmes waved me to silence.

"Pray proceed, Mr. Ellis. I am intrigued,"

"I told the inspector that I had posted the packet off to my bank that very morning to await my instructions. I added that I was not aware of the contents, thinking this would make me less blameworthy if the matter was pursued. At this he became angry, demanding that I get it at once, which was ridiculous. I pointed out that there was no way I could lay my hands on it before Monday, which is today."

"And where in fact are these letters that have aroused such interest?"

"Why, I have them here." Ellis fished in his pocket and took out a small American-cloth package which he handed to Holmes, who gave it a cursory glance before stuffing it into the pocket of his dressing-gown.

"What followed from that?" he prompted our caller.

"Inspector Gregson seemed baffled but accepted what I said. He told me I must get the packet first thing today and hand it over. After various objections on my part, it was eventually agreed that I would meet him at one-thirty today to pass it over. At first I suggested that I could take it to a police station, but this he flatly refused to countenance, insisting the whole business must be between the two of us. This made me think, but to be rid of him I consented to meet him in a public house, the Black Boy at Catford, at the time agreed. I thought furiously about it over the weekend and decided the whole business smelt fishy, so knowing your interest in bizarre events, I took the liberty of approaching you in the hope of you being able to untangle it."

"You should have come earlier, Mr. Ellis," said Holmes petulantly. "Valuable time has been wasted."

"I had no wish to intrude on your Sunday, and I was on your doorstep before eight o'clock this morning, but feared you would find the matter too trivial to contemplate. It must have been then that I lost my pipe, and it was only after purchasing a replacement that I plucked up the courage to return."

Holmes sprang to his feet, his earlier lethargy gone as he rubbed his hands briskly together.

"We must lose no time," he snapped. "Watson, I need you to make an exact replica of this package." He tossed it to me. "We have a piece of American cloth somewhere about the place and a few sheets of folded newspaper will suffice as padding. Then you and Mr. Ellis will make your way to Catford so that he may keep his appointment at the Black Boy, but not in company. Unless he appears to be in physical danger, you will be as complete strangers. Do you follow?"

I nodded as I began to tear newspapers to make the dummy package,

"What will you be doing in the meantime, Holmes?" I looked up just in time to see his back before his bedroom door closed on him, and with a resigned shrug continued my task. I remembered that somewhere in our rooms I had seen an old American cloth shopping-bag and began to search for it. I had completed the package when Holmes reappeared, freshly shaven and dressed for the street. He took the parcel from me and weighed it in his hand then compared it with the original.

"Excellent, Watson, excellent. Here, Mr. Ellis, do you take this while I retain yours for the time being. Catford is about twenty-five minutes from London Bridge, so I suggest that you depart from the station at about a quarter-to one. Time your departure to allow you ample time, but not so much as to attract attention by loitering around. Under no circumstances must you and Watson be seen together. Keep your appointment, but not one second before one-thirty, as I need all the time available to me. You will leave here first with Watson after, but I repeat, give no sign that you are in company. Do you understand?"

Not awaiting a reply, he seized his hat and stick and bounded from the room, leaving Ellis and me to stare at one another.

"He seems to think there is some urgency in the matter," our client remarked with a puzzled frown. "What is he about?"

I was as much in the dark as was he, but with no wish to admit it, I contented myself with a vague generality and checked my watch against the one on the mantelpiece. It was a trifle past eleven-thirty and our Bradshaw told me that the twelve-forty-six would have us at Catford in comfortable time.

As I replaced the volume something struck a chord in my memory, and with a muttered apology to Ellis I leafed through Holmes's collection of common-place books until I found what I sought. It led me to other references and I marked them all with slips of paper before indicating to Ellis that it was time to leave.

A passing growler stooped at my hail, and bundling Ellis into it I told him to wait by Euston Station for ten minutes and then have the driver proceed at a leisurely pace to London Bridge. Soon after I procured a hansom and dawdled sufficiently to allow him his ten minutes start, so that by the time we had Euston in sight I could make out the four-wheeler moving off. Luckily my jarvey was given to minding his own business, so when I told him to follow the other cab but to get no closer than fifty yards he contented himself with a laconic, "Right-ho, Guv'nor," and no more.

At London Bridge Station, I saw Ellis entering the booking hall and, giving him time to get clear, I followed suit, buying myself a first-class ticket to Catford. I sauntered casually along the platform, seeing my man seated in a second-class compartment and passing him without a glance. I was satisfied that neither of us had been followed and I settled back in my seat to savour the memories of my all-too-short holiday in the Midlands,

My day-dreaming almost caused me to miss my station, and I scrambled out just as the train began to move. Ellis was already at the ticket barrier, but once out in the street he stopped to ask a patrolling constable for directions and I overtook him. Pretending interest in the window of a gentlemen's outfitters, I saw his reflection pass me, and I fell in behind him for the seven or eight minutes that brought us in sight of the sign of The Black Boy.

It still needed a few minutes to the half-hour and, remembering Holmes's decree that he should not keep his appointment until the last possible moment, he continued walking and was lost to sight round the next corner. My friend's strictures did not apply to me, and I turned into the only bar of the tavern and ordered a pint of the best bitter.

It was not a very cheerful place, but it was clean and the beer was cool and frothy. The landlord was a taciturn fellow so, carrying my pot to a table by the window, I picked up a copy of *The Pink'un* let by a previous patron.

From behind its cover I surreptitiously studied the only other customer. He was a dark-visaged plump individual with thinning black hair, tallying well with Ellis's description of the man who called himself Inspector Gregson, and as I watched him he began to evince signs of

20

impatience, his eyes darting from the door to the fly-spotted clock over the bar and every so often hauling out a watch which he compared with the time shown by the clock.

It was after twenty-five minutes to the hour when Ellis put in an appearance, casually buying himself a drink before going to sit down with the other man. By straining my ears I could just catch their low-voiced conversation, urgent and angry on the one part while Ellis remained calm and unruffled.

"You're late," growled the dark man.

"A little. I had to find the place and I spent a long time in the bank. I also have a business to run." Ellis was acting handsomely.

"Have you got it?"

Ellis gave the other a long cool look before replying.

"I assume," he said, "that as you had no wish for me to take it to the police station, you are pursuing the matter in a private capacity?"

"What is it to you?" asked the man sharply.

Ellis spread his hands and smiled ingratiatingly. "I thought there might be a little recompense for my trouble. After all, my business is at a standstill and I've had the expense of coming all this way."

"Oh, I see," sneered the other. "Well, there's a sovereign in it once I have the packet in my hand, but hurry up with it."

Ellis took the package from his pocket but made no move to hand it over. Instead he leaned back in his chair, tapping the parcel against the fingers of his other hand. Impatiently the man threw a coin on to the table, and unable to delay any longer Ellis put out his hand to deliver the object under discussion.

However, his procrastination was repaid, for as the man reached out to grasp the packet, the door opened to admit Sherlock Holmes, and hard on his heels a tall pallid man with wisps of yellow hair escaping from beneath the bowler he wore set squarely on his narrow head.

Ignoring my presence, Holmes gave a simulated exclamation of surprise, at the same time going across to clap Ellis on the shoulder.

"Why, Mr. Ellis!" he cried. "Fancy running into you in this quiet suburb. You remember me, I hope? John Verner, who bought that magnificent sideboard from you at Easter."

Ellis played his part as if born to the stage, grasping Holmes by the hand and shaking it vigorously.

"Why, of course, sir, and I hope you are well satisfied with it."

"Indeed I am, Mr. Ellis. Will you not introduce your friend?"

"Just an acquaintance, actually. This is Inspector Gregson, a detective policeman from Scotland Yard who has been good enough to take me into his confidence."

Holmes affected astonishment as he looked at Ellis's companion who was edging nervously towards the end of his chair.

"Now there's a coincidence," he remarked, smiling broadly. "It so happens that this gentleman with me is also Inspector Gregson of Scotland Yard – Ah, no you don't!" He lunged forward to grasp the bogus inspector by the collar as the table went over with a crash, glasses smashing on the floor.

In a split second Gregson produced a set of handcuffs which he clapped smartly on the impostor's wrists, whereupon the latter slumped back into his chair with a defiant snarl.

"You can't touch me. I've done nothing against the law," he spat. Gregson shook his head sadly as he surveyed his captive. "How about impersonating a police officer for a start?" he suggested. "No doubt we can think up a few other charges if we try hard enough. Unless, of course, you think your pals are not worth protecting – then we might make things a little easier for you."

"I've nothing to say except that I've done nothing." The man clamped his mouth shut and shot a venomous glare at Ellis, who wisely ignored him.

Holmes collected the packet from where it had fallen to the floor in the scuffle and the prisoner's eyes grew fearful as Holmes turned it over speculatively before addressing himself to Gregson.

"I think we should see what all the fuss is about, Inspector, don't you?"

Not waiting for a reply, he took out his pocket-knife to cut the binding, then unwrapped it to reveal a neatly folded selection of pages from *The Daily Post*, scattering them on the table which had been set back on its legs. The handcuffed man's mouth fell open at the sight and a stream of vile curses issued from his lips, while Gregson looked on, perplexity written all over his pasty features.

"Is that all?" he said in a tone of disappointment. "Are you trying to make a fool of me, Mr. Holmes?"

The prisoner gave a start at the mention of my friend's name, then he leered at the inspector who was scowling angrily.

"Make a fool of you, Gregson?" murmured Holmes with a hint of irony. "Certainly not. All I said was that a well-known criminal was making use of your name and threatening one of my clients. That is exactly what has happened. The fact that he was trying to get hold of a lot of old newspapers is neither here nor there. Watson." He acknowledged my presence for the first time. "Tell Gregson how all this came about."

I joined the group to give a carefully edited version of events, with no mention of the letters and our substitution of the fake package, and by the end Gregson was looking completely at sea.

"Why all the fuss over this rubbish?" He waved a contemptuous hand at the heap on the table.

Holmes shrugged and began to stuff the pieces of paper into his pocket. "Probably they thought it was a bundle of money. This, in case you have not recognized him, is George Bentley, a known associate of Charlie Dickson and the late Ned – or 'Nobby' – Clarke. I'm sure there are a few things he can tell you if he puts his mind to it."

"We shall see." Gregson turned to Ellis who was sitting quietly in his chair. "You will be needed to give evidence, sir, but I see no charges that you can press. You have lost nothing over this matter?"

"Only my time, and it was worth that to see Mr. Holmes at work." I hid a smile as Gregson's neck took on a reddish hue, but he contented himself with a grunt before hauling the sullen Bentley none too gently to his feet and took him off in search of a conveyance.

Holmes turned to Ellis and clapped him on the back. "A superb performance, my dear sir."

"I've not enjoyed myself so much in years," Ellis confessed with a chuckle. "Let me buy you a drink, gentlemen. It's an excellent brew, and I am a sovereign to the good by dealing in old newspapers."

"I was afraid Gregson would spoil our story by spotting those scraps were all from today's paper," Holmes remarked. "You should have thought of that, Watson."

"Did you, Holmes?" I replied, but he affected not to hear me.

With the incurious landlord compensated for the commotion and with drinks before us, Holmes related how he had caught Gregson about to leave his office, and on hearing that his name was being used, had willingly accompanied Holmes to lay the transgressor by the heels.

"I cannot recall when Gregson was more keen to follow me," said Holmes, "but I fancy he thinks there is more to it than we have told him. My one fear was that our bird might have flown before we arrived, but thanks to you, Mr. Ellis, all was well."

"I gather there was nothing said of the genuine package?" I put in.

"I thought it better not to confuse Gregson by introducing too many complications. I have them in my pocket, Mr. Ellis, so you may carry out your first impulse to destroy them."

Ellis shook his head emphatically. "No! If it is all the same to you, Mr. Holmes, I never want to see them again. Burn them. Throw them in the river if you will, but I want nothing to do with them,"

Holmes drained his glass and set it down on the table. "Tell me this then," he said gravely. "Do you know to whom they were written, or by whom?"

"No. There was nothing in them that revealed the name of the writer or the recipient. I can say that they were in an educated hand, although Heaven help us if that is the result of education."

"Then, Mr. Ellis, I shall attempt to find the rightful owner and hand them over. It is clear that someone is being kept in a state of fear that they will be made public, and whatever our personal views on the character of the writer, I hold blackmail to be a despicable crime, second only to treason against our country. Destroy these letters and the unhappy victim will still be living in fear, so with your approval, I shall do my best to return them to the person who wrote them and set her mind at rest."

"The matter is in your hands, Mr. Holmes, but let me hear no more of it, I beg you. Now, as one professional man to another, there remains the matter of your fee to be discussed."

Holmes gave a shrug and mentioned a small sum which was paid over with a will. Soon afterwards we went our separate ways, Ellis to take an omnibus to New Cross and vanish forever from our lives, while Holmes and I strolled slowly towards the station.

"I suppose," Holmes said gloomily, "I must peruse these letters to see what may be gleaned from them, but if they are indeed as friend Ellis describes them, I have no taste for doing so."

"Perhaps I can help you there," I said casually enough.

He gave me a sour look and his lips compressed into a thin line. "I knew you to be a man of the world, Doctor," he said in a frosty tone, "but I never counted prurience as one of your weaknesses."

I found myself shocked and angry at his words, hurt that my old friend could have so low an opinion of me.

"Neither is it," I snapped. "I am no more desirous of reading that filthy muck than are you. I had another string to my bow."

He stopped in his tracks and stared at me, a contrite expression on his face as he laid a hand on my arm.

"My dear fellow. I do most humbly apologise. I withdraw my words absolutely and abjectly. I should have more faith in your probity."

"That's all very well," I said furiously. "That was the most hurtful thing you have said in the nine years of our association." I fell back on a sulky silence and stalked on ahead of him.

Once seated in our compartment, Holmes, with the unfailing charm that he could produce on occasion, soon restored my humour, so that by the time we arrived at London Bridge, a normal relationship prevailed.

24

However, it was not until we sat at the tea-table that the matter was again raised.

"Now I that am forgiven, Watson," said Holmes, "enlighten me as to how we may trace the owner of this property we have come by."

I sat back smugly. It was so seldom that I managed to be one step ahead of Holmes that I meant to extract the maximum enjoyment from it.

"If you recall," I commenced, "Ellis bought the desk at an auction of the effects of one Edwin Clarke, and you identified that scoundrel Bentley as an associate of Ned or Nobby Clarke – presumably the same man. Is that not so?"

"Yes, yes, Watson, of that I am aware. Pray get on with it."

I refused to be ruffled and continued at my own pace, "After you left to find Gregson – not seeing fit to advise me of your movements – I had a stirring of memory and spent what time I had in looking through our collection of scrap-books. I came across an entry pertaining to an Edwin Clarke."

Here I paused to light my pipe and was gratified to see a light dawning in my companion's eyes as he assessed the import of my words,

"By Jove!" he cried. "That was brilliant work, and I think I begin to see what you are driving at, but please proceed."

"As you can verify," I went on, "Edwin Clarke was employed until five years ago as valet to Count Mikhail Pindarus, a diplomat in the service of one of those Central European states that no one can ever find on the map. Clarke was arrested on a charge of demanding money with menaces from his master and collected four years in prison for his sins.

"Bear in mind," I added, "I had little time to delve into your journals, but I did ascertain that the Count is a bachelor and something of a ladies man, although no scandal has ever attached to his name. He lives in his Embassy in Belgrave Square, but seems to incline more to the social round than to diplomatic business. As Clarke, a proven blackmailer, was once his servant, I suggest it might pay to put an ear to the ground in that direction. What say you?"

"I say Watson is a jewel!" he cried, springing to his feet. "Never underestimate yourself, nor permit me to do so."

He swept the remnants of the meal to one end of the table and shouted for Mrs. Hudson to clear the debris. Tossing his jacket on to the sofa, he urged me to bring down the volumes that had provided my information, and I laid them before him open at the relevant pages.

For upwards of an hour he sat at the table scribbling on sheets of paper, every so often curtly demanding I fetch another scrap-book but otherwise not saying a word.

Eventually he collected his notes together and, leaving the books in wry confusion, he retired to his armchair. Filling his old clay pipe with the rank black shag so beloved of him, he sat puffing furiously with his chin sunk on his chest.

Recognizing the signs, I quietly replaced the books on the shelves, and the evening being still young, took myself off for a walk in the park, knowing full well that I would get nothing from him until his deliberations were concluded. I returned as dusk was falling to find him still in the same attitude, and as I put a match to the gaslight he looked at me ruefully.

"A three-pipe problem, Watson, and although partly unraveled, we are not yet home and dry."

I waited for him to go on and, after a glance at the bundle of notes in his hand, he did so.

"It has become clear to me that the letters in our package were written by one of two ladies, but turn things around as I may, it remains no more than an even choice. As much as I shun the idea, there is nothing left but to but to approach one or the other and invite a confidence, hoping that the first will prove to be the one."

I stared at him in amazement, for never had I known him act in such a haphazard manner, and at the risk of offending him I said as much.

"Then perhaps you have an alternative?" he said waspishly. I shook my head regretfully, and as a sop to his pride, observed that if a brain as keen as his could not resolve the dilemma, then who else in London was there to turn to? For a long minute he stared at me, and then a smile of pure joy spread across his lean features as he smacked one fist into the palm of the other.

"That's it, Watson!" he cried. "That is the answer I need!"

With no word of explanation he dashed into his room, to emerge twenty minutes later in full evening dress, an opera cloak over his arm, and silk hat in his hand.

"Bless you, Watson!" he threw over his shoulder as he made for the door. "Wait up for me. This is your case and all credit is yours."

The door slammed, leaving me to stare at the blank woodwork, wondering what I had said to trigger this sudden activity. Picking up a yellow-backed novel, I tried to interest myself in the banal story, but my mind refused to concentrate and I found myself looking constantly at the creeping hands of the clock and reading the same passage without taking in in a single word. I suppose I must have dozed, for all at once the time seemed to have jumped forward two hours and stood at almost half-past midnight. I stood up to stretch my cramped limbs and almost at once heard the street door open and close, followed by Holmes's familiar tread on the stairs.

I looked at him expectantly as he entered, but with infuriating casualness he removed his hat and cloak and, settling himself in the basket chair, took two cigars from the coal-scuttle and handed me one.

He smiled cheerfully at me, but on my pressing him for the details of his expedition, he ignored my plea completely.

"Be a good fellow, Watson," he said. "Go down to the kitchen and make a pot of tea. I think Mrs. Hudson has retired and my throat is absolutely parched."

I gave him an exasperated scowl, but knew that if I was to get satisfaction, the quickest way was to indulge his whim, so putting the best face I could on it, I did as he requested.

When I returned he had removed his tie and shirt-front with the evident intention of making himself comfortable while he talked, and with a steaming cup in his hand he began.

"Well, my dear Doctor, where do you think I have been?"

"As you did not see fit to confide in me, Holmes, anything I said would be merely surmise, and I know how you abhor that,"

"Oh, don't be so stuffy, man. It ill becomes you, but as it was you who sent me off, I thought you might have put two-and-two together."

I shook my head impatiently and said nothing, until taking pity on me he unfolded the steps he had taken.

"It was your remark, Watson, that gave my brain the necessary jolt to get it working again. If I remember rightly, you said that if a brain as keen as mine could not resolve the matter, then who in London could. A piece of blatant flattery, but it served its purpose. Whom do I acknowledge as my peer in the realms of deduction and analytical reasoning?"

I began to get his drift and it showed on my face as he went on,

"Yes, my brother Mycroft, who you will recall meeting in the affair of Mr. Melas, the Greek gentleman who sought our aid last year.

"In the hope that Mycroft would see what I had failed to see, I took myself off to the Diogenes Club and laid the problem before him. With his involvement with so many odd people, I hoped that he might be able to tell me something of Count Pindarus that might help. I trust him implicitly and had no qualms when it came to taking him step by step through the whole case up to the point where I had reasoned that these letters must be returned to one of two ladies. But which?"

"'What do you want of me, Sherlock?' he asked when I had finished.

"'Why,' I said, 'your considered opinion as to a way out of my dilemma. It is far too delicate a matter to be left to pure chance, but I freely admit to being stumped.'

"He thought this over before answering, and when he did his manner was grave and portentous. 'Sherlock,' he said, 'if I aid you in this, I must

27

have your solemn word that the Count's name will never appear in any way whatsoever. If through your involvement any scandal attaches to him, you will be answerable to the very highest authority. Do I have that assurance?'

"I gave my word as the only way of getting what was required and he gave me two slips of paper, bidding me write one of my two names on each. Much puzzled, I did so and handed them back, at which he looked briefly at them before putting a match to one and handing me the other. Then without another word he stalked from the room."

"Good Lord!" I exclaimed. "Do you mean to say that your brother knew of this matter all along?"

"So," Holmes replied emphatically, "I had deduced it to be one or the other, and when I told him the story, he knew instantly which one it could not be. How, I neither know nor care, but it has raised the curtain on the final act of the drama. On my way home, I sent a telegram from the all-night office at Charing Cross, and I expect our mysterious young lady to come here as early as young ladies can ever do."

"Lady!" I muttered. "If all Ellis said of those letters is true, lady is the last word I would apply to her."

"And the man who debauched her? Is he not as culpable, or do different standards of morality apply to our sex?" I was lost for an answer and took myself off to bed, leaving Holmes to linger while he considered his attitude to our expected visitor.

We breakfasted unusually early, and by ten o'clock Holmes was pacing restlessly back and forth across the room like a caged tiger. I was accustomed to his nervous tension as a case approached its climax, but I was thankful when the sound of carriage wheels sent him to the window and I saw an expression of satisfaction on his face.

"Quickly!" he rapped. "Seat yourself as unobtrusively as possible, and on no account utter a word until I give you leave."

He arranged the chairs to his liking, sitting himself down with his back to the window in the pose he was wont to adopt when conducting one of his searching inquisitions. No sooner was he seated than Mrs. Hudson knocked on the door and announced that a lady had an appointment with Mr. Holmes. Then she ushered in a heavily veiled woman.

She entered hesitantly as if fearing a trap and advanced to the centre of the room where she stood like a frightened animal, ready to run at the first hostile move.

"Pray be seated, Miss Lawler," said Holmes in a gentle tone. "I am Sherlock Holmes. The other gentleman is Dr. Watson, my friend and colleague from whom I have no secrets."

She sat on the only available chair, so placed that the light fell on her face, and then raised her veil to reveal the features of one of the most truly beautiful women it has been my fortune to see. Her face was pale and drawn, but this only served to enhance her beauty. I judged her to be no more than twenty-two years of age, and I marvelled that, if the account of the letters given by Ellis was to be credited, so lovely a face could hide a soul as depraved as any trollop to be found in the houses of ill-repute that abounded in both the West and East Ends of London.

"Well, Mr. Holmes?" Her voice was low and well-modulated. "Your summons has brought me, but had I not been aware of your reputation and status, I would not have allowed your hint of 'urgent and private matters' to induce me to come. Please be good enough to enlighten me at once."

"I shall do so, Madam," said Holmes. "I shall be brief and factual, one might almost say brutal, but I see no merit in false delicacy in the situation in which you find yourself. No, do not interrupt, I pray you. A few years ago as a very young girl, you were on terms of the utmost intimacy with Count Mikhail Pindarus, were you not?"

At the mention of the Count's name her eyes widened, her already pale face turned a chalky white, and she swayed in her chair as though on the point of swooning. Recovering herself with an effort, she spoke in a haughty voice, albeit with a slight tremor of anxiety.

"Mr. Holmes, I fail to see why you should be prying into my private life, and I am not answerable to you for my conduct in the past."

"Do not think to play the grand lady with me, Miss. I am trying to help you, and your private conduct, as you put it, has for some time been in jeopardy of being made public, as we both well know. In short, Miss Lawler, there are in existence certain letters written by you to the Count that, if published, would blast your reputation for all time. Am I right?"

She looked at him defiantly for some seconds before all resistance crumbled and she broke down into a piteous sobbing that was heart-rending to hear and see, I made to go to her, but a look from Holmes pinned me to my seat, and I was compelled to watch her distress with a sorrowful heart. Despite my earlier strictures, no man worthy of the name could fail to be unmoved by her pitiful state – except Sherlock Holmes, who waited impassively for her to compose herself.

Presently she became calmer and, taking a wisp of lace from her reticule, dabbed her eyes dry before raising them to my companion to await whatever blow was to fall.

He spoke with a gentleness totally unlike his usually cold manner, and a faint smile of sympathy touched his thin lips for a brief moment.

"There, my dear young lady. Now it has been said, let me set your mind at rest." He held out the packet containing the letters. "These, I

29

believe, are the cause of your anxiety and are for you to dispose of as you will. Take them, do,"

She sat in dumbfound amazement until the packet was thrust into her hands, when she turned it over and over as though unable to take in the meaning. She turned her gaze back to Holmes and spoke in a shaky voice.

"Have you read them, Mr. Holmes?"

He shook his head. "I give you my solemn oath that neither I nor the good Doctor has opened the package. It came into my possession just as you see it. We were asked to take whatever steps we deemed proper for the disposal of it by a person who has, for honourable reasons, no desire to be identified. As we have had no sight of the contents, I suggest you examine it to satisfy yourself that all is well. Dr. Watson and I will retire while you do so, and when you have verified the contents, please tap on the door to the left of the fireplace. Come, Watson," and so saying, he led the way into his bedroom and closed the door firmly.

Once inside I turned to him with a look of disbelief. "I say, Holmes, what a stunner! I find it hard to credit that she should be the author of the sort of thing attributed to her."

He gave me one of his sardonic grins and clapped me on the back.

"Good old Watson! Ever an eye for beauty – but let me remind you that some of the world's most evil women have been renowned for their beauty. Not that I think her evil, but if we can induce her to tell her story, we may be better able to form an opinion."

We passed the next ten minutes in desultory talk before a light tap on the door recalled us to the other room.

Miss Lawler stood with flushed cheeks, her bonnet discarded carelessly while in the grate a blackened pile of smouldering ash gave testimony to the disposal of the package and its contents. Approaching Holmes and much to his confusion, she seized his hands and squeezed them fervently.

"However can I thank you for what you have done, Mr. Holmes? I was at my wits end with worry and shame, but now I can look forward to a new life, thanks to you."

"Please, Madam, do not over-estimate my part." He gently disengaged himself. "Dr. Watson played an important role. If you want to show your appreciation, may I suggest that you give us an account of how you came to this predicament. Watson is my amanuensis and keeps a meticulous chronicle of all our cases, and he alters names and places to ensure no one is identified."

She looked at me questioningly and I added my assurances.

"Very well," she said at last. "I know you both for men of honour, and if by speaking I can make you think more kindly of me, then I will do so."

She settled herself down and began her story in a low voice, avoiding our eyes as she began her unhappy tale.

"I will be completely frank, gentlemen, and you must judge me according to your lights, but I vow it will not be a crueller condemnation than I have made on myself. As you must know, my father is highly placed and we move in the topmost diplomatic circles. I was but sixteen when I first met Count Pindarus and, at that impressionable time of life, I found him exercising an incredible fascination over me. In spite of his well-known reputation as a philanderer, I threw myself at him, and he is not the man to refuse that which is offered to him gratuitously. To my everlasting shame, long before my seventeenth birthday, I became his paramour, or as I found out later, one of them. Such was the intensity of my passion that all sense of decency was thrown to the winds and for some months, I became the most abandoned creature imaginable."

She paused, and in her downcast eyes was written all the agony and shame that she now felt, then pulling herself together she continued.

"Like all bright flames, my obsession died as quickly as it had flared, and I became sensible of the depths of depravity to which I had sunk.

"My conduct had inevitably become the subject of gossip, although its full extent was fortunately never known. My father, scandalized by my behaviour, took me off to the Continent for three years and we both believed that the whole matter to be forgotten.

"Whilst in Italy I met a young man in our diplomatic service, and a mutual attraction made us constant companions. It became accepted that he would ask for my hand in marriage, to which I was by no means averse. He approached my father, and it was arranged that when he returned to England after his time in Rome, our engagement would be announced. I came home in January to await his coming, and that is when the agony began."

Again she stopped, the strain of confessing her fall from grace beginning to show, and at a sign from Holmes, I went to request Mrs. Hudson to bring a tray of tea. Miss Lawler remained silent until it arrived, then somewhat recovered she went on with her narrative.

"Whatever my past sins, I have prayed for forgiveness, and my remorse has surely earned me that, but it was not to be. I had not been back in London above three weeks when I was approached in the street by a man I knew as Edwin Clarke, formerly valet to Count Pindarus during our association. He told a story of having fallen on hard times and solicited my aid, so out of charity I offered him a couple of half-sovereigns. He rejected them contemptuously and said that if I really wanted to help him, I could buy some letters from him – letters written by me to the Count which I might like to have returned. At first I affected indifference, but when he quoted some passages from them, I knew how deeply I was compromised, and if any folly was discovered, I would be an outcast forever.

"The amount he demanded was quite beyond my means, and I was afraid that if I paid, it would not be the end of it. To gain time, I arranged a meeting with him and, in desperation, I went to Miki – Count Pindarus – and poured out the whole story. Whatever you may think of him, he is not without finer feelings, and he was angry and concerned on my behalf, although for his own reputation he cares not a jot. I learned that the man Clarke had tried to blackmail the Count some years previously but without success. The Count had handed him over to the police and the last he had heard of him he was serving a stiff prison sentence.

"Miki persuaded me to accept a sum of money to keep the scoundrel quiet while machinery was set in motion to lay him by the heels with the recovery of the letters the prime consideration.

"I kept my appointment with Clarke, paying fifty pounds without receiving the letters, and this happened twice more until I despaired of ever being free of his clutches, Then early last week, he failed to turn up for another appointment. Whatever relief I may have felt was dispelled when the following morning a letter was delivered to me saying that Clarke was dead, but the writer as his business associate expected the same arrangements to continue, and told me to meet him on Thursday."

Holmes interrupted her story for the first time. "Tell me, Miss Lawler, where were these meetings?"

"Once in a tea-room off the Strand, once in St. James's Park, and the third at Victoria Station. The one that was not kept was to be on the Embankment by Cleopatra's Needle. Last Thursday's, which again was not kept, was to have been in Trafalgar Square."

"And what was the Count doing all this time?" asked Holmes.

"I went to see him on Thursday after my fruitless wait and he knew Clarke was dead, but he was perturbed that the threats continued, not having anticipated that others would be privy to the matter. After all, blackmail is not as any other crime, is it?"

Holmes remained silent, and after a moment Miss Lawler continued.

"As I said, he was already aware that Clarke was dead, but how he came into possession of the knowledge he did not reveal. He did his best to reassure me, promising that the matter would be resolved with no involvement on my part, but believe me, gentlemen, I have spent the intervening days in deepest despair, my mind becoming almost unhinged.

Castigate me as you will, but no words can describe the degradation I have brought on myself through my own abandoned behaviour."

"No one here will condemn you, Miss Lawler," said my companion. "To commit folly is one thing, but to recognize and regret it requires more character than many have. You may be of easy mind and tell the Count that neither you nor he has anything further to fear. Now go and put all this behind you, and we both wish you a happy future."

He bowed and turned away, plainly no longer interested now that the matter was concluded. I escorted the lady downstairs and saw her into a cab, ascending back to our rooms to find Holmes standing before the fireplace with his hands thrust deep into his pockets.

"By Jove!" I exclaimed. "Who would have guessed that that angel-faced woman would be capable of committing to paper the words that so shocked Mr. Ellis? It was a stroke of luck that the letters came into the possession of an honourable man after Clarke's fortuitous death."

"Fortuitous?" said Holmes quizzically. "Do you see it so?"

"Was it not? Of course, he must have had Dickson and Bentley in his confidence – " I stopped, suddenly grasping the meaning of my friend's last words. "Holmes!" I cried. "What are you suggesting?"

"My dear Watson, do you seriously think that a man like Pindarus would let matters take their own course?"

"Do you mean to say that Clarke's death was deliberately contrived by the Count?" I stuttered.

Holmes gave a dismissive shrug and turned away impatiently. "One can only surmise," he said. "Quite frankly, I care neither one way nor the other what becomes of these leeches as long as they are not free to ply their evil trade. Now, I have a feeling that Lestrade will put in an appearance before the day is out. He is completely at sea over that little matter of the Brieland abduction and he will swallow his pride and come to me to throw him a hint."

He drew the bow across the violin strings, and after a moment of hesitation, I beat a retreat up to my bedroom before he got down in earnest to his caterwauling, shutting the door firmly behind me.

The Case of the
Woman at Margate

I was sitting alone over an early breakfast, drawn from my bed by the promise of a fine day. The summer lingered as though reluctant to give place to autumn, and I was torn between the rival attractions of Middlesex playing at Lords and a thoroughly idle day in Regents Park. My friend and colleague, Sherlock Holmes, was still abed, nursing his ill humour at the inordinate amount of political comment that monopolised the daily press,

"Confound it, Watson," he had railed. "Five governments in little more than a year is no way to conduct the business of our great country. It reduces us to the level of a Latin republic floundering from one crisis to another." He had scattered the offending papers with a petulant scowl.

"Politics! It makes small difference to the criminal classes which party is in power. Does a footpad or swindler care if we have a Conservative or Liberal administration? Does a murderer or burglar pause to reflect who leads the country? Of course not. Yet because our press is so preoccupied in influencing the minds of a fickle electorate, those parasites of society pursue their nefarious calling without the glare of publicity that is such a deterrent."

Wisely I had held my peace and waited for his peevishness to abate. Notwithstanding his discontent, the year had been a busy and productive one for Holmes. His standing had never been higher, and in the five-and-a-half years our association, I had seen his reputation flower from that of an obscure consulting detective to become the most sought-after figure in the history of criminal investigation. His services were in demand from the highest in the land as well as from the official police, yet would he be just as willing to help the poorest and most abject citizen if the case offered stimulation and challenge to his restless mind.

I reached for the last piece of toast, pausing as my ears caught the sounds of an altercation from below, Mrs. Hudson's indignant tones punctuated by those of a man. Soon the good lady's firm tread approached our door and I opened it on her knock to find her flushed and angry.

"I'm sorry, Doctor. There is a *gentleman* – " She gave the word a disparaging sound. "A gentleman who insists on speaking to Mr. Holmes and refuses to be put off." She snorted. "Barely seven of the clock, indeed!"

I gnawed at my moustache. I knew my friend had no pressing cases in hand, hence his irritability. Perhaps this was what would divert him from his present lethargy.

"Who is he, Mrs. Hudson?"

She pursed her lips and handed me an engraved card.

"'Mr. John Ruddy'," I read. "'East Kent Manager, Rural and Urban Insurance Company, Margate'." I tapped it with my thumb and spoke ruefully to our landlady.

"Well, Mrs. Hudson, if he will not go, then for the sake of peace and quiet I suggest you bring him up."

She sniffed and turned away, grumbling beneath her breath. Soon the importunate caller was shown in. He was a sallow-featured fellow, some forty years of age, thin and with lank black hair plastered damply across his narrow skull. But for his rounded shoulders he would have been as tall as Holmes, and his eyes burned feverishly as he fidgeted with the brim of the brown billy-cock hat held in nervous fingers.

Hardly was he in the room before he burst into impassioned speech.

"Mr. Holmes, you must help me or I am ruined!" he cried in a high-pitched voice. "Perhaps I am ruined anyway, but – "

"Mr. Ruddy, I am not Mr. Sherlock Holmes," I broke in. "I am Dr. Watson, Mr. Holmes's colleague and confidant. Please calm yourself and be seated while I find out if he will consent to see you."

He stared at me wildly and almost danced in his agitation. "He must hear me, Doctor! My whole career hangs by a thread!" He grasped my arm and I shook him off impatiently.

"Sit down, sir," I said with some asperity. "'Must' is not a word to be used to Sherlock Holmes. I will speak to him, but he is a busy man."

I gave our visitor a stern look, then knocked on my friend's door.

His querulous voice bade me enter.

"What the deuce is going on, Watson?" he demanded. "I could find more peace in the monkey-house at the Zoo."

"You have a client," I said, nettled by his tone. "He insists that you alone can rescue him from whatever dilemma he finds himself in. He is quite unnerved."

"At this ungodly hour? Send him away, there's a good chap. Tell him to return at a more civilized time." His eyes suddenly lit up. "No, wait. This may provide some small diversion. Ring for fresh coffee and entertain him until I am fit to appear."

Turning back into the sitting room, I found John Ruddy pacing the carpet, his sallow skin flushed with emotion as he spun round to face me.

"You are a fortunate man, Mr. Ruddy," I said, not waiting for his query. "Mr. Holmes will attend you shortly. Meanwhile I shall send for

35

fresh coffee. No doubt you left – " I looked again at his card. " – Margate well before breakfast."

"Indeed I did, Doctor. I slept but little last night and, deciding my only hope of succor lay with Mr. Holmes, I caught the milk train at the crack of dawn."

"Then some toast to stay you." I rang for Mrs. Hudson, and despite the man's protests, he attacked the food voraciously when it arrived.

It was twenty minutes before Holmes appeared, his old purple dressing gown flapping around his lean shanks. Our caller looked up, hastily swallowing a mouthful of toast, but ere he could speak Holmes held up an admonitory hand, the force of his personality imposing itself at once.

"Wait, my dear sir," he commanded. "I too have my needs." He poured coffee and picked up the card from the table where I had laid it.

He looked at it carelessly, then with great deliberation began to fill a pipe from the dottles of the previous day that were drying on the mantelpiece. Not until his head was wreathed in a halo of pungent smoke did he speak.

"Well, Mr. John Ruddy from Margate, what is the purpose of this early intrusion? Be brief but explicit and tell me why the death of Mr. Elias Burdick should cause you such unrest."

Our visitor's eyes started from his head and his hands trembled. "How – *how* – do you know that, Mr. Holmes?" he stuttered in amazement, while I struggled to contain my own astonishment as Holmes turned a sardonic eye in my direction.

"Come, sir," said my friend, "Dr. Watson and I read our newspapers, and when we see that on Monday a body was taken from the sea at Margate, and is identified by Mrs. Emily Burdick as that of her husband Elias we take note. Hard on that I receive a visit from the East Kent representative of an insurance company. Why, what could be plainer?"

Ruddy's face cleared. "Of course, Mr. Holmes, it must be obvious," he cried, and I saw the flicker of annoyance in Holmes's eyes at this casual dismissal of his powers of deduction.

"Then pray proceed," said the latter coldly. "Watson, yesterday's *Morning Post* and *Evening News*, if you will be so good. Go on, sir. My time is valuable."

His pipe gurgled as he laid back in his chair with hooded eyes while our client began to speak, Holmes's calm demeanour having a steadying effect on the man.

"As you see from my card, Mr. Holmes, I manage the East Kent region for my employers. All my working life has been spent in the insurance business, from office boy to my present position, albeit with several different companies as opportunity offered me advancement. My

36

present post I have occupied for some three years, and the company, although small and relatively new, is both progressive and efficient."

"Yes, yes," Holmes interrupted. "Please come to the point,"

"As you say, sir. Just over three weeks ago, I had a request through the post to provide life cover for this Elias Burdick, his wife to be the beneficiary. Imagine my astonishment when the sum involved was no less than six-thousand pounds, the largest single piece of business that had come my way. Most of our policies are small affairs, what we regard as burial funds, with premiums of but a few cappers weekly, but they add up, sir, they add up. I replied at once, enclosing the appropriate forms and pointing out that I would require medical confirmation of his good health. Within forty-eight hours I had the papers back, together with a doctor's certificate of recent date and the first monthly premium of thirteen-pounds-and-ten."

As Ruddy had been speaking, I had been busy with the newspapers and found the items that Holmes had tucked away in his memory. I marked them with a pencil and gave him a brief nod.

"One moment, Mr. Ruddy," Holmes was saying. "From whence did this request emanate?"

Our client looked slightly sheepish. "From Ashford, but it was *poste restante* at the main post office in that town. Burdick explained that he was an actor with no fixed address, travelling wherever work was offered. I realise now that I should have been more cautious, but in my anxiety to secure the business, I was less so than usual."

"Indeed you were," murmured Holmes. "The certificate of health – who issued that?"

"I don't know. The signature was indecipherable, as so many are. Begging your pardon, Dr. Watson," he added hastily. "It was from rooms in Wigmore Street, though, which is a reputable address."

"Quite," said Holmes drily. "At least near enough to Wimpole and Harley Streets to inspire confidence. You have it with you?" Ruddy delved into a pocket and handed a paper to Holmes, who glanced at it and passed it to me. The signature was indeed unreadable, but something in the address disturbed me and I went to the bookshelf for the London street directory.

"By George, Holmes!" I cried. "This – " but he silenced me with a finger to his lips and I subsided into my chair.

"Pray continue, Mr. Ruddy," Holmes urged.

"On Sunday night, a pile of clothes was found on a deserted part of the beach. It was reported in the stop press of the Monday morning's paper, but it was badly smudged and I took little heed of it until in the local evening paper I read of a man's body being recovered from the rocks. Even

37

then I had no more than a feeling of sympathy for a stranger who had been foolhardy to get out of his depth and had met his fate alone and unnoticed. However, on reading further, I was shocked to find that the pile of clothes found earlier had been identified by the contents of the pockets as belonging to Elias Burdick, an actor who had that day been reported missing from his lodgings. Moreover, it was being assumed that the body was his."

"So in all probability it was your client," mused Holmes, "You had no knowledge of his presence in Margate or the reason for it?"

"No. My only contact with him had been by post, and that not for three weeks since," Ruddy took out a handkerchief and mopped his brow. "Worse was to come. Imagine my dismay when yesterday noon a policeman escorted a lady to my office. He introduced her as Mrs. Emily Burdick, who had lately been to the mortuary to identify the drowned man as her husband."

"A prompt appearance indeed," observed Holmes. "So you saw a huge claim looming up. But surely, my dear sir, that is one of the hazards of your profession, unwelcome as it might be from your point of view."

"If that was but all! Oh, Mr. Holmes, it has placed me in the most ghastly predicament. Never in my twenty years in the insurance business have I done anything dishonest or indulged in sharp practice, and even now I have behaved with perfect probity."

"Then what is your problem?" asked Holmes with some impatience.

"As I have said, this was the largest single policy I have ever been asked to issue, and in my anxiety to secure it I acted somewhat precipitately. It is a company rule that any exceptional circumstances should be referred to Head Office for approval. Nothing specific is laid down, it being left to local judgement, and I have a certain amount of discretion."

"Ah, I begin to get your drift," my colleague put in. "You conducted this matter on your own initiative and responsibility, and now you fear the wrath of your superiors."

"Exactly. My career will be finished – in ruins." The poor fellow sobbed and wrung his hands in anguish."

"But surely you hardly expected your Head Office not to perceive this large transaction? Would you not be taking commission on it?"

"Indeed, and it would have appeared in my monthly report due this very weekend. Had there been no claim, I could expect at the most a mild reprimand for excess of zeal. I was dazzled by the thought of my own cleverness, but now – "

"I appreciate your position, Mr. Ruddy, but what can I do?"

"I have misgivings as to the validity of the claim," replied the other fiercely. "My whole instincts and experience tell me it is wrong, yet I fear to approach the Board without firm evidence. Why, it may even be regarded as collusion on my part to defraud them. It is an immense sum."

"I see." Holmes steepled his fingers and dropped his chin onto them. For a long time he remained motionless, lost in thought. Ruddy made as if to speak, but I silenced him with a shake of the head. At last Holmes looked up, and when I saw his eyes with the old familiar light, I knew he was intrigued.

"Let me expound, Mr. Ruddy," he said. "Three weeks ago you agreed to insure the life of one Elias Burdick for the sum of six-thousand pounds, payable in the event of his death to his spouse, Emily Burdick. The business was conducted by post with no personal contact. Your client gave no fixed address, preferring to use the G.P.O. at Ashford as his postbox."

Ruddy nodded and Holmes continued. "Last Sunday, Elias Burdick is fortuitously drowned on your very doorstep, and within thirty-six hours his widow is at your office to establish her claim. It does appear that a few inquiries would not come amiss."

"Then you will help me, Mr. Holmes?" The man's eagerness was pathetic.

"I shall seek the truth, no more and no less. Tell me, did the lady offer any explanation for her late husband's presence in Margate?"

"She was very distraught, but I gathered he had come hoping for some part at a local theatre."

"She had accompanied him?" asked Holmes with a frown.

"I think not. What few words we exchanged led me to believe that she had read the newspaper accounts and had followed. The constable gave me to understand she was taking a room at the very lodgings that he had occupied. A respectable boarding-house run by a Mrs. Ellis."

"Most interesting," said Holmes, rising to his feet. "Very well, Mr. Ruddy, I shall look into the matter. "Return to Margate by the first available train and carry on as if nothing out of the ordinary had occurred. Do not under any circumstances get in touch with Mrs. Burdick or allow her to speak to you."

"But will you not come with me?" demanded Ruddy, his face falling.

"No one must know of my involvement in the matter at this stage, but rest assured that Dr. Watson and I will be on the spot later today."

"You will not approach my Head Office? That would surely bring about my downfall."

"Trust me, sir," Holmes said sternly. "Only by doing so have you any hope of retrieving your position. I shall telegraph my time of arrival. Watson, be so good as to see Mr. Ruddy to the door." When I returned it

39

was to find Holmes on his knees, the newspapers scattered about him. He looked at me severely as I came in.

"I marked the relevant paragraphs. Have you found them?"

"I have, and also the one you chose to ignore."

"I saw nothing else of importance," I replied huffily.

"You saw but did not observe. Look, man, here." His finger stabbed at a small item tucked away on the second page of Tuesday's *Morning Post*.

"Read it, my friend."

A few lines sufficed to report that a waiter from the Stanton Hotel, Margate, one George Monk, had been missing since Sunday afternoon. All his effects remained in his room and nothing had been stolen from the hotel.

"How does that concern us?" I asked. "A coincidence, nothing more."

"I distrust coincidences, even while admitting them," Holmes said pettishly. "Two men missing on the same day from the same town with no apparent connection between them is indeed coincidence. Now, my dear fellow, you were going to tell me that the Wigmore Street address is nonexistent." I nodded and he reached out to take his book of cuttings from the shelf.

For a considerable time he leafed backwards through the pages, sometimes lingering over one page or another then moving on with a mutter of frustration. At last he gave a cry of triumph and scribbled on the back of an envelope before turning the pages more rapidly. He made one more note, then closed the book with a snap.

"The case proceeds and the sea air beckons," he cried. "Watson, the *Bradshaw*!"

By eleven o'clock, our train had left behind the sulphurous fumes of London and we were looking out on the green fields of Kent, the hops coming to fruition on the vines and the conical oast houses waiting patiently to begin their labours. Holmes had despatched three telegrams from London Bridge, announcing that one was to John Ruddy, but remaining coyly mysterious regarding the others. We had the compartment to ourselves and, defying all my efforts at conversation, my companion stared fixedly out of the window. The amber stem of his brier was clamped firmly between his teeth, only being removed to be stuffed afresh with his noxious black shag.

At last I was constrained to lower the window, and the tang of salt in the air told us we were approaching the popular seaside resort that was our objective. The train clanked to a halt, the engine giving what sounded like a sigh of relief at having completed the journey. We made our way out of the station and Holmes raised a finger to the driver of a four-wheeler who, oblivious to the soft warm atmosphere, was muffled to the chin in layers of coats and comforters.

"The Stanton Hotel, cabbie, and take your time." My friend clambered in beside me and made himself as comfortable as possible on the lumpy horse-hair cushions.

"You have pondered much," I ventured to observe, nettled by his taciturnity. "Have you reached a conclusion?"

"Have you?" He turned his beaky nose towards me, "You have the same information as I, so what do you make of it?"

"Very little" I confessed. "It is plain that Mr. John Ruddy suspects or perhaps even hopes for some irregularity in the claim, and also that you support him, but on what grounds?"

"Were it only that I would be easier in my mind," he said sombrely. "No, old friend, I fear we fish in far murkier waters, but I must have more facts. Facts, Watson, are crucial."

"Is it not possible that Ruddy, with the well-known reluctance of the insurance world to disburse money, is grasping at straws? Added to which is his fear of the consequences of his unorthodox transaction?"

"That is his primary concern," agreed Holmes. "That is indisputable. A policy holder dies soon after the first premium is paid and his widow and beneficiary is on the spot almost at once to lay her claim. That is enough to disturb any responsible agent. But consider, Watson, how did Ruddy describe her?"

I thought back. "He said very little of her except that she was distraught. Surely that is natural?"

"Natural, yes, but think, man, think! We have this lady straight from seeing her husband's body on a mortuary slab making a bee-line for the honey-pot of the insurer's representative," He gave the rusty chuckle that served him for a laugh. "A neat turn of phrase, Watson. Mark it well." His face sobered. "Does that strike you as the actions of a grieving widow?"

"I suppose not, unless there was little affection between them and she was playing the part expected of her."

He bent forward and tapped me on the knee with the stem of his pipe. "There you have it. Playing the part – but what part?"

Before I could digest this, the cab drew up before an unpretentious but pleasant hotel and we alighted to climb the three wide steps to the entrance. A young woman presided at the reception desk, and on our approach she looked up with an engaging smile.

"Good afternoon, gentlemen," she said. "You require rooms?"

"No, miss." As ever Holmes remained impervious to feminine charms and his face was stern. "I wish to see the manager at once." His tone had undergone a subtle change, no more than a slight coarsening of

41

accent, but I knew it foretold a slipping into one of those parts which he so easily assumed.

"I'll see if Mr. Hardy is free, sir," said the young lady. "Who shall I say wishes to see him?"

Holmes leaned forward confidentially and lowered his voice. "I am Inspector Lestrade of Scotland Yard, but the name is not to be bandied about. Please inform Mr. Hardy. Our business is urgent."

The young lady's eyes widened, but she hurried away without a word.

"Holmes!" I hissed in his ear. "You go too far. What if he asks for identification?"

He patted his pocket and his lips twitched mischievously. "Be easy. I am well prepared. Just back me up like a good fellow."

The young lady was back in a flash. "This way, sir," she said in an awe-struck voice.

My companion turned on the charming smile of which he was capable when it served his ends, placing a finger to his lips in a conspiratorial fashion. We found ourselves in a small office with a rotund grey-haired man rising to greet us from behind a desk.

"James Hardy, Inspector. I trust nothing is amiss?" His chubby face was creased into an ingratiating smile and a pink tongue moistened his red lips.

"Nothing to cause you worry, sir, and I'd take it kindly if you will forget that we are police officers. We are here *incognito* on an extremely delicate business in which you may assist us." The story fell easily from Holmes's lips as he fixed the manager with a penetrating look.

"Of course, gentlemen. Please be seated and tell me how I may help."

Holmes folded his long frame into a chair and brusquely signed for me to sit beside him. From his pocket he took a notebook which he studied for a while. I could see he had it open at a blank page, but his performance was impressive.

He looked up at last. "I understand, Mr. Hardy, that last Monday you reported that one of your waiters, a George Monk, was missing."

"That is correct, Insp – er – " Hardy paused uncertainly.

"Mr. Smith will serve, and my colleague is Mr. Brown." Holmes laid a finger alongside his nose, a vulgar gesture, but well in the character of Lestrade whose name he had so lightly taken. "Tell me, sir, when did this man's absence first come to your attention?"

"It was tea-time on Sunday. He had served lunch as usual, and then from two until four he was free. It was his habit, if the weather was clement, to take a stroll on the sea front each afternoon. It is but five minutes gentle walking from here."

"And on Sunday he followed his normal practice?"

42

"To the best of my knowledge," the manager replied. "Miss Hillman is positive that he went out at twenty minutes after two o'clock. She spoke to him as he passed her on the back stairs."

"Miss Hillman is the young lady at the desk? How was he dressed?"

"I questioned her and she told me he was wearing a blazer, flannels, and carrying a straw hat. Quite the young blade. But surely, Mr. Smith, all this is known to the local police from the statement I made to Sergeant Lane on Monday?"

"That's as may be, sir," said Holmes gruffly. "This is a far deeper matter that I am pursuing. Be so good as to answer my questions without wasting time." He wrote something in his notebook. "So twenty-past-two is the last known sighting of him by your staff?"

"Exactly." Hardy frowned at being thus admonished. "When he failed to appear at tea-time, I was at first most angry, assuming he had absented himself willfully, but when he did not turn up at dinner I became rather more worried." The manager picked up a pen and rolled it in the palms of his hands. "I had gone to his room at quarter-past-four, but it told me nothing. His suit was on a hanger ready to be donned, and there was no hint that he had not expected to return. Several times during the evening I looked in, but nothing had changed."

"So when he remained absent on Monday you went to the police. You have had no word from them?"

"Sergeant Lane came to interview us all – most discreetly, I may add – but I have heard nothing since."

"Was Monk a satisfactory employee?" asked Holmes.

"He would not have remained otherwise. He was my only resident waiter, all the others being local men who come in daily."

"What was his background?"

Hardy smiled faintly. "Rather unusual for a waiter. He had spent some years at sea as a steward on steamers to the East, but he had wearied of the life and, to use his own phrase, swallowed the anchor. I had one occasion to reprimand him when he first came, but he took it in good part. He wore a ring in his left ear, a common practice among seafaring men, but most improper in an hotel of this class."

"Of course," murmured Holmes. "Now, sir, first a word with Miss Hillman and then I shall want to see the man's room. Will you fetch the young lady, please?"

When the latter came in, Holmes gave her his chair and stood looking down at her. She sat with neatly folded hands, her clear grey eyes looking out from a frank open countenance that in other circumstances would have been ready for laughter.

"Now, Miss Hillman, listen carefully," Holmes began. "My name is Smith, and this other gentleman is Mr. Brown." A small wrinkle of perplexity passed across her smooth brow as my friend continued. "You will forget any other name you may have heard, Miss, for I am here on more important matters than you can conceive. No word of this visit must pass beyond these four walls. Do I make myself clear?"

She nodded gravely. "I am not a simpleton, Mr. Smith. Neither am I a chatterbox. What do you want of me?"

"I understand you were the last person at this hotel to see Mr. George Monk before he vanished. That is correct?"

"I believe so. I had been to the kitchen for a cup of tea, leaving the porter at the desk, when Mr. Monk came down the service stairs on his way out. It was precisely twenty past two when I left the kitchen."

"You spoke?"

"Briefly. He said 'Good afternoon, Miss Charlotte,' that being my name, and I replied, 'Good afternoon, George. Mind you keep out of the sun' It was a very hot day," she added. "He went out, never to return."

"You were on good terms?" asked Holmes.

"Oh, yes. He was a widely travelled man and told marvellous stories of his times when we were together in foreign parts."

"Close friends, in fact?"

Miss Hillman blushed prettily. "On friendly terms. No more than that, Mr. Smith."

"Thank you, miss, that is all. Remember, be circumspect." He waited for the door to close on her then turned to the manager. "Now, sir, the missing man's room."

We were conducted to a small room under the eaves, the door of which Hardy unlocked and threw open. When he made to enter, Holmes put out an arm to bar his way and stood surveying the cramped quarters from the threshold.

"Nothing has been removed?" he asked.

"Nothing. Sergeant Lane made a thorough search but took nothing."

Holmes sighed. "Then I doubt if there is much left for us. The trail is cold, but we may find something. Come, Brown, and do you, Mr. Hardy, remain here."

We went in and Holmes allowed his eyes to wander over the room, touching nothing. Then turned to me with a snort.

"I think we will learn more of Sergeant Lane than of George Monk," he said in a low voice. He opened the cupboard that served as a wardrobe and went through the pockets of the few clothes hanging therein, producing only a German silver pencil case and a soiled handkerchief. He dropped to his knees to examine the half-dozen pairs of boots and shoes in the bottom before looking over his shoulder at the manager who hovered uncertainly in the doorway.

"Mr. Monk was not a small man, judging by his apparel, yet his feet were not large."

"Indeed not," Hardy agreed. "It was a conceit of his that a size six boot left ample room to wear two pairs of socks in the worst weather."

Holmes nodded absently and, still on his knees, let his eyes travel over the floor. Suddenly, like a rabbit darting into its burrow, he dived full length beneath the bed to came out with a small object in the palm of his hand. His eyes twinkled at me as he rose to his feet and dusted the knees of his trousers.

"So the good sergeant did leave us something," he murmured. "Tell me, Mr. Hardy, could this be the ear-ring worn by your man?" He held out his hand and the light caught a glimmer of silver. The roly-poly manager shrugged. "Possibly, but I could not take an oath on it. All I can say it is similar."

"But distinctive," said Holmes. "Come, there is no more to be had here. I need not repeat, Mr. James Hardy, I require your discretion."

"In my profession one learns discretion very early," Hardy said pompously. "My lips are sealed." He followed us to the hotel entrance and watched us descend to the street and vanish from his sight.

"Well," I asked, "what now?

"I fear we have much to do and luncheon must be a casualty to our industry. The police station is our next objective. I believe I observed it on our journey from the station."

Five minutes later we walked into the bastion of Margate's law and order and found a uniformed inspector talking to a young and intelligent looking sergeant, both looked up as we entered and the senior man turned away towards an inner sanctum.

"A moment, Inspector" Holmes said authoritatively. "A word with you, please."

"Cannot the sergeant deal with it, sir?" The inspector frowned. "I am a very busy man."

"Not too busy to speak to me, I hope." My companion took a card from his pocket to hand to the inspector, at the same time placing a finger to his lips.

The other glanced at the card then raised his eyes and spoke with alacrity. "Of course I will be pleased to speak to you, sir. Nothing will give me greater pleasure. This way, if you will. Lane, I am not to be disturbed." This last to the sergeant who nodded impassively.

No sooner had his door closed on us than he stretched out his hand.

"My dear Mr. Holmes, this is indeed an honour and a delight. Inspector Griffin, my old colleague at Sevenoaks, has spoken most warmly of you. Please sit, gentlemen, and tell me how I may assist you. My name is Purdew."

"First I must make a confession," Holmes began when we were seated. "I am guilty of posing as a police officer and of using the name of Inspector Lestrade of Scotland Yard in order to obtain information quickly."

Purdew's eyes twinkled. "I'll make a bargain with you, Mr. Holmes: If you promise to tell no one, neither shall I, Now, what brings you to Margate?"

"Two crimes which may be connected." The inspector's look invited my friend to go on, which he did. "The disappearance of George Monk from the Stanton Hotel and the alleged drowning of Elias Burdick."

"'Alleged drowning'?" Purdew looked blank. "With respect, Mr. Holmes, I see no room for doubt. The body was identified by his widow and our surgeon certified drowning as the cause of death. As for Monk, we think it probable that he has returned to his old calling of ship's steward."

"Inspector, are you aware that the Rural and Urban Insurance Company is liable for a very large sum in respect of Burdick's death?"

"I knew them to be involved, but not to what extent. A constable escorted Mrs. Burdick from the mortuary to the agent's office. I know Mr. Ruddy well."

"Mr. Ruddy is not a happy man, Mr. Purdew. He has doubts about the validity of the claim."

"As these people so often have," replied the inspector. "It is in their nature."

"I believe he has good cause in this instance," said Holmes, and went on to relate the woeful tale told us by the unhappy man.

"It seems Mr. Ruddy acted somewhat irresponsibly and is now anxious to retrieve his position." Purdew plucked at his moustache. "However, Mr. Holmes, I am at your disposal. What do you want of me?"

"What happened to the body of the drowned man?"

"Why, it is still at the mortuary pending Mrs. Burdick's instructions."

"Excellent!" Holmes clapped his hands. "May I inspect it?"

"As you wish. I should like to accompany you if I may." On receiving a nod, the inspector reached for his cap and we followed him out into the street, he pausing for a brief word to the sergeant as we passed.

"Rather young to be a sergeant, is he not?" Holmes remarked casually.

46

"A bright and ambitious young man," Purdew agreed. "Would that I could recruit more like him, but on the pittance a constable is paid, it is hard to do so." He shrugged and lengthened his stride. "The mortuary is but two streets away."

"Sergeant Lane investigated the business at the Stanton Hotel," said Holmes. "What were his views?"

"We agreed that it seemed an impulsive action on Monk's part," said the inspector thoughtfully. "However, if he suddenly made up his mind to return to sea, there was little we could do."

"And you think that is what happened?"

"In the absence of more evidence it seems likely."

"Then perhaps we shall find more evidence," Holmes replied, but refused to enlarge on his remarks.

I congratulated myself on the fact that I was following my friend's reasoning thus far, and permitted myself a little smile. So often had I been dragged along at his coat-tails and left in the dark by his incisive brain that to find myself keeping abreast of his thoughts for once afforded me no small satisfaction. He must have divined my feelings, for as we reached the doors of the gloomy building he gave me one of his thin smiles while Inspector Purdew applied himself vigorously to the bell.

The wicket-gate was opened after an interval by a shirt-sleeved man who wore a leather apron and carried an enamel mug of tea. He was of indeterminate age and had a suitably lugubrious expression on his battered features.

"Not another customer, Guv'nor?" he said complainingly.

"Not this time, Charlie. We want another look at the one brought in on Monday."

"Number seventeen." Charlie gave a jerk of the head, "This way, if you please." He led the way through the gloomy precincts and into a large cavern-like room where three or four shrouded bundles lay on slabs ranged against the wall. "There he is. Number seventeen."

At a murmured word from Holmes the inspector dismissed the attendant, leaving us looking down at the pathetic heap before us.

"Are you squeamish, Purdew?" asked Holmes, one hand on the corner of the covering sheet.

"I've seen enough in my time to be inured," said the other.

"This is your province, Watson, so I'll not ask you." He drew the sheet back to reveal a face battered beyond all recognition, at which he whistled softly.

"And this is the body identified by Mrs. Burdick as that of her husband? On what grounds, pray?"

"She said she would know him anywhere, but she pointed out the silver ring on his left hand. See, it is embedded in the swollen flesh." The inspector pulled the sheet down and pointed.

Holmes produced his magnifying glass and peered closely at the ring, mumbling under his breath the while. Presently he turned his attention to the rest of the piteous remains, first turning the head from side to side then touching and probing the torso as he would a joint of meat.

His eyes narrowed in satisfaction when he finally threw the sheet to the floor and stood back.

"There is no doubt as to the cause of death, Mr. Purdew?"

"Our surgeon, Dr. Stubbs, has no doubt," replied the inspector, "and he is a very competent doctor."

"Watson? Would you agree?"

"If Dr. Stubbs made a thorough examination, and I see by the incisions that he did, I would not dream of contradicting him," I said stiffly,

My friend gave and ironic smile at my defence of a professional colleague before turning back to the policeman. "The clothing recovered from the beach," he queried. "Where is it?"

"Back at the station in the property store. It will be returned to the widow after tomorrow's inquest."

"Then we must make haste. Come." Leaving the uncovered corpse as it was, he made his way out into the street, his long legs striding out as we kept pace with him as best we could. "I must see that clothing," he flung over his shoulder to the perspiring Inspector Purdew as we entered the station. "Have it brought in at once, please."

His tone was peremptory and Purdew looked at me in bewilderment, but I could only shrug and he gave the necessary orders to Sergeant Lane before leading us into his office. When the sergeant appeared laden with a linen sack, he hesitated nervously and looked uncomfortably at his superior.

"Excuse me, sir," he said in a reverential voice, "but is one of these gentlemen Mr. Sherlock Holmes"

"What the deuce is it to you, Lane?" snapped the inspector. "Do not be impertinent."

Holmes stepped forward. "I'm sorry, Mr. Purdew," he said wryly. "I forgot to tell you I asked for two telegrams to be addressed to me here. It was most discourteous of me. They have arrived, Sergeant Lane?"

"Five minutes since, sir. I thought it might be a practical joke, but I wanted to be sure. Here, sir."

He pulled them from his top pocket and Holmes snatched them from his hand, tearing them open feverishly and giving a small cry as he read the contents. "I am right, Watson, I am right." He smiled grimly and tucked the telegrams away before turning his attention to the sack of clothing.

Tipping the contents on to the floor, he crouched down to paw through them, for all the world like a rag-picker at an East End street market.

The inspector looked at me with raised eyebrows and I gave him what I hoped was a knowing smile before giving my attention to Holmes, who was wrapped in concentration.

"Jacket, trousers – nothing in the pockets – linen, socks, cap." He stood up, still talking to himself. "As I expected, no boots or shoes. Everything is here, Inspector?"

"Everything." Before more could be said, there was a knock on the door and at a sign from Purdew the sergeant answered it. He exchanged few words then brought in a constable who had what appeared to be a bundle of dirty rags under his arm.

"I think you should see this, sir," Lane said to the inspector. "Denton found these stuffed down a rabbit-hole by the big copse. Show the gentlemen, Denton."

The embarrassed constable shook out the bundle to reveal a striped blazer, once-white flannels, and various other items of men's apparel, including a pair of tennis-shoes upon which Holmes pounced avidly.

"Tell us, Denton," the inspector was saying. "How did you come to find these?"

The constable shifted his feet and looked rigidly ahead. "Sir, at one-fifty p.m. I was patrolling – "

"Yes, yes," Holmes interrupted impatiently. "You are not giving evidence in court, man. Tell us a quickly as possible."

"Do as the gentleman says, Denton," added Purdew.

"Well, sir, I'd been round the copse and was going back to make my point with Sergeant Hoskins when I saw this flapping from a rabbit-hole." He indicated the blazer. "I dragged it out and found the rest of the stuff farther in. Sergeant Hoskins told me to bring it back here straight away."

"This is all there was?" asked Holmes keenly,

"All I could see and reach, sir."

Holmes and the inspector exchanged glances and, at a nod from the former, Purdew dismissed the constable with a brief word of commendation.

Holmes swung round sharply on Sergeant Lane, who was exhibiting signs of wanting to speak. "Come along, Lane, out with it," he urged.

"I am correct in thinking that these clothes belong to the missing waiter, sir?" Holmes remained silent and the sergeant continued. "If so, then should there not also be a straw hat?"

"Perhaps it is still in the burrow. A thorough search will show us."

"Organize it, Lane," said Inspector Purdew. He waited until the man had left, then turned a worried look on Holmes. "It looks as if we must look for another body. Two men drowned within hours of each other!"

"Another body, Inspector? Whose, pray?"

"Why, George Monk's, surely. Do we not agree that these are his clothes?"

"Most certainly. His name is on the laundry label inside the jacket, but I do not think a man taking an afternoon bathe would stuff a pair of pristine white flannels into a rabbit-hole, do you?"

The inspector rubbed his chin thoughtfully, then his face brightened. "Then he was not drowned. He changed into more appropriate attire before making his way to a port where he would find a ship."

"Mr. Purdew," Holmes said patiently, "we know that when Monk left the hotel he was carrying nothing, else the lady clerk would have remarked upon it to your sergeant or myself."

"Then he purchased them in town and changed in the copse?"

My friend turned to me. "What do you say to that, Watson?"

I shook my head. As much as I deplored this baiting of the inspector who had received us in such a fine spirit, I was unable to keep a note of smugness from my voice. "I think we were looking at the mortal remains of George Monk not half-an-hour since," I answered, and Holmes gave a delighted chuckle.

"Capital, Watson. You learn apace." He turned to the inspector, who had dropped into his chair wearing a thunderstruck expression.

"Are you saying, Mr. Holmes, that the body in the mortuary is not that of Elias Burdick, but that of George Monk?"

"Exactly." Holmes became apologetic. "Forgive me, Inspector. I had no intention of keeping you in the dark, but I like to verify facts before committing myself."

"Then you suspected it from the first? Why?"

Holmes seated himself opposite Purdew and began to explain. "I learned from Monk's employer that when he first came to Margate, he had cause to reprimand him for wearing an ear-ring, as is the habit of many sea-going men. Sergeant Lane was not told of this? No, but I found this under the bed in Monk's room." He produced the small silver object from his pocket.

"I think Watson will confirm its origin."

"Benares work," I said. "I saw much of it when I passed through India on my way to Afghanistan."

"We were told that Monk had extremely small feet of which he was somewhat vain," continued Holmes. "The corpse we saw had such small feet and his ear was pierced to accommodate an ear-ring." Holmes leant forward and tapped the table. "But, mark this, Inspector – the ring so deeply embedded in his finger was of Benares silver-work also."

"You make a case," said Purdew, "but how do you account for the fact that Mrs. Burdick identified the ring as her husband's?"

"Remember the face was so disfigured that it was unrecognisable. The ring was probably too tight to be removed even before the body was swollen in death, so needing to make a positive declaration, she seized on the ring." Holmes sat back complacently and eyed the inspector.

"I begin to understand," said the latter. "You believe that Burdick disposed of Monk with the intention of letting his wife claim the insurance money by identifying the body as that of her husband." His face went red with anger and jumped to his feet. "What a pair of monsters! We must take her and force her to reveal her husband's whereabouts."

"All in good time," said Holmes urbanely. "Inspector Purdew, you have been very patient with me thus far. Will you trust me farther?"

The policeman hesitated briefly before sitting down again. "What do you want of me, Mr. Holmes? I trust you implicitly."

"Then listen carefully. This is what you must do." Holmes began to speak tersely, receiving an occasional nod of understanding from the inspector. "Be sure of this, Mr. Purdew," he concluded, "I have no wish for my name to come into this matter, and any credit accruing is yours alone."

"It shall be as you say," replied the gratified inspector. "What will you do meanwhile?"

"I shall attend Mr. John Ruddy, who must surely be impatient to hear of my progress. Then we shall proceed to Mrs. Ellis's boarding establishment, where I understand the so-called widow is lodged. Remember, Inspector, be prompt, but do nothing until you have my signal, or all may be lost."

He stood up. "Mr. Ruddy's office is close?

"But five minutes' walk. Turn left out of the station. The third turning on the left is Priory Road, and his office is halfway up on the right above an empty shop. You will see his plate at the side door."

When five minutes later we came into the office to find our client impatient and anxious. He sprang up from his desk to grasp my colleague eagerly by the sleeve.

"Mr. Holmes!" he gasped. "At last! What news have you for me?"

Holmes shook himself free. "Compose yourself, sir," he said crisply. "I can guarantee your six-thousand pounds is safe. What account you will give your superiors of your actions is for you to determine, but I'm sure a little judicious wording will ease your path. At the same time, I hope this will serve as a lesson to you."

"Indeed it will, Mr. Holmes," Ruddy said fervently. "My ambitions outran my judgement, but I know better now. But what happens next?"

"We have the final act to play out – but meanwhile there is the matter of my fee."

"Ask what you will and I will gladly double it," cried Ruddy.

"That is unnecessary," replied my friend coldly. "My charges are fixed and not open to discussion. However, if you will write a cheque now you may hand it to me in exactly one hour's time when you are relieved of your troubles." He named a sum which was accepted without demur. "Now we pay a call on Mrs. Emily Burdick, to whom you present me as a financial secretary to your company." Again his impish humour showed through as it so often did when we neared the end of a case. "Mr. Gregson is a capital name for me, I think. Mr. Ruddy. Whatever you do, say nothing to alert the lady to the fact that you are anything but the sympathetic agent of the insurance company. Can you play the part?"

"Mr. Holmes, I could play Hamlet himself with what is at stake!"

"I hope so. Watson, you look put out."

"Is there no part for me in what you term 'the final act'?" I asked.

My friend laughed and laid an affectionate arm across my shoulders.

"My dear fellow, where would I be without you? Of course you have your part, but more of that later. Let us proceed."

Our objective was a neat villa a few hundred yards from the sea-front. A card in the window proclaimed vacancies, and the door was opened by a plump jolly-looking woman who smiled brightly at us.

"Good afternoon, gentlemen," she said. "You require rooms?"

"I'm afraid not, Madam," Ruddy replied in solemn tones. "You are Mrs. Ellis?" She nodded. "I am Mr. Ruddy, and I believe I am expected by Mrs. Burdick."

Her face took on an expression of sympathy. "Oh, the poor woman! How I feel for her in her grief. Come in, gentlemen, please."

We were ushered into a comfortably furnished parlour and invited to sit down. Mrs. Ellis stood in the doorway, her fingers twisting the rings she wore on both hands.

"A moment, please." Holmes took immediate charge. "I am an associate of Mr. Ruddy's. Sit for a moment and tell us about Mr. and Mrs. Burdick."

"There's not much to tell." She took a chair and continued to play with her rings. "Mr. Burdick came to me before lunch on Sunday asking for a room. He told me he was an actor from London hoping for a few weeks work at a local theatre before the season ended."

"Did he say which?" asked Holmes.

"No, I had very little speech with him. Within an hour of his arrival he went out, to get the lie of the town, he said, and told me he would be in for tea. That was the last I saw of him."

"He went out empty-handed?"

"He carried a Gladstone bag," She sniffed and dabbed at her nose with a wisp of handkerchief. "He had not returned by eleven o'clock, which is when I start locking up, and by midnight I thought he had fallen in with friends and was sleeping elsewhere. It happens with actors,"

"You went to bed?" Holmes encouraged her. "Go on, please."

Mrs. Ellis nodded unhappily. "I never dreamt anything was amiss. How could I? Well, Monday came and he hadn't come back, so I went to his room. I found a suit and pair of boots in the wardrobe and his razor on the wash-stand. Then I got worried and went to the police."

"Where you were told that Elias Burdick's clothes had been found on the beach," Holmes finished for her.

"Not only that," she cried dramatically. "Even whilst I was at the station, it was reported that a body had been taken from the sea and was assumed to be that of my lodger. They wanted me to look at it, but as I told them, I'd hardly seen the man and they could do without my help."

She shuddered. "What would I want with corpses I hardly knew?"

"You were well spared," agreed Holmes. "And Mrs. Burdick?"

"That was Tuesday. All of a twitter, I was, and this lady came to the door with a policeman who said she was Mrs. Burdick and she wanted her husband's old room. Not a word had she to say for herself, she was so upset, and I didn't have the heart to refuse her. I took her up, and over a cup of tea the policeman told me she'd come straight from identifying her husband at the mortuary."

Holmes pinched his long nose thoughtfully. "Tell me, Mrs. Ellis, how was the lady dressed?"

"All in black, head to toe just like a widow would be, and so heavily veiled that I marvelled she could see where she was going, Within five minutes she was down again, asking the policeman to take her to Mr. Ruddy's office." Mrs. Ellis lowered her voice. "Do you know, since she came back I've not seen hide nor hair of her. Stricken with grief, she is, and takes all her meals in her room. I just knock on her door and leaves the tray on the landing table. Number three, it is. I must say," she added, "her appetite hasn't suffered at all."

"Grief takes on different forms," Holmes observed sententiously, "Now, Madam, be good enough to inform the lady that Mr. Ruddy is here to do business with her. Say no more than that, you understand?" He eyed her sternly and with a nervous nod she left.

"Remember your part, Mr. Ruddy," said Holmes in a low voice. "Watson, I shall leave the door open that you may see from a suitable vantage point but not be seen. Be on your guard, old chap." He went to the window and gave a twitch of the curtain as the landlady returned,

"I'll take you up, gentlemen," she said, but Holmes shook his head,

"No, Mrs. Ellis, you will remain here. Have you any other guests in the house? No? Good, then you will lock yourself in this room and not come out until I or my other colleague tell you to." He inclined his head towards me. "It is for your own safety."

Such was the force of his personality that she nodded meekly and we heard the key turn as soon as we were in the hallway. Holmes went to the front door and quietly slipped the catch. Then we made our way silently up the narrow stairs.

We found ourselves in a poorly lit passage with several doors on either side. Number three was at the end, the door set at an angle, and at a sign from Holmes, I took up a position in the gloom where I could command a view of the room once the door was opened. Ruddy knocked on the door and a muffled voice from within bade him enter, which he did with Holmes hard on his heels.

I could see clearly into the room where a veiled figure sat in an upright chair placed with its back to the only window. As Holmes stepped over the threshold, I saw him check his stride for the merest fraction of a second, then continue.

"My dear Mrs. Burdick," said Ruddy, his voice oozing sympathy. "This is a sad occasion indeed. May I present Mr. Gregson, our head cashier?"

"Very sad," said Holmes evenly. "However, your husband's forethought and prudence must provide some small consolation." There was no reply and Holmes advanced farther into the room. "Do you not find the atmosphere somewhat close?" he went on, and not waiting for an answer, he stepped swiftly past the woman and threw the sash open to its fullest extent.

A strong breeze from the window rushed through the room and the woman turned her head in alarm. The draught took her veils and she frantically pulled them back over her face as Holmes slammed the window down. His long legs took him back to face her, his eyes blazing triumphantly.

"The game is up, Elias Burdick!" he cried. "Will you come quietly?"

54

With an unladylike oath the figure leapt from the chair, taking Holmes off balance and cannoning him into to Ruddy, who stood paralysed.

"Watson!" shouted my friend. "Seize him!"

I bounded forward and received a violent blow on the shoulder, but I grappled with the black-clad figure, realising at once that this was no woman who fought so desperately. I got in a telling punch to the ribs before a pair of sinewy hands took me round the throat and slammed me against the wall, driving the breath from my body. My assailant dived for the stairs, but hampered by the long dress was not quick enough to evade my clutching fingers which took hold of the streaming veil. It checked him for an instant then Holmes was on him and I was left gasping with the veils in my hand, together with a long black wig.

"Stout work, Watson," panted Holmes, applying a vicious arm-lock to his captive and receiving a stream of invective in return. He took a whistle from his pocket to blow a shrill blast, and within seconds Inspector Purdew pounded up the stairs with Sergeant Lane and a constable at his heels.

Not wasting time on questions, Purdew clapped a pair of handcuffs on the writhing man and left the sergeant and constable holding him in a rough grip.

"Well done, Inspector." Holmes straightened his coat. "Meet Elias Burdick, the murderer of George Monk. Also known as Luke Henry and Josiah Larkin, under which names he committed similar crimes. There are bodies buried under those names in Essex and Hampshire, but he can only hang once, unfortunately."

The prisoner continued to struggle violently until a tap from the sergeant's truncheon persuaded him of the futility of resistance, and at a signal from Purdew he was hustled downstairs to the waiting van.

"Is there anything more I should know, Mr. Holmes?" asked the inspector.

"I think not. You have a grasp of the situation that would make your London counterparts blush with shame." He thrust out his hand. "Goodbye, sir. It has been a delight to work with you."

After fulsome thanks, Inspector Purdew departed with his prisoner, leaving Ruddy to come forward to express his gratitude in more tangible form.

"I do not know how you did it, Mr. Holmes," he said wonderingly. "I can never thank you enough."

"I have my methods," smiled Holmes as he folded the slip of paper into his pocket book. "Watson, my dear fellow, are you injured? I should have inquired sooner."

"There is nothing wrong with me that a belated lunch will not cure," I complained. "Do you realise we have had nothing since breakfast? Also we still have Mrs. Ellis locked in her parlour."

"So we have. Good Lord, I had quite forgotten. The poor lady must be frantic."

In the event, the good lady was reasonably composed, and a few judicious words giving a bare outline of events was sufficient to soothe her ruffled feelings.

"You will read of it in the papers, and Inspector Purdew will want a statement from you," ended Holmes. "Meanwhile, speak to no one of it. Now, Watson, I believe you mentioned lunch." An hour-and-a-half later we were on our way back to London. With my notebook open, I was sketching in the affair with it still fresh in my memory, and I paused to chew my pencil when I caught my friend's eye.

"Still puzzled?" he asked with one of his impish smiles. "Why, you were with me every step of the way."

"I thought so, but I must confess I became somewhat confused towards the end." I tapped my notebook. "We knew that the body in the mortuary was that of George Monk, and it was meant to be taken for Burdick. Also it was reasonable to assume that Burdick had murdered that poor fellow in order to claim the insurance money."

"Very good, old chap. Go on."

"That is where I lose the thread," I said. "I expected to find the villain's wife there as his accomplice. Where is she?"

"There is no wife, and there never was." He pulled out his pipe and began to fill it.

"Ah, those telegrams!" I exclaimed. "You kept me in the dark."

"Not really. The telegrams were mere confirmation of similar cases I found in my commonplace book."

"Then how the deuce did you know that the supposed widow was Burdick in woman's guise?"

Holmes applied a vesta to the tobacco and surveyed me through a blue haze. He turned to look out of the window, and at first I thought he wasn't going to answer me. He sucked at his pipe and for a full minute he remained stubbornly silent. Then he turned back to me with a wry smile.

"Confound you, Watson," he said pettishly. "You have a facility for asking the most awkward questions. The whole truth of the matter is that I didn't know that until the very last minute!"

"What!" My pencil fell from my fingers to roll unheeded on to the floor. "Are you telling me – "

"Yes, Watson. Right up to the moment I stepped into that room, I fully expected to find Burdick's female accomplice."

"Then what changed your opinion?"

"You will recall that the supposed Mrs. Burdick was seated with her back to the window with her face heavily veiled and in shadow. As I went in, I saw a pair of boots peeping out from below the dress and to me they seemed somewhat over-large for a lady. There are some unfortunate women so endowed but it set me off on a new train of thought. You saw me open the window?"

"Yes, and caused a most infernal draught."

"Precisely my intention. The breeze disturbed the veils swathing the woman's head and in that fraction of a second I saw the nose."

"The nose!" I echoed. "Surely, Holmes, a nose is a nose, is it not?"

"Oh, yes." He gave me a thin smile. "You, my dear fellow, are more familiar with the whims and caprices of the fair sex, but even I am aware that no lady, whatever her other pre-occupations, would neglect to powder her nose to receive visitors, although she would remain veiled. That nose, Watson, was as shiny as a new sovereign, and at that moment the whole matter became clear."

I recovered my pencil from beneath the seat and directed a quizzical look at my companion, "So you admit to a certain amount of luck at the end?"

"I admit nothing of the sort," he said testily. "It was observation and deduction that brought the business to a satisfactory conclusion, and will hang Burdick under one name or another. Now let me relax for the remainder of the journey. I fear Lestrade will be at our door this evening. He has quite lost the scent in the matter of the vanishing shop at Highgate."

"You owe the poor fellow something for the use of his name," I said drily, but he closed his eyes and uttered not another word until we came to London Bridge.

The Grosvenor Square Furniture Van

The first day of October, and already winter signalled its approach with a chill wind that rattled the windows and sent puffs of smoke into the room from the newly-lit fire to mingle with the haze of our post-breakfast pipes. For once the table was cleared before nine o'clock, and Sherlock Holmes, my friend and fellow-occupier of the rooms at 221b Baker Street, had discarded his old blue dressing-gown to assume his outdoor clothes.

I raised a querying eyebrow as he chose a stick from the collection in the stand, receiving a negative shake of the head in response.

"No, I have no special need of your company, but of course, you are quite welcome to join me in a brisk walk to Bradley's for a pound of shag."

"In that case I shall remain here," I replied as I settled back behind the pages of *The Daily Telegraph*. "This wind promises to do my shoulder little good. Bring me half-a-pound of Arcadia Mixture if you will be so good."

The door had not closed on him before I sat up with yelp of excitement. "Holmes!" I shouted loudly, and he reappeared with a look of amused annoyance on his face.

"Really, my dear Watson, must you shout at me as though you were hailing a cab? What is so urgent?"

"This." I thrust the paper at him and stabbed a finger at it. "It sounds right up your street, or I'm a Dutchman."

He took the paper from me and ran his eye over the item I indicated. It told of the mysterious disappearance of the well-known and highly respected Sir Peter Fawkus from his home in Grosvenor Square. His butler, one Thomas Moscrop, was also missing, and the matter was made more bizarre by the fact that a large sideboard had vanished from the dining room, leaving its contents strewn on the floor.

He returned the paper with a shrug. "Nothing there for us. I see Lady Fawkus has sufficient influence for Scotland Yard in the person of our friend Gregson to show an interest. I don't doubt he will blunder his way to a solution, given time."

This time he shut the door firmly, and I was left with only the sound of his footsteps on the stairs, I went back to the paragraph and tried to fit the bare facts into some kind of logical order by using my friend's methods, I was still cogitating when Mrs. Hudson announced Inspector Gregson.

"Come in, Inspector," I said. "Holmes is out at present but should be back shortly. A glass of beer while you wait?"

"Thank you, Doctor. Most welcome." He spread himself comfortably in front of the fire. "Your very good health, Doctor Watson."

Holmes was back within ten minutes of Gregson's arrival. He divested himself of his coat and threw it on to the settee, along with his hat.

"Now, my dear Gregson," he smiled, "how may I assist you in the matter of Sir Peter Fawkus?"

The officer grinned ruefully, "Always one jump ahead, Mr. Holmes, though I'll not deny being grateful to you for that more than once. I expect you've seen what the papers have to say, and between the three of us, there's a deal of pressure from above to get the thing sorted."

"Tell me what you know," said Holmes as he filled his pipe. "Leave nothing out, however trivial you may think it to be."

"Well, sir, it's like this: On Wednesday night, Lady Fawkus returned from the theatre to find the house in darkness, the only servant in evidence being her personal maid who was dozing in her mistress's bedroom. She told Lady Fawkus that the butler, Moscrop, had told the rest of the staff that Sir Peter had given orders for them to remain in their quarters, as he was expecting important visitors. However, there was no sign of Sir Peter, nor of Moscrop. This was well past midnight, and Lady Fawkus decided that her husband had for reasons unknown left the house, taking the butler with him,"

"Surely a very casual attitude," Holmes put in. "What opinion did you form of conditions within the household?"

"I got the feeling there was something on the lady's mind. She's a handsome woman, barely thirty years of age, while her husband is all of seventy. What little I could get from the servants made me think she spends a lot of time with her own friends, while Sir Peter is at his club most evenings. Anyway, it wasn't until yesterday morning that it became clear that neither Sir Peter nor Moscrop had returned, and a footman found that a large sideboard had gone from the dining room. Lady Fawkus waited until mid-day, and when Sir Peter hadn't come home and a messenger had ascertained that he had not been to his club, she took herself straight to the Yard to demand something should be done. I've been landed with it, and quite frankly, Mr. Holmes, I don't know where to start."

Holmes gazed into the fire as if for inspiration. Then he looked up at Gregson. "What of the butler? Has he been long with Sir Peter?"

"No more than a couple of weeks. He's only there temporarily, as the regular man is in hospital recovering from an accident. Got himself knocked down by a cab in Orchard Street. Old fellow, name of Clarke – been with Sir Peter twenty years and more."

"Then," said Holmes, "I suggest you turn your attention to this fellow Moscrop. It will also be fruitful to give some thought to the matter of the sideboard and why it is missing but the contents left. That is all I can think of at the moment."

Gregson nodded gloomily, obviously disappointed that my friend had nothing more to offer. He was given some consolation by the promise that Holmes would give the matter further thought and get in touch if anything should occur to him.

Once the inspector had left, Holmes slumped into his chair with his old cherry-wood pipe clamped between his teeth, a frown of concentration furrowing his brow. He remained so even when Mrs. Hudson tapped on the door again, so I took it upon myself to ascertain her mission.

"It's a lady asking for Mr. Holmes," she whispered, casting a wary glance over my shoulder at the motionless figure.

"Who is she?" I found myself whispering also.

"Says her name is Mrs. Hebden, and her husband has gone missing. She seems a respectable body."

"Oh, for goodness sake show the lady in!" Holmes called impatiently. "Anything is better than this infernal whispering and hissing."

With a helpless grimace, the good lady turned to usher in a short dumpy middle-aged woman whose plump face was creased in lines of worry. Holmes rose to his feet, his former irritability replaced by a smile of sympathetic kindness.

"Pray forgive my ill-humour, Madam," he said gently. "I was faced with a problem that nags like an aching tooth, and any distraction can only be a relief. Be seated and I assure of you my undivided attention."

Mrs. Hebden smiled nervously and lowered her comfortable body into the chair indicated, where she sat with hands folded primly in her lap.

Meanwhile I ventured to open a window to dispel the acrid fumes of Holmes's foul pipe.

"Now, dear lady," he said soothingly, "make me privy to your problem, and I shall endeavour to advise you. A missing husband, I believe?"

"That's right, sir. I took the liberty of coming to you 'cos Harry Murcher said if anyone could help it was you. Harry's a policeman, and by way of being a friend of me and my John, lives near the Elephant."

"Ah, yes, the Lauriston Gardens affair, if my memory isn't at fault, eh, Watson? Proceed, Mrs. Hebden."

"Well, my husband has a small furniture van that gives us a comfortable-enough living. We'll never make a fortune, but he gets lots of

60

jobs the big firms won't bother with, and as there's only me and the horse to keep, along of the occasional help, he can do things cheaper than most. On Wednesday, he was engaged to make a collection in the West End, and was to be told his destination when he had his load. Also, he needn't hire any labour, as that'd be supplied. He thought it a bit queer, and the lateness of the hour, too. He was to be in Grosvenor Square at exactly nine o'clock where he'd be met." At these last words my head jerked up, and Holmes leaned forward tensely.

"Grosvenor Square, you say?" he asked. "Did he tell you the address?"

"He wasn't told. Just to be there at nine, not a minute either side, and he'd be told where to go. He'd been given a goodly sum in advance, so he made no objections, and he told me to expect him when I saw him.

"Like I said, that was Wednesday, and I've heard nothing of him since. It was yesterday afternoon when I got really worried, so I spoke to Harry Murcher, and he says you might be able to help." The poor woman was about to burst into tears, and Holmes patted her gently on the shoulder.

"The good constable counselled you well, Madam, for what you tell me may have some bearing on my earlier problem. I shall not give you false hopes, for there is much that is still unclear, but leave me your address, and I promise you shall hear from me immediately I have news for you."

He led her from the room, murmuring words of comfort as he did so. No sooner had the front door closed on her than he bounded back up the stairs and into our sitting room like a whirlwind.

"Come, Watson, stir yourself! The game's afoot, and I pray we may be in time!"

He tossed my boots towards me, and I was still struggling into my ulster when he was halfway down the stairs, calling impatiently for me to make haste. By the time I reached the pavement he had secured a hansom, and seconds later we were rattling down Baker Street and crossing Oxford Street in the direction of Grosvenor Square, to be deposited at the door of the missing baronet.

"Look around you," he said, waving a hand to embrace the solid bastions of wealth and respectability. "Behind those façades exists as much hate, passion, and human frailty as you will find in Seven Dials or Whitechapel, albeit in a more genteel guise, and without the excuse of poverty and deprivation that may be advanced for the less salubrious quarters of our great city. At times I despair for the future of the human race." He turned to stride up to the front door where he applied himself to the bell-pull. The door was opened by an elderly woman, whom I judged from her attire to be the housekeeper. We were left standing in the hall

61

while she disappeared bearing Holmes's card, but our wait was short, for she quickly returned to conduct us to a small drawing room.

A few minutes later the door opened to admit Lady Fawkus. "Mr. Sherlock Holmes," she said, tapping his card on her fingers. "I have heard much of you."

Holmes bowed. "To my credit, I hope, your Ladyship. This is Dr. Watson, my friend and confidant, whom I fear is inclined to romanticise my modest achievements. Inspector Gregson has seen fit to seek my advice in the matter of your husband's disappearance, and I deemed it best to hear the circumstances from your own lips."

Lady Fawkus nodded and invited us to sit down. "Smoke if you wish, gentlemen, and I trust you will not think too hardly of me if I indulge in a cigarette."

She was a truly beautiful woman, with large violet eyes set below the most striking crown of chestnut hair I had ever seen, while her lips were full and sensuous beneath a straight patrician nose. The only flaw in this vision was a suggestion of hardness at the corners of the mouth.

The story she told was in substance the same as we had heard from Gregson, and at its conclusion, Holmes rubbed his chin thoughtfully.

"Did Sir Peter's absence cause you immediate concern, or was it nothing out of the ordinary?"

"Well, he sometimes spent the night at his club if affairs delayed him, but he would usually contrive to apprise me if he was going to. I was more mystified by the fact that the butler wasn't to be found."

"Ah, the butler. He was a newcomer to your household, and here on a temporary engagement. How did Sir Peter come to engage him?"

"I engaged him. My husband is a very busy man, and when Clarke was injured, the arrangements were left to me."

"His references were satisfactory, of course? I assume you took them up?"

"It was unnecessary," Lady Fawkus said. "He came with a personal recommendation." She looked away as if wishing to avoid the subject.

"From whom?"

"A friend."

The name, please," Holmes insisted.

"Mr. Fulton Braddock, if that is of any importance,"

"And this Mr. Braddock is well known to you and your husband?"

"To me, Mr. Holmes." She turned her beautiful eyes on to Holmes's face. "I think you should understand that my husband and I move in our own circles. He is forty years older than I, and is occupied with affairs of national and international importance. I ensure that this establishment runs smoothly and perform the duties of hostess when it is required, but otherwise we have few acquaintances or interests in common. Do I make myself clear?"

"Quite," said Holmes austerely. "So Mr. Braddock is a friend of yours rather than your husband's, and he came to your aid when you required a temporary butler." He seemed to lose interest in the matter. "The articles from the missing sideboard were left on the dining room floor. Was anything at all taken?"

"Only Moscrop or Clarke could answer that," she said coldly. "I am not in the habit of counting the spoons daily."

"Of course not. Does Sir Peter have a valet or personal servant?"

"He had, but he was discharged a week ago for theft. My husband missed some money from his room, and Moscrop found a large sum hidden in the man's wardrobe. He denied it, naturally, but the evidence was plain enough."

"How long had he been with Sir Peter?"

"Oh, well before my marriage to him. My husband was grieved that such an old and previously honest retainer should betray his trust."

"I see," Holmes said slowly. "And except for Moscrop, the only occupants of the house would have been the servants who had been told by the butler to remain in their quarters, allegedly on orders from Sir Peter."

"Apparently so, except that Mrs. Murgatroyd, the housekeeper, had permission to visit her niece in Wandsworth and stay away overnight. The police inspector examined all the servants and learned nothing."

Holmes stood up to leave and I followed suit. "One thing more, Madam. It was past midnight when you reached home. You did not come straight back from the theatre?"

Lady Fawkus turned to the bell-rope and remained with her back to us when she answered. "No, not directly. I had supper with a friend." She turned back with a bright spot of colour burning on her cheek. "I hope I can rely on your discretion, Mr. Holmes. I wouldn't welcome the attentions of gossip-mongers, and neither would Sir Peter."

"I am always discreet," said my friend icily, "but the truth must be paramount. Good day to you. Lady Fawkus."

He was tight-lipped as we looked for a conveyance, and I was about to comment on the remarkable beauty of the lady whose presence we had just left when a growler pulled up and Gregson's head appeared at the window.

"Well met, Mr. Holmes," he cried. "I thought I might find you here, as you weren't at Baker Street. Great news! We have found the sideboard missing from here – at least, I hope there isn't more than one floating about."

63

"Where? Tell me the circumstances, Inspector," said Holmes sharply.

"In an abandoned pantechnicon on Plumstead Common. It was seen by a patrolling constable yesterday with the horse munching away at the grass. When it was still there this morning he thought it strange, and had a look inside. The doors weren't locked, and all it contained was a large sideboard. He reported it to his station, and a sharp sergeant connected it with the description of the one we circulated as missing from here and got in touch with us."

"The van, no doubt, had the name of John Hebden painted on the side?" said Holmes eagerly.

Gregson's jaw dropped and he stared in amazement. "Lord save us, Mr. Holmes!" he gasped. "Sometimes I think you to be in league with Old Nick himself! How did you know that?"

"Are you going to Plumstead? Good. We shall accompany you and explain as we go."

On the way to London Bridge Station, Holmes told him of the visit by the worried Mrs. Hebden, at which the inspector gave a lop-sided grin.

"So our interests coincide. You think the van has a connection with what has happened to Sir Peter? Is this Hebden part of the plot?"

"You know I dislike theorising without sufficient facts to build on," my colleague said seriously, "but I fear that Hebden may turn out to be the innocent victim of some deeper conspiracy. Once we are at Plumstead, it may be that a few more pieces of the puzzle will fall into place – but let us not rush our fences."

We had the good fortune to catch a train to Plumstead almost at once, and a short walk brought us to the police station where Gregson made himself known to the sergeant at the desk.

"Where is the van now, Sergeant?" asked the inspector.

"Still on the Common, sir. I was going to have it brought in, but young Hopkins who found it reckoned it might be best to leave it where it was in case someone turned up for it. He's as keen as mustard, and quite bright, even if he has been educated." The sergeant sniffed. "He should've been off duty now, but he wanted to stay with it"

It was a weary uphill climb to the Common, but Holmes stepped out to such effect that Gregson and I were left puffing in his wake, while every so often he would stop impatiently to exhort us to greater effort. At length we came to the Common and, following the sergeant's directions, struck off to the right. Soon we came to our objective, a smartly turned-out pantechnicon with a hobbled nag cropping away at the short scrubby grass.

A uniformed constable was patrolling back and forth some yards away from the van, and on our approach stepped forward with an admonitory hand upraised.

"I'm sorry, gentlemen," he said civilly enough. "I'm afraid you aren't allowed to approach this vehicle."

"Quite right too," Holmes said approvingly. "Has anyone else shown an interest in it while you've been here?"

The young officer looked at us doubtfully. Gregson produced his warrant card, at which the constable sprang to attention and saluted smartly.

"Sorry, sir. I took you to be members of the public, and it'd not do to have them trampling all over the place."

"You've done well," Gregson commended him. "These two gentlemen are Mr. Sherlock Holmes and Dr. Watson. Answer them as you would me."

"Tell us what first aroused your curiosity," Holmes put in.

"It was yesterday evening, sir, and my beat covers this part of the Common. I saw the van and thought nothing of it, for it certainly hadn't been there an hour earlier when I came by. When I came on again late this morning it was still here, and I began to think it may have been stolen and abandoned. I decided to have a look inside, and there was this massive piece of furniture, not even covered up. Well, I recalled some talk at the station of a stolen sideboard, so I gave a boy a couple of pennies to take a note to the station asking what I should do. Sergeant Wells came to see what it was all about and reckoned Scotland Yard might be interested."

"And so we are," said Gregson warmly. "You did everything right, Constable – Hopkins, isn't it?"

"That's right, sir. Number R989, Stanley Hopkins."

"Has anyone been near the van since you stationed yourself here?" Holmes inquired.

"No one until you, the doctor, and the inspector arrived, sir,"

"Have you?"

"Once when I looked inside, and again when Sergeant Veils looked."

Holmes gave a grunt of satisfaction, then he began a slow perambulation around the vehicle, his eyes darting hither and thither as each circulation took him closer until he stopped with a hand resting on the lever to release the doors. Signalling us to remain at a distance, he clambered in to commence a systematic search of the interior. The sideboard, a substantial piece of furniture, stood at the far end, and Holmes gradually worked his way towards it, sometimes stretching up to peer at the sides and roof of the van, then dropping to his knees to crawl on the floor with his lens to his eye. He was in this latter position when he gave a small cry of triumph.

"Quickly, your knife," he called over his shoulder. I climbed in and approached him gingerly, handing him the knife with the large blade already open. He inserted it in a crevice in the floor and worked it to-and-fro. Then he turned to me with a small object lying in the palm of his hand. Carrying it to the light, I saw it to be a grubby wooden button, the kind often found on the jacket of a labouring man.

Gregson looked at it and gave a sniff. "I see no help coming from that," he said dismissively, handing it to Hopkins, who studied it closely.

"If I might be so bold, sir," the constable said tentatively, "I think this could have come from a waterman's coat – what is known as a pea-jacket. See, there is a smear of tar at the edge of it."

Holmes descended from the van, taking the button to examine under his lens. He looked at Hopkins with new respect. "Go on, Constable," he urged, "What are you thinking?"

"Well, sir," the young man replied, embarrassed by the attention he was attracting, "I remember that a lot of barges tie up at nearby Erith Wharf, and there are one or two shady characters among the bargees that need watching, although most of them are decent hard-working men."

"How do you come to know that?" growled the inspector.

"I was born at Erith, sir, and my mother still lives there, running a little coffee-shop for workmen."

"We shall bear that in mind," said Holmes. "Come into the van now and tell me what you observe."

We crowded in behind him, and my nostrils were assailed by the faint but unmistakable odour of the operating theatre.

"By George, Holmes," I said, "that smells like chloroform or I've never used it!"

He forebore to answer, but began searching the interior of the sideboard with his long sensitive fingers. After a while he withdrew his hand to show us a glistening object, which on closer examination proved to be the broken portion of a cuff-link bearing the initials *P.F.* The significance of this find wasn't lost to us, but further searching revealed nothing more of value.

Outside once more, Holmes mounted to the driver's perch, the old nag turning his head to cast a disinterested eye at him before going back to his browsing. My colleague sat with a look of deep concentration, as if willing the vehicle to yield up its secrets. Suddenly he bent to retrieve a scrap of paper adhering to the footboard. He smoothed it out and studied it. Then to Gregson's offended glare, he handed it to Hopkins.

"What do you make of that, Constable?" he asked. I peered round his shoulder and saw it was part of a leaf torn from a penny notebook. Written on it in a shaky uneducated hand was part of the one word: *"Cordwainer"*. The remainder of the word was torn off.

The young man frowned, then spoke in a tone of suppressed excitement. "Why, sir, there's a public house called The Cordwainer's Arms in Erith. It sits opposite the jetty, and it's where most of the barge people gather when they aren't working."

"Capital!" said Holmes, rubbing his hands together gleefully. "The scent grows stronger." He dragged his watch out. "It approaches five o'clock. You and I must return to London, Watson. Gregson, can you arrange to have the van and nag taken care of at the police station?"

"Of course, Mr. Holmes. What have you in mind?"

"Meet us at Erith Police Station at eight o'clock. Hopkins, if you aren't averse to some extra duty, you can be there too."

Hopkins assented eagerly. Then in response to Holmes's query, he pointed out the shortest way to the railway station. We set off briskly, and soon after six o'clock, a cab set us down in Baker Street,

Holmes vanished into his room, emerging very quickly dressed in the manner of a Thames waterman, and sporting an unkempt moustache under a reddened nose. From his writing desk he took a revolver which he dropped into the capacious pocket of his reefer jacket, and taking my cue from him, I armed myself with my old service revolver, adding a stout ash-plant from the stand for good measure.

He gripped my shoulder and smiled warmly. "Good old Watson. I hope we need have no recourse to firearms, but come what may, I couldn't wish for a stouter comrade at my side. Now to Erith, for I am sure you realise that the solution to both problems lies there."

It was almost on the stroke of eight when we walked into the police station at the small riverside village in Kent where Gregson and the young Hopkins awaited us. The local man, Inspector Wray, who had been deep in talk with the Scotland Yard officer, gave a bark of laughter when introduced to my disreputable companion and shook his head in wonder.

"I must say, Mr. Holmes," he chuckled, "I would have warned my chaps to keep a very sharp eye on you, did I not know who you were. Will you be needing any assistance from us?"

"I will be grateful to have two or three of your most solid men on hand, Inspector. I trust Gregson has told you what we seek? Watson and I will make our way to this Cordwainer's Arms, and leave the official force to dispose themselves within easy hail of the tavern. Can you suggest who is the most likely candidate for our attention?"

"Sam Levett is the biggest thorn in our flesh," Wray said promptly. "A big ugly brute of a man with a temper to match. You'll not miss him with his red face, piggy eyes, and broken nose. He knows the insides of our cells well enough for his violence. Jem Milton is his lap-dog, a little weasel-faced character who's nothing on his own."

"Thank you, Inspector. That is most useful. Now, Watson and I shall see what we may stir up at the jetty."

We made our way to the waterfront and found the public house we sought directly opposite the wharf. Several moored barges bobbed gently on the river, giving the occasional creak as they rubbed sides against the wharf or each other.

Holmes whispered in my ear, then pushed his way through the entrance of the public bar, giving me a brief glimpse of a sawdust-strewn floor before the door closed on him. I entered the small private bar, which was reasonably clean and comfortable, the floor covered in brown linoleum, and with four or five chairs, their padded seats covered in American cloth.

By leaning on the counter, I could peer round the dividing partition and discern Holmes taking his first pull from a tankard of beer.

"What's it to be, mate?" The voice was that of a surly-looking man who moved along to eye me with suspicious curiosity,

"Whisky, I think, Landlord. A large one," I replied. "Quite a nip in the air tonight. Will you take something yourself?"

"Thanks, Guv. A drop of rum'll go down nicely." He brought the drinks, then leaned on the bar to eye me speculatively. "Stranger in these parts, Mister?"

"That's right," I said, improvising quickly. "I am a doctor and a bit fed up with London, so I thought I might find a nice little practice in the country. I've been scouting around this area, but without any luck."

He nodded, appearing to lose interest, then turned away at the importunate hammering of a beer-mug on the counter of the other bar.

"Come on, Charlie," a whining voice called. "Move yourself. We're all dying of thirst in 'ere."

"You mind your lip, Jem Hilton," growled the landlord. "You'll wait until I'm ready to serve you." But despite his declaration of independence, he went to obey the summons with some alacrity. I positioned myself so that by looking into the fly-spotted mirror over the bar I obtained an excellent view of the adjoining room. Holmes was leaning negligently against the beer-stained counter nursing his tankard, and next to him was the Jem Milton who had been so accurately described by Inspector Wray. He was attired in a similar manner to my colleague, and as I watched, Holmes turned to speak to him.

"I see you've lorst a button orf yer coat, mate," he said, his rough accent coming clearly to me.

"What's it to you?" Milton retorted belligerently.

"Would this be it?" Holmes held out his hand,

"I dunno. Where did you find it?"

Instead of answering Holmes placed the button against one on Milton's coat and nodded. "Looks like it," he said, "'Ow did you come to lose it in a furniture van?"

The weasel-faced man paled beneath his grime and shot out a hand to snatch at the button which was withdrawn too quickly for him to grasp,

"Wot's yer game, cully?" he rasped menacingly. "You lookin' fer trouble, 'cos yer in the right place to get it. So gimme the button an' sling yer 'ook."

"You are the one in trouble," said Holmes in his normal voice. "I know all about your game at Grosvenor Square on Wednesday, so why don't you come quietly and save us all a lot of bother?"

Milton gave a shout of rage as he aimed a futile blow at Holmes, at the same time yelling for the company at large to come to his aid.

"Come on, mates, 'e's a peeler!" But the words had scarcely left his mouth when a crisp upper-cut from Holmes laid him stretched out on the floor. Some of the men in the bar showed signs of joining in, and I sprang to the door where I raised my voice to summon Gregson and his party,

Not pausing for a reply, I erupted into the other bar, barging my way through the threatening mob to stand at Holmes's side. For a brief moment my sudden arrival took them by surprise, and before they could gather their wits the door again burst open for Gregson, Hopkins, and three powerfully built constables to charge in.

There was a sudden hush, and the circle around us drew back sullenly.

Holmes bent down to snap a pair of handcuffs on the recumbent Milton, whose eyes still held a glazed look. The local officers surveyed the room grimly, and the would-be assailants slunk sheepishly back to their tables. Any who attempted to leave being turned back by Hopkins who had stationed himself at the door.

"Anyone else you need, Mr. Holmes?" asked Gregson.

My colleague looked at the oldest of the local policemen. "What do you think, Constable?"

The man scanned the room before shaking his head. "I think not, sir. Most of these are straight enough. Just a touch excitable where strangers are concerned. There's no sign of Sam Levett, but our chum here could point you in the right direction." He prodded the prone figure with a not-too-gentle boot. "That's right, isn't, Jem lad?"

"Well, my man, where do we find Levett?" asked Holmes.

"Go to the Devil!" was the sullen reply.

Holmes shrugged. "No matter. Inspector, I think you can charge this pitiful specimen with the murders of Sir Peter Fawkus and John Hebden."

There was a howl of terror from the wretch on the floor. "You can't do that! They ain't dead! They're still – " He broke off as if suddenly realising he had said too much, his eyes on Holmes's impassive features.

"I am afraid you will have to convince us of that," said the latter in a hard voice. "Landlord, is there a quiet room where I can have a few words with this scum?"

The landlord became obsequious in his anxiety to please, the very mention of murder having reduced him to a quivering wreck.

"Of course, sir. You can have my sitting room at the back. You won't be disturbed there. I don't know nothing of what's going on, and I always try to keep – " He stopped as one of the constables stepped forward.

"Shut it, Charlie Higgins, and show the gentlemen through. We know all about you, so just watch your *P*'s and *Q*'s."

The flap of the counter was lifted, and Holmes dragged the thoroughly cowed Milton to his feet and pushed him through into a small shabby room, with Gregson and myself following, the constables remaining in the bar to ensure that nobody left to raise an alarm. The prisoner was thrust into a rickety chair while Holmes studied him coldly before starting his interrogation.

"So you would have us believe that Sir Peter and the van driver are still alive?" he asked. "How do you know that?"

The handcuffed man wetted his lips and looked up slyly. "If I peach, will you promise to go easy on me?" he whined.

Gregson thrust his face close to the other's, speaking in a dangerously soft voice. "All I promise you is an early morning walk if we don't find them alive, so if you've got anything to say, get on with it."

Milton's brief show of resistance melted away, and he raised his manacled hands as if in supplication as the rest of us stared at him.

"I'll tell yer all I know," he quavered, "They're on Sam Levett's barge just over the road, and they was both alive and kicking when I was there not an hour gorn. That's the truth, so 'elp me it is."

"Who is guarding them?" asked Holmes.

"Sam, Tom Moscrop, and the toff what paid us to take the old'un from that big 'ouse."

"Moscrop!" gasped Gregson. "Was he in it too?"

"Of course he was," said Holmes impatiently. "Come, we have no time to lose. Get one of the local men to take this rat to the lock-up, and we shall tackle those on the barge."

A few minutes later, having ascertained the exact location of our objective, our small party consisting of Holmes, Gregson, myself, Hopkins, and the two beefiest of the local men made its way quietly down to the waterfront. There was a slight rise and fall of the moored vessels as the tide turned, the noise made as they chafed against the wharf effectively masking any sound of our stealthy approach.

We found the barge in question, and Holmes held out a restraining arm. A small cabin perched at the stern showed a thin ray of yellow light, and my colleague pointed to it. When sure that we understood, he moved swiftly along the jetty and, abandoning any further pretence of silence, he sprang lightly on to the deck and charged the door of the cubby-hole with his shoulder.

I was on his heels, my pistol at the ready and the others crowding me from behind. The door burst open, and in the dim light of a smoky lantern I saw three figures frozen into brief immobility, while on the floor were two more bodies bound and gagged. The paralysis of the three was but momentary before they exploded into violent action, leaping at us with fists swinging wildly. Holmes struck the leading man full in the face with his clenched fist, but the man's momentum carried him on to crash into Holmes, who in turn cannoned into me so that I fell to the floor, A heavy boot swung towards me, and in a reflex action I grabbed the ankle above it to hang on desperately, bringing a heavy body down on top of me.

I wriggled out, and as I struggled to regain my feet, I heard Gregson call to someone to stop. Then came a loud splash followed by a terrible scream that was suddenly cut off. Supporting myself with a hand on the wall, I found Hopkins sitting on the man I had brought down, a big hulking brute who I took to be the notorious Sam Levett. Holmes had in his grasp a pale-faced weedy character whose teeth chattered with fear, while out on the deck I could just make out Gregson and the two local officers staring over the side into the murky water of the Thames as it sucked at the piles of the wharf.

"Quickly, Hopkins, 'cuff this pair together." It was Holmes who spoke as he came over to where I stood, concern showing on his face. "Watson, you aren't badly hurt, I trust?"

I smiled, denying any serious damage.

"Then come. Your professional skills may be needed here."

We set about releasing the two trussed men. Both were conscious, and they took deep gulps of air as I removed the filthy gags from their mouths. One was a white-haired man of advanced years. He was clad in a dress shirt and smoking-jacket, while the other man was much younger, wearing the corduroy breeches and leather gaiters favoured by cab and van drivers. They gasped for breath and flexed their cramped limbs, groaning with pain as the circulation returned. Holmes, satisfied that I was able to manage, patted me on the shoulder.

"I leave them to you, Doctor. I assume, of course, that you are Sir Peter Fawkus and Mr. John Hebden?"

71

A nod from each confirmed his surmise, whereupon my companion went out to the fresher air of the deck, My cursory examination told me that neither had sustained serious injury, and as soon as they were able to stand, I assisted them to rise and move out into the cool night air, where I found Gregson and Holmes gazing sombrely into the dark waters below. Of the two scoundrels who had been apprehended there was no sign, but Hopkins and another stood on the jetty, fishing with long poles by the light of a bulls-eye lantern.

Cutting short any attempts at questions or explanations, Holmes insisted on an immediate adjournment to the nearby Railway Hotel. Neither would he permit any talk until Hebden and Sir Peter, fortified with stiff brandies had removed the accumulated grime of their captivity, and were ravenously devouring a plate of sandwiches.

There was a knock on the door, which turned out to be Hopkins with the announcement that the search of the river had been unproductive.

"The tide's in full ebb now," he explained, "Anybody in there would be well on the way to Gravesend by now."

"Very well, you've done your best," Gregson replied. He was about to dismiss him when Holmes spoke mildly.

"I think Hopkins should hear the rest of the story, Inspector," he said. "After all, his contribution has been most valuable in this matter."

Gregson was plainly of the opinion that young policemen shouldn't be allowed to get above themselves, but he gave his grudging consent, and Hopkins placed himself unobtrusively in a corner of the room. With pipes and cigars drawing nicely, Holmes set the ball rolling.

"Now, gentlemen, pray let me hear your own accounts of your misfortunes so that I may compare my own conclusions. Will you begin, Sir Peter?"

The elderly baronet began to speak, hesitantly at first but with increasing fluency as his tale progressed,

"It was Wednesday evening, soon after nine o'clock, and I was settled in my study with a glass of whisky. My wife had gone out, and I was looking forward to a quiet couple of hours when the butler, Moscrop, entered to announce that two gentlemen insisted on seeing me. I wasn't best pleased, but even as I demurred, two rough characters pushed their way in and advanced towards me.

"'What is the meaning of this?' I demanded. 'Moscrop, show these persons the door.' He made no move, and to my horror I was seized violently to have a filthy rag forced into my mouth to stifle any outcry that I might make. During this outrage Moscrop stood by passively, making no move to assist me. I should add that he was a temporary – "

"Yes, yes," Holmes put in. "We know he was engaged on the recommendation of Fulton Braddock, a friend of Lady Fawkus's."

"That is so," Sir Peter said bitterly. "Have you secured the scoundrel?"

"He is dead," Gregson stated flatly. "In attempting to escape, he fell between the barge and the jetty, and was crushed to death. We haven't yet recovered his body."

A glint of satisfaction showed in Sir Peter's eyes. "Then that may save the washing of dirty linen," he said grimly. "But to continue. I was trussed up like a chicken and taken to the dining room, where a pad soaked with what I assume was chloroform was clapped over my mouth, and the next thing I knew I was in a coffin-like container being transported in some kind of vehicle. I lost consciousness again, and recovered as I was being manhandled on to that filthy barge, where I was thrown on to a pile of sacks in the hold. Shortly afterwards this gentleman," he nodded towards Hebden, "was pushed in to join me."

His face showed anger at the memory, but he took a sip of his brandy and went on. "How long we were left I have no notion, but it must have been a full day, for when the hatch again opened it was dark. To my astonishment, who should climb down was none other than Fulton Braddock. My spirits rose, thinking deliverance was at hand, but my hopes were dashed by his first words." His voice trailed away to a whisper.

"You may speak freely, sir," Holmes said earnestly. "Nothing that you say will go beyond these four walls, other than is required to serve the ends of justice, and Braddock is beyond reach of that." He looked round the room, his stern face willing Gregson and Hopkins to nod agreement.

The baronet seemed reassured by my friend's words, and after a short pause he took up his tale again, telling of how Braddock had taunted him with his wife's infidelity, before going on to describe how the old man's body would be found in some obscure reach of the Thames, when it would be assumed he had taken his own life. After a decent interval, it was Braddock's plan to marry the grieving widow, thus gaining not only a respected place in society, but a considerable fortune to boot.

During the latter part of this recital, Gregson's face had taken on a look of incredulous anger and, unable to contain himself, he now broke in on Sir Peter's narrative.

"Are you implying that your wife was party to this conspiracy?" he stuttered.

"Of course I am not, Inspector!" snapped the baronet angrily. "She may be a slut and an adulteress, but never a murderess!"

"I think we can trust Sir Peter's judgement in the matter," declared Holmes. "It grows late, so if you will allow me to round things off. we

73

may save time and get back to London before midnight. I take it, Mr. Hebden, you were seen as a danger to these villains, so they intended to make away with you to ensure your silence?"

"That's about it, sir. I was uneasy about this job from the start, and must have showed it, for no sooner had we reached Erith than I was knocked on the head and found myself in the same case as this gent. They took us up top when it got dark, and I don't mind saying I thought my last hour had come. How was it you found us in the nick of time?"

Holmes told of Mrs. Hebden's appeal, and then went on: "It was too much of a coincidence that Sir Peter Fawkus and a sideboard should vanish from Grosvenor Square on the very same night that a furniture van and its owner were last heard of in that very Square. When the van was found abandoned with only the sideboard in it, the inference was certain. You both owe a lot to Mrs. Hebden's wifely concern, and to this very acute police constable whose aid was invaluable.

"Now, I am sure Mr. Hebden is keen to put his wife's mind at rest, and Sir Peter has no wish to linger at the scene of such an unpleasant experience, so if Inspector Gregson will agree to leave the formalities until tomorrow, we can doubtless secure a carriage, and any further details can be cleared up as we travel."

The hotel landlord was able to find us a not-too-dilapidated carriage complete with driver, and leaving Gregson and Hopkins to their own devices, the four of us were soon on our way. The elderly baronet, exhausted by his ordeal, fell into a fitful doze, and as we clattered through Plumstead, Holmes drew Hebden's attention to the police station where his van was held, assuring him that it would be well cared for until collected.

"One point I must reiterate, Mr. Hebden, is that you must exercise absolute discretion in the matters that have been revealed tonight."

"Trust me, sir," the man replied. "I see and hear a lot in my job that's best kept mum about." He laid a finger along his nose and winked.

Sir Peter opened his eyes and favoured him with a weary smile. "I'll not forget you, Hebden," he said. "You were a great comfort to me in our predicament, and with your permission, I will call on you as soon as I have recovered from the events of the past few days." He turned to Holmes. "After we have restored Mr. Hebden to his hearth, I have a request to make of you which I hope you will not refuse." Holmes inclined his head, and the rest of the journey passed in silence until we turned into the mews that was the van-driver's home. The wheels hadn't stopped before Hebden leapt from the carriage. He was half-way across the cobbles when Mrs. Hebden rushed from a doorway to throw herself into her husband's embrace.

"We aren't needed here," chuckled Holmes, rapping on the carriage roof with his knuckles.

"Would that such a homecoming awaited me," Sir Peter said wistfully. "Will you oblige me by taking me to my club in St. James's?" He laid back, his head in shadow. "May I impose on you to go on to inform my wife of my well-being? I am in no frame of mind to face her this night, and I fear I may say things that should be left unsaid. I leave it to your good sense as to what explanations you make, but I beg of you not to judge her too harshly."

I could see from my colleague's face that the task was distasteful to him, but he accepted the mission before lapsing into a brooding silence, his head sunk on his chest, not speaking until we turned from Pall Mall into St. James's and stopped before Sir Peter's club.

Refusing assistance, the baronet descended and leaned in to shake us by the hand. "Thank you both for all you have done. I would count it an honour if you will lunch with me on here Monday. There are matters to be discussed between us, not the least of them financial."

We watched the old man make his way up the steps of the building, and a few minutes later we reached Grosvenor Square, where the carriage was dismissed with a handsome gratuity for the driver.

"I shall not enjoy this encounter," Holmes muttered. "Don't hesitate to restrain me should my feelings betray me."

The door was opened by Lady Fawkus in person, and her hands flew to her bosom at the sight of us.

"You have no news?" she said faintly, "You haven't found my husband?"

"Sir Peter is safe," Holmes answered frigidly. "He has been saved from those who would harm him, but he elected to spend the night at his club, where we left him not ten minutes since. I think you should hear of the events that brought him near to death, but resulted in the death of his would-be murderer, Fulton Braddock."

Her beautiful face turned a ghastly pale and she clutched at the doorpost for support, her eyes widening in shock and horror at my friend's harsh tone.

"What are you saying?" she said in a strangled whisper. "You must be mad to speak so!"

"Let us enter, Madam, and I shall lay the facts before you. Then you may pronounce on my sanity."

He took a pace forward and she retreated into the hallway. I followed and kicked the door to behind me. Lady Fawkus hesitated as if to defy us. Then we were led into the same small drawing room as on our earlier visit.

75

As she turned up the gas-light, our dishevelled appearance caused her to look askance. She faced us with a thunderous frown.

"Now, Mr. Sherlock Holmes," she demanded. "I will ask you to account for the vile and slanderous statement you made. I warn you, sir, my husband has much influence, so have a care."

"Very well, Lady Fawkus, I will be completely frank with you, and then you may take what steps you will. This afternoon you told us that on Wednesday night you had supper with a friend. Was that friend Fulton Braddock? Ah, I see it was. Have you seen him since Wednesday?"

"He called on me this morning to offer his sympathy and support, but what signifies that?"

Holmes's eyes were like chips of ice as he answered. "While you were being entertained by Braddock – no doubt to more than supper – his minions, one of whom one was your butler Moscrop, were abducting Sir Peter with a view to encompassing his death." She looked wildly from one to the other of us, then collapsed into a chair. Fearing her about to swoon, I stepped forward but was waved away.

"You have taken leave of your senses!" she cried. "Even if what you say is true, what advantage would Mr. Braddock get from my husband's death?"

"A wealthy widow is an attractive proposition to a man without honour or scruples, and he wasn't one to let a little matter of a husband stand in his way."

Lady Fawkus stood up and faced us with blazing eyes. "Mr. Braddock is a gentleman for whom I have the highest regard, and it ill-becomes you to impute such base conduct to a man who isn't here to defend his honour!"

"Honour?" sneered Holmes. "A man who would conduct a liaison with a married woman can have little of that, I declare."

For a moment I thought she would strike him. Then her body slumped as she recalled his earlier words.

"You said he is dead. Is that true?"

He nodded and she dropped back into her chair. Burying her face in her hands, she began sobbing loudly.

Holmes watched her bleakly until she regained control and looked up with reddened eyes.

"Tell me what you believe to be the truth, Mr. Holmes, but spare me your views on my personal conduct. That is between me and my conscience."

My companion began in a cold and detached tone as Lady Fawkus listened with a look of ever-increasing horror as the sordid tale unfolded. When all was told she sat rigidly in her chair, her lovely face ravaged by the conflicting emotions that passed over it. When she at last spoke, it was in a low humble voice.

"I cannot believe that these terrible events are a figment of your imagination, Mr. Holmes, and I presume there is evidence to substantiate it?"

"Indeed. Three scoundrels are in custody, and will be quick to confess and mitigate their own part, but Sir Peter and Mr. Hebden are alive, and will tell as much of their own story as the authorities deem necessary, so there can be no doubt of the facts."

"Oh, God!" she cried piteously. "What have I bought about? Will I ever be able to face that good man again?"

"That, Madam, is out of my hands," replied Holmes as he prepared to leave. "However, I don't think Sir Peter is a vindictive man, so there may yet be hope for you both. Good night."

We set off to walk briskly in the direction of Baker Street, Holmes now recovering his spirits. He paused under a lamp-post to light a cigarette.

"For your records, I think it will transpire that Clarke's accident, and the dismissal of the valet, were engineered to leave the gang a clear run when the time came to put Braddock's scheme into effect. Watson, is something amusing you?" he said sharply.

"I hope we don't meet a zealous policeman," I chuckled.

"Good Lord, why should that concern us?" he asked in a puzzled tone.

"Do you not realise, my dear Holmes, that apart from that outrageous moustache that was lost in the struggle, you are still attired as a Thames bargee? Hardly the type of person to be seen after midnight in this part of town."

He looked down at himself, and then joined in my merriment.

"Should that arise, old chap, we could always ask Gregson to vouch for us, and that would give great satisfaction to his sense of humour."

Still laughing immoderately, we resumed our homeward progress.

The Merton Fiends

As the reputation of my friend and colleague, Mr. Sherlock Holmes, grew, so did the number of cases in which he was consulted. Many were so mundane that he either provided the solution without stirring from his favourite chair, or the applicant was dismissed with the icy contempt he reserved for obvious time-wasters. Nevertheless, his work-load was prodigious, and as one case followed on the heels of the last I found little opportunity to flesh out the skeletons from my notes and diaries.

However, there is one case that will forever remain vividly in my memory – not so much for its complexity as for the sheer callousness and inhumanity displayed by the perpetrators, and also for the sense of remorse engendered in my companion.

"If only I had foreseen the course of events and taken up the case at once," he said later, and no words of mine could lift his burden of guilt.

It was a fine morning in early summer, and we hadn't long returned from Hampshire where we had extricated Miss Violet Hunter from the peril of the Copper Beeches, The lady was both courageous and beautiful, and her sweet face lingers yet in my memory. Mrs. Hudson had removed the remains of our breakfast, casting an exasperated eye on the tangle of newspapers at my friend's feet. I could never fathom how a mind so orderly as his was incapable of keeping a newspaper together. We had filled and lit our post-breakfast pipes when the muted jangle of the doorbell was shortly followed by the reappearance of our good landlady to announce that a Mr. Marcus Perry waited below.

"Will you see him, sir?"

"Why not?" replied Holmes carelessly. "Nothing else presses."

The caller, somewhat less than thirty years of age, was of medium height and build, with a frank, open face. His brown, curly hair was unruly above eyes of the same hue, and a fine moustache adorned his upper lip. His expression would have been pleasant but for the lines of worry and anxiety that now shadowed it, and his whole bearing had the signs of suppressed agitation. "Come in, sir!" cried Holmes, unfolding his long limbs to greet our visitor with a vigorous handshake. "You are most welcome. Be seated, I beg you."

Perry lowered himself into the chair so placed that the light from the window fell directly on to his face. "Thank you, Mr. Holmes. It is very good of you to see me so promptly, for I know you must be a busy man."

"Nonsense, Anything you have to say may be said in the presence of my friend and confidant, Dr. Watson. Pray feel free to fill your pipe with the Fantail Mixture which you favour, and then tell me what brings you from Bromley so urgently."

Our caller's jaw fell in amazement, "I have read of your powers of deduction, sir, but it is beyond belief that you could have read so much within minutes of my entry."

My companion shrugged. "It was no great feat. The distinctive aroma of your tobacco clings to your garments. That particular blend of burley, latakia, and fire-cured leaf is peculiar to John Myers, who has a small shop in the Market Square of Bromley, and isn't widely known farther afield." He smiled. "I venture to suggest that while your eyesight is reasonably good, you occasionally wear *pince-nez*, denoting an acquaintance with books. You are a bachelor, and your hurried breakfast included a soft-boiled egg. Beyond that I know nothing of you."

"You are correct in every detail, but how – ?"

"Merely logical observation. The faint but definite marks on the bridge of your nose, and the black ribbon leading from your lapel to your breast pocket suggest the *pince-nez*. A trace of egg on your moustache points to a hastily eaten breakfast, and no caring spouse would allow you to leave home thus adorned." He raised a hand to stop further comment. "Now, sir, to the purpose of your visit, if you please. You have my full attention."

Perry began to charge his pipe from a soft leather pouch. "I own a small bookshop in Bromley, but my concern is for my sister Charlotte," he began. "Some two-and-a-half years ago, at the age of twenty-four, she formed an attachment for a Mr. Julius Swan, much against the wishes of my mother and myself. On her twenty-fifth birthday, she announced her intention of marrying him, and as she was of age we were helpless."

"You disapproved of her choice?"

Our visitor shifted uncomfortably in his chair. "We didn't like the man, and we found him most unpleasant in an oily way. Also he was reticent regarding his antecedents. But then we had never envisaged marriage for her at all."

"Come, sir, I don't think you are being completely frank with us," said my companion sharply. "What are you concealing?"

Marcus Perry showed signs of agitation as my colleague eyed him severely, then he went on in a low voice. "Charlotte is a good, sweet girl, and I love her dearly, but she isn't as other women. She has never matured, and although it pains me to say so, she is physically unattractive and of limited mental capacity." He leaned forward and spoke with a fierce intensity. "Do not mistake me, Mr. Holmes. She isn't an imbecile, but she needs constant care and supervision in the most simple of tasks. And," he added, "a great deal of love and affection."

79

"Which no ordinary husband could be expected to provide?"

"Least of all Julius Swan!"

"Yet he took her as his wife. Was there an ulterior motive? Did she take a sum of money to the marriage?"

"A tolerable amount. When our grandfather died soon after Charlotte was born, she and I had eight-hundred pounds apiece placed in trust until we were of age. That appreciated over the years, but I have never touched mine." His face saddened. "As I grew older I came to believe that my poor sister would always need caring for."

"And she took her portion to her marriage?" said Holmes keenly. "But what is your problem?"

"I am her only living relative. Father has been dead several years, and Mother died soon after Charlotte left us. I am convinced that it contributed to her death. After she married Julius Swan, she went to live at Morris Drive, Dulwich, in a household that included Julius Swan's brother Patrick and his wife Caroline. Since then I have been barred from any contact with her, even by letter, and she wasn't even at Mother's funeral! I have called at the house on several occasions, but have always been rebuffed in the rudest fashion – in most cases by Patrick Swan, who went so far as to offer me physical violence. I was told that my opposition to her marriage had embittered her, and she wasn't in a fit state to see me. Two weeks ago I made one last effort to see her, but I found The Walnuts closed and empty, and no one could tell me to where they had moved."

"So you wish me to trace her for you." My colleague shook his head. "No, Mr. Perry, I need more than that to tangle in a family dispute. Have you evidence to suggest your sister may be in danger?"

The other shook his head. "Not directly, but since I last spoke to Patrick Swan, almost a month ago, I am convinced that I am being watched and followed. I know he trailed me from Dulwich on my last encounter with him, and this very morning I saw him in the crowd at Charing Cross."

"Has he followed you here?" Holmes sounded dubious. "What would be his object in acting thus?"

"If I knew that, Mr. Sherlock Holmes, I wouldn't need your advice," Perry said with some asperity.

At a sign from my companion, I got to my feet and looked down on the busy street, but saw no furtive figure lurking below, I gave an imperceptible shake of my head and returned to my seat.

"Listen, Mr. Perry," said Holmes. "I believe you are overwrought and seeing danger where none exists."

"You don't believe me?" He seemed on the verge of tears. "You refuse to help me?"

"I did not say that. Let me have twenty-four hours to consider the matter, and I promise you shall have my answer by this time tomorrow. More than that I cannot say."

Perry stood up to leave. "Very well, sir. I cannot force you to take my worries on yourself, but you will give it due thought?"

"I have promised to do so. Good day to you, sir. Watson," he said with a lift of his eyebrows, "be so good as to see Mr. Perry to the street door and summon a cab for him." When I returned Holmes was turning from where he had been looking down from the window, his brow furrowed with thought. He raised an interrogative eyebrow at me.

"No obvious followers. I watched the cab out of sight, so perhaps the gentleman has an overactive imagination."

"And the bicyclist on the corner who pedalled off so energetically in the same direction?" he asked drily.

"I saw no cyclist," I protested.

"Perhaps I had a better vantage point at this window." He lowered himself into his chair and for more than an hour-and-a-half he remained lost in reverie, sucking furiously on the unsavoury old pipe which accompanied his deepest meditations. It wasn't until the shrill cry of a paperboy drifted up from the street that he sprang to life.

"'Orrible accident at Charing Cross! Man falls under train! All the latest!"

"What was that?" he cried. Then he was on his feet and clattering down the stairs. He came back with the paper clutched in his fist, and a grim look on his face.

"Confound it!" he said savagely, "I have been a fool! A blind, culpable fool!"

He thrust the paper at me, a bony forefinger jabbing at the smudged print of the stop press. I read it through in stunned silence:

A terrible accident occurred at Charing Cross Station when a man fell in front of an incoming train and was killed instantly. The platform was crowded at the time, but no one could tell the cause of the man's fall. The contents of his pockets showed him to be a Mr. Marcus Perry, a bookseller from Bromley in Kent.

"Good Heavens above!" I gasped as I looked up at his set features. "Do you think – ?"

"What am I to think?" he replied bitterly. "How far can coincidence stretch? That man came to me for help and left to meet his death. I owe Marcus Perry a life, a debt which I shall repay."

81

Seldom had I seen my friend so consumed by angry remorse, and twenty minutes later we had brushed by an outraged Mrs. Hudson, who was about to convey a succulent steak-and-kidney pudding up to our rooms. A cab took us to London Bridge Station, and not until we were on our way to Dulwich did he utter a word.

"I misread the urgency of this matter," he said glumly as we passed through Bermondsey. "Had I but heeded Mr. Perry, I may have saved his life, and perhaps delayed the peril to his unfortunate sister."

"His sister? She too is in danger?"

"Of course she is!" he said impatiently. "You took notes this morning. Marcus Perry told us he and his sister each inherited eight-hundred pounds. The lady's naturally went with her on her marriage, while his was invested against the time when he was unable to care for her, and must have appreciated considerably over the years."

"And she being his next of kin, that sum will now go to her," I said as I followed his reasoning. "You believe that her brother was murdered, and Mrs. Swan is now in considerable danger of meeting a like fate?" I shook my head. "Two deaths for less than two-thousand pounds?"

"Murders have been committed for as few pence, and it is an assumption I dare not ignore. If I err, nothing is lost."

Two other passengers alighted at East Dulwich, and the short journey to Morris Drive took less than ten minutes in the ancient station fly. The Walnuts was a square, yellow-brick pile with its windows shuttered and bearing obvious signs of neglect. It was screened from view by a high wall, with the nearest dwelling set fifty yards away.

"What now?" I asked. "Shall you enter?"

He shook his head. "No, I think not. If these people are as cunning as I think, they will have left no clue behind them." He looked along the road. "Perhaps this honest fellow can give us some information."

He pointed with his stick to the figure of a postman heading towards us.

"Good day to you, Postman," he said as the man drew near. "I wonder if you can help me." He jingled some coins in his pocket.

"What's your problem, sir?" The postman seemed prepared to talk.

"It's Mr. Swan at The Walnuts. He seems to have left in some haste."

"Them?" The man laughed scornfully. "The Lord alone knows where they went. D'ye know, in two whole years I never took above a dozen letters up there."

"Did you ever see the people?"

"I've seen them come out when I've been passing, Two blokes and a young woman – nice looker, too."

"No one else?"

82

"Not to say seen, but a couple of times I caught sight of a woman's face at that attic window." He nodded towards the house. "Kind of scary, it was, with a dead white face sand her hair all tangled."

"Do you know when they left?"

The postman tugged at his beard. "Now, today's Tuesday, and it wasn't last week. That's it!" he cried. "Two weeks last Saturday. I always walk through here on my way in, and I was on early turn so it must've been about five in the morning. There was a plain black van at the door, and the two blokes were loading up. They were gone by the time I'd sorted and started my walk, and that's all I know."

"No name on the van?" Holmes asked sharply. "No driver with it?"

"No, sir. Like I said, that's all I saw."

My colleague pressed a florin into the postman's hand. "What do we do now?" he said when the man was out of earshot. "It is evident they intended to slip away leaving no easy trail. Think, man, think."

I thought, but no bright flash of inspiration came. "I have only one idea," I said tentatively. "What about the cabbie at the station? Could he have picked up anything?"

"A forlorn hope, but it is more than I have come up with, so I suppose it's worth a try." He lengthened his stride, his lips set in a thin line, and we were back at the station almost as quickly as the hackney had brought us away.

The driver of the decrepit old cab was dozing in his seat, opening his eyes reluctantly when Holmes called to attract his attention.

"The house in Morris Drive you took us to. Do you remember it?" The man nodded. "Have you been there before?" Holmes flipped him a coin.

"Time or two," the driver said taciturnly.

"Do you know the folk who lived there?"

"Not to say 'know'. There was two gents and a young lady I took out there now and then, but they've been gone a couple of weeks or more, I reckon. Old Tom in the booking office might know a bit more."

We entered, and my companion put his question to the booking clerk, who scratched his head thoughtfully.

"Queer lot, them," he ruminated. "One gent used to go up to town regular, but later it was the other. Could be brothers." He frowned.

"Funny thing is he had a return ticket until he started buying a single just before they stopped coming a couple of weeks back. Charlie out there – " He jerked his thumb. "He reckons they just upped and went."

"Were there ever any women with them?"

"One young'un, but I don't know which one she was with. Tell you what, though. The taller one did ask me to look up the best way to get to Merton. About a month ago, that'd be."

"Not much to go on, but it's all we have," Holmes mused when we were on the train back to London.

"I fail to see that we have anything," I objected.

"Merton, my dear chap, Merton. A small village just beyond Wimbledon, best known for its association with Lord Nelson. It could be where the Swans have gone to ground. Have you a better idea?" he said snappishly.

I had to admit I hadn't. "But it is a long shot," I added huffily. Conversation languished. From London Bridge, we took a hansom straight to Scotland Yard where we found Inspector Lestrade in his shabby office.

Ignoring the latter's less-than-enthusiastic greeting, Holmes came straight to the point. "A man was killed this morning at Charing Cross Station," he said abruptly. "For how long can you delay the inquest?"

"Why on earth should I want to do that?" Lestrade asked with a scowl.

"Because I suspect foul play, and because a woman's life may be at risk if a verdict of accidental death is recorded now. I can say no more yet, Inspector, but trust me as you have done in the past."

"I must have more than that to interfere, Mr. Holmes."

"Say that you haven't yet notified the victim's next of kin. That should suffice, and also bring my suspects into the open."

Lestrade shook his head, then capitulated with a sigh. "Very well, Mr. Holmes. You've never let me down in the past. But," he added grimly, "I want to know the facts sooner or later."

"And so you shall, along with such credit that accrues. When will the inquest open?"

"Thursday. I shall need a word with the constable who was at the scene, but there will be no difficulty there."

We left the gloomy building and, to my relief, took the first cab that appeared to return to Baker Street, and the prospect of food."

"What now?" I asked.

"We wait. Before long those we seek must reveal themselves, or the whole business would be pointless."

At my colleagues behest, I attended the inquest, seating myself as unobtrusively as possible. The first witness, a P.C. Parsons, affirmed that he had been on duty in the precincts of the station at the time of the incident, and was drawn to the scene by the screams and shouts of the horrified crowd. "No, sir," he answered in reply to a question from the coroner, "nobody I spoke to could say how the man came to fall."

84

Next, the police surgeon confirmed that he pronounced Marcus Perry dead at the scene, and he was followed by a man whom I recognized as one of Lestrade's sergeants. Due to the multiple injuries to the victim, the identification had only been possible by the contents of the victim's pockets, and in view of that, an adjournment was requested until the next of kin could be traced and informed.

At this point a surprise development occurred. A youngish, fair-haired man rose and, with great respect, asked that he might be heard.

"You have some relevant information, sir?" asked the coroner.

"Indeed I do, sir. My name is Hector Moscrop, and I am the Perry family solicitor. At this moment I am endeavouring to trace a Mrs. Julius Swan, the deceased's sister, and his only living relative. I would welcome an adjournment until such time as she can be told of this unhappy occurrence."

"Then so it shall be, Mr. Moscrop. I shall adjourn this inquiry for seven days, and I suggest you liaise with the police in the matter."

We all rose, and on leaving the room I found Moscrop closely engaged in talk with the plain-clothes sergeant.

"Why, Dr. Watson," he grinned as I approached. "I thought there was something in the wind when Inspector Lestrade spoke to me. Perhaps you would like to join Mr. Moscrop and me at the Yard."

I thought rapidly. "Why not come to Baker Street, Sergeant Groves?" I suggested. "I'm sure the good Lestrade can spare you for an hour, and you may glean something of interest from Mr. Sherlock Holmes."

Hector Moscrop's eyes widened. "You are *that* Dr. Watson?" he gasped. "The great detective's friend?"

"I have the honour of his trust and confidence, sir," I said modestly. "He is most concerned over the manner of your client's death."

Both men acquiesced eagerly, and a little later a four-wheeler dropped us at 221b Baker Street, where I found my colleague pasting cuttings into his commonplace book.

"Sergeant Groves! You are quite a stranger these days. And this gentleman – no, don't tell me. He is a lawyer representing the late and unfortunate Mr. Marcus Perry."

"That is so, Mr. Holmes. Hector Moscrop, Solicitor, of Bromley. In what manner may I assist you – or you me?" His manner was brisk and business like.

Holmes considered the attorney for some seconds. Then, liking the man's approach, he waved him and the sergeant to chairs. "Tell me, sir, without betraying confidences, how well did you know Mr. Marcus Perry?"

85

"Barely at all, Mr. Holmes. Of course, I knew of him as the family had long been clients of my late father, who passed on five years since, but it wasn't until the death of Mrs. Perry that I had any dealings with young Mr. Perry." He hesitated before going on. "Do I gather that you suspect an irregularity in the manner of my client's death?"

"I think we must be frank with each other, Mr. Moscrop," Holmes said. "It is my firm conviction that Marcus Perry's death was no accident, but a deliberate act of murder."

Moscrop gasped, but Holmes pressed on.

"My problem is to trace the miscreants quickly before another crime is perpetrated. Oh, I am pretty sure of their identity, but not their present whereabouts. That is why I need your help. Be assured anything you say will be treated with the utmost circumspection, and I speak for Dr. Watson and Sergeant Groves."

"Ask away. I have absolute faith in your discretion, Mr. Holmes,"

"Thank you, sir. I believe Marcus Perry's sole surviving relative is his sister Charlotte, who is now Mrs. Julius Swan. Unless he made other provisions, his whole estate goes to her. Is that correct?"

"It is. He rewrote his will at the time of his mother's death, and that is the only time I net the poor fellow. It came as something of a surprise to learn that Miss Perry had married. Let me elucidate. When I went into partnership with my father with a view to eventually taking the practice, we discussed the clients, among them the Perrys. I learned that Miss Perry was somewhat – to be blunt – less than bright."

"If we are to be blunt, I would say closer to feeble-minded," said my companion brutally. "However, she did marry, and that started a chain of events that led to her brother's death. She now inherits a considerable sum of money that Marcus had invested for the future when he thought his sister would need the care and attention he couldn't give."

Moscrop nodded. "The total sum when all is settled is likely to be well in excess of three-thousand pounds. That is taking into account the fact that he owns the freehold of his shop and living quarters at Bromley, and anything his stock may realize."

"As much as that," murmured Holmes. "A tempting sum indeed."

"What do you require of me? Anything I can do that is within the law I shall consider, if you can convince me of the necessity."

"Let me say this, sir: The longer the settlement of the estate takes, the longer Charlotte Swan may live. Can you see your way to delaying probate for as long as possible?"

"That will need little help from me." The attorney smiled thinly. "I am sure you are familiar with the leisurely processes of the law."

"I'm not so sure I should be listening to this," Sergeant Groves put in uneasily.

"Then close your ears," Holmes said dismissively. "In any case, Inspector Lestrade has been acquainted with my fears, although I have no evidence to present." He turned back to the young lawyer. "When the result of the inquest is made public, you may expect a visit from those whom I wish to trace. I need to know precisely where they are hiding out. Keep me informed of all that transpires – every little detail as far as you think is proper to your integrity as a man of law. Much depends on it."

"If a crime is contemplated, it is my duty to take all practical steps to prevent it." Hector Moscrop spoke earnestly. "I am honoured to be of assistance to you, Mr. Holmes, and you, Doctor."

In the days that ensued my colleague was restless and jumpy. When I suggested that we might hasten events by going out to Merton to make our own inquiries, he gave me short shrift. "Use your head, do," he snapped. "If these people had so much as a hint that I'm involved, the whole business could run out of control. No, we must wait." It was early forenoon on Tuesday that a telegram came from Moscrop.

Holmes threw it across to me and sprang to his feet. "Stir yourself!" he cried. "The game's afoot!"

The telegram was terse and to the point. "*Developments. Must see you here. Moscrop.*" By the time I had read it, Holmes was on his way downstairs and, grabbing my hat and stick, I hastened after him.

A train for Bromley was about to leave, and we managed to tumble into a carriage even as it began to move. Holmes uttered not a word until we alighted more staidly at our destination and had secured a four-wheeler to convey us up the hill to the town centre where Hector Moscrop had his office. We mounted the stairs to be greeted excitedly by the solicitor.

Immediately we entered he took us to his inner sanctum, telling his clerk and office boy that under no circumstances was he to be disturbed.

"You have news for us?" said Holmes as soon as the door closed.

"Indeed I have." Moscrop had an air of satisfaction about him. "It was as you surmised, but I confess to some perplexity."

"Pray continue, sir. Perhaps I can explain."

"I arrived at the office to find I had been preceded by callers whom my clerk had admitted to wait in the outer office. They announced themselves as Mr. and Mrs. Julius Swan, brother-in-law and sister of the late Marcus Perry."

"Naturally," said my companion drily. "No doubt they were eager to hear when they could expect to get their hands on your late client's money, and how much to expect."

87

"Indecently so, and when I explained that It could be some weeks, the man became agitated. What puzzled me though, was the lady's appearance. I had been led to expect a very different woman from the one before me."

"You interest me, sir." Holmes leant forward intently. "Describe them to me, please."

"As one would expect from a woman in mourning, she was dressed in black and heavily veiled. Nevertheless, beneath her outer garments I could discern a slim and graceful form." Moscrop blushed and hurried on.

"Although she spoke in a low voice, she was lucid, and with an instant grasp of what I said – not at all as I had been led to believe. Naturally, I asked if she had the necessary proof if her identity, and from her capacious bag she produced a birth certificate and marriage licence, together with such other documents that, had you not aroused my suspicions, would have left me in little doubt that she was who she claimed to be." He paused to sip from a glass of water at his elbow.

"What followed then?" my colleague prompted.

"The man asked what would happen now, and I explained that Mrs. Swan would have to attend the resumed inquest, and give evidence of her relationship to the deceased. At this he appeared uneasy, and the lady asked nervously if she would be required to view the body of her brother. When I said that the injuries were so extensive that identification was only possible by the possessions found on him, and also the fact of his absence from his business, both seemed most relieved." Here the lawyer gave us a self-satisfied smirk. "What I did next was to have her swear on oath an affidavit of all she had told me, which she did with same reluctance, but when she raised her veil to affix her signature I saw her to be an attractive, almost beautiful young woman."

"She actually signed the affidavit? It was properly witnessed in your presence?" Holmes's eyes gleamed.

"Of course." Moscrop sounded offended. "She signed fluently as 'C. Swan, née Perry' in the presence of my clerk and office boy."

"Capital!" Holmes rubbed his hands together almost gleefully. "If my theories are correct, we have them for misrepresentation and perjury to start with. You have done well. Now, sir, did you get an address where they might be contacted?"

"I fear that was more difficult," Moscrop confessed. "They inquired as to the amount that might be expected from the will. I was deliberately vague, and also warned them to expect some delay in obtaining probate. That was when they showed agitation. I said I would get in touch with Mrs. Swan when I had more information, but they demurred on the grounds that their movements were uncertain. They proposed that they called on me at regular intervals, but I replied I didn't conduct business like a tradesman awaiting casual callers." He drummed his fingers on his desk. "Finally the man – with marked reluctance – agreed that I should contact them by writing to Wimbledon *poste restante*. Beyond that he wouldn't go. I'm sorry, Mr. Holmes, but it was all I could do."

"So be it. They will be at the resumed inquest on Thursday, of course. Describe the man to me, Mr. Moscrop."

"Tall, almost your height, with fleshy features and eyes that were cold, and never still for a minute. When he spoke his voice was harsh."

My friend pondered for a few seconds before coming to a decision. "I think the matter gathers pace. I assume that once the inquest has passed a verdict of accidental death, and accepted Mrs. Swan as Perry's next of kin, she is his sole legatee. If she dies even before the will is proved, her husband will inherit." The lawyer nodded, and Holmes went on. "This is what you must do: Write to Mrs. Swan at Wimbledon on some pretext or other, but don't post it until after the last post tomorrow. Then tell her a letter is on its way to Wimbledon. Do you follow?"

"I don't pretend to understand, but it shall be as you say. Shall I see you on Thursday?"

"We shall be there, but on no account must you acknowledge us. You will hear from me in due course. Come, Watson. There is nothing more to do immediately, so we can call on the tobacconist, John Myers, to see if his reputation is justified."

We emerged from the cramped shop some half-an-hour later, each with a new pipe and half-a-pound of tobacco apiece blended to our own taste. I had some inkling of the manner in which Holmes meant to proceed, but it came as a surprise when, on Wednesday morning, he disappeared without a word, leaving me to my own devices. It was tea-time before he returned, flopping loose-limbed into a chair to gulp thirstily at a cup of tea.

"Old friend," he said, placing his cup on the floor, "I fear there are some members of your profession unfit to called doctors."

I bristled. "That is a sweeping generalisation, Holmes! Pray explain yourself."

"I said some," he replied urbanely. "Surely you wouldn't defend Palmer, Pritchard, and their like? Of course not, but I speak of those who by reason of age or infirmity are no longer competent to continue to practise their art."

"You have a point there," I admitted. "Why did you make it?"

"Let me start at the beginning. My first call was on our old friend Lestrade, and I think I have persuaded him that a particularly callous crime is in the offing, and also that Marcus Perry's death was part of the plan. Next I went to Merton." He smiled at my raised eyebrows. "I was careful

89

not to advertise myself, but my inquiries showed that there were but two practising medical men in the area. One, a Dr. Stevens, is young and energetic. The other, Dr. Drury, is an octogenarian, almost blind and frequently the worse for drink."

"That is indeed disgraceful," I said. "But what does it signify?"

"Suppose you needed a death certificate properly issued without too many questions being posed? Would you send for a young, alert doctor to issue it when an old and senile practitioner is at hand?"

I thought for a few seconds. "I see your point, but if the doctor was new to the case, a second signature would be needed."

My companion looked nonplussed, then dismissed the objection with an impatient gesture. "If the stakes were high enough, a cunning and ruthless man could find a way around that – more so if the doctor had paid several visits to the deceased. We must proceed on that assumption."

The next morning, Thursday, we were at the venue of the inquest early, remaining outside in a convenient doorway to watch the trickle of arrivals. Hector Moscrop was among the first, followed some ten minutes later by a couple who we recognized from the lawyer's account as the pair who had visited him on Tuesday. It was easy to see why Moscrop had been surprised by the woman's appearance, for under her shapeless mourning apparel and heavy veil I could discern a woman in no way resembling the picture Perry had drawn of his unfortunate sister. The only others to enter were P. C. Parsons and Sergeant Groves – the latter, Holmes told me, sent at his insistence by Lestrade.

My colleague consulted his watch. "Now," he said, "our birds are caged for at least an hour, and for as long as Mr. Moscrop can delay them afterwards." He hailed a passing hansom which took us to Waterloo where we boarded the first train to Wimbledon. Once there, we ensconced ourselves in a pleasant tea room that commanded a view of the post office and settled down to wait. I had a fair inkling of what we were about, but it proved a long wait, and by the time our quarry appeared, I was awash with tea.

"At last," breathed Holmes, his elbow digging me sharply in the ribs. Peering through the lace curtains at the window, I saw our quarry alight from a four-wheeler. The man paused to speak to the driver, and the woman had raised her veil to reveal her as being even more lovely than Moscrop's description, although even at this distance her face showed lines of strain.

I became aware that Holmes was speaking. "As soon as they enter the post office, secure a conveyance as quickly as may be. We dare not lose them at this stage. Now!" he said urgently.

I was already on my way, and luckily secured a four-wheeler that had dropped its fare at an adjacent bank. Even so, the pair we meant to follow had already emerged from the post office and re-entered the cab that had waited for them. As it drove off, my colleague came out and said a few words to our jarvey before climbing in beside me.

We drove through the busiest part of the town, and eventually came to more open country when our cab slowed perceptibly. Holmes ducked his head out of the window and called to the driver before casting a quick look behind us. He sat down with a faint smile curving his thin lips.

"I may have maligned Lestrade in the past," he murmured, "but this time he must be commended."

"Lestrade?" I frowned. "Where does he fit in?"

"Oh, he took me at my word, and even now he is close on our heels."

"Good grief!" I exploded. "You said nothing of this! I swear there are times when you don't trust even me."

"I am sorry, old friend. With the best will in the world, I cannot think of everything, and I wasn't even sure that the good Inspector would appreciate the urgency of the matter." He looked so abject that I couldn't hold my wounded dignity, and contented myself with a snort.

After some twenty minutes, during which Holmes took frequent glances out of the window, our cab stopped, and the driver got down to speak to us.

"What now, Mister?" he asked. "They've turned off down a lane that don't lead nowhere except for one old house that was empty last I heard. They'll spot us for sure if I carry on after them." He grinned knowingly. "What's the caper, Guv – a bit of hanky-panky?"

"More serious than that," Holmes said as we got down. "This gentleman will tell you as much as you need know." Lestrade had also alighted from his following vehicle and was approaching in the company of two uniformed constables and a solidly built middle-aged woman whom I guessed to be a police matron.

"Trouble, Mr. Holmes?" asked the inspector. My companion explained the situation as Lestrade looked sharply at our driver, who appeared to be an intelligent young man.

"I am Inspector Lestrade of Scotland Yard," announced he. "These gentlemen are Mr. Sherlock Holmes and Dr. Watson." The driver caught his breath as Lestrade went on. "We are engaged in official business of the utmost importance, and you, my man, will do exactly as you are told."

"Always ready to help the law, Mister. Stand on me – Bert Scroggins won't let you down."

Holmes took charge smoothly. "Good man! Wait here, but be ready to come to our assistance if you are needed." He drew Lestrade to one side. "Who is your driver, Inspector?"

"Got him and the others with the wagon from the local police station. Mrs. Russell, the matron, came down from the Yard with me. What next, Mr. Holmes?"

"Better you remain in ignorance until Watson and I have the lie of the land, but be within calling distance. If I'm right, you will have the pleasure of arresting three of the most heartless and callous people it has been my misfortune to encounter in many a year."

"And if you're wrong?"

"Then you may have to arrest Watson and myself for breaking and entering, but I don't anticipate that."

Before Lestrade could remonstrate, Holmes had seized my arm to propel me quickly out of sight down the narrow lane, but we had gone less than fifty yards when we were alerted by the crunch of wheels on the pot-holed surface. I found myself dragged willy-nilly into the cover of a hedge just as the cab we had followed from Wimbledon hove into view.

"Lestrade will deal with him," my colleague said as it passed. "Hurry, time is of the essence."

We pressed on. A few minutes later we saw the house, an old, decaying two-storied place with small attic windows set in the slate roof, one of which was closely shuttered. Through the uncurtained ground floor window to the left of the front door, we could see shadowy figures moving to-and-fro, apparently engaged in an animated discussion.

"I would give a lot to hear what they are saying," Holmes muttered fractiously. "We must gain entrance to the house somehow."

"What about the rear?" I suggested. "There appears to be a path on the far side that might lead in that direction,"

"Well observed, Watson. Let us explore."

The path showed little evidence of recent use, overgrown with hawthorn bushes that tore at our clothing as we made our stealthy way along it until we came to the end of the rotting fence where the track ended. A loose board came away easily in my hand, and we crept silently up the neglected garden until we reached the wall of the house, with a locked and unpainted door set in. My companion pressed his ear to it, then took out the set of lock picks he had acquired by his own mysterious methods. The door yielded in seconds, and we were in a dirty stone-floored outhouse or scullery. Now we heard voices, and although the words were muffled, I decided that they belonged to two men and a woman. With infinite care we crept closer towards the point from where the sounds came and found ourselves facing another door which appeared to lead into the house.

"They aren't in there," Holmes breathed in my ear. He opened the door a fraction to peer through the gap before easing it wider. Looking over his shoulder I glimpsed a sparsely-furnished hallway that had a flight of stairs ascending to our left, while on the other side there was a half-open door through which the voices came, raised in contentious argument.

"I did what I thought best, Julius," a man said pettishly. "We need the old fool to visit a time or two more before she gets worse. She is in a bad way."

"I'm sure Patrick was right," a woman said nervously. "He couldn't let things slide."

"And what if that confounded letter was a plot to discover where we are?" said the man called Julius in harsh, grating tones. "There was no need for Moscrop to write vague nonsense when he knew Caroline and I would be at the inquest."

"Were you followed?" asked Patrick anxiously.

"I think not, but I don't like it. Caroline, go up and put her in the next room before Drury gets here."

Holmes pulled back swiftly, leaving the merest slit through which to observe the hallway beyond. There was the sound of a door shutting, then footsteps on uncarpeted stairs.

"Our chance to see what devilry is in train," he said. "Quickly, not a sound."

He was through the door as he spoke, leaving me to follow as he tiptoed lightly along the hallway and up the stairs. He paused on the first landing, then carried on up another steeper flight that could only lead to the attic rooms before coming to a sudden halt. My view was blocked by Holmes's body, but I heard the scrape of a vesta being struck, then a metallic clink as of a key being inserted in a lock. My companion continued up, testing each tread carefully before allowing it to take his weight. We reached the top where the yellow glow of a guttering candle came from a doorway which I guessed to be the attic with the shuttered window we had seen from the front of the house. Holmes extended an arm to hold me back. Then came a stifled cry from the attic.

"Charlotte!" The woman's voice rose. "Charlotte! Wake up!" Footsteps hurried over the bare floor, succeeded by a low whimper as of an animal in distress.

"Quick!" Holmes leapt forward as if propelled by a spring, I close on his heels, all caution thrown to the winds. As we exploded into the room the woman turned, her mouth opening in a silent scream.

"Quiet," my colleague almost snarled. "Quiet, if you wish for any mercy. Doctor, there is work for you."

In the brief second that followed I saw it was the woman we had followed from Wimbledon. She had discarded her veil and outer clothes to reveal a shapely form and features that would have been almost classically beautiful in other circumstances. Now her face was chalk white, her large luminous eyes wide with fear. I took this in at a glance, but my attention was drawn to the far corner of the room to a scene the like of which I wish never to see again.

The light from single candle hardly reached the corner, but I could just discern a low truckle bed with the vague outline of a body covered by a ragged blanket. The stench in the room was well-nigh unbearable, and I hurried to open the window, throwing back the shutters to admit light and the sweet summer air before turning again to the bed. As daylight flooded in, I saw it was a woman lying there, though barely recognizable as such. The matted grey hair hung about her gaunt face like tendrils of weed, and her eyes were sunk deep in their sockets. A thin dribble of saliva ran down her chin, but apart from the faint fluttering of her eyelids there was almost no sign of life in the wasted form.

Drawing back the filthy verminous covering, I found her clad in a once-white nightgown even more soiled than the blanket. Taking her wrist to feel for a pulse, I was shocked by the fragile bones and the blue veins that stood out starkly against the paper-thin skin. Behind me, Holmes was speaking to the woman in a low, intense voice, but the words passed over me as I concentrated on my search for a flicker of life. The seconds ticked away until I looked over my shoulder to where my companion held the woman's arms in a steel grip.

"She's barely alive," I said, hoarsely, "She needs more attention than I can give – urgently,"

He dragged the woman over to the fouled bed, his face a mask of anger.

"If you have a spark of humanity in you, Mrs. Patrick Swan, you will obey my every word. It is your only hope of escaping the gallows. Do you understand what I am saying?" She nodded fearfully and he went on. "You will control yourself and summon your husband and brother-in-law. They must be together. Can you do that?"

Again she nodded, and Holmes led her to the door, still maintaining his grip on her arm. She was near to swooning, but he looked at her implacably until she took a deep breath and called out in shrill tones.

"Patrick! Julius! You must come! Patrick! Julius!"

Almost at once a harsh voice came up the stairs. "What the deuce is it, Caroline? Drury should be here any minute."

"Please, you must come!" she cried in response to a shake from Holmes. There were some muttered words from below, then footsteps pounded on the stairs. Holmes thrust the woman away and shot me a meaningful look.

I rose and retrieved my stick as two figures appeared in the doorway. On seeing me they halted their headlong rush, but my colleague shot out an arm to seize the first man and flung him across the room for me to deal with. Even as I raised my stick, Holmes was leaping at the second man.

For the next half-minute I was fully occupied. My opponent was strong, and his momentum sent me reeling backwards. He grabbed at me instinctively, partly to keep his balance, partly to ward me off. It was his undoing. His arms flailed wildly as he ran full tilt into my half-raised stick which caught him squarely in the mid-riff. The breath was driven from him, and before he could recover I felled him with an upper-cut that snapped his teeth together with a satisfyingly loud click. As he dropped to the floor, I snatched a quick look to see how Holmes was faring, but he had his man in a vicious arm-lock which forced the cursing man to his knees. The whole affair was over in less than a minute.

"Nicely done, old chap." My friend grinned wolfishly as he dragged his opponent roughly to where my victim lay with eyes glazed over. With his free hand he took a pair of handcuffs from his pocket. "Just slip these in to our two beauties, then do what you can for that poor creature." It was soon done. Then Holmes went to the open window to blow a shrill blast on a police whistle. I turned back to the pitiful object on the bed, but as I bent over her I saw now she was beyond any aid that I or anyone else could give. The pale lips fluttered in a last expiring breath, and I knew it was over for her.

I stood up and looked with loathing at the manacled figures, one still unconscious, the other mouthing a stream of obscenities. A red mist swam before my eyes and, losing all control, I drove my fist into his evil face.

While this had been going on, the woman had cowered in a corner, her face buried in her hands, and now Holmes turned to her.

"The police will be here within seconds," he said in clipped tones. "Your husband and his brother are sure to hang, but you may save yourself by turning Queen's Evidence. Are you prepared to do so?"

She raised her tear-stained face to him. "Yes, I never wanted this," she sobbed. Then she smiled slyly. "They wouldn't hang me in any case."

Before any more could be said, the front door crashed open, and a babble of voices came from the hallway below.

Holmes went to the top of the attic stairs. "Up here, Lestrade!" he called. "Bring all your men and the matron."

Soon the room was filled to overflowing, for not only had the inspector brought his own team, but had included our cabbie to add to the numbers.

While Holmes spoke to Lestrade, I took the police matron to view the poor dead woman who at last lay at peace. Death had softened her features, but even before the terrible suffering she had endured, she could never have been at all attractive.

"What killed her, Doctor Watson?" asked the matron shakily. "I've never seen a sight such as this."

"I think starvation along with general neglect, but the *post mortem* will tell us for sure." I felt revulsion and rage at the thought of so-called human beings acting thus towards this helpless woman.

"Leave it to me, sir. I'll do what is necessary." Mrs. Russell, the matron, sensed my anger and eyed me sympathetically. "She'll be avenged, have no fear."

By now the unconscious man, whom I learned was Patrick Swan, had opened his eyes. Finding himself manacled to his brother, he glared balefully at the woman, Caroline, who returned his look defiantly before turning her head away. Holmes and Inspector Lestrade concluded their brief conference, and the latter went over to the two men.

"Patrick Swan," he intoned, "I arrest you for the murder of Marcus Perry." He went on to recite the usual caution, ending with: "Other charges may follow. Julius Swan, you will be charged with being an accessory before and after the fact. Other charges may follow."

"What about her?" spat Julius.

"Mrs. Swan will be charged in due course," Lestrade said coldly. "Take them away, Constable."

Some months later, we were visited by Inspector Lestrade, who had come hot-foot from the trial of the Swan brothers.

"They'll swing, Mr. Holmes," he announced, taking a pull from the tankard of beer I had placed before him. "The woman got off, though."

My colleague nodded. "Naturally. I never believed she thought matters would turn out as they did. She was happy for Julius to marry Charlotte Perry to gain her money to share among them, but that was all. In any case, she had no idea at the start that murder was planned, and when it became obvious to her, she was afraid of them both. Besides, she did give you a lot of help, did she not?"

The inspector shrugged. "We had a case anyway, but two things tipped it her way: First, she has a pretty face, but mainly because she is in an interesting condition. What first alerted you, Mr. Holmes?"

"Elementary, Inspector. Why would any man marry an unattractive, feeble-minded woman, and then cut her off from her family other than for mercenary reasons? It was obvious from the start, but I was slow off the mark. Marcus Perry's visit to me precipitated matters and made the Swans move faster than they intended. If I had grasped the urgency of the case at once, both Perry and his sister may have survived."

"Maybe." Lestrade wiped his lip and rose to his feet. "Well, I have work to do. This will make interesting reading when I retire to pen my memoirs. Good afternoon, gentlemen."

As the slam of the door was followed by his footsteps on our stairs, my companion raised a mocking eyebrow towards me. "Another triumph for the great Inspector Lestrade, eh, Watson?"

I contented myself with a snort of disgust.

The Addleton Tragedy

The months following Sherlock Holmes's miraculous reappearance after his supposed death at the hands of Professor Moriarty were busy enough to keep even his questing mind at full stretch. I have seldom seen him in better spirits than in that summer of 1894. I had lately disposed of my Kensington practice for a gratifying sum, once more taking up my old familiar quarters at 221b Baker Street. With an unusually healthy balance to my name with Cox and Company. I was free to fall in with whatever whims of fancy took my friend's attention, and I accompanied him on the majority of his cases where my presence was requested.

It was early June and we had lingered over the morning papers until Mrs. Hudson drove us from the breakfast table with clucks of disapproval at the sheets of newsprint scattered on the floor by Holmes's chair. I was as yet unshaven, but Holmes, unpredictable as ever, was fully dressed, having already been abroad on some errand of his own which he hadn't seen fit to confide to me. In fact, he hadn't uttered a word since his return, and I knew better than to intrude on his silence until I received the necessary encouragement. About to retire to my room, I was stayed by him addressing me sharply.

"What do you know of Wiltshire, Watson?"

The apparent irrelevance of the query took me unawares and I paused to arrange my thoughts.

"Come, my dear fellow," he said, a hint of amusement in his voice. "You must have heard of that pleasant county."

"Of course I have," I retorted impatiently. "All it means to me is Stonehenge, the Great Western Railway, and the great cathedral of Salisbury. Otherwise, it is somewhere to pass through on the way to the West Country. Is there a reason for your inquiry?"

He thrust a newspaper at me, jabbing a tobacco-stained finger at a column headed: "*Gruesome Find in Ancient Burial Chamber*".

"What do you make of that?"

I ran my eyes down the page to read that a party of archaeologists engaged in excavating a historical site near Devizes had come upon five skeletons, only four of which belonged to the period of the chamber. The fifth was of more recent origin, and among the bones was a rotting sack containing a quantity of gold plate, identified as the proceeds of a robbery which had occurred four years earlier at nearby Addleton Hall.

The report continued:

Inspector Blane of the Wiltshire Constabulary is satisfied that the remains are those of Edgar Barton, who vanished at the time of the robbery and was suspected of being responsible for the crime. He was the nephew of Mr. Willis Barton, the owner of the Hall.

I looked at my companion with eyebrows raised. "It seems plain enough," I said. "I see nothing here to excite your interest."

"Do you not? Come, my dear fellow, you have seen sufficient criminal activity to know when a matter feels right. Why should this man commit a burglary, then hide himself to die with his booty hard by the location of his crime? No, my good Doctor, it will not do."

I shrugged the matter aside and went to complete my toilet, and I had forgotten it completely by lunch when Mrs. Hudson announced a visitor.

"Miss Elizabeth Barton," she said, standing aside to allow entry to a young woman.

The name didn't at first register with me, but Holmes sprang to his feet to greet her effusively.

"My dear Miss Barton. Come in and be seated, I pray you. I trust you had a not too unpleasant journey from Wiltshire?"

She looked startled by his words, but lowered herself into the basket chair and watched Holmes take his place facing her. She was tall and slim, some twenty-five years of age, with warm brown eyes that held signs of deep sorrow. When she spoke her voice was quiet, but with a firmness that would hold the attention of those she addressed.

"I have heard of your powers of deduction, Mr. Holmes," she said. "And this must be Dr. Watson, who acts so ably as your chronicler." I bowed and she continued. "Yes, I have travelled from Wiltshire, but whether the journey was pleasant or otherwise I didn't notice in my agitated state of mind. I come to beg your help, sir, to clear my brother's name of a foul calumny, yet I can offer no concrete facts for you to build on, other than my own firm conviction of his innocence and integrity."

She paused and looked beseechingly from one to the other of us and I, a widower of more than two years, felt a surge of compassion and chivalry at her distress. Holmes, practical as always, leaned back with hands clasped behind his head.

"Your brother being the late Edgar Barton, whose remains were unearthed in the Bronze Age burial chamber?"

She nodded sadly, her eyes dry but holding a look of fierce pride. "Then," said Holmes, "I will hear your story, and we shall see if logic and reason can come to the aid of sisterly trust. Pray make me familiar with the events that have brought you so much distress."

"Edgar, who was four years my senior, and I lost both parents in a typhoid epidemic ten years ago, and our uncle, Mr. Willis Barton, gave us a home at Addleton Hall, some two miles from Devizes. I should add that Uncle Willis Is a very wealthy man who made his fortune in the African colonies before returning to England to enjoy the fruits of his labours. He bought the Hall on the death of the last Lord Addleton some two years before we went to live under his roof. He never married, and it was made clear to us that Edgar was to be his heir. Indeed, Uncle Willis treated us as his own flesh and blood, and in the six years that we lived there, he denied us nothing."

Here Holmes interposed a question. "You say six years. Am I to understand that you no longer reside there?"

"That is so, but I shall explain that shortly if you will bear with me. Due to our uncle's generosity, Edgar had no need to work, but he repaid that generosity by taking on the responsibility for the management of the estate, while from the age of sixteen, I was the virtual mistress of the Hall, taking complete charge of all domestic arrangements. It was a happy time, and the only cloud for me was the advent of an unwelcome suitor."

"Surely," said I, "there was no shortage of the young men of the district knocking at your door?"

"I accept the implied compliment, Doctor," she said modestly. "I fear there is a marked lack of eligible bachelors around Addleton and I had very little company of my own age of either sex. But to continue. The suitor of whom I spoke was a Mr. Elliot Langley. He was the son of my uncle's late partner during his Colonial days, and when he turned up at the Hall unannounced, he received a warm welcome. When he first showed an interest in me, I was flattered, despite he and Edgar having little liking one for the other.

"He had been with us for some two months when he showed himself in his true colours and – " Here Miss Barton averted her eyes and spoke in a barely audible voice. "He behaved towards me as no gentleman should."

"Did you tell your uncle or brother of his conduct?" asked Holmes.

"There was no need. Uncle came upon us as I struggled with him in a corridor and at once ordered him to leave the house. There was an angry scene of which I heard but part as I fled to my room, and I never set eyes on the wretch again."

My friend shot me a glance and, satisfied that my pencil was busy, he turned back to our client. "When did this disgraceful incident occur?"

"A month before Edgar's disappearance, four years ago this week, so Mr. Langley departed in the May. When my brother heard of it, he was for going after him to chastise him, but he allowed my uncle to placate him –

although Edgar vowed that if he ever set eyes on the man again, nothing would stop him."

"This Langley," asked Holmes. "What was his physical appearance??

"Tall, well-set up, and of a similar cast of countenance to my brother – so much so that on more than one occasion they had been taken for brothers or cousins, much to Edgar's chagrin."

"Thank you, Miss Barton. Now proceed to the night of the burglary."

"It was discovered by George, my uncle's personal servant, but neither I nor Uncle Willis heard anything unusual during the night. George had cause to go to the large drawing room to find the cabinet in which the plate was kept open and empty. He rushed to inform my uncle, who sent him to fetch Edgar, but my brother wasn't in his room. This gave no immediate concern, as he as often out and about the estate at the crack of dawn, but after the groom had fetched the police from Devizes and he was still absent, the inspector seized on the obvious and suggested that Edgar was the culprit."

Holmes frowned as the lady paused, and I ventured a query of my own. "You told us, Miss Barton, that your uncle had treated you both very generously, and your brother was his appointed heir. Did no one think it unlikely that he would sacrifice his future for a relatively small amount of gold plate?"

"Hardly a small amount, Doctor. The plate was worth more than three-thousand pounds and consists of five very fine pieces. However, I take your point. I think the police had it fixed firmly in their minds that such a sum would tempt anyone, and didn't see it in relative terms."

"And your uncle's view?" asked Holmes sharply.

"To give him his due, he resisted the idea most strongly until he was persuaded that with Edgar's sustained absence there was no other answer, and only then did he accept it with the deepest sorrow."

"But you did not." It was a statement rather than a question, and the lady at once concurred.

"No. At no time did I harbour the slightest doubt of my brother's innocence, and even this latest discovery does nothing to shake my belief. Let me say at once that I hold no animosity towards my uncle for his attitude, for there is no reason other than my stubbornness to think otherwise. "

Holmes got up and walked to the window where he stood looking down at the traffic below. Then he turned to face Miss Barton.

"Did Mr. Willis Barton ask you to leave Addleton Hall after this sad occurrence?"

"Indeed, he did not. He showed the utmost compassion for me, but with my feelings such as they were, I felt my position to be intolerable and

101

was unable to be under any further obligation to him. I went to Marlborough and secured a post as companion to a widowed lady, hoping vainly to clear my brother's name. For four long years I have prayed for Edgar to return with a credible explanation, but the events of this week have plunged me into the depths of despair." Her eyes filled with tears, and she began to sob. "Am I foolish to still believe in him even after his death?"

I went to fetch her a glass of water while Holmes allowed her time to recover before going on.

"Pray forgive me if some of my questions are painful, but I am anxious to do what I can, and must have all the facts at my disposal. Who identified these bones as being your brother's? Was it you or your uncle?"

She looked at him blankly for several seconds.

"I don't understand, Mr. Holmes. Can a skeleton be recognized?"

"That is my point. Dr. Watson will tell you that without a precise medical and dental history, it is only possible to say that the remains are male or female and fall within approximate limits of height and age at the time of death. Again I ask: Who made the identification?"

"Are you saying that these remains aren't my brother's?"

My companion raised a cautionary hand. "I wouldn't have you delude yourself with false hopes, Madam. All I suggest is that those concerned have taken the obvious view that your brother vanished at the time of the robbery and now a skeleton has been found with the proceeds of the crime, so it follows therefore that the remains are those of Mr. Edgar Barton. That assumption would be tenable if there was one scrap of supporting evidence, but thus far I have heard nothing to point in that direction. I keep an open mind. Have the police spoken to you since the discovery?"

She shook her head. "There has scarcely been time. I saw the account in this morning's paper and knew it was my last chance to clear Edgar's name. I spoke to my employer, Mrs. Widgeon, and she readily gave me leave to come to London. Can you – will you help me, Mr. Holmes?"

"The matter intrigues me," he said. "Watson, the *Bradshaw*. We shall accompany Miss Barton back to Marlborough and then proceed to Devizes. I must warn you, young lady: I promise nothing, and it may well be that the truth will not be to your liking. Can you accept that?"

She lifted her chin bravely. "I am in your hands, sir, and will abide by your findings. You have my complete confidence."

During the journey Holmes remained deep in thought, often ignoring or not hearing words addressed to him. It was early evening when we alighted at Marlborough and, having sent the lady off in the station fly to her place of employment, we sought rooms at the Western Hotel.

102

"Nothing is to be gained by unseemly haste," my friend observed. "This is one case where a few hours makes little difference to our investigations, so I let us enjoy a good dinner and a night's sleep before proceeding further."

Eight o'clock next morning found us bowling along in trap with Holmes at the reins. Addleton Hall was located on the Marlborough side of Devizes beyond the village of Bishop Cannings. The house was approached through an impressive set of wrought-iron gates, with a broad drive curving expansively to the main entrance. It was evident that the owner of this magnificent pile had spared no expense in its upkeep. A tug on the bell-pull brought immediate response from a butler, who took the card presented by Holmes before standing aside to permit us entry.

"If you will be so good as to wait here, gentlemen," this august personage intoned, "I shall ascertain if Mr. Barton is free."

As we stood there, I gazed round the spacious entrance hall, noting the innumerable trophies of the chase adorning the walls, the most eye-catching of which was a mummified crocodile all of fourteen feet in length staring malevolently at us from a glass case. I was still looking askance at the fearsome memento when the sound of footsteps drew our attention to the man approaching us with a look of surprised welcome on his deeply tanned features.

"Mr. Holmes!" he cried. "This is indeed an unexpected pleasure, but I confess I am at a loss as to the reason for your visit. Nevertheless, you are welcome, and your reputation is well known to me."

Holmes introduced me, and soon we were sitting in deep leather chairs puffing appreciatively at the excellent cigars that our host pressed on us. Willis Barton was some sixty years of age, as tall as Holmes but of much heavier build, his muscular frame and shock of dark hair conceding nothing to his years. His eyes were bright and keen, giving the impression of gazing into far distances.

Dispensing with any small-talk, Holmes came straight to the point.

"My visit is occasioned as the direct result of an appeal made to me by your niece, Miss Elizabeth Barton, who is intent on removing the stigma attached to the name of her brother. I realize that the subject must be distasteful to you, sir, but the lady will not accept the general opinion that your nephew was the perpetrator of the theft that took place four years ago. To ease her mind, I have undertaken to review the matter while warning her that my findings may be disagreeable to her, but such is her faith in her brother that she discounts the risk."

A look of ineffable sadness came over Barton's bluff features and he drew deeply on his cigar.

"I will not pretend that I welcome further probing into this old wound, but recent events have made it inevitable. I admire Elizabeth for her loyalty, and it was with the greatest reluctance that I came to believe the Edgar had betrayed my trust. Even that reluctance worked against me, for had I thought from the start that he had stolen the property, I would never have made the matter public."

"You would have condoned the offence?"

"I would have pardoned him freely. Edgar was as a son to me, as Elizabeth was and still is a daughter, but there was never any need for him to steal from me. Had he been in any sort of trouble, I would have given him such help as he needed and asked no questions."

"Then you were persuaded of his guilt against your own instincts and your knowledge of his character?" Holmes asked keenly.

"I resisted the thought as long as possible, but the police presented an incontrovertible case, and at last I yielded to the evidence. Poor Elizabeth was distraught, and although she bore me no ill-will, she saw it as unfitting that she should remain under my roof." Willis Barton lowered his voice confidentially. "Between these four walls, I made an arrangement with the lady with whom she stays as a companion to pay her a more generous salary than is usual, but that isn't for her ears."

Holmes nodded absently. Then with an abrupt switch of direction asked, "I believe you spent much of your early life in Africa, Mr. Barton. Your entrance hall hold many trophies of your sojourn there."

"Thirty years I lived and worked there, from my eighteenth birthday until I returned to the Old Country in '82 following the death of my partner, Bob Langley. I made my pile and looked after it, but Bob died as broke as when he went out. Money ran through his hands like water, and every time we hit town after a few months in the bush, he threw his share around with both hands."

"What business were you in, Mr. Barton?"

The man chuckled reminiscently as he replied. "Nothing shameful by the standards out there, even if we did sail a bit close to the wind at times. Ivory, skins, and the odd bit of gold. Sometimes a diamond or two, but we always gave the Kaffirs a fair deal. A rusty rifle or an iron pot meant more to them than the occasional gold nugget they turned up with."

Once again Holmes changed tack. "Your late partner had a son who stayed with you for a while, I believe?"

Willis Barton nodded reluctantly. "That is so. Elliot called on me when he came to England and found himself down on his luck. Naturally I made him welcome, but we had a disagreement and he left."

"Due to his behaviour towards your niece," Holmes murmured, then went on without waiting for confirmation. "Had he no mother living?"

"She died at his birth, but I fail to see why that is pertinent."

"You haven't heard from him since his departure?" Holmes pressed.

"The last I heard of him he was in Chippenham, and that was a few weeks after he left here." Barton made it plain that the subject of Elliot Langley wasn't to his taste and Holmes appeared to drop it.

"What a magnificent set of fire-irons," he remarked, nodding towards the huge grate. "Such a pity the poker should be missing. That quite destroys its value. No doubt you are relieved to have your collection of plate restored to you at last."

The older man seemed bewildered by my friends' apparent inconsequential manner, but he managed a bitter laugh at the last sentence.

"I would give ten times its worth if that would restore my nephew and niece to my hearth, and without bragging that would still leave me a very wealthy man. I shall not keep those trinkets, Mr. Holmes, for they would serve as a constant reminder of what I have really lost."

There was a slight pause before Holmes spoke again. "This burial chamber – is it on your property?"

"Yes, two fields away towards Devizes. The excavations have been suspended while the police make their inquiries, but poor Edgar's remains have been removed to the mortuary at Trowbridge."

At that point a discreet tap on the door was followed by the butler entering to whisper a few words in his master's ear. The latter threw a hesitant glance at us and spoke apologetically.

"It seems that Inspector Blane is wanting a word with me. Would it embarrass you to be present, gentlemen?"

"Not in the slightest!" Holmes cried heartily. "I welcome the chance to meet the inspector and hear what he has to say. It will save us the time of seeking him out elsewhere."

Inspector Blane was young to be holding the rank that he did, but his eyes were alert beneath sandy eyebrows that matched his close-cropped hair. I put his age at a year or two either side of thirty-five, and he was plainly a man who knew his business and wasn't to be trifled with. He paused when he saw that Barton already had visitors, but was waved in to be introduced to us.

"Of course I know of you, Mr. Holmes, and Dr. Watson also, but what is there to interest you in this matter?"

Holmes gave a succinct account of our reason for being at Addleton Hall, and Blane spread his hands expressively.

"You're welcome to make any inquiries you wish, sir. It will be a great pleasure to see you at work, and you may call on me for anything you may wish to know. Alas, I fear your labours will be in vain, much as I would desire otherwise." He turned to the owner of the house. "I called on you, Mr. Barton, to let you know that the inquest on your nephew will be held tomorrow, and you will be required to attend to identify the remains. Eleven o'clock at the Golden Hind in Devizes. I would spare you, but the law must be observed."

Willis Barton's shoulders sagged despondently. Then his head jerked up as Holmes intervened.

"Can you state definitely that this collection of bones was once Edgar Barton, Inspector?"

"Who else can they belong to?" asked Blane. "All the evidence points that way."

"Then it doesn't need Mr. Barton to state the fact. You or I or Dr. Watson could say so with equal truth."

Blane stared incredulously. "Are you suggesting otherwise, sir?"

"Not at all. All I say is that the evidence is purely circumstantial, and these remains could be those of any male person of similar age and build to the young man in question."

"Then where is my nephew if that is not he?" Barton cried urgently. "Who else could have perished in that horrible tomb, and why has he not been seen these four years past?"

Holmes made no reply to this, addressing himself to Blane instead. "Is it possible to view this burial chamber, Inspector? I assume that your investigations there are complete."

"I'll take you there myself, but don't expect too much of it. It is very insignificant compared with the great barrow at West Kennet, and was only uncovered by chance. We can go at once if you're ready."

Accepting Willis Barton's fulsome invitation to return for luncheon, we followed Inspector Blane over the fields until we came to the site of the excavations. It was indeed insignificant by any standards, a low hump some three feet high, almost covered in bushy scrub, and with a raw scar where the explorers had entered by way of a low tunnel sloping down to the interior. Holmes halted some yards short, his keen eyes darting hither and thither before he began to circle the mound, scrutinising it intently until he arrived back at his starting point.

"Who was responsible for opening the chamber?" he asked Blane who had watched his every move.

"Members of the local Historical Society. They had been interested in it for years, and had tried to attract the attention of professional archaeologists without success. I heard they even went so far as to write to Professor Challenger and had a very dusty answer from him."

Holmes chuckled. "They would. Challenger wouldn't see enough fame or notoriety in this to tempt him. Unfortunately, these well-intentioned people were more enthusiastic than expert. However, one must

106

not be too critical of them if they had tried to arouse interest and failed. May we go inside?"

"You will find candles just inside if you think it worthwhile. I've seen enough of the dismal place, so I shall await you here."

"Come then, Watson. You'll not refuse to bear me company, will you?"

Bent almost double, we ducked into the gloomy hole, our candles guttering. To my inexpert eye there was little to excite the interest, and apart from a jumble of old bones at which the rawest medical student would have turned up his nose and a few bronze artefacts, it was to me no more than a dank hole in the ground. My companion shuffled forward then squatted on his haunches, his neck twisted to inspect the roof, moving his candle in all directions. A muttered exclamation escaped his lips, but although my eyes followed his, I saw nothing to take my attention.

We retraced our steps and took in deep gulps of the sweet air without. Then Holmes shot off to scramble in the scrub growing on the mound, returning with twigs and grass stains on his trouser-knees and a look of smug satisfaction on his face.

He approached Blane and laid a hand on his arm. "Inspector, have you sufficient influence to have tomorrow's inquest adjourned for a week?"

"I shall need a reason," the inspector frowned. "Can you offer me one? I don't relish being kept in the dark."

"Well said!" cried Holmes, clapping him on the shoulder. "Let me speak to Mr. Barton over luncheon, then I promise to tell you what I propose. Can you be at the Hall at two o'clock?"

"I shall be there, Mr. Holmes, and if by throwing a different light on this sorry affair you can bring happiness to Miss Barton, I'm your man." He coloured to the roots of his sandy hair as he uttered these last words.

We ate a simple but satisfying meal, and as soon as the cloth had been drawn, Holmes got straight down to business.

"Mr. Barton," he began, "if I can clear your nephew of this shadow hanging over you all, how far are you prepared to go to help me?"

"I would go to Hades itself or perjure myself in any court in the land. Do that and I will meet any account that you see fit to render."

"The first two are quite unnecessary, and for the third my professional charges aren't such as to damage your credit. All I ask is that if I am to bring this matter to a successful conclusion, you will answer truthfully any questions I may put to you, with my word on absolute confidentiality."

"You have my hand on it, sir," said Barton.

"Then listen to what I have to say," and without more ado my friend proposed a plan so audacious that even I, used to his ways, was astounded.

107

Our client heard him in silence, consternation written all over his bluff features, but at the end he blew out his cheeks in hearty laughter.

"By George, sir! You ain't one for half-measures, are you? I'll go along with it gladly if it will clear Edgar's name and restore Elizabeth to my hearth."

"Then it only remains to secure Inspector Blane's agreement, and we may go ahead. Ah, I believe that is his hand on the bell now."

"Leave Blane to me," said Barton. "Nothing would suit him better than to have a hand in clearing my nephew's name. It would stand him in good stead with Elizabeth, if you take my meaning."

The policeman's first reaction to Holmes's extraordinary proposal was to mount a vigorous protest, but under pressure from the uncle of the two young people he at last capitulated, albeit with deep misgivings.

"If this goes awry," he said gloomily, "I can throw my career out of the window. The Chief Constable will demand my head on a plate."

"Then come, Watson!" cried Holmes clapping his hands. "The game's afoot!"

We made our best speed back to Marlborough, where I was set to packing our bags while Holmes busied himself by sending several telegrams to London and a note to Miss Barton which he had delivered by hand before hustling me willy-nilly to the railway station.

We caught the London Express by the skin of our teeth, and by half-past seven a hansom had deposited us at the door of our Baker Street rooms. I snatched an evening paper from a passing news-boy and trailed Holmes up to our sitting room where I thrust the paper at him. The black headlines shouted their message at us:

Arrest Likely in Wiltshire Skeleton Mystery

"It worked! They swallowed it!" I exclaimed gleefully.
He took the paper from me and began to read aloud:

It is learned by our correspondent that it is probable that Mr. Willis Barton of Addleton Hall in the county of Wiltshire will shortly be arrested in connection with the murder of his nephew, Edgar Barton, whose remains were discovered earlier this week.

He perused the remainder of the paragraph in silence before throwing himself into his chair, where he began stuffing tobacco into the bowl of an amber-stemmed briar.

"The morning papers will make more of it, you may be sure," he opined as the blue smoke wreathed around his head. "We must bestir ourselves early tomorrow. It would never do for us to be in disarray if we have a caller at the crack of dawn, as I hope we shall if my ploy bears fruit."

So it was that well before seven next morning our sitting room presented an unaccustomed aspect, our breakfast-table cleared, and even the newspapers folded neatly after we had read each in turn. They all carried similarly sensational stories as the one we had read the previous evening, although much amplified by speculation as to the course of events. Each one treated the matter in its own style, but all made a big play of the fact that the local police were acting on the advice of Mr. Sherlock Holmes, the renowned consulting detective of Baker Street.

For upwards of an hour we waited in silence, Holmes consuming pipe after pipe of tobacco and evincing signs of mounting impatience. I tried once to divert him, only to be quelled by a withering look. Then soon after eight o'clock a furious ringing of the doorbell brought him to his feet.

Heavy footsteps on the stairs preceded the violent bursting open of the door with the indignant protests of Mrs. Hudson pursuing the dishevelled figure that confronted us brandishing a copy of *The Daily News* in a shaking hand. Holmes strode across to placate our outraged landlady before turning to face the agitated intruder who was a young man of about thirty years, whose eyes blazed hotly in a face that in other circumstances could fairly have been described as good-humoured if not handsome.

"Sit dawn and compose yourself, Mr. Edgar Barton," commanded Holmes ere the man could recover his breath from his precipitate rush up the stairs. "I have been expecting you this past hour or more."

Our visitor appeared stunned by Holmes's words and the latter gently took his arm to propel him towards the basket chair and ease him dawn into it. "The brandy, Watson, if you will be so goad. Our guest seems to be somewhat confused. Here, my dear fellow, drink it down, then together we may unravel this four-year-old mystery. A cigarette, perhaps?"

With the brandy gone and a cigarette held in trembling fingers, the man had regained same measure of control. He thrust the newspaper forward, his eyes still wild and furious.

"Mr. Sherlock Holmes, for you must be he, what terrible thing is this that you have brought about? By what right do you scheme and connive with the police to place in jeopardy the life of a good and honourable man?" He half rose, and for a moment I thought he was about to launch himself in an assault on my friend.

Holmes fixed him with a compelling stare, and he subsided back into his chair, still white and shaking.

"Calm yourself, sir," Holmes admonished him. "Your uncle is in no peril from me or the police. Moreover, I suspect that your fears for your own liberty are quite unfounded, but until you tell me frankly of the sequence of events on that night four years ago, I shall reserve judgement."

"Then what is the source of these infamous stories in the newspapers?" demanded the man Holmes had addressed as Edgar Barton, and who hadn't denied the appellation.

"Merely a ruse on my part to bring you forward so that this whole sorry business may be resolved. Have you no care for the grief and heartbreak suffered by those who love you best? The uncle who was your benefactor was ever willing to accept you back into his house, while your faithful sister has never wavered in her belief of your innocence of any crime. Do you not owe it to them to stand forth and let the truth be known?"

Edgar Barton turned a haggard face towards us before dropping his head into his hands in a gesture of despair.

"Alas, Mr. Holmes," he groaned, "I fear I should give even greater sorrow to those of whom you speak, for although I am guilty of no great crime, the very course of events points an accusing finger. If you would spare them, let me return to the limbo from whence I came and say nothing of my continued existence."

"Pull yourself together, man," Holmes said sternly. "I already have a fair grasp of what happened on the night of the robbery. If my deductions aren't at fault, you may walk out of here to rejoin your family with a lighter heart than you have known these past years. Tell me your story, remembering that I am not a minion of the law but a seeker after truth and justice. There are no policemen lurking behind the curtains with handcuffs at the ready, so I implore you, trust me and all will be well. If you choose silence, I shall consider it my duty to tell the world of the facts and let things fall as they may."

The unhappy man looked at Holmes for a long minute, gnawing his lip in an agony of indecision. Then, with a resigned gesture, he nodded his head.

"So be it," he almost whispered, "I see I must needs trust you, but how did you arrive at the conclusion that I was still alive?"

"That I decided very early on. I became involved as the result of a plea by your sister, who has remained steadfast in her loyalty to you. Even before she approached me, I found it hard to believe that even had you been guilty of the theft as the newspapers suggested, it was against all reason to find your remains together with the booty so close to the scene of the crime. When Miss Barton told me her story, I asked myself who was likely to have been mistaken for you, and one name came to mind. Do I need to speak it?"

Edgar Barton shook his head and his cheeks flushed in anger. "No, you have the rights of it, but I am no felon, as you will see if you believe the story I tell."

"Then let us have some refreshment before we commence. Watson, pray ask Mrs. Hudson for coffee and some of her excellent plum cake."

A quarter-of-an-hour later the room was filled with the fragrant aroma of coffee, and we settled back to hear young Barton's narrative.

"You will have heard that on the death of our parents, Elizabeth and I were taken in by our uncle. He is a year or two my father's elder, and a finer man never set foot on earth. We were treated as his own, and we in turn did what we could to repay him, although that was little enough. The only discordant note came with the advent of Elliot Langley, the son of Uncle's late trading partner. He turned up with a story of being down on his luck, and our uncle's generous nature impelled him to offer the fellow a roof. It soon became obvious to me that he was no more than a parasite, his only goal being to extract as much as he could from Uncle Willis. He was selfish and lazy, and when I remonstrated with him about his conduct, he laughed in my face and told me to keep my nose out of his business, hinting that my uncle had swindled old Bob Langley out of his share of the partnership. I was patently untrue, and I was hard pressed to keep my hands off him."

Young Barton drained his cup, controlling his anger with an effort. "You gave no credit to the allegation?" Holmes interjected.

"None whatsoever. I knew my uncle well enough by this time to know that hard-headed business-man though he was, he was no swindler. After that, barely a civil word passed between Langley and me, but Elizabeth seemed to have a certain kindness towards him, despite my disapproval. However, a month or so after Easter, I returned one tea-time from a business trip to Trowbridge to find Langley gone, sent packing by my uncle. Both Uncle Willis and my sister were angry and distressed, but their wrath was nothing beside mine when I learned the reason for his dismissal."

"Miss Barton has apprised us of the incident," I said grimly.

"Well, gentlemen, you will also know that I was dissuaded from seeking him out with a horse-whip, but I vowed to exact retribution if he ever crossed my path again. After that, life settled down to what it had been before his arrival, but I detected a certain reserve in my uncle's demeanour. Reports reached me that Langley had been leading a life of debauchery in Chippenham before absconding with a trail of debts in his wake. I heard rumours that my uncle had made himself responsible for those debts, which was well in keeping with his generous nature.

"But to get on to the night of the burglary – that dreadful night forever stamped on my memory. I was working late in the library, preparing the accounts for the coming quarter-day, and finding myself drowsy, I thought to make myself ready for bed. It was my invariable habit to go round to ensure that all was secure for the night, and this I began to do. Imagine my surprise when I saw a moving light reflected on the terrace outside the large drawing room! I was still in the library and, seizing the poker from the grate, I stepped cautiously out on to the terrace in time to see a dark shape emerge from the drawing room. I must have been heard, for the figure turned to look in my direction. There was enough moonlight for me to recognize the features of Elliot Langley, and on seeing me, he at once took to his heels and with me in pursuit ran across the lawn and into the rough fields beyond."

"You made no outcry?" asked my colleague.

"I saved my breath. Besides," added the young man, "I wanted the satisfaction of dealing with him myself. He had a good start, but was hampered by a bulky sack slung over his shoulder, and I caught him as we crossed the second field. I grabbed his coattails and hurled him to the ground. I threw myself on him, expecting a desperate struggle, but to my total astonishment I met with no resistance. I sat astride him with my knees planted in his chest, but he made no move. Then it was I saw his face was suffused and his eyes wide open in a ghastly stare. I realised I was kneeling on a corpse, and I sprang to my feet in horror. Imagine if you can the scene there in the pale light of the moon, with me standing over a dead man on whom I had sworn vengeance for his insult to my sister and a poker in my hand. What interpretation would be put on it? For ten minutes I wrestled with my conscience before making a decision that I now know to be cowardly and foolish. I resolved to dispose of the body and vanish."

"Your reasoning was at fault," observed Holmes, stuffing tobacco into the bowl of his largest pipe. "Even if you were afraid of the truth not being accepted, you could have gone to your bed as if nothing had happened and be there when the burglary was discovered in the morning."

"That did occur to me, but I am no hand at dissembling, and most surely would have given myself away."

"Then you could have told your uncle the facts and relied on his trust."

"Oh, that's easy enough to say now," Edgar Barton retorted hotly. "Then I was in a state of terror and panic, and my thoughts weren't so logical."

"Logical enough to cast it into that hole," Holmes said severely. "Did you have any notion what it was?"

"No. It wasn't until I read of the discovery of the bones that I knew it to be an ancient burial chamber. The hole was covered by scrub, so I put a large flat stone over it, hoping it would never be found. The clothes I stuffed into a convenient rabbit-hole, together with the poker, and to the best of my knowledge they remain there still. Taking to my heels, I made my way by devious means to London, having enough money in my possession to maintain me until I obtained employment in a counting-house which paid sufficient to keep body and soul together. Oh, how often have I mourned my foolish and impulsive actions! I wanted to make a clean breast of it, but the more I procrastinated, the less likely it was that I would be believed. It was only this hare you started that brings me here now." He sat up and faced Holmes squarely. "Well, there you have it, Mr. Detective. What do you propose to do now?"

Holmes leaned back, his fingers stroking his long nose. "I believe your account, Mr. Barton, but you acted rashly and precipitately. As I see it, the only offences you have committed are failing to report a death and concealment of a body. Reprehensible as it is, I don't think the law will demand great retribution of you, but in my eyes the greater crime is the pain given to those who love you. Are you prepared to be guided by me in order to bring about a felicitous conclusion?"

"It seems that I am in your hands," said young Barton with a bitter laugh. "What have I to lose now? My own stupidity landed me in this muddle, and all I desire now is to have it over and done with. Have I your word that my uncle is in no danger and that the only purpose of the newspaper story was to induce me to reveal myself?"

"You have. Are you able to travel with us immediately to Wiltshire?"

"The sooner the better." He stood up. Now that a decision had been made it, was a different man now facing us from the wild figure that had burst into our chambers not an hour ago. His jaw was set in a firm line and his eyes were bright with a hope that had been lacking before. Holmes eyed him steadily, then gave him an encouraging nod.

"Good. Watson, do you run downstairs and secure a four-wheeler while I compose a couple of telegrams to prepare the ground ahead of us. I believe there is an excellent train at eleven o'clock"

So it was that we again found ourselves stepping from the train at Marlborough, making our way at once to the Western Hotel, where the manager greeted us warmly.

"The sitting room for which you wired is ready, Mr. Holmes," he said. "The young lady arrived not ten minutes since and awaits you there. Will you go straight up?"

"Not I," my friend replied. "Be so good as to conduct this gentleman to her at once. Is the dog-cart at hand? Good. Then the doctor and I will be on our way." He slapped the young man on the back. "Go on up, sir. I have one theory still to confirm, but we shall rejoin you later."

We never knew what took place between brother and sister, for five minutes later we were clip-clopping along the road to Addleton Hall. Holmes was in a blithe mood and refused to discuss the case, saying that if I hadn't grasped the situation yet, then I must wait upon events. We were met on the steps of the Hall by an excited Willis Barton, whose face fell when he saw but the two of us step down from the wagon.

"Where is Edgar, Mr. Holmes? Your telegram led me to look for him to be with you. Has something gone amiss?"

Holmes freed his arm from the other's importunate grip. "Curb your impatience, sir, I beg you. All is well, and your nephew is at this very moment with his sister. They are in Marlborough, but they will join you ere long. Before they do so, there is a matter that I would resolve between us – not only for my own edification, but to enable the good Watson to tie up the loose ends when he records the case in his chronicles."

"Ask what you will, and I shall answer if it is within my power to do so." He led us into the library, producing cigars and whisky before giving us his full attention. "Now, gentlemen, what would you know?"

"We have established that the skeleton in the barrow isn't that of your nephew," Holmes began blandly. "The question remains as to whose it is. Do you have any thoughts on that, sir?"

Willis Barton's eyes flickered, and he shifted uncomfortably in his chair. "Why, I assume it to be that of the burglar, but I can only surmise how it came to be there."

"I have the advantage of knowing that," said Holmes. "Let me tell you at once that the remains are those of Elliot Langley, buried in panic by your nephew."

Our host's face was ashen, and his big frame appeared to shrink before our very eyes. He took a huge gulp of whisky and immediately refilled his glass with a shaking hand.

"Tell me all, Mr. Holmes," he said when he had recovered somewhat. "Is Edgar still in peril?"

"I doubt it. He acted unthinkingly, but I think his offence will be looked on with compassion."

Holmes went on to relate the course of events as told by young Barton while the older man listened in silence. As the story drew to a close, he stared down at his hands with an expression between relief and sadness.

"So Elliot Langley is dead," he whispered. "God rest his soul, and God forgive me. I began to suspect as much when you displayed such confidence that it wasn't Edgar, but I feared to speak. What led you so quickly to the truth?"

My companion smiled. "The first hint came when Miss Barton told me that her brother and Langley were often mistaken for close relatives, and your tolerant attitude to his abuse of your hospitality confirmed my suspicion that he had Barton blood in his veins. Am I correct?"

Barton squared his shoulders and gave us a defiant look. "You are, Mr. Holmes. There is no point in denying it, as I am the only concerned party still living, but I would ask your discretion, Doctor, if you set this story down on paper."

"Be easy, sir," I replied. "I am adept at disguising places and people when preparing my stories for publication. I merely try to place before the public my colleague's unique powers, and I defy anyone to identify the players in these little dramas."

"Say on, Mr. Willis Barton," Holmes encouraged him. "Our discretion is absolute."

"Very well." Barton's eyes held a faraway look as he embarked on a tale that had its beginnings on the Dark Continent thirty years ago. "You will recall that I told you of my time in Africa and how my partner, Bob Langley, would go through his money as fast as he made it. We worked well together, but our temperaments were as chalk and cheese. I was ever a sober and prudent man, and it fell out that while we were in the Transvaal – Pretoria to be precise – disposing of our goods and laying in supplies for the next trek I met a lady with whom I fell deeply in love. My love was returned in full until I introduced her to Bob. You can imagine that I suffered by comparison with him – he with his zest for life and me so staid and careful. The upshot was that he couldn't tear himself away from her, and I couldn't bear to see them so happy together, so by mutual agreement between Bob and myself I went up-country alone. I returned four months later to find them married. You can picture my feelings, but I put the best face on it and wished them all the luck in the world."

Here he stopped to blow his nose on an outsize handkerchief.

"Worse was to follow," he resumed. "I hadn't been back in town many days when Mrs. Langley called on me at my hotel, and what she told me turned my world inside out. Marriage hadn't changed Bob in any respect, and he was out of funds and deeply in debt. He had approached me to get another safari under way, but I had no idea just how desperate

115

he was for money until his wife told me. I wasn't reluctant to leave, as it wasn't the easiest situation for me to see the woman I still loved with my partner, although I bore them no grudge. As I mentally began to plan how I could stake Bob until we had made few sovereigns, and that without giving it the appearance of charity, she began to sob hysterically and upbraid me for going off on my own.

"I pointed out that as she and Bob were so wrapped up in each other, I felt my absence to be the wisest course, and the fact that I had returned to find them married confirmed it. 'You fool?' she cried. 'Why do you think I married him? Was I to wait indefinitely for you to come back and have my shame revealed to all?' At first, I didn't grasp her meaning, but eventually she made me understand that I was the father of the child she was expecting. I was stunned and ashamed, even though she convinced me that Bob had no inkling of the truth, and she wouldn't have come to me now if they weren't in desperate straits for money."

Holmes made no comment when the other paused, but I sensed disapproval in his somewhat Puritan nature.

Willis Barton began to speak again. "To cut a long story short, Bob and I went off, with me making him an advance on our expected profits and leaving his wife enough to support her. We were gone about six months and returned to find her dead and her baby son being cared for by a kindly old missionary and his wife. That was in '64, and four years later Bob got himself killed by a mad rogue tusker when his gun misfired. As you may guess, he left nothing and I made myself responsible for the boy's upbringing and education, but there was a fatal flaw in his character, and by the time he was seventeen, he had been in all kinds of trouble. I'll not go into any details, but he eventually went up-country on his own, and all I heard of him were a few discreditable stories that filtered down.

"I came back to the Old Country in '82 a disappointed man, for I had hoped that Elliot would become the son I had always wanted, but I had never had the courage to reveal the truth of our relationship."

"He must have learned it somehow," I hazarded. "His behaviour indicated that he had some hold over you."

"That is so. He came to England some four-and-a-half years ago and sought me out. By then my brother and his wife were dead and their children were living with me. When Elliot made himself known, I was unable to turn him away, and it wasn't long ere he saw Edgar's remarkable resemblance to him and put two and two together. When he confronted me with it, I couldn't in all conscience deny the truth, but surprisingly enough he wasn't interested in having the facts made known. Instead, as the price of his silence, he prevailed on me to make a larger allowance – much more than Edgar received. His conduct grew more and more intolerable until the incident with Elizabeth came as the final straw. I told him to leave my house and never show his face again, defying him to do what he would about our relationship." Willis Barton sighed. "Can you conceive of the pain and agony that decision caused me?"

Neither Holmes nor I replied, and the older man continued.

"Strangely enough, he went with nothing more than veiled threats, and for the next month I waited for his next move, but except for regular demands for money I was left in peace. Then came the burglary and my mind was on Edgar's apparent betrayal of my trust to the exclusion of all else. After that I heard no more of Elliot, other than he had left Chippenham with a trail of debts behind him which I felt honour-bound to settle."

Holmes rose to his feet, and I closed my notebook and followed suit.

"I don't think we need pry more," said my companion. "I think I hear the sound of wheels on the gravel, so we will leave you in peace with your loved ones. I believe you have sufficient influence in the county to have your nephew's impulsive actions dealt with sympathetically, but I see no reason for the distant past to be raked over. Is there an anteroom where Watson and I may wait until the two young people are safely in here with you and we can depart unobserved?"

We drove to Devizes, Holmes concerned that Blane's mind should be put at rest with a judicially edited story of events. We found the inspector at the police station, and between us we concocted the fiction that Holmes had been in the district on an entirely different matter and that the papers had wrongly made a connection with the four-year-old crime, leading to their false assumption that Willis Barton would soon be arrested.

"It's your case, Mr. Blane," my friend said. "Take what credit you can from it, but I would beseech you to spare the Bartons as much unpleasantness as you can.

"Rely on me, sir, and it has been an education to me to see your methods. One thing I would ask, though: What first put you on the track of the real truth?"

"Oh, that was the roof of the burial chamber," Holmes answered vaguely. "There was an obvious difference in the soil immediately over the skeleton indicating that it had been disturbed much later than the Bronze Age."

On our return journey to Paddington, Holmes sat huddled in a corner of the compartment, humming quietly to himself. It wasn't until we approached Newbury that I ventured a question.

"One small point: How will you account for the telegrams to the newspapers that hinted of Willis Barton's imminent arrest? Will not your reputation be damaged now that events have turned out differently?"

117

He turned a bland smile in my direction. "My dear Watson, those wires must have been sent by some malicious person using my name. They cannot be laid at *my* door. If newspaper editors are so gullible as to print that kind of thing without verifying the facts, it is their misfortune. I shall issue a firm denial and demand that they publish a retraction and apology immediately and prominently."

"Really, Holmes, you are incorrigible." I laughed. "Have you no shame?"

Thus, what started as a tragedy came to a happy conclusion, with Holmes opening a letter a week later to find a cheque enclosed, the amount of which caused me to whistle when he showed it to me. It was signed *"Willis Barton"*.

Three months had elapsed when an item in *The Morning Chronicle* came to our attention. It announced the engagement of Chief Inspector Blane of the Wiltshire Constabulary to Miss Elizabeth Barton of Addleton Hall in that county, and in the next day's mail came invitations for Holmes and myself to be guests at the forthcoming nuptials.

"Blane has taken another step on the ladder of promotion," Holmes remarked. "A wife such as Miss Barton will be invaluable in his career."

However, events intervened which took us to Paris on the case of Huret, the Boulevard Assassin, in consequence of which we were forced to miss that joyful occasion, much to my regret.

The Crown of Light

It was a close and humid day in the August of 1896. Holmes and I were returning on foot from an expedition to Bradley's the tobacconist where I had replenished my supply of Arcadia mixture and Holmes had obtained a fresh stock of the abominable black shag whose fumes he inflicted on all and sundry. We were in no hurry, the oppressive atmosphere making the slightest exertion a labour, and as we rounded the corner into Baker Street a cab was seen to be standing before our door.

"I say," I noted, "we appear to have a visitor."

He paused to look at me sardonically. "An excellent deduction, Watson, and worthy of further exposition,"

"Really," I said acidly, "I fail to see what other inferences are to be drawn from the mere fact of a hansom waiting before our chambers. Perhaps you will be good enough to enlighten me."

He moved on slowly and I hastened to catch up with him. "Well, I would suggest that it has been there more than a few minutes. The horse has provided its own evidence of that, and since the beast is munching contentedly on its nosebag and the jarvey isn't in view, it seems that the caller is the cabbie himself, either on his own behalf or as a messenger for a third party."

"Of course, but that is so obvious that it scarcely warrants comment."

"Then, my dear fellow, it must be equally obvious that the cab is there, so why mention it if you aren't prepared to take the matter to the end?"

I knew from experience that when my friend was in a disputatious mood there was nothing to be gained by verbal fencing, so biting my tongue, I preceded him to our door to use my key. On our entering the hall, a man who could only be the cab driver sprang from the wooden chair on which he was sitting and looked from one to the other of us,

"Mr. 'Olmes – Mr. Sherlock 'Olmes?" he asked eagerly.

Holmes stepped forward. "I am he, and this is my colleague. Dr. Watson. Pray tell me in what way I may be of assistance to you."

"I need 'elp, Mr. 'Olmes, desperate 'elp, and I can't think of no one else to turn to! I took the liberty of coming 'ere, 'oping you can advise me."

Holmes gave the man an appraising look, then gestured to the stairs. "Come, I shall hear what you have to say, but I promise nothing at this stage."

119

He led the way to our sitting room and, divesting himself of his coat, sat down with his back to the window with our visitor facing him. The man was agog to begin his story, but Holmes wasn't to be hurried. "Fill the briar which protrudes from your waistcoat pocket. I think you will find the good Doctor's special blend both soothing and stimulating at the same time."

Taking the hint, I brought out my newly replenished pouch and passed it to our guest. Holmes filled his cherry-wood with his own pungent shag while I, on retrieving my pouch, selected the inscribed silver mounted briar presented to me by my brother officers of the 66th.

"Now, my good fellow," said Holmes when our pipes were drawing, "I beg you to state your problem, and I promise to listen with all attention. The doctor will make notes against the unlikely event of my memory being at fault, then I shall decide if you can be helped."

The man took a deep breath and loosened his neckerchief. "Well, Guv'nor, it's like this. My name is Pritchard, Lewis Pritchard, and I'm the owner of the cab standing out front. I do very nicely at my trade, and live out Deptford way in as neat a little two-up, two-down as you could wish for. A few weeks back, I was asked if I'd be interested in buying the house at a very fair figure and I said I was. As I said, I make a good living from my cab and it's a poor week indeed when I clear less than three pounds after all expenses, although it means being out in all weathers."

"A man of industry," Holmes murmured as Pritchard paused to relight his pipe. "Proceed, I pray you."

"I married about three years ago, and although to our sorrow we as yet have no children, we are both young and pray that time will be kind to us."

Here my companion interrupted him. "I take it you purchased your cab on your discharge from the Royal Artillery?"

Pritchard looked startled. "Why, yes sir, I did. But how do you know my regiment when I said nothing of it?"

Holmes waved a deprecatory hand. "Your bearing indicates you have seen military service, almost certainly overseas, and when you reached for Watson's tobacco pouch, I observed the regimental crest tattooed above your wrist. The tattoo is of a style common to India. May I also venture to suggest that as you chose to drive a cab on your discharge and your horse looks particularly well-cared-for, you were most probably a driver."

The man eyed Holmes with new respect as he nodded. "Right on target, Mr. Holmes, and if I say it myself, no finer lead driver ever took a gun into action. But if I may continue, you will have gathered that I made a very happy marriage, and all was well until some four months back, when I found on several occasions my wife was absent when I returned

120

home at night. At first I paid little heed, until I noticed these absences took on a regular pattern of occurring every Tuesday and Thursday. I sought an explanation, but beyond saying she had been visiting friends, she offered nothing. When I pressed her, she became agitated and accused me of base suspicion and lack of trust. I protested strongly, yet her very words aroused in me those very feelings of which I stood accused."

At this juncture Holmes, who had been listening intently with closed eyes, leaned forward and spoke sharply. "Tell me, sir, why do you represent yourself as something you are not?"

For brief moment the man looked confused, but recovered quickly. "I don't understand. What do you mean?"

"Come now," said Holmes with some asperity. "I beg you, don't take me for a complete dunderhead. You are a man of some education which was probably acquired at a minor public school, although you didn't reach university. Why present yourself as of the labouring classes? You play your part well, but to one who has made a study of philology, your deception is apparent. I warn you, Mr. Pritchard – or whatever your name is – I'm not to be trifled with, and unless some very good explanation is forthcoming, I must bid you good day." He rose to his feet and looked down sternly at the man who had the grace to look abashed.

"I crave your pardon, sir," said he. "You are in the right, although what you see as a deception was in no way intended to fool you. If you will allow me to tell something of myself, you might understand the reason for this masquerade."

Holmes surveyed him keenly, and apparently satisfied resumed his chair. "Very well." He nodded curtly. "Pray proceed."

"I will not affront you by asking for a pledge of secrecy," said our visitor. "I have every confidence you will appreciate my position when I tell you that I am the youngest of three sons from a prominent and well-respected family. My father and one brother hold important posts in the Civil Service. Not in the public eye but working, if I may put it so, behind the scenes. Whatever administration is in power, they are there to guide and advise the government to the best of their ability. My other brother is a lawyer with a leaning towards politics and a lot of ambition. When young, I led a wild and dissolute life, often causing my family acute embarrassment, and this culminated in my father disowning me completely, cutting me off without even the proverbial shilling.

"This shocked me into realising the dangerous path I was treading, and I sought to redeem myself by enlisting as a private soldier in the Royal Artillery. As you may well imagine, the lot of a gentleman ranker isn't an easy one, and very early on I found it expedient to adapt my manner and speech to that of my comrades. I confess I never quite succeeded in mangling the Queen's English as did some of my fellows, excellent chaps though they were. When I took my discharge the same considerations applied, and thus I came to you as that which I in fact have become. Does that explain my little deception?"

Holmes smiled faintly. "It is understandable in the circumstances, but what of your wife? How much of this does she know?"

Pritchard rubbed the bowl of his pipe against his cheek before answering slowly. "She is aware that I was once a gentleman, but of my family she knows nothing. She is a person of some education herself, her father being a wealthy clothing manufacturer who – although a self-made man – ensured that she and her older brother had the advantages denied him. As with a number of men who rise above their humble origins, Joe Smithers is still something of a rough diamond, but hoped his children would move up the social scale, and when his only daughter announced her intention of marrying a common cabman – to say that he disapproved is to understate the case. As Freda, my wife, was of age, he couldn't forbid the match, but from thence on he has neither spoken nor made any effort to contact her in any way. In all fairness," added the man, "I must make it clear that he settled the very handsome sum of two-hundred pounds a year on her, which is more than my father did for me. Of course, the money is hers to use as she sees fit, and I lay no claim to any part of it. Yet it is that very money that has precipitated the present crisis and brought me to your door." His voice broke and he hung his head to recover his composure.

Holmes's pipe gave forth a chorus of obscene gurgling noises and he laid it aside reluctantly, spilling ash down his waistcoat in the process. "Continue, Mr. Pritchard – if that is indeed your name."

"It's the name I've been known by these ten years past, so I can fairly call it my own. As I said, I was given the option of buying the house in which we live, and yesterday the offer was put on a firm footing and a price quoted which was more than fair. The present owner is advanced in years and is to spend the remainder of his days with a daughter in Sussex, so he requires a quick decision from me. Freda and I have often talked of owning our own home, and I was keen to get back to talk it over with her. As it happened, I picked up a fare who kept me darting hither and thither until quite late, and in consequence it was past ten o'clock before I'd seen to the nag and made my way home. Freda was home, but I knew she had been out as her boots stood in the passage showing signs of damp from the summer shower that had fallen earlier that evening."

"A piece of deduction worthy of yourself, Holmes," I chuckled.

He flung me an impatient look and urged our visitor to continue.

"I was too full of my news to make an issue of it then," Pritchard went on, "but when I announced our good fortune, I was disappointed at her

122

lack of enthusiasm. It wasn't that she raised any objections, but neither did she seem to have any joy from it. It was when I came to speak of financial matters that things came to a head. As I mentioned, she has her own income, paid monthly through her father's solicitors, and I have never inquired how she disposed of it. She isn't prodigal or extravagant and I assumed she invested it safely, so when I suggested that a small portion of her money should be loaned to me to effect the purchase of the house, I was floored by her reaction.

"At first she was evasive, then when I pressed her for an answer, she became extremely agitated, and eventually refused point blank to lend me a penny. In vain I pleaded, pointing out that it would be a loan on strictly business terms, but she was adamant. I was set on having the property and with my own modest savings short of my needs, my only other resource was to obtain a loan for the remainder, but why should they have the interest when she might do so? Her response was to say that I must do as I saw fit, and at that I lost my temper, using harsh words that only served to reduce her to tears, with the result that for the first time in our marriage we retired to bed in an atmosphere of anger and hostility. I spent a restless night and rose well before dawn. I knew Freda was awake, for I heard her sobbing into her pillow, but I was still angry and went to prepare my breakfast without a word to her."

The unhappy man paused and shook his head sadly before proceeding.

"It was while searching in the kitchen drawer for a knife that I came across this pamphlet." He pulled from his inside pocket a creased piece of paper and held it out.

Holmes took it and unfolded it. Looking over his shoulder, I saw a cheaply-printed sheet headed "*The Crown of Light Mission*", exhorting those in need of spiritual comfort to seek solace and guidance at the above on Tuesdays and Thursdays with Mr. and Mrs. Lester Burton, followed by an address in a less salubrious part of Bermondsey. Holmes perused it with an expression of distaste, then laid on the arm of his chair and sat back with a sigh.

"Apart from what we are meant to read," he said, "it tells us little. It was produced on a small hand-press, not by a firm of commercial printers. The paper could have come from one of a hundred stationers and was cut to size by a pair of not over-sharp scissors, so I suggest it wasn't intended for mass distribution, but run off as required to be given to selected persons. Did you ask your wife if she had knowledge of it?"

Pritchard nodded. "I went to her at once. At first she feigned ignorance, but when I pointed out that I hadn't seen it before, and as she and I were the only people in the house, it followed that she must have put it in the drawer. Again she resorted to tears, saying I was determined to make her unhappy, but I still insisted on an answer. At last she said, not very convincingly, that it had probably been pushed through the door and she had put it away without reading it. At that I flung out of the house and went to my work a bewildered and unhappy man. As I prepared my cab for the day's work, I fell to brooding on her conduct and decided that her refusal to be frank with me was in some way linked with her absences from home and that piece of paper.

"I left the mews and, ignoring any prospective fare who tried to hail me, I drove at my best pace to the address in Bermondsey to see if any clue might be gleaned. The place was an old warehouse, and as I entered the gate, I was accosted by a rough-looking character reeking of beer whom I took to be the caretaker. I attempted to question him about the mission, but all I got was foul abuse and told if I didn't push off I'd be out on my ear. I saw no profit in trying to reason with the lout so I left, and it was then that your name came to mind. I thought there was nothing to be lost by entreating your help, or at least advice, and here I am. It may seem a trivial domestic matter to you, Mr. Holmes, but I'm at my wits end and know not where to turn for relief."

Holmes raised his eyes broodingly to our caller. "As you say, it may well be a trivial matter, but my instincts warn me that there are deeper waters and bigger fish than may be apparent to us now. If you will give your consent to let me take whatever steps seem good to me, I shall be most willing to attempt to throw some light on to your problem. I believe your wife to be in grave trouble – so grave that she feels unable to confide in you, and may be driven to desperation if the matter isn't resolved quickly."

Pritchard blanched under his tan. "What can it be, Mr. Holmes?" he cried. "Freda is as pure and honest as the day is long. How could she be in serious trouble?"

"That we must discover, sir," Holmes replied austerely. "I can make no judgement until I'm in possession of all the facts. There is nothing more you can tell me?"

"I have told you all I know. What must I do now?"

Holmes stroked his long nose. "Do nothing and go about your business as usual. Above all, put no further pressure on your wife, for I fear she is near breaking point. Leave me your address and that of the mews where you keep your equipage and I will be in touch. Now, good day to you, Mr. Pritchard, and be of good heart."

The door had barely closed on our client before Holmes had vanished into his own room, reappearing ten minutes later as a completely different person. He wore a decrepit billycock hat and a shabby buttonless coat secured at the waist by a length of frayed string. He carried an old carpet-bag which clanked as he put it down, and a straggly moustache adorned his upper lip. I marvelled at his facility in changing his whole appearance and personality with a few simple accessories and to become the very essence of the character he purported to be.

"Come, Watson, we must move apace," he cried. "Be so good as to secure a four-wheeler for our journey. No self-respecting cabbie will stop for such as I."

Resigning myself to another missed lunch, I preceded him down the stairs and was lucky enough to find a growler discharging its passengers on the other side of the road. The driver looked askance at my disreputable companion but offered no objections, and on a muttered word from Holmes I directed the man to Bermondsey. Holmes slouched pensively in a corner, only rousing himself as we rattled over London Bridge, when he turned a quizzical eye on me.

"Well, what is your reading of the case?" I, too, had been pondering, but was forced to admit that I had no substantial theory to offer. Nevertheless, I made the effort.

"Obviously there is some threat hanging over Mrs. Pritchard, but on the present information I cannot conjecture what it can be. Apart from marrying in defiance of her father's wishes, she seems to have led a blameless existence, and even her father wasn't so uncaring as to cut her off completely. In fact, her allowance is very generous – as much as my wound pension from a grateful government. By Pritchard's account, they are a loving couple and hitherto have had no secrets between them,"

"Excellent, my dear fellow. So we need more data to build upon, and perhaps it may be found in this squalid neighbourhood. Ah, we approach our destination, and that unprepossessing iron hut is the address we seek. Continue for two-hundred yards that I may alight unremarked, and wait where you can see without being seen."

I rapped on the panel with my stick, and as the cab slowed, Holmes slipped nimbly on to the cobbles, his carpet-bag clinking in his hand. I told the driver to take the next turning and stop and, handing him a half-sovereign as earnest of good faith, bade him wait upon my return. I walked back to the corner in time to see Holmes shuffle up to the iron gate of the mission and enter. Crossing the road, I strolled in the same direction and, on coming level with the gate, I paused to fill and light my pipe, keeping a covert eye on the entrance. Less than a minute passed ere I heard the sound of voices raised in altercation. Then Holmes came into view, pursued by a large uncouth-looking figure uttering threats of violence bestrewn with some of the foulest oaths it has been my misfortune to hear. He slammed the gate behind Holmes, who retaliated with a shake of his fist, and to my dismay added his own comments in language that matched that of the other man. Never in the whole course of our association had my friend inclined to coarseness of expression, and to hear it now was a shock to my sensibilities. I excused him now on the grounds that it was in keeping with the character he was presenting and that he must deplore it as much as I. So reflecting, I turned back to where I had left the cab, throwing a quick glance over my shoulder to ascertain that my companion was following. On entering the cab, Holmes delved into the depths of his carpet-bag to produce a loosely-wrapped parcel from which he took a pair of boots and a light jacket.

"I fear the trousers must do," he said, peeling off his moustache. "The absence of a hat can be accounted for by a gust of wind from the river. Have the cabbie drive to the nearest police station and we shall see if they have any useful facts about this so-called mission." As we went, he told me of his encounter and its outcome. "I posed as an odd-job man seeking work, and found our repellent friend drinking beer in a back room. I recognized him at once as a notorious bully-boy from the Elephant and Castle, and I know for a fact that he has several counts against him for violence and petty thieving. It owes more to the constitution of his victims than his own restraint that he hasn't faced a more serious charge than assault and battery. However, I asked fairly enough if there was any work to be had and I was told to push off, but I began to walk round and point out that the place could do with a few touches here and there. At that he became aggressive and offered to throw me out if I didn't 'sling my 'ook', and I became equally offensive with the result that you observed."

"Good Heavens!" I gasped. "You could have come to serious harm at the hands of that brute!"

"Really, Watson, have you so little faith in me that you fear I couldn't hold my own with such a crude rascal as he? You have remarked on my mastery of the noble art on more than one occasion. But here we are at the bastion of law and order. Be good enough to keep me company and be ready to stand surety for my respectability, dressed as I am."

We entered the police station where a sergeant was writing laboriously in a ledger. He laid his pen aside with the air of one glad of the excuse to be relieved of his task and greeted us civilly.

"Good afternoon, gentlemen," then a surprised look came to his face. "Why, it's Mr. Sherlock Holmes and the Doctor! What brings you to this part of the world?"

I remembered him as the constable who had discovered the body of Enoch Drebber on that memorable first occasion when I had been privileged to see Holmes display his remarkable powers, and although unable to put a name to him, I recalled my friend anathematizing him as a

126

blundering fool who would never rise in his chosen profession. I was human enough to be mildly gratified that the sergeant's stripes proved my colleague to be even so slightly fallible. He could have read my thoughts, for he gave me a rueful grin before addressing himself to the sergeant.

"Rance, is it not? John Rance?"

"That's so, sir. Sergeant Rance these two years past, thanks to you."

Holmes looked mystified. "I recall nothing I have done to advance your career, pleased as I am to note it."

"Not directly, Mr. Holmes, but I knew you thought I should have recognized that drunk in Lauriston Gardens that night as the murderer, so I got to thinking about smartening up my ideas and this is the result, while Harry Murcher still pounds a beat down Brixton way, so it's you what takes the credit."

"Then I congratulate you, Sergeant, and perhaps I may draw a little on that credit by asking you for some local information."

"Anything I can tell you I will, sir, and perhaps there may be a good word in it for me. I'll not presume to put myself alongside of Inspectors Lestrade and Gregson, but a favourable mention in my record can do no harm."

At the mention of the two Scotland Yard inspectors, Holmes smiled sardonically and contented himself with a non-committal grunt. "What do you know of The Crown of Light Mission along the road from here?"

Rance sucked on his moustache and pondered the question before answering.

"Well," said eventually, "I know nothing that gives us any concern – except for that caretaker they've hired."

"You mean Bert Carver?" Holmes put in quickly.

"That's him, and I give a lot to feel his collar, but since he come out of Pentonville last spring he's had that job and never a sign of old ways. The job was found for him by a prison visitor and he reports to us once a week. Not very willingly, I may say, but so long as he don't give no bother, there isn't much I can do about him."

"What of the minister, or whatever he calls himself?"

"All I know is what I hear from the beat man. This bloke turns up with a woman said to be his wife about six o'clock every Tuesday and Thursday and leaves just after nine. Where they live I've no idea, and I've had no call to ask. That's all I can offer, Mr. Holmes, and I wish it could be more."

"Ah, well," sighed Holmes. "Not as much as I had hoped, but I shall remember your willingness to help, Sergeant." A couple of florins slid across the desk to vanish quickly, and with Rance's expression of goodwill echoing in our ears we made our exit and returned to Baker Street.

127

Over our belated lunch, my companion was taciturn, paying little heed to the handsome pork-and-veal pie provided by Mrs. Hudson. Eventually he pushed his plate to one side with the meal barely touched and went to the window, where he stood for some time gazing broodingly down at the street. I observed his back for some minutes before venturing to break in on his thoughts. "I say, if you aren't going to finish that pie, I see no point in letting it go to waste."

He turned to stare at me blankly for some seconds. Then, like a dog ridding itself of fleas, seemed to shake himself into the present.

"By all means, my dear fellow, make of it what you will, but be hasty, for we must go out again."

My surprise was evident and he explained impatiently.

"Don't you see, Watson?" he said irritably. "This is Wednesday, and tomorrow there is another meeting of this so-called mission. I feel it to be imperative that we prevent Mrs. Pritchard attending, and indeed to put a stop to its activities once and for all. I intend to see the lady and induce her to lay her trouble before me, that it may be lifted completely."

"Do you think she will confide in you?" I said through a mouthful of pie. "If she will not trust her husband, why should she trust you?"

"It is possible. I'm a stranger to her and she has no reason to fear my censure or disapproval. I think that fact may persuade her to unburden herself if I can convince her that I can hold out hope of relief."

"Can you promise her that?"

"There is blackmail involved, and you know my views on that. I will strain every nerve and sinew to bring to book those foul predators on human frailty. Now do hurry. I wish to talk to the lady before her husband returns home."

Still chewing, I pursued him down to the street, and soon we found ourselves crossing to the south side of the river for the second time that day. Our journey took us through a succession of mean streets to Rotherhithe, and thence to the outskirts of Deptford where our driver halted to ask directions of a patrolling constable.

As we approached our goal, Holmes bade the cabbie stop and, after alighting, we watched the vehicle out of sight before we proceeded on foot. Holmes looked approvingly at our surroundings, and indeed the district was less sordid than those we had just traversed. It hadn't yet lost the battle against the ever-encroaching octopus of London, and there was still a rural feeling to this little corner. The house we approached had gleaming brass-work on the newly painted door and gay curtains hung at the windows, evidence of the loving care lavished on this humble dwelling, The door was opened by a woman in her late twenties, as neat and tidy in her person as the exterior of the house, yet her eyes showed strain and worry foreign to the pretty features.

Holmes raised his hat. "Mrs. Pritchard?" he asked on her look of inquiry.

"Yes, that is my name. What can I do for you?"

"I am Sherlock Holmes, of whom you may have heard, and this is my friend and colleague, Dr. Watson." He indicated me, and I in turn raised my hat.

Her face took on a guarded look, but Holmes continued ere she could speak.

"I beg of you to forgive our intrusion, and rest assured we wish to cause you no distress. If you permit us to enter, I shall explain our business."

After a momentary hesitation she stood aside. Then, closing the door behind us, led the way into a small but comfortable parlour.

"Be seated, gentlemen," she said. "I know of your reputation, Mr. Holmes, but I'm at a loss to understand your interest in me."

"I will be quite open with you, Madam," began Holmes when we were seated. "I can but hope you will be as frank with me, for only the truth will serve to raise the shadow of anxiety from which you suffer."

"I fail to see – " she began, but Holmes held up an admonitory hand.

"Hear me out, I pray you, if not for your own sake then for the sake of your husband. My reasoning leads me to believe that you are being blackmailed, and the source of the blackmail is The Crown of Light Mission. If you will give me your complete confidence, I pledge myself to the downfall of the villains who batten on the fears of such unfortunates as yourself. I have no connection with the official police, and whatever you tell me will be safe with the good Doctor and me."

She stared at him in amazement overlaid with fear and anguish, but my companion wasn't to be diverted.

"You are being bled white by these people, and unless you confide in me, there can be no end to it until you are penniless and your marriage destroyed. Is that what you desire?"

Mrs. Pritchard had turned a deathly pale, her eyes fixed on the stern features of my friend. At length she made a gesture of resignation and spoke in a tone of great bitterness.

"How this came to your notice I don't know, but you are correct in your assumption of blackmail. Not through any fault or misconduct on my part, but because of one who is very dear to me. I refer to my brother."

She paused to take a deep breath, and then the words spilled out from her as water from a broken pitcher. "It began some four months ago when I received call from a man who purported to be collecting on behalf of The

Crown of Light Mission. I have little time for these mendicants who seem to divert the larger part of the offerings into their own pockets. I refused instantly, but the creature had his foot in the door and said if I wouldn't contribute on my own behalf, it would be to my brother's advantage to do so. Of course, this held my attention and I demanded an explanation of his words." She paused and looked at us defiantly. "Perhaps I should tell you something of my family to make the subsequent events clear,"

"I know you to be the daughter Joseph Smithers, a clothing manufacturer," Holmes interposed. "I also know that you have an older brother, and that you married in defiance of your father's wishes, but nevertheless he settled a generous allowance on you and that allowance is being filched by this so-called Crown of Light. Pray continue with your account, Madam."

"Very well, Mr. Holmes." She moistened her lips. "This person told me that Marcus, my brother who virtually runs the business now, has been embezzling large sums of money from the firm and spending it in dubious pursuits, and unless I wished my father to hear of it. I would be wise to contribute to their poor mission."

Holmes frowned. "Surely in that case there would be more profit in going to your brother?"

"That was my first thought, but the man forestalled me by saying my brother was being taken care of and my small contribution was but a make-weight. I was bemused and near collapse, but I told him I had no money in the house. He smiled – oh, what a terrible smile! He told me to attend the next meeting of the mission and bring fifty pounds in gold. I was almost out of my mind and to get rid of him I acceded to his demands. Little did I know what it was to lead to, for since that day I have been paying three pounds at each and every meeting of that evil mission, twice a week."

"Good Lord!" I exploded. "That's more than your whole allowance!"

"You are well informed, Doctor," she said bitterly. "I'm rapidly reaching the end of my resources, and what will then ensue I fear to contemplate."

"What does your brother say of this?" asked Holmes. "Have you told him?"

The lady shook her head vigorously, "I was forbidden to tell him that I was also being made pay on the threat of the whole matter being exposed. What induced him to commit such folly is entirely beyond my comprehension."

Holmes rose abruptly, taking me by surprise, but I could sense from his attitude that he was steps ahead of my thoughts.

130

"Thank you, Mrs. Pritchard. I think it safe to say that you have made your last payment to these leeches, and I may even offer some hope that you will see the return of at least part of your money. Come, Watson, time presses."

He paused in the doorway to add almost as an afterthought: "Where might your brother be found at this hour?"

She hesitated. Then, convinced of my colleague's integrity, she spoke. "He has his own establishment at Blackheath overlooking Greenwich Park. He is unmarried, but prefers to live away from home. My mother is a strong-willed woman who terrorises even my father so that he spends as much time as he can at the Walworth factory for the sake of peace and quiet." She gave her brother's address, which I scribbled into my notebook.

"Then be of good heart, Madam," said Holmes. "Say nothing of this to your husband at this juncture, although I feel you would have been wise to confide in him from the first moment."

We had the good fortune to find a cab-driver willing to take us up the steep incline of Blackheath Hill to the Heath, but it was a painfully slow journey. Dusk was falling as we were deposited at the gate of a neat little villa commanding a fine view over the park to the twinkling lights beginning to appear on the river beyond. Holmes pull on the bell was answered by an elderly woman of upright carriage. She took Holmes's card and conducted us into an anteroom. We weren't left to kick our heels for long before the door opened to admit a pleasant-looking fellow whose features proclaimed his kinship with Freda Pritchard.

"Mr. Sherlock Holmes?" he asked, twisting the card in his fingers.

"I am he," my friend replied.

"Then this other gentleman can only be your biographer, Dr. Watson, whose accounts of your exploits I devour avidly. I'm honoured to meet you in the flesh, but I am at a loss to divine the reason for your presence. But be seated, I beg you. I usually indulge in a small drink at this hour and I hope you will join me."

Once we were seated with a generous measure of Scotch whisky in our hands, Holmes came straight to the point.

"First of all, Mr. Smithers, I'm going to ask you a question that you will find insulting and impertinent. Please bear with me and take no offence, for once I hear the answer I expect to hear from your lips, I will reveal the purpose behind it."

Smithers looks mystified but inclined his head in acknowledgement. "Fire away, Mr. Sherlock Holmes. I know you do nothing without good reason, and you have fairly set my curiosity afire."

"Very well, I will be blunt. Are you being blackmailed?"

131

Our host's mouth fell open and he stared at Holmes in amazement. "Blackmailed?" he stuttered. "Why should I be blackmailed? My life is an open book, and though I have all the minor vices of most men of my age and position, there is certainly nothing that I'd pay to have hushed up."

"Thank you, sir," said Holmes. "That is as I thought, and now I can tell you the reasons behind my offensive question. Before I do so, I must ask for your assurance that I shall be left to deal with the matter in my own way, and that you will not try to take matters into your own hands."

His grave tone impressed itself on the other who nodded a grudging consent, and Holmes went on to lay all the facts before him. Smithers listened with growing horror that quickly changed to rage and indignation as Holmes described the pitiful state to which Freda Pritchard had been reduced. At the end of the recital he sat pale and tight-lipped, his fists clenching and unclenching as the full enormity of the situation sank in.

"Good God, Mr. Holmes, why did she not come to me at once? I could have set her mind at rest and showed her the falsity of the charge."

"That was the cunning part, sir. She was told that you too were paying for silence, and if she let it be known that she also was paying, all would be revealed. It was a plot to keep you apart, and that is why I came here tonight, certain that you were an innocent party. Who would know enough of your family circumstances to be so convincing?"

Smithers left his chair and paced rapidly back and forth, his brow corrugated in concentration before stopping to face Holmes.

"Tell me, sir, does the name Lester Burton strike a chord?"

Holmes looked up sharply, his eyebrows raised. "It does, but where did you hear it?"

Our host resumed his seat and laid his head back as if to collect his thoughts. Then he began to speak in a low voice.

"What I have to say is in the strictest confidence, which I'm sure you will appreciate. When my sister declared her intention of marrying Lewis Pritchard, it wasn't the most welcome news to my father, but for all his faults he loves Freda and desires her happiness. The main opposition was from my mother, and you may think me lacking in proper respect when I say she not the most lovable of women, but it is a fact. Even my father fears her. She was a machinist in his first factory and was astute enough to see that he would rise in the world with the right encouragement, so she married him." He grinned boyishly. "I was born five months after the wedding, but she wouldn't thank you for reminding her of the fact. She has aspirations to be the great lady and saw Freda and me as stepping-stones into society, and you can imagine her chagrin when my sister remained obstinate and I showed no interest in the girls paraded before me."

132

He sat up and fixed us with a firm look. "Don't misunderstand me, gentlemen. I'm not averse to the company of the fair sex, but I prefer them to be of my own choosing."

"We hadn't thought otherwise," said Holmes. "Proceed, I pray you."

"Well, when Freda wouldn't submit, my father forbade her the house – on my mother's orders, of course – but to salve his conscience, he secretly made her an allowance. Mind you, I thought she could have done better, but for all I know he may be a most worthy fellow,"

"Doubt it not, sir," my friend put in. "Until this business cast its shadow, they were the happiest couple alive. But forgive me, I interrupt."

Smithers continued. "A few months ago I was at Croydon races, where I made a bit of a killing. I threw a celebration party at a nearby hotel, and among those present was Lester Burton, He seemed a stout-enough fellow and we travelled back together somewhat the worse for wear, as happens on these occasions. I must have found him a good listener, for I later recalled bemoaning the rift with my little sister. By morning it had gone from my mind until shortly before lunch, when who should turn up at the office but this Burton on the pretext of asking after my health. We went out for a steak pudding and a glass of porter, and out of the blue he asked if I would like to be reconciled with Freda and offered to act as intermediary.

"Against my better judgement I became interested, but had to point out that I knew nothing of her whereabouts except that it was in these parts. He waved my objections aside and I agreed to let him see if he could trace her. A week later he approached me again with the story that he had spoken with Freda and the message she sent was that she wanted to neither hear nor see anything of me nor of the rest of the family, and would I please leave her alone. Does that fit in with your theory, Mr. Holmes?"

"As I surmised, the idea was to prevent any communication between you. But now that the truth is out, we can bait the trap to catch our rat. Time is of the essence. Your sister cannot tolerate the strain much longer, and there are others in like situation."

"What can I do, Mr. Holmes? I place myself at your disposal and will follow your instructions to the letter." Holmes studied the man before giving a nod of agreement. "Your aid would be invaluable, but do nothing on your own initiative or the consequences may be dire. Be at my chambers at eight o'clock tomorrow morning. Do you know where this man Burton has his quarters?"

"Not the actual address, but although he was very close about himself, he did make a rather bad joke about having a fine view of Smithfield, Barts, and Newgate from his window."

133

"That narrows the field. Now we must go, and we shall see you in the morning."

"I'll send the boy for a cab to take you to Blackheath or Maze Hill – whichever station is your choice." Smithers rang the bell and gave the necessary orders, and ten minutes later we were on our way. At London Bridge, Holmes made straight for the all-night telegraph office, then mystified me by taking a cab to the General Post Office in St. Martin's-le-Grand, where he disappeared for twenty minutes. He returned humming tunelessly to himself and spoke not a word for the rest of the journey. At Baker Street he jumped from the cab, leaving me to pay, and by the time I reached our sitting room he had gone into his own room, closing the door firmly behind him, and that was the last I saw of him that night.

Over an early breakfast he was more forthcoming. "Mr. Marcus Smithers will be on our doorstep shortly, as will our client, whom I telegraphed last night. I rely on your down-to-earth common sense, Watson, to see that the two get along together, for I hope that some part of the family feud may be settled out of this sordid affair."

"That sounds like one of them now," I said as a cab stopped outside.

The doorbell pealed faintly and my friend looked at me with a roguish smile.

"Would you venture to say which?"

I shrugged. "As I cannot see through walls it could be either, but no doubt you know differently."

"It is certainly Smithers. If it was Pritchard arriving in his hansom, he would take time to settle his horse before leaving it. The gentleman whose tread is now on the stairs paused only long enough to pay the driver, who immediately drove away. Come in!" he called as a knock came on our door.

Smithers entered. "Good morning, gentlemen," he said. "What's afoot?"

"Pull up a chair, my dear sir," said Holmes, "Allow me to pour you some coffee while we await another guest. In fact, I believe he is even now below.

A few minute elapsed before Pritchard appeared, pausing on the threshold at the sight of our other visitor, but Holmes waved him to a chair and supplied him with coffee. He raised an eyebrow in my direction before taking a seat for himself and stuffing tobacco into his pipe.

I cleared my throat. "I think, gentlemen, this meeting is long overdue. Mr. Marcus Smithers, this is your brother-in-law, Mr. Lewis Pritchard." I sat back to watch the conflicting emotions chase across the faces of the pair.

134

Smithers recovered first, getting to his feet to thrust out his hand. "My dear Pritchard!" he cried. "As Dr. Watson says, this is a long overdue meeting, and I'm delighted to make your acquaintance at last!"

For the merest fraction of a second our client hesitated, then he rose to clasp the proffered hand. "You are right, sir. This is a long-delayed meeting, but through no wish of mine. Your sister would have welcomed a sign from you, but alas, it never came." He turned to me. "However, I fail to see how this concerns the matter in the forefront of my mind."

"I think I do," said Smithers, turning to look at Holmes and myself.

"It does indeed," I said in my role of mediator. "You both have Mrs. Pritchard's welfare at heart, and neither of you has the slightest cause to feel antipathy towards the other."

Holmes intervened brusquely. "Please, gentlemen, let us proceed to the matter in hand, and explanations can come later. You will make your way to Deptford, where Mrs. Pritchard may have comfort from the knowledge that her conflict of loyalties is over. You, Mr. Smithers, know how all this came about and can lay the whole story before Mr. Pritchard and your sister. I enjoin all three of you to remain at Deptford until I telegraph, you, and above all you must convince the lady that she has nothing to fear. Now away with you. Watson and I have our own furrow to plough."

As soon as our visitors had left, Holmes sprang to his feet and, ignoring the coffee cup he overset in his sudden access of energy, threw off his dressing-gown.

"Come. Mr. Lester Burton is due a visit from us. I think we can be certain of finding him at home at this hour."

"I may be obtuse, Holmes, but do we know where to find him? The casual description he gave Smithers of the view from his window is vague enough and there must be a goodly number of locations with such a view."

Holmes chuckled. "What do you imagine I was doing at Post Office headquarters as we came home last night?"

A light dawned on me and I could have kicked myself for not deducing the reason for my prolonged wait, but his tone piqued me.

"I didn't think you to be bribing Crown servants to betray their trust and duty," I snapped.

"Neither was I," he snapped back. "It so happens that the authorities have cause to be grateful to me for a service I rendered them some months back, and they aren't averse to aiding in the downfall of any miscreants if it's in their power to do so."

He chattered inconsequentially as we trotted along Oxford Street in a growler, but said nothing of the matter in hand until I asked who would be paying his fee in this messy case.

He smiled thinly. "I'm hopeful that Lester Burton will be persuaded to make a significant contribution once I have him in my grasp. I see by the set of your coat that you aren't armed, but no doubt our sticks will serve if it comes to it. Ah, I think we may alight here."

The sight of Barts Hospital revived memories of my first meeting with the man with whom my life was to be so involved, and divining my thoughts he clapped me affectionately on the shoulder. "Much has happened since that January day long ago, old friend. I shall never cease to be grateful to young Stamford for bringing us together. But come, the weather is about to break and we have no waterproofs with us."

The sky had assumed a leaden hue presaging the imminence of heavy rain. Holmes hurried us down Old Bailey and into a doorway, the entrance to a block of service flats. He approached the porter ensconced in his cubbyhole and, after a few quiet words, a coin changed hands before the man resumed his perusal of the racing pages in his newspaper. We then made our way up the stairs to stop before a door on the second floor. Holmes pulled at the bell, then leant on his stick until the door partially opened and a plump face surrounded by side-whiskers peered out at us.

"Mr. Lester Burton?" said my friend ingratiatingly.

A wary look came over the suety face and the man licked his lips nervously. "Who are you? What do you want?"

"My name is Sherlock Holmes, and I wish to have a few words regarding The Crown of Light Mission. Ah, no you don't!" Holmes thrust his stick into the gap in time to prevent the door slamming on us, then applying his shoulder to it burst into the apartment, forcing its occupant back several paces. I followed Holmes inside and shut the door behind me, leaning my back against it to preclude any escape.

"This is an outrage!" spluttered Burton, for I was sure it was he. "Leave at once or I shall call the police!" He retreated as Holmes advanced on him menacingly.

"Yes, by all means call the police, and a pretty story there will be to tell them. They take a very poor view of blackmail."

"I have no idea of what you are talking about," the man blustered, but his eyes were filled with fear as he edged back, followed inexorably by Holmes.

"Don't trifle with me," said Holmes, "At this very moment, a lady is on her way to lay information against you, but her husband and her brother, suitably equipped with horsewhips, will precede the minions of the law."

Sweat beaded the plump features and Burton began to speak, but his words were drowned by a violent clap of thunder following the lashing of rain on the window. He began again and the pause had given him back some confidence.

136

"I refuse to bandy words with you, sir. I have heard of you as an interfering busy-body, and I can only conjecture that what little notoriety you have achieved has gone to your head. Withdraw at once, or I shall call the porter to eject you."

Holmes glared at him with loathing and contempt. "How dare you attempt to outface me, you despicable cur!" he almost snarled. "I'm here to break you and ensure your evil trade is brought to an end. I'm not bound by any rules that may prevent the police treating you as you deserve."

"And how do you propose to do that?" Burton sneered.

"That is your choice: Either surrender all the material that gives you power over your unhappy victims and sufficient funds to make at least some restitution, or be prepared to have me beat it out of you."

"You wouldn't dare. Even were your wild accusations true, what proof can you have?"

"All that I require." Holmes loomed menacingly over the cowering figure. "Come, accept that the game is lost and you may yet take flight before the police arrive."

The blackmailer put on a show of bravado. "Threaten all you will. You will find nothing here that you want. Get out!"

Taking a pace forward, Holmes grasped Burton by the shirt-front and shook him until his teeth rattled. Rarely had I seen my friend in such a cold rage and I feared that he would lose control entirely, but at last he flung the wretch into a chair where he huddled, his breath coming in shallow gasps. Holmes took a grip on himself and cast an eye around the room.

"Watson, do you go through that coat that hangs behind the door and see what you may find."

My search produced a bunch of keys, a small diary, and a pocket book containing a number of bank-notes. I passed it all to Holmes who made a cursory assessment of the money then threw the keys back to me.

"See if you can match one of these to the safe that stands in the corner. I suspect its contents will prove illuminating."

Burton made to protest, but a threatening gesture from Holmes made him subside fearfully in the chair.

The safe was an early model by Chubb, and the second key I tried allowed me to swing the door open. I was faced by two large ledgers, a bundle of papers, and a leather bag which on being opened revealed a considerable sum in sovereigns and half-sovereigns. Holmes pounced on the ledgers and swiftly turned the pages for several minutes before slamming them shut with a grunt of satisfaction.

"This is what we need," he said grimly. "The bank-notes and gold will provide some recompense for such victims as can be traced and furnish my fee into the bargain. As for the papers – well – "

"You can't do that!" Burton screeched. "That's theft!"

"Then tell the police," Holmes replied contemptuously, turning away in disgust.

With a speed born of desperation Burton sprang from the chair and snatched at the pocket-book which Holmes had laid on the table. I leapt to stop him and he aimed a blow that caught me on the shoulder that sent me cannoning into Holmes. By the time we had recovered, our blackmailer had grabbed his coat and was halfway through the door. With a frantic lunge I tried to hold on to his arm, but he slipped through my grasp and ran for the stairs, leaving me staring at the pocket-book which was all that I retained of him.

"Let him go," said my colleague. "We've drawn his teeth, and you did well to hang on to the money. If Mrs. Pritchard can be induced to lay information against him, he will not get far."

I admit yielding to the temptation to keep to myself the fact that my rescue of the pocket-book was less deliberate than he assumed, but no harm was done by that. I went to stand beside my friend at the window to look down at the street. The rain had stopped and people were hurrying to get their business done before the next downpour. Suddenly, Holmes gripped my arm and sucked in his breath.

A running figure dashed into view at the very moment that a brewer's dray lost a wheel immediately below us. The loaded cart tipped over, shedding its load, and the running man disappeared from sight beneath the heavy casks. The cries of horror from the horrified onlookers reached us through the closed window, and as the crowd congregated Holmes turned away.

"I think we would do well to leave before we are implicated," he said quietly, and taking the ledgers and papers he pushed me towards the door. Pausing only to collect my stick, I followed him down the stairs and through the entrance hall, where the porter had deserted his post to see what was happening in the street. Crossing into Newgate Street we found a cab, and stopping only at the Strand telegraph office to send a wire to the Pritchards, proceeded back to our rooms.

I stopped suddenly as we entered the sitting room. "Holmes!" I gasped.

"The bag of gold!"

"Really, Doctor, do you think me so careless?" He threw the leather purse on to the table. "We have an hour before lunch, which I shall occupy by going through these books while you count the money."

We applied ourselves thus, and the total sum staggered me. The pocketbook yielded £2,400 pounds in notes of various denominations, while there was a further £120 and ten shillings in gold coins. When I reported the amount to Holmes, he nodded his satisfaction,

"It seems Mr. Burton had no faith in banks, which is fortunate. At least a hundred-and-fifty of it belongs to Mrs. Pritchard, but it will be the deuce of a job to apportion the remainder. It seems that no sum was too insignificant for that creature to reach for, and his accounts show amounts a small as five shillings from more than one of his victims. I hope that some can be induced to come forward at tonight's meeting if they can be persuaded they have nothing to fear. I shall enlist Mrs. Pritchard' aid in that, as they may trust her as one of themselves."

"But what hold could he have over all these people?"

"Who knows? If a duchess wished to conceal an indiscretion, she would be no more anxious than the wife of a market porter to pay for silence. It is a matter of degree. Where one would find five-hundred pounds, the other would struggle to raise five shillings. I'm not interested in the details. Blackmail is a dirty business whatever the sum involved, and I rank it as more evil than a murder committed in a moment of passion."

"What of the papers?" I ventured.

"I shall destroy them unread. I've no desire to have people's weaknesses laid before me, and whomever cannot be traced through the ledgers will have no more demands made on them. A prominent advertisement in the newspapers announcing that The Crown of Light Mission has sufficient funds for its needs should be enough to relieve the minds of most contributors."

We didn't linger over lunch and, as we hailed a cab, Holmes took a paper from a passing newsboy.

"I say, look at this," he chuckled, passing the paper to me."

The headlines shouted at me. "*Man Killed by Falling Beer-Barrels*". I read on:

> *A man identified as Mr. Lester Burton was killed in an accident in Old Bailey when the wheel of a brewer's dray collapsed and dislodged its load as a man ran by. He was killed instantly. Alfred Huggins, the porter at his residence, said Mr. Burton was a quiet gentleman who gave no trouble. It is believed that the deceased had two callers shortly before he met his death, but no trace of them can be found.*

"No more than he deserved," Holmes said, then leant back with closed eyes until our cab dropped us at the Pritchards' house. Pritchard himself admitted us, and before he conducted us in, Holmes handed him the newspaper.

"It's all over, then?" asked our client.

"Apart from some loose ends, but your wife has nothing to fear and never did have, as I expect you now know. However, with your permission I will ask a small service of her."

"Ask what you will, Mr. Holmes. Anything to repay our debt to you. But come, she is waiting on you."

With the advent of Holmes and myself, the small parlour seemed very crowded. As well as the Pritchards and Smithers, a thick-set elderly man stood squarely in the middle of the room, his ruddy face glistening with perspiration.

"So you're the famous Sherlock Holmes," he said before anyone else could speak. His eyes latched on to my friend's lean figure, "I'm Joe Smithers, and a confounded old fool I've been."

Holmes inclined his head. "Most of us are at times, even my friend Dr. Watson," he said urbanely, obviously not including himself in that and ignoring my splutter of indignation."

We disposed ourselves on the chairs brought in by Pritchard and the assembly looked expectantly at my colleague.

"You had something to ask my wife," Pritchard said tentatively.

"I have indeed. Now the threat to your happiness is lifted, Mrs. Pritchard, do you have the courage to attend at the Mission tonight and help me do likewise for those others who were in the same situation? I have a number of names, and if you will identify those whom you know, I think they will trust you rather than myself."

"There is no more danger?" the lady asked fearfully.

"None. Burton is dead and all his records are safe from revelation."

"Then I will do it gladly. A number of poor wretches will have as much cause for gratitude as I. You understand that none of us knew any of the other's secrets and we all went in fear of exposure, and also we had been threatened with physical violence if we talked between ourselves or failed to meet that man's demands."

A steely glint came into Holmes's eye. "Ah, our friend Carver. I promised a police sergeant a good turn, and I found an interesting piece of information among Burton's papers. He also had a hold on Carver over the matter of a night watchman who was killed in a robbery at a bonded warehouse. He deserves to be thrown to the lions, and Sergeant Rance will take great pleasure in feeling Carver's collar, as he so elegantly puts it."

He thought for a moment. "One loose end remains, and that is the woman calling herself Mrs. Burton. What do you know of her?"

140

"She hasn't appeared these three weeks past," replied Mrs. Pritchard. "I doubt she was his wife, for she seemed as cowed as the rest of us."

"Then you have anything against her should she appear?"

"Nothing."

"Then let us give her the benefit of the doubt." Holmes cast his eye benignly on the gathering. "Can it be that I have also effected a family reconciliation?"

It was the elder Smithers who replied. "You have, Mr. Holmes. That is what I meant when I said I had been an old fool. Freda has chosen well, and all that I can do now is to make up for the lost years as best I can. One thing has come out of this, and from henceforth I shall be master in my own house. Too long have I been weak and skulked in my works for the sake of peace and quiet, but no longer. Freda and her husband will always be welcome in my home, and I hope I can persuade Marcus to return until such time as he finds a wife of his own choosing."

Holmes rose to his feet. "Then we shall meet at Bermondsey at six o'clock tonight."

There was but a limited response to Mrs. Pritchard's attempt to return as much of the money as possible, the majority of the victims being happy to slink away, relieved to know that they were no longer menaced. Even Holmes was unable to trace all of Burton's victims, and eventually a well-known charity received a handsome anonymous donation.

What fee Holmes awarded himself I don't know, but some weeks later I was astonished to have in the post my not insignificant bookmaker's account marked "*Paid, with thanks*". I knew better than to raise the matter with my friend, for he can be very touchy at times.

It was several years later that I saw an item in *The Daily Telegraph* that raised my eyebrows. It announced the purchase of Lewis Pritchard's cab firm by Tilling's, the gigantic cab company. No mention was made of the price that was paid, but the paper's business correspondent seemed to think that Pritchard had done very well out of the deal.

When I showed the paragraph to Holmes, he responded by pointing to the obituary column where I read of the death of Sir Charles Richards, a high-ranking official at the Foreign Office. My expression remained blank until Holmes gave me a hint.

"Richards? Pritchard? Come, Watson, I knew who Pritchard was right from the beginning. I thought even you could put two and two together and come up with the right answer."

The Adventure of the
Silk Scarf

Sherlock Holmes was never an easy person to persuade that, although his powers of observation and deduction were far superior to those of most other people, his body was subject to the same laws as were lesser mortals. It was therefore to my relief and satisfaction that he gave in to my urgings to spend the night at a very comfortable hotel in the pleasant Kentish town of Sevenoaks. He had brought to a successful conclusion the gruesome murder of the Hopfield murderer, thereby saving Inspector Griffin from a mistake that could have blighted the remainder of his career.

We were sitting in the smoking room over brandy and cigars, having enjoyed a most excellent meal, with Holmes more relaxed than I had seen him for many weeks, He was chaffing me over my concern for his health and well-being, and I was happy to have him in such good spirits.

"I do vow, Watson, no mother hen clucks more assiduously over her chicks than do you over myself," he observed.

"Ah, but you must understand that I have a double responsibility. Firstly as a medical man and then as a friend, so I must be doubly watchful."

"And thirdly," he said with a chuckle, "should anything happen to deprive you of my company, you would be unable to afford to remain at our present address on your own."

"Really, Holmes!" I exploded. "That is a most outrageous remark, and not a matter for levity."

He was instantly contrite and spoke in a conciliatory tone. "Forgive me, my dear fellow. I do appreciate your concern and know your advice is of the best, even if I do not always follow it. But wait – I see we have a visitor,"

I turned my head to see the solid figure of Inspector Griffin bearing down on us. He was out of uniform and, in his suit of heavy tweed, he looked the very model of a country squire.

"Good evening, gentlemen," he said as he neared us. "I hope I don't intrude?"

"On the contrary, Inspector," smiled Holmes. "Your arrival is most opportune. I fear that without your advent, the good Doctor was about to consign me to bed for my health's sake. I count you a veritable saviour."

"Pay no attention to him, Inspector," I said when he looked blank. "He is in a puckish mood tonight and will take nothing seriously. Let me get you a glass of this fine brandy, for I see you are off duty."

I rang for the waiter and Griffin sank back into a deep armchair across from Holmes and me. He said nothing until our order had been fulfilled, and even then seemed to take an inordinate time to get his cigar drawing to his satisfaction.

Holmes eventually gave him an opening. "I divine, Inspector, that your visit here isn't just for social purposes?"

Griffin fingered his moustache and spoke apologetically. "Well, sir, I must confess to an ulterior motive, and I hope you will not take it amiss or think me presumptuous in seeking your counsel."

Holmes waved his hand. "Feel free to speak, I beg you."

"The fact is I have been asked to find a missing person, but as the person concerned is of age and seems to have disappeared of her own free will, there is nothing I can do in my official capacity."

"Then what is your problem?" Holmes asked with a frown,

"Let me put the whole story to you. I was approached this evening by Major-General Romney, who resides at Brent Croft, Foxford. That is about four miles from the town off the London Road. He bought the property some six years ago on his retirement from the army." Griffin took a sip from his glass. "The household consists of the General and his wife, his daughter Ellen, and the usual complement of servants, among them his former batman Ted Lennard, who is valet, groom, orderly, and self-appointed bodyguard. The daughter is a handsome girl of twenty-three, engaged to a Mr. Peter Witham, whose grounds of Witham Court adjoin the General's. I should add that Mrs. Romney is the General's second wife, and is some years his junior." Here the inspector paused as ash from his cigar dropped on to his waistcoat. He brushed it away and proceeded with his account.

"Some time after tea yesterday, Miss Romney took it into her head to vanish from home, leaving only a short note for her father. In it, she stated that she needed to be alone to resolve a problem, and he wasn't to worry about her. Her fiancé knew nothing of this until late last night when the General's man was sent to make inquiries of him, and also in the village, all to no avail. General Romney waited throughout today for some news or communication, and having neither, he called on me late this afternoon to obtain my help, I pointed out that the girl was of age and therefore a free agent, and as there was no evidence of foul play or coercion, I could take no official steps. Being an old soldier, he understood I was bound by rules and regulations, but he is an influential man, being a magistrate and a member of the police committee. I knew that if I could help him it would

143

do my career no harm, and I hinted that I might be in a position to give him unofficial assistance. To be blunt, sir, I had you in mind, knowing you to be staying here tonight. If I have presumed too much on such short acquaintance don't hesitate to reprimand me, but if you can see your way to speaking to the General, I shall be eternally grateful and forever in your debt."

Holmes studied the policeman thoughtfully before replying.

"As you are aware, Inspector, although I'm a professional man and look to my fees for a living, I only accept cases with intriguing or unusual features, which your problem doesn't obviously have."

Griffin's face fell, but before he could speak Holmes continued.

"However, in view of our pleasant and fruitful association of the past few days, and taking into account the fact that Watson will be more than pleased if I spend more time away from the polluted atmosphere of London, I see no reason to turn down your request. Who knows – we may find more meat on the bone than is apparent at first sight." The inspector leaned across to grasp my friend's hand.

"Bless you, Mr. Holmes!" he said fervently. "You have taken a weight from my mind, and I appreciate it."

"Do not count your chickens, Inspector Griffin. There may be no more to the matter than appears on the surface, but at least I shall breathe more of your sweet country air while keeping my mind active, eh, Watson?"

I knew any objections I might make would be brushed aside, and I contented myself with a grunt as Holmes at once became business-like.

"Have you given me all the facts as you know them?" he asked.

"I have related all that passed between me and the General not two hours since. I cannot vouch for the General telling me every detail."

"It is too late to do much tonight," Holmes reflected. "Can you arrange for us to meet General Romney in the morning? I prefer it to at his house, as the trail must begin there." Griffin nodded and my friend went on. "Meanwhile, if you will be good enough to impart all you know of the Romneys, I shall have something on which to ponder."

The inspector looked round to ensure we weren't overheard and began slowly as he arranged his facts.

"As I said, the General came to Brent Croft on his retirement, which I understand was hastened by the death of his first wife. The present Mrs. Romney was the widow of an officer killed in the Zulu Wars, and is a good thirty years younger than the General. They were married soon after his retirement, and as you may guess, the marriage gave the local gossips a field day. If Miss Ellen had any feelings towards a much younger woman taking her mother's place, she gave no sign of it, and they have always appeared to be on the best of terms." Here the inspector paused to take out a stubby pipe, accepting the pouch offered by me with a nod of thanks. We all lit up and a blue haze soon hovered over our heads.

Griffin took up his tale again. "The indoor servants number four: A cook-housekeeper, a housemaid, a parlour maid who also attends Mrs. Romney, and the General's man Ted Lennard, of whom I spoke earlier. He occupies a privileged position, having served his master since the war in the Crimea, and subsequently during the Mutiny and all the other campaigns in which the old man was involved. Rumour has it that he isn't overly fond of the present Mrs. Romney, but naturally, the General wouldn't countenance any show of disrespect from him,"

"You are remarkably well informed," Holmes put in.

Griffin smiled and permitted himself a wink. "I owe that to George Izzard, the village constable. I allow him a certain amount of discretion on his patch, but I insist he keeps me posted on events in the village. I don't use him as a spy," he hastened to add, "but I do like to be forewarned of any likely trouble. Not that we have much, apart from the occasional bout of fisticuffs outside The White Horse on a Saturday night, and a little not-too-serious poaching."

"You have said nothing of the missing girl's fiancé, Peter Witham," remarked Holmes. "Is he well-thought-of in the neighbourhood?"

"He inherited Witham Court on the deaths of his father and older brother from typhoid." Inspector Griffin's tone was neutral. "Until then, he lived in chambers in London, and I understand he was regarded as something of a Champagne Charlie. He looks to have settled down since coming in to the estate, although he still spends a considerable amount of time in London. The General seems to accept him as a potential son-in-law, having shown marked disapproval over a previous suitor for his daughter's hand. That was John Paxton, a not-very-successful writer who lives with his mother on the edge of the village. As for Witham, my private information is that Ted Lennard has little regard for him, but my belief is that in Ted's view there is no man good enough for Miss Romney."

Holmes stood up and rubbed his hands. "Thank you, Inspector. You have painted a very clear picture of the situation, and I assure you that it will receive my very best attention. You will arrange for us to meet General Romney tomorrow morning?"

"Indeed I will. A message will be sent to him first thing, and I shall await you with a wagonette at nine o'clock if that suits."

"Excellent. Is accommodation available at Foxford?"

"Tom Rudge at The White Horse keeps a good house, and his wife is renowned for her table."

"Then Watson and I will bring our bags, and should it be necessary to spend another night in your pleasant countryside, we shall stay there. Now we will bid you goodnight."

We watched the inspector's departing back and my companion turned to me with a smile.

"The very best type of police officer, Watson," he said. "Would that we had more of the same kind. Now I shall seek my room and over a pipe or two reflect what may be drawn from this apparently mundane affair. Sleep well, old friend."

Holmes was in a pensive mood at breakfast, but later as we stood on the hotel steps to enjoy the first pipe of the day he turned to me.

"You have more experience of the fairer sex than I, Watson. Here we have a young lady whom to the best of our knowledge has a happy home and is engaged to an apparently worthy gentleman of her own choice. Why does she suddenly take it into her head to disappear, leaving only a brief note to her father indicating that some problem is exercising her and no word to her fiancé?"

The same thought had occurred to me as I lay in bed trying to apply my friend's methods to such information as we had, and I could only arrive at one conclusion.

"It could be that she is having some doubts in respect of her prospective marriage, and wishes to review her feelings with no pressure being brought to bear upon her."

"Quite so. Your reasoning is faultless as far as it goes – but what has encouraged such doubts? Are they newly risen, or have they been harboured for a period? If the former, what recent event is responsible? If they are of long standing, is there a connection with her previous suitor, the one discouraged by the General? Did she – ?"

"Steady on, Holmes!" I protested. "One question at a time. You have chided me often enough on the folly of speculation unsupported by facts."

"Indeed I have, and rightly so, but my questions are rhetoric and merely indicate that they must be asked and answered before we can begin to proceed to a theory. But here is the inspector, and it may be we can think of further questions during our journey."

On arriving at Brent Croft, a trim parlour maid conducted us to a large comfortable study, book-lined and smelling of leather and cigars – obviously the old soldier's retreat. The General, a broad upright figure with a closely trimmed white moustache standing out in his mahogany features, rose from a deep armchair to be introduced to us by Griffin.

"Of course I have heard of you, Mr. Holmes," he said in a clipped voice. "I gather Dr. Watson is an old frontier campaigner, as well as being your chronicler and confidant." He invited us to be seated. "I'm grateful

146

for your interest in my daughter's disappearance, and you will not find me ungenerous toward your efforts."

Holmes frowned. "Let us be quite clear on this, General: My fees reflect the time spent and the difficulty of the task and aren't variable, unless I decide for my own reasons to waive them altogether."

The General flushed under his tan. "I crave your pardon, sir," he said stiffly. "I had no intention of patronising you, but this matter is disturbing for me, and I spoke thus out of anxiety."

Holmes acknowledged the apology and came straight to the point, his tone brisk as he asked his questions.

"Tell me, General, what positive steps have you taken to trace your daughter's movements since Sunday night?"

"When she didn't return yesterday, I sent a telegram to my sister in Surbiton inquiring if she had received any visit or communication from Ellen. They are very fond of each other and my daughter stayed with her aunt for some months after the death of her mother. The answer was negative, and having no other relatives or close friends to whom she might have gone, I could think of nothing further than to consult the good Inspector Griffin. He explained the official position, but thankfully he prevailed on you to offer your services."

"I understand you made inquiries of your daughter's fiancé, and also in the village, without success."

"My first steps. Now Lennard, my factotum, has on his own initiative taken the dog-cart to ask at the railway stations if she had been observed on Sunday evening. You may be aware that we are distanced almost equally from two stations, and she is well-enough known to have been noticed if she had purchased a ticket from either."

Holmes stroked his chin and looked at the older man. "Tell me, General, did anything suggest to you that your daughter wasn't in her usual spirits?"

The General considered this for a few moments before speaking, frowning as he strove for recollection,

"Let me see," he said slowly. "On Sunday she went to evening service at the village church. We had all been to morning service, but I'm sorry to confess that I find one helping of our vicar as much as I can digest in one week. I had retired to this den of mine where I was putting the finishing touches to my memoirs, which I hope to publish next year. The time was well past nine when my eyes told me I had done enough and I went to the drawing room just before my wife came in. She said it was such a beautiful night that she had taken a walk in the grounds, and the maid told me that Ellen had gone to her room directly after coming in from church, and that was the last time she was seen by any of us."

147

Holmes steepled his fingers, his eyes narrowing in thought. "Tell me, sir, exactly what steps you have so far taken, in the greatest detail. There is another point which may prove to be vitally important: How was it possible for her to leave the premises unbeknown to anyone?"

"Her room is in a passage to the left of the stairs, while the rooms of myself, my wife, and my man are to the right. When she failed to come down to dinner, I sent the maid up to see if she had fallen asleep, but her room was empty."

"What time was that?"

"We dine at seven, so it would have been a few minutes after that. A back staircase leads to the yard and stables, and if the servants were busy in the kitchen, it would have been easy for her to slip out unobserved had she so desired."

"Has she done that before?"

"Not to my knowledge. Why should she?"

Holmes shrugged the question aside. "Then the hours between four o'clock and dinnertime at seven must be our starting point. The sun sets a few minutes after seven, so it is reasonably light for half-an-hour after that. Inspector Griffin tells me that you made some inquiries as to whether she had been seen in the village, or by Mr. Witham."

"That is so, but with no result. Young Witham was as much in the dark as the rest of us. It wasn't until later that I found this note addressed to me. It was on my dressing table."

The General took an envelope from his pocket, passing it to Holmes, who inspected it closely before removing the single sheet of paper within.

"There is no doubt that this is Miss Romney's hand?" asked Holmes.

"I would recognize it anywhere," the General said firmly.

My companion began to read aloud the brief note:

Father Dear,

I must go away for a short while to consider a problem that only I can resolve. Please do not worry. I shall return very shortly.

All my love,
Ellen

Holmes produced his magnifying glass and subjected the letter to an intense scrutiny before passing the paper and lens to me.

"What do you make of it, Watson?" I looked at him reproachfully, knowing that whatever deductions I might make he would turn inside out.

148

However, I tried do my best not to seem too obtuse and applied myself to the task.

"Well, what do you see?" Holmes spoke sharply.

I passed the items back him. "Beyond the fact that it was written with a fine-nib pen on good quality paper, it tells us very little."

"Little enough," agreed Holmes, "As you say, it was written with a fine steel nib by someone who was under great stress and was acting on impulse. I would suggest that the ink used was Valkden's blue-black."

We all waited on further revelations and he quickly obliged.

"The type of nib is obvious, but if you examine the paper closely, you will observe that sufficient pressure was applied to cause parallel grooves on the down strokes. The users of fine pens are invariably light of touch. It is undated and the last line is paler, showing the use of blotting paper, which indicates haste and impulse, while the pressure of the pen leads me to deduce emotion and stress."

"That's all very clever," growled General Romney. "I concede that the paper and ink is ours, and the pen is of the kind favoured by my daughter, but does that bring us nearer to finding her?"

"Would you describe your daughter as an impulsive woman?"

"Indeed not. Neither would she procrastinate if a decision had to be made."

"Then it is reasonable to assume that something occurred just prior to her departure to precipitate it, and if we discover that occurrence, we have made a step forward,"

At this juncture, there was a knock on the study door and the pretty parlour maid entered hesitantly. Behind her loomed the burly figure of a police constable, ruddy and perspiring, his helmet under his arm.

"Please sir," said the girl, "George – Mr. Izzard – says he must speak to the inspector. I told him he was engaged with you, but he won't take no for an answer."

Griffin rose with a word of apology and glared at the constable. "This had better be important, Izzard. Out with it, man."

"Beggin' your pardon, sir, I think I should speak to you alone."

Izzard fixed his superior with a hard look.

The inspector hesitated, then turned to us deprecatingly. "Will you excuse me, gentlemen?" He followed the policeman from the room, returning some few minutes later with a sombre expression. When he spoke it was as though a bomb had exploded in our midst.

"A most terrible thing has occurred," he said tightly. "Mr. Peter Witham has been found dead in the woods adjoining his estate, almost certainly murdered. I know nothing beyond that, but Miss Romney must be found and apprised of the tragedy. I can now take official action in the search for her, but I hope I may still look for your co-operation, Mr. Holmes?"

"Most certainly," replied my friend. He turned to the General who was sitting rigidly in his chair. "When do you expect your man to get back from his inquiries, sir?"

The old soldier took a grip on himself. "If he had news from Shoreham, he would have been back half-an-hour since. I assume he drew a blank there and went on to Otford. We may expect him soon. He drives the dog-cart at a fair clip."

"I shall await him," said Holmes. "Proceed to your duties, Inspector, but disturb nothing until I join you."

Griffin gave my companion a hard look. "As you say, Mr. Holmes. You will find the place? It is on the path near the stile where a hedge divides the Witham estate from the General's."

"Someone will show me, but I reiterate, nothing must be disturbed before I arrive, do you understand?" As the door closed on Inspector Griffin, an angry snort came from the General.

"Damnation, man, you take a cavalier attitude towards Griffin. Were I in his place, I would consign you to Hell."

Holmes eyed him coldly. "General Romney, I wouldn't presume to question your military judgement. Pray extend the same courtesy to me. What was a domestic inquiry has now become a criminal matter in which my expertise has been sought, and I must apply my own methods."

The old man bowed his head. "I beg your pardon, sir. I have a high regard for Inspector Griffin and wouldn't otherwise have spoken thus. You must proceed in your own way, of course." He looked up. "I believe I hear the dog-cart outside. Perhaps Lennard has some news for us."

Very shortly a perfunctory knock on the door was followed by the entry of a stocky well set-up man. He ignored Holmes and me and spoke directly to the General.

"Otford, sir. Eight-thirty-four to Holborn Viaduct. Could have changed at Bromley for Victoria. Sunday night, that was."

"Thank you, Lennard. You have done well. Meanwhile we have had some terrible news. Mr. Witham has been found dead in the woods between our properties – murdered, by all accounts. I have only the bare facts. These gentlemen are Mr. Sherlock Holmes and Dr. Watson, who were asked to help find Miss Ellen and now assist Inspector Griffin in his investigation in finding the perpetrator of this foul crime." The manservant's leathery face was expressionless, showing no sign of shock or even surprise at the news. He stood waiting for the General to issue instructions.

"Mr. Holmes wishes to question you," said the latter. "Answer him as truthfully as you would me."

The man turned to look at Holmes with eyes that bordered on insolence.

"Ask away, Mister, if the General says so, but I don't know nothing about Mr. Witham."

"We shall see," said Holmes, clearly nettled by the man's attitude. "You say Miss Romney caught the eight-thirty-four from Otford. Who told you?"

"It was Bert Carter, the booking clerk. He remembers the time, as he'd just bagged up his small change and Miss Ellen had nothing smaller than a sovereign, so he had to count it all out again."

"What condition was she in? Composed? Agitated?"

"Bert noticed nothing amiss, but she was heavily veiled."

"How would she have reached the station? Obviously you didn't drive her, and nothing has been said of any carriage being taken."

"She must have walked. Taken her about an hour or so. She had a small travelling bag with her, so Bert says."

"Where were you between tea and dinner on Sunday night?" Holmes's voice was suddenly sharp.

"Me?" Lennard scowled. "I saw to the mare and washed the trap, then went to the kitchen for a cup of tea and a chat with Mrs. Hodge, the cook. At six or just after, I brought the General a whisky-and-soda water in here. Then I went up to lay out his mess-kit for dinner. After he'd dressed and I'd tidied up, I went back to the kitchen for my own dinner, and it was about half-after-seven I first heard Miss Ellen was missing."

"Were you surprised?"

"Worried and surprised. It was never Miss Ellen's way to be less than considerate towards others, She'd never give no one trouble. Anyway, I had a word with the General, and he sent me off to ask Mr. Witham if he'd seen her, He said he'd brought her home from church in the morning and didn't expect to see her until he come to dinner Tuesday."

"That is correct," the General affirmed. "He was going to London yesterday morning and expected to stay overnight."

"He still intended to go despite his fiancé's mysterious absence?" My friend sounded incredulous. "He made no further effort to ascertain if she had returned or sent a message?"

"No doubt he had his reasons." The old soldier sounded unconvinced by his own utterance and looked at Lennard appealingly.

"I called at Witham Court yesterday afternoon," said the latter quickly. "The housekeeper said she'd seen neither here nor hide of him since early morning when he went to catch the train."

"So you saw him on Sunday night, but not since?" The man nodded and Holmes continued. "You didn't think to inquire about him when you visited the stations?"

"Why should I? I was only concerned with Miss Ellen."

Before more could be said, we were joined by Inspector Griffin who exhibited a certain amount of impatience. "Mr. Holmes! How much longer must we wait? I have Dr. Marsh standing by to officially confirm death, although there is no question about it. He is a busy man and has living patients to attend to."

"A few minutes more, Inspector," my friend replied soothingly, then broke off as the door opened to admit a pretty fair-haired woman whom I adjudged to be some thirty years of age.

"Edward!" she cried with an edge to her voice. "Will you kindly tell me what is happening? You have been closeted with these people for more than an hour, and there is a policeman clumping about in the hall." She paused for breath. "I'm entitled to know what is going on in my house."

The General advanced to take her by the hand. "Inspector Griffin you know. These other gentlemen are Mr. Sherlock Holmes and Dr. Watson, who came to assist in finding Ellen. Brace yourself, my dear. We have lately received some terrible news."

"Not Ellen?" she gasped, wide-eyed.

"No, thank God, but tragic enough. Peter has been found dead in the lower wood – murdered."

As her husband finished speaking, the lady's face blanched and giving a low moan she crumpled to a senseless heap on the floor. I knelt down beside her and took one of her hands. It was cold and clammy, with the pulse shallow and rapid, as was her breathing.

"She is in a state of shock," I announced. "Have her put to bed and kept warm, with hot drinks when she regains consciousness, and send for her own doctor."

With the assistance of Lennard, I got her to her room, where we left Mrs. Hodge and the parlour maid to get her into bed. When we came out, we were met by Holmes at the head of the stairs.

"General Romney has given me permission to inspect Miss Romney's room and any other parts of the house that I may so wish," he said to Lennard. "Will you be my guide?"

The man gave a surly nod and led us along the corridor to throw open a door at the opposite end. "This is Miss Ellen's," he said grudgingly. It was a light and airy chamber, feminine without being fussy. Holmes stood in the doorway before entering, his keen eyes taking in and recording everything. He then went to a small escritoire under the window and picked up a leather writing case which he examined under his lens.

"This is the only occupied room this side of the staircase?" he asked Lennard, who stood glowering at us suspiciously.

"The others are guest rooms. Miss Ellen did have the one corresponding to this on the other side, but when the new mistress came she took that, and Miss Ellen moved into here."

"Now show me the other rooms – without disturbing Mrs. Romney."

We went back to the other corridor, stopping at the third door. The end room, from which I had lately emerged, was Mrs. Romney's, and the chamber we now entered was obviously the master's. Holmes looked around and raised his eyebrows.

"I see there is no communicating door to Mrs. Romney's room," he said mildly.

"That's right," Lennard said sourly. He pointed. "That door there leads to the Guv'nor's dressing room, and another beyond to my billet."

Beyond a cursory glance around, Holmes showed little interest in the bedroom or dressing room, but on reaching the man's quarters he stared curiously. "You are snug enough here," he offered. "I don't think the other servants are so well provided for."

"They haven't been with the General for thirty-six years, nor campaigned over three continents with him," said Lennard proudly.

"I'm not criticising," smiled Holmes. "He is fortunate to command such devoted loyalty. I see you have some mementoes of your adventures." He indicated a collection of trivia displayed about the room.

"They've all got a story," said the man, his animosity falling away. "That lump of lead we found in the General's map-case at Inkerman – Major Romney he were then – and that wicked looking knife gutted his horse in the Ashanti fight in '73."

Holmes picked up a length of silk from beneath a chair and ran it through his hands. "Indian, of course."

Lennard's scowl returned as he nodded. "Took it off a Pandy at Meerut in '57. Mind you, I had to take his head off first. He come at us waving a *tulwar* with no good intentions." He took the scarf or turban from Holmes and draped it over two pegs on the wall.

"One last thing," said my companion. "Is it possible for anyone to pass along this corridor without you knowing, if you are in here?"

"Absolutely impossible. There is a floorboard that creaks whenever anyone passes, and I hear it, awake or sleeping."

Holmes frowned. "I didn't hear it. Did you, Watson?"

I shook my head. "Not a sound."

The manservant explained. "That's because a weight on the board in the passage makes it creak this end, right under the head of my bed. Let me show you." So saying he walked out into the passage and took a few

153

steps in either direction. Sure enough, when he reached a certain point a faint creaking came from where he had described.

"Your own private alarm system," remarked Holmes as we joined Lennard outside. "Who knows of this?"

"Just me and the General, and now you two gents. I hope you'll keep it so. I don't want no one else in on it. I'd do anything for the Guv'nor, and for Miss Ellen too. Anything," he said passionately. "You don't think any harm has come to her, do you?"

Holmes looked him straight in the eye. "Not in the physical sense, but something occurred to worry her enough to make her need to be alone while she thought it over. If we knew what that was, we might know where to start looking."

The man's face was expressionless as he turned away. "Then if that's all, I must get back to the General. Do your best to find her, sir."

We followed him down the stairs where he turned into the study, and as the door closed on him, Holmes looked thoughtful.

"That man knows more than he is saying, Watson. I wonder what he's hiding? But come," he went on briskly. "The inspector grows restless."

The latter was indeed edgy and hurried us incontinently to the location of the crime, passing on the way an old and abandoned stone cottage. The stolid Constable Izzard stood on guard, and beside him a bearded man whom I at once recognized as a member of my own calling. Hovering in the background was a foxy-faced character wearing a corduroy jacket and moleskin trousers, both items which would have benefited from a wash, as indeed would have their wearer.

"Dr. Marsh," said the inspector in an apologetic tone, "I crave your pardon for the delay, but Mr. Sherlock Holmes," he indicated my friend, "is assisting me in this matter and was adamant that nothing should be disturbed until his arrival."

"The blame is entirely mine, Dr. Marsh," Holmes put in smoothly. "It is imperative that I should examine the ground ere it is trampled over."

"I know you by repute, Mr. Holmes," replied Marsh stiffly. "No doubt this other gentleman is Dr. Watson. I hope I shall not be detained unnecessarily, for I'm a busy man."

"That I appreciate," said Holmes. He stood motionless, scanning the surroundings keenly before taking his lens and bending his lean frame to scrutinise the ground leading to where the body lay sprawled on its back, partly hidden in the undergrowth.

On reaching the dead man he dropped to his knees, his beaky nose inches from the corpse, all the while muttering under his breath.

Presently he stood up and beckoned to the police surgeon. "Make your examination, Doctor, but be good enough to follow precisely in my footsteps. Will you permit Dr. Watson to view the body with you?"

"Of course. Anything to hasten matters."

We approached cautiously to find ourselves gazing down on the corpse of a well-nourished man whose ghastly features and protruding tongue gave unmistakable evidence of the manner of his death.

"Not much doubt there, eh, Watson?" said Marsh as he set about his task. "Strangulation. Dead about twenty-four hours or a little over." He rose to his feet and brushed the knees of his trousers, eager to be about his rounds. "Nothing more you want from me, Inspector?"

"No, Doctor, except to ask you to look in on Mrs. Romney. I fear that this news on top of the mystery of her step-daughter's absence has been something of a shock to her."

Marsh had obviously been made aware of Ellen Romney's disappearance, and without comment gave us a curt nod and took his leave.

"Do you agree with the findings, Watson?" asked Holmes.

"As far as it goes," I said cautiously, not wanting to openly criticize a professional colleague, and earning myself a sharp look from Holmes.

"Who found the body?" he asked, "Was it you, Izzard?"

The constable shook his head. "No, sir. It was Joe Bennett here." He bent a dark look on the rough-looking man who stood nearby. "Says he was out for a walk and saw a boot sticking out from the bushes. More like he was up to no good setting snares. Tell the gentleman about it, Joe, and no nonsense."

Bennett looked as if to deny the accusation but thought better of it.

"Well, sir," he said in an injured tone, "like George says, I were just taking a morning stroll when I sees this boot. I grabbed hold and pulled, and out 'e pops. I could tell 'e were a goner, so I runs to get George Izzard afore he started 'is beat."

"You moved nothing after that?" Holmes queried, and got a shake of the head in response. "I didn't touch nothing neither, sir," offered Izzard. "Just took a quick look and came straight to the Croft where I knew Inspector Griffin was."

My companion nodded his approval. "Good man. Now, Watson, take a closer look at the body, and tell me truthfully what you see."

I knew he had detected my previous reticence, and this time I made pretence of a more thorough inspection, even though I knew what I had seen. I looked up to meet his sardonic eyes.

"Dr. Marsh's findings were correct as far as they went," I said slowly. "The man most certainly died of strangulation, but there is no evidence of finger or thumb marks that would have been apparent if it had been done

155

manually, although there are signs of bruising around the front and sides of the neck. Therefore I deduce some other means was employed."

"You mean a rope or cord?" Griffin hazarded.

"I doubt it," said I, shooting a meaning look at Holmes,

"It's your body, Inspector," the latter put in. "What do you make of it?"

Inspector Griffin look mildly shacked by my companion's flippant tone, but collected himself and spoke thoughtfully. "Well, sir, the man was obviously strangled, and we have the word of two doctors on that. As Dr. Watson says, there is no evidence to suggest an assault with bare hands and rules out choking from internal sources, the bruising must be significant. If not a cord or rope, then what?" He paused and snapped his fingers. "I remember now! Some years ago when I was at Gravesend, I dealt with the case of a Spanish seaman who was strangled by one of his mess-mates using a length of window-cord. 'Garrotting', I believe they call it, and that left a distinct weal, just like a red necklace."

"Excellent!" cried Holmes. "You are right in every detail, except for the points you haven't yet had brought to your notice. Bear with me just a while longer, Inspector," he added as Griffin's face darkened. "I shall hide nothing from you, that I promise."

"We haven't searched his pockets," said the inspector. "Perhaps robbery was the motive, although I confess I find it hard to believe that any footpad would be here on the off-chance of finding a victim."

"Quite," said Holmes. "Nevertheless we may learn something from the contents that is of use, but not just yet."

He took his magnifying glass and commenced a systematic examination of the surrounding area, gradually widening his circles, pausing now and then as his eye was caught. Once he stooped to retrieve an object from the ground to slip into his pocket, and again to produce a pair of tweezers with which he delicately removed something invisible to us from a low branch of a bush. He returned to where we stood with an air of satisfaction and took Griffin by the arm. "There is nothing more to be discovered here, Inspector. Let me draw the picture for you," He led the other over the ground he had covered.

"We know that the killer was a fairly powerful man. Witham was of good physique, yet he made little attempt to defend himself. Just here on our right, as you will observe from the trodden state of the turf, is where the assailant lurked in wait, probably for more than a few minutes. He allowed his victim to pass, springing from behind to do his terrible work. When his object was achieved, which I deduce was very quickly, he dragged the body to where it was partially hidden before making off along the path, which is too well used to afford us any clue as to direction."

156

"But you discovered more than that," Griffin stated flatly.

"Indeed, but first let us see what the poor fellow's pockets may tell us, if anything."

The inspector set about the task, which yielded a sovereign case containing nine sovereigns and three half-sovereigns. There followed a cigar-case, a silver box of wax vestas, an assortment of silver and copper coins, and a small bunch of keys. In the corner of a waistcoat pocket, wrapped in tissue paper, was a handsome diamond ring, and from another came a slim silver watch which showed the correct time.

Holmes seized on the last item, opening the back to reveal the inscription "*To Peter with all my love*". His face darkened, but he made no comment. Finally the inspector brought out a pocket-book, the only contents being a couple of bills and a letter. Griffin, after slowly reading the letter, stared at my companion open-mouthed. The latter took it from him, and over Holmes's shoulder I was able to read the few lines inscribed thereon. It was dated for Sunday and began without salutation or preamble:

> *I deem from this moment our engagement to be terminated. Your scandalous and despicable conduct has made it impossible for me to ever meet you again. You will not need me to specify the base conduct to which I refer, nor can I expose you without bringing pain and anguish to the one I love above all others. I pray that your sense of shame tells you to avoid meeting any of my family again, and that you have sufficient honour remaining to repent and mend your ways.*
>
> *Ellen Romney*

"That explains why she left in such a hurry," observed Griffin sagely.

"Not quite," Holmes demurred, "What was the scandalous conduct that led her to write the letter, and how is it connected with Witham's death?"

"So you think we must find the girl to get these answers?"

"Not necessarily, although she must be found sooner or later." He lapsed into deep thought, chin on chest and hands clasped behind him, only roused when the inspector asked if the body could be taken away.

"What? Oh, yes, of course," said Holmes absently.

Griffin had a whispered colloquy with Constable Izzard before joining Holmes and me, and then addressing my friend with an edge to his voice.

"Now, Mr. Holmes, you hinted at information which I don't share. If you will be so good as to let me in on it, I may possibly be bright enough

157

to make something of it off my own bat. I welcome your co-operation, but I don't want to be made a fool of."

Holmes looked shocked. "My dear Inspector! Nothing is farther from my thoughts, but first I would ask you to examine this." He took out his pocket-book to reveal a yellow filament, so fine that a breath would have taken it away. "I removed it from a low bush adjacent to the body. What do you see?"

"Why, a thread of silk. Has it significance to our matter?"

Holmes fished in his pocket and produced a rough pebble, somewhat smaller than a golf ball. "And this? It was also close by, and the only one to be seen on the leafy mould."

Inspector Griffin stared at it, then shook his head despondently. "Perhaps I'm not so bright after all. Explain, I beg you."

"Do not blame yourself. I may have missed the point had I not already had my wits jogged at Brent Croft. Tell me, Inspector: What do you know of *Thuggee*?"

Griffin removed his cap and scratched his head. "Very little, except that it was a form of murder once practised in India and we now apply the term of '*thug*' to any brutal and violent character,"

"Quite so. Strangulation was the Thugs' method, achieved by throwing a strip of cloth round the victim's throat to thus cut off his breath. A turban was the instrument employed and it could then be wound back on the head leaving no sign of a weapon. A few coins in the end of the cloth gave it weight so that when lashed at from behind the victim's throat was encircled as with a whip. Watson will bear me out, I think."

"That's true," I agreed. "But surely the sect was eliminated years ago? Are you suggesting a gang of Indians is operating here?"

The inspector's face lit up. "I think Mr. Holmes means that whoever did this employed the same tactics, and that pebble was the weight. It also implies that the silk thread was from the other part of the weapon, and the killer had some knowledge of this *Thuggee*."

Holmes didn't reply and Griffin stopped short to stare at him aghast.

"Good Lord!" gasped the latter. "Do you mean you suspect the General of this? Why, it's unthinkable! What reason could he have?"

"Reason enough if what I think is correct, but no, he isn't the only one who is familiar with the subcontinent,"

"You mean Lennard? But why? I know he had little regard for Witham as Miss Romney's fiancé, but surely he'd not take such drastic action?"

"I shall say no more until I have all the facts. You will see for yourself shortly. Then, if you have an alternative theory, don't hesitate to voice it. I have been wrong before. Norbury – eh, Watson?"

158

We strode on in silence until we once more stood in the entrance to Brent Croft. Our arrival coincided with the appearance of the station fly, from which alighted an elegantly dressed young woman carrying a small travelling case.

Griffin at once strode forward and addressed the woman sharply.

"Miss Romney! Wherever have you been?"

She drew herself up to look at him coldly. "I see no reason to account to you for my movements, Inspector. Have I committed some crime by making a journey without your permission?"

Griffin flushed. "I beg your pardon, miss, but your father has been extremely concerned by your unexplained absence and came to me for assistance. I in turn enlisted the help of this gentleman, Mr. Sherlock Holmes, who was aiding me in another matter. I'm sorry to say that since then events have taken a more tragic turn."

She reached out to grasp his arm. "My father!" she gasped.

He hastened to reassure her. "The General is quite well, miss, but it is bad enough. May we go into the house?"

She led us into a drawing room where she threw back her veil and looked at us from dark-shadowed eyes that showed signs of stress. Before she could ask the questions trembling on her lips, Holmes spoke.

"I think your first consideration, Miss Romney, must be to relieve your father of the anxiety engendered by your absence. He will doubtless make you aware of the other reason for our presence here. Afterwards, Inspector Griffin and I would have a few words with you."

She nodded. "Of course I must see my father." She gave us a hard look and turning on her heel went out.

"A 'determined young woman',", my companion murmured. He looked found a bell cord which he pulled, and shortly the parlour-maid came in.

"Do you know where Mr. Lennard may be found?" Holmes queried.

"Yes, sir. He's in the kitchen having a cup of tea along of Mrs. Hodge."

"Then pray ask him if he will be good enough to join us at once."

Holmes turned to the inspector. "Will you trust me to conduct this interview in my own way and not intervene until I give the word?"

"I hope you know what you are doing, Mr. Holmes. I'm content to give you some leeway, but I remind you that I shall be the one to get it in the neck should things go awry."

"Be easy. We are too near the truth for things to go wrong now. Ah, Lennard, I wonder if you will oblige by giving us another sight of your room? Inspector Griffin wasn't with us earlier, and I'm sure he will find much to interest him."

The man looked at us steadily for a few seconds. "If you must," he said ungraciously, turning to lead the way upstairs.

On entering the room, Holmes went to the length of silk that still hung on its pegs. Taking it down, he handed it to Griffin, then produced the thread from his pocket-book for the inspector to compare. Next he took out the pebble and held before Lennard, who blanched at the sight.

"Well, Lennard?" said Holmes quietly. "Your silence will serve no purpose now, except to cause more distress to those you would protect."

The man eyed us stonily. Inspector Griffin's brow was creased in a frown as his eyes darted between Holmes and Lennard, while the former waited for a reaction from the manservant. I began to see the pieces fall into place as Lennard looked straight at my friend, defiantly at first, then his shoulders sagged in resignation.

"I suppose it had to come out sooner or later," he said at last. "I've no regrets for what I done. The blighter got no more than he deserved."

"Are you confessing to the murder of Peter Witham?" said Griffin in his most official voice. "If so, I must caution you – "

"Save your breath," replied the unhappy man. "Yes, I killed him, swine that he was."

"Why?" asked the inspector.

"If you don't know, then I'm not about to tell you." Lennard sat on the edge of his bed, obstinacy written in every line of his face.

"Ah, but I think I know," put in Holmes, "and I'm pretty sure that Miss Romney also knows, although she may be unaware that it was your doing." He went to stand before the man. "Have you considered that it may be that she suspects her father?"

"That's impossible!" Lennard stood up agitatedly. "Why, the General'd never be capable of doing what I did, and in any case he don't know why I done it, and I pray that he never finds out."

"Inspector Griffin stepped forward. "Edward Lennard," he intoned solemnly, "I'm charging you with the murder of Peter Witham. Have you anything to say?"

There was no reply, and Holmes shook his head.

"Then let me reconstruct events leading up to the murder," he said. "I think it was on Sunday that Miss Romney came into possession of evidence that made her aware that her fiancé wasn't an honourable man. It was more than the revelation of some minor peccadillo that might be readily overlooked and excused. We can be sure of that from the tone of the letter in which she renounced her engagement to Witham, and from the phrase she used to indicate that if the facts were made public it would give distress to the one she loved most. That could only be her father, so I asked myself what it implied.

160

"She was in turmoil, unable to face her family with the secret locked inside her, so she decided to go away to compose her thoughts in some privacy. Unbeknown to her, what she had discovered was also known to Lennard, and had been for some time. He was fiercely loyal to the General, and when Miss Romney fled, he divined that she too had become aware of the situation."

At this point, Holmes paused and looked at Lennard sadly.

"Witham was having an illicit relationship with Mrs. Romney, was he not?" he asked. "You knew of it, but couldn't bear to see the General hurt and humiliated. Am I correct?"

The wretched man nodded. "Aye, that's about it. I've seen 'em in that old cottage together behaving like a couple of animals, night after night when the Guv'nor was shut away in his study. I never knew Miss Ellen'd found out, though. Not 'til she went off, leaving that letter for her dad."

"So you took matters into your own hands, hoping that with Witham's death, she would have no cause to make her father aware of the matter,"

Not waiting for a reply, Holmes continued, addressing himself now to Inspector Griffin. "Lennard knew from his inquiries that Witham was taking the early train to London and, from his local knowledge, that his intended victim would take the path between the two properties. Taking that scarf," he indicated it, "he went to lay in wait, probably picking up the pebble from the drive where they lie in profusion along the edge."

"And he knew of this Indian business from his time there with General Romney," Griffin chipped in.

Before Holmes could continue the door burst open to admit Ellen Romney. She was pale but composed, and stopped to survey the solemn group gathered in the room.

"Father has told me of Peter's murder," she said icily. "What steps are you taking to apprehend his killer, Inspector?"

"That is done, miss," Griffin replied with some embarrassment. "Lennard has confessed to the crime and is now under arrest."

"No!" she burst out angrily, "That is ridiculous! What reason would Ted have for committing such a crime?"

"The same reason that sent you away, Miss Romney, and caused you to break your engagement," said Holmes, "He has been aware of what was going on for much longer than you, and feared that your discovery of it would force you to confide in the General."

The young woman swayed on her feet and I took her arm to lead her to a chair. She collapsed limply and looked dazedly at Lennard,

"Is this true, Ted?" she whispered. "You'd known all along?"

"That's right, Miss Ellen. I was hoping you'd realise he weren't good enough for you and give him the shove afore the truth come out." His eyes

161

showed some animation. "John Paxton – he's the one for you, even if he ain't got much money,"

"Oh, Ted," she sobbed, the tears running down her cheeks. "It wasn't needed. I'd never have told Father what that woman was doing." She turned her face up to look at us angrily. "I'll deal with her in my own way and Father will never know of her shameful deceit." Her anger turned suddenly to fear. "He needn't know, need he? He mustn't!"

"That depends on what Lennard says in court, Miss Romney," said Holmes. "He's admitted the murder, but if he refuses to give reasons, well – " He shrugged. "I think if Inspector Griffin is prepared to take a fresh statement covering the bare facts of the murder, it may well be seen as personal animosity." He carefully avoided the inspector's eye.

"I shan't say nothing to damage the Guv'nor, rely on that, miss," said Lennard stoutly, seemingly uncaring for his own predicament, "You go on and tell him old Ted's blotted his crime sheet at last."

Inspector Griffin jerked his head, and the still-sobbing Ellen Romney ran from the room, only to return within minutes with a wrathful General Romney on her heels.

"Griffin, you oaf!" he roared. "What in God's name has got into you? And you, Mr. Sherlock Holmes – whatever reputation you had is shot to pieces by this stupidity!"

"I beg your pardon, General," said Griffin with dignity. "I must do my duty, whatever the circumstances. Lennard has admitted to killing Mr. Peter Witham, and I have no choice but to take him into custody."

"That's true, sir," said the accused man. "I done him in, all right."

"Nonsense!" boomed the General. "You've been bullied into saying this!"

The inspector looked outraged and Holmes intervened coldly.

"With all deference due to your age and former rank, sir, I assure you that is no room for error. The matter is quite clear, and if you would help your loyal servant, I suggest you procure for him the finest legal advice that you can. Your opinion of me I discount, but the aspersions you have made regarding Inspector Griffin's integrity do you no credit."

For what seemed minutes the old man simmered, finally speaking in a more composed manner. "So it's true, then? But why, Ted, why?"

"It were for Miss Ellen, Guv'nor. He were never right for her and would only have made her life a misery." Lennard was speaking calmly and with confidence. "I think she guessed it, but was too much of a lady to face him with it."

The General snorted, "If she had something to say she'd say it, lady or no lady." He swung to face his daughter. "Wouldn't you, girl?"

"Perhaps." Her eyes fell, but already the General had turned away.

"Inspector, I spoke unjustly and in haste. Will you accept my humble apologies? And Mr. Holmes, will you also be so generous?"

Holmes smiled faintly, while Griffin inclined his head gravely.

"You were shocked and under a strain, sir," said the latter. "Now I must ask Lennard to accompany me to the police station."

General Romney gnawed at his moustache. "What will be the outcome, Griffin?" he asked.

"There can only be one, sir. Unless," Griffin added, "he can make a plea of insanity which the court will believe."

"I'm as sane as any of you lot," Lennard said furiously. "I knew what I was doing and why, and I ain't going to snivel for no one."

The General seemed to have aged a decade since entering the room. Now he turned almost pleadingly to the inspector. "I know this is irregular, but will you allow me a few minutes alone with Ted? I give my word he will make no trouble, and you may post a man outside my study door and on the terrace." He turned to his servant, "You'll not let me down?"

"Never have done yet, have I, sir?"

With the briefest hesitation Griffin agreed, "Of course, General, and I'll not insult you by placing sentries. Ten minutes, sir?"

The two old soldiers, both holding themselves rigidly, made their way down to the study, leaving Ellen Romney to gaze tearfully after them until Holmes sought her attention.

"One point I would clear up, Miss Romney," he said. "Will you be so good as to tell us when you first became aware of your step-mother's involvement with your fiancé?"

She looked at him dully before speaking in a low husky voice.

"It was on Sunday evening. Peter had brought me back from church and I had gone to my room feeling unwell. Soon afterwards I went to open the window for air and I saw Charlotte – Mrs. Romney – hurrying down the drive. Although I maintained a superficial show of amity towards her for Father's sake, I was never comfortable in her presence for reasons I was unable to explain to myself. On a sudden impulse, I decided to follow her. Nobody saw me leave and I was some thirty yards behind her when I saw her enter the old cottage. Have you seen it?"

We murmured assent and she went on.

"I was intrigued enough to approach cautiously and peer through one of the glass less windows. What I saw horrified me! She and Peter were locked in a passionate embrace, and even as I watched they displayed such abandonment that my senses reeled. I began to feel physically sick, yet I was mesmerised, unable to drag myself away from the ghastly sight."

She shuddered at the memory and Holmes laid a hand on her arm.

163

"Do not distress yourself, Miss Romney. We follow your meaning. Pray tell us of your subsequent actions."

"At last I forced myself to flee back to the house, shamed and disgusted by what I had witnessed. That my father's wife should give herself so wantonly to the man to whom I was promised was unbelievable, yet I had the evidence of my own eyes. My first thought was to denounce her to Father, but the idea of inflicting pain and humiliation on him gave me pause.

"I knew I couldn't face her without my anger betraying my knowledge, so as I became calmer I decided to go away until I could make up my mind as to a course of action. I wrote a note to Father, which you will have seen, and also a letter to Mr. Witham in which – "

"We have seen that also, miss," put in the inspector. "From the contents of his pockets, we deduced that the affair was of long-standing."

"There isn't much more to tell," said Ellen Romney, "I sneaked out down the back stairs like a thief, and caught the train to London, where I spent two nights at an hotel for ladies before coming back to this."

"What decision had you made?" asked Holmes, ever anxious to have a story complete.

"I was going to confront her with what I had seen, and warn her that unless she mended her ways I must tell my father. Whether I could ever bring myself to do so I know not, but be assured, gentlemen, I shall use all my wiles to bring her to heel," she concluded grimly.

There was a period of silence before Griffin moved towards the stairs.

"Then the case is closed," he said heavily, "I can feel pity for the man whose loyalty drove him to extremes, but the law must be upheld. I think the General should be left in the belief that Lennard was actuated by concern for his master's daughter and last his self-control through an excess of zeal."

Holmes made no sign of agreeing or disagreeing, and we arrived at the lower floor just as the General came out of the study, closing the door behind him. His shoulders were bowed and his eyes spoke of unshed tears. He came towards us and with an effort straightened up to become the very picture of the gallant old campaigner that he was. He looked at his daughter for a moment, then spoke in his usual crisp voice.

"Go to your room, my dear," he said in a tone that brooked of no argument. "I have something that must be said to these gentlemen before the final act."

"Where is Lennard?" Griffin asked sharply.

"Have no fear, Inspector. He remains in my study with pen and paper to write his statement." The General gave the travesty of a smile. "He knows his duty and will do it."

164

Even as he spoke there came the sound of a shot, muffled by the heavy door, but nevertheless unmistakable. With an oath Griffin sprang forward and flung open the door, Holmes and I crowding on his heels.

"God d--- it!" roared the inspector, stopping in his tracks. "This is an outrage!"

I wasn't unprepared for the sight that met our eyes. Lennard sat at the desk with the muzzle of a revolver in his mouth and the back of his head completely blown away, the window behind him spattered with blood and brains. Inspector Griffin stared at the macabre sight before turning to face the General, who stood calmly beside Holmes. "Confound it, General!" he cried furiously. "You connived in helping this man evade justice. How could you abuse my trust so?"

"I sir?" said the General with dignity. "I merely left him here to write his statement. He must have found my old service revolver in the desk drawer and decided to take this way out. I cannot pretend regrets that you were baulked of your prey, though."

"He was my prisoner and it will reflect on me!" Griffin almost snarled.

"I shall see no blame attaches to you, Inspector," replied the General soothingly. "We value you too highly to see your career ruined." He sat down heavily on the nearest chair. "The real tragedy is that it need never have happened. You see, I knew all about my wife and Witham and had the matter under control."

"You knew?" Griffin and I stared at him, but Holmes showed no sign of surprise whatsoever.

"Gentlemen," said General Romney patiently, "I may be older than you, but I'm not blind, and neither am I in my dotage. Very early in my marriage, I knew I was mistaken in taking a wife very near my daughter's age, but I had enough pride and self-esteem to keep it to myself."

"She knew that you were aware of her unfaithfulness?"

"I was about to confront her with it when Ellen's disappearance took precedence in my thoughts. When Witham came to dinner on Tuesday, I was to present my ultimatum."

"Which was?" This from Holmes.

"He would break off his engagement to my daughter. Charlotte would have a reasonable but not overgenerous allowance provided she left my roof and didn't reside within ten miles of Foxford. Ellen is a mature woman and would be capable of taking events in her stride when told the true facts. Witham was never but second choice for her, thanks to my meddling in her life." He dropped his head into his hands and sighed.

I jumped as my companion touched my arm. "Come, Watson, old friend," he whispered. "There is no more for us to do here, and the General and Miss Romney have the strength of character to survive this tragedy. If only he had confided his knowledge to her and Lennard earlier."

We crept out unnoticed, and it wasn't until we had retrieved our luggage and settled in the train to London that he referred to the matter again.

"We shall hear more of Mrs. Romney, Watson. She will not sink into obscurity, mark my words."

"And perhaps under another name," I said, my contempt showing in my tone, at which he laughed and resumed his study of the evening paper.

The Bickstone Lodge Affair

A Novella

Chapter I – The Mystery in the Woods

"Y ou realise, Watson, that it would be injudicious to reveal the full story of our little adventure at Stoke Moran for some years yet?" Sherlock Holmes looked up from his task of pasting cuttings into what he liked to call his common-place book.

"Little adventure!" I echoed, wiping my pen before laying it down. "Scarcely a little adventure by any standards. Apart from the appalling danger to Miss Stoner and ourselves, there was also the death of the lady's stepfather into the bargain."

"Dr. Grimesby Roylott is no loss to the world," he said severely, "and I assure you my conscience troubles me not at all on that score."

"Nevertheless, I fear your actions would find little favour in official quarters, however justifiable you may consider them."

"Precisely, my dear fellow, and that is why the business must remain between ourselves for the present." My companion gave me a mischievous smile. "Bear in mind, Watson, you too played a not inconsiderable part in the matter and would most surely be regarded as an active accessory both before and after the event. However, those footsteps on the stairs can belong only to Lestrade, so I suggest we change the subject. Come in, Lestrade," he called, not waiting for the knock.

The inspector entered, his ferrety features set in a look of wary amusement as he laid his hat on a small table.

"I'll not play your game, Mr. Holmes. Even you cannot see through solid oak doors, so you must have seen me coming up the street. Good morning, Doctor." He turned to me, thus missing the sardonic gleam in my friend's eye.

"Sit down, Lestrade," said the latter with a quiet chuckle. "No doubt you have at last arrested Dixon, the night watchman, for the Lambeth murder?"

"How the deuce do you know that?" said the detective, a note of resentment in his voice. "It is but a half-hour since I clapped the darbies on the villain."

"You look well pleased with yourself," replied Holmes. "Besides, it was obvious from the outset that he killed the woman. He maintained he

167

had made his rounds every hour. The body was in full view of the gateway where she had been strangled three hours earlier, yet it was left to a passing labourer on his way to work to report it."

"That's all very well, Mr. Holmes," growled Lestrade. "You have only to theorise, but we have to produce hard facts in court."

"The facts spoke for themselves," Holmes said dismissively. "However, you got there in the end. What of the Highgate affair? Is that settled?"

"Gregson is blundering about on that," said Lestrade with a snort.

"Tell him to direct his attention to a short left-handed man who has a smattering of Latin," said Holmes. "There is no need to mention my name."

The inspector's dark eyes looked out suspiciously from under his beetling brows. "You would not be having me on, Mr. Holmes?"

"Come, Lestrade, you know me better than that," said Holmes blandly.

"There you are, Inspector," I cried. "A chance for you to score off Gregson." I broke off as Holmes directed a frown in my direction.

"A glass of beer, Lestrade?" offered my companion.

"Not now, thank you all the same. I must get back to the Yard to make out the charges against Dixon." Lestrade got to his feet and recovered his hat. "I only dropped in as I was close by, seeing as we had not rubbed shoulders lately." He hesitated on the threshold as though he would speak further, then with a shake of his narrow head he took his departure.

The street door slammed and Holmes returned to his paste-brush and cuttings, ignoring the look of annoyance that I directed at him and it was left to me to break the silence.

"Really, Holmes," I expostulated. "I think it too bad of you to mislead poor Lestrade in so blatant a manner."

"Mislead? I do not follow," He looked up blankly. "In what way did I mislead the fellow?"

"Why, that piffle about a short left-handed man with some knowledge of Latin. You know nothing of the Highgate case apart from what you have gleaned from the newspapers."

"You think not?"

"You have not been within a mile of Highgate these past three days. In fact, your only excursion outside these rooms was yesterday when we went to Bradley's for our tobacco."

"And what else occurred during our perambulations?" He raised an eyebrow.

"Nothing," I replied promptly. "Oh, you bought a box of matches from that shifty looking pedlar on the corner of George Street, although why you could not have done that at Bradley's, I do not know."

"That shifty looking pedlar happens to be one of my most reliable sources of information," he said. "It was he who told me that Bossy Simons was trying to dispose of a number of enamelled miniatures."

"Bossy Simons? Who the devil is he?"

"Just a petty thief who seems to have ideas above his station. He began life as a schoolmaster, but when a few sovereigns vanished from the headmaster's study, that career came to an end. Since then he has become a veritable magpie, but this time he has over-reached himself."

"How so?" I asked.

"Those miniatures are worth several thousands of pounds, and I know for a fact that a certain big organisation had them marked down. If Bossy is not taken up quickly, he is liable to find himself with two broken legs or worse. He will be much safer in one of Her Majesty's excellent prisons than if he is on the loose."

"And he is short-statured, left-handed, and has some Latin," I said. "But why not give Lestrade a name rather than an oblique hint?"

"It maintains my reputation," my friend replied smugly. "Confound it, man, they cannot expect me to do all their work for them. Perhaps Mr. Abel Vineberg may now have the sense to take more stringent precautions against a break-in than he has hitherto. Some folk positively invite a visit from the criminal fraternity."

My companion rose to his feet to prowl aimlessly around our sitting room. I recognised the signs. His restless nature craved the stimulation and excitement of a challenge to his amazing powers and, without that, he became fretful and edgy, liable to outbursts of impatience. As I watched him, I again had the fleeting notion that he used some form of narcotic to curb his boundless energy, and again I dismissed the thought as unworthy.

Surely one of his intellect would not risk blunting his razor-sharp brain in so dangerous manner, and I berated myself for my suspicions. I returned to my notes, re-reading them to pick up the thread. From the corner of my eye I saw Holmes go to the window embrasure, where he remained to stare abstractedly down into the street.

"Watson!" His sharp tone brought my head up with a jerk. "We have a visitor."

The faint jangle of the doorbell came to confirm his words, followed after a brief interval by Mrs. Hudson's firm tread on the stairs and a knock on the door which I answered.

"A Miss Celia Winsett asking for Mr. Holmes," announced the good lady.

169

"Show her up, please, Mrs. Hudson," I said on a confirmatory nod from Holmes, who rubbed his hands in anticipation.

The lady was young, no more than twenty-five years of age, with keen intelligent eyes set in an oval face that was pale with worry. She looked from one to the other of us as if unsure whom to address.

"Come in, Madam. I am Sherlock Holmes, and this is my trusted friend and colleague, Dr. Watson." He swept a pile of mutilated newspapers from the basket chair and waved a hand. "Pray be seated and tell us what drove you to walk to a railway station so early in the morning following after a sleepless night."

"Is it so apparent, Mr. Holmes?" she said with a wan smile as she sat.

"To me it is," said my companion, returning her smile. "The faint traces of leaf-mould in the welt of your boot, the smudge of soot on your glove that came from opening a carriage door, together with a weariness of feature all speak for themselves. Watson, be so good as to ask Mrs. Hudson to bring some refreshment. Miss Winsett has not broken her fast."

He sat back, refusing to allow her to speak until we were all provided with steaming cups of coffee and a rack of buttered toast was placed on the low table beside our visitor's chair. Some of the colour returned to her face as she smiled her gratitude.

"Now, Miss Winsett," said Holmes, "how may we be of service to you?"

She smoothed her dress over her knees and spoke somewhat diffidently.

"It is hard to know where to begin, Mr. Holmes. I do not wish to take up too much of your valuable time, and yet – " She hesitated and turned her soft brown eyes from Holmes to where I sat with a notebook poised on my knee.

"My time is at your disposal," my companion said encouragingly. "Tell me about yourself and permit me to decide what is relevant. Better too much information than too little."

"So be it," she nodded. "I was born in France of a French mother and an English father, and lived in Paris until the age of twelve. Both my parents died of cholera during the siege of 1870, and I was brought to England by my uncle, James Winsett, who stood as my guardian until his death in 1878."

I made a murmur of sympathy, but Holmes remained impassive as the lady continued.

"I had become engaged to Lieutenant Philip Martin of the Royal Artillery. We intended to marry in the autumn of '78, but my uncle's death caused us to delay our plans. Before new arrangements could be made, he was suddenly posted to India." There was a catch in her voice and a look

170

of ineffable sadness came over her features. "I never saw him again. He was killed within a few weeks of arriving in Bombay."

Even my cold-natured companion was moved by this pitiful recital and he spoke with unusual gentleness. "You have borne much, Madam. It must be painful to relate such a catalogue of misfortune."

"It was a bad time for me," she admitted. "However, I resolved to put the past behind me, although not forget it, and I came to terms with myself. My uncle had left me an annuity of two-hundred pounds a year, but I was not content to live in idleness until I became soured and self-pitying. Due to my parentage, I speak French and English with equal facility, so I was able to obtain a post as reader and translator for a well-known publishing house. I was living in lodgings in London, but it was ever my desire to move to the country. Shortly after last Christmas, I obtained the lease of a cottage near the village of Bickstone, which is close to Bromley."

Miss Winsett paused, her features becoming animated. "Oh, it was so lovely, gentlemen," she cried. "All I had ever dreamed of, set quietly amid woods and glades, yet still within easy reach of London for the few occasions that demanded my presence here. It is on the estate of Sir Charles Listel, who resides at Bickstone Lodge, and the rent is extremely moderate. I counted myself fortunate in finding it, and the past three months have been some of the happiest I have known in recent years."

Her tone became suddenly angry. "That is, until last Tuesday."

Holmes leaned forward, his eyes alert as they scanned our visitor's face. "Something occurred to upset this idyllic scene?" he prompted.

"Indeed it did. You may dismiss it as the fears of a lonely woman, but I am certain in my own mind that something mysterious is going on."

"I do not think you are of a nervous disposition, Madam," Holmes replied. "Tell me what disturbs you."

"Thank you for that, Mr. Holmes." She looked up at the mantelpiece and smiled. "Please smoke if you so wish, gentlemen. My uncle was an inveterate consumer of Navy plug, and the aroma will bring back happy memories for me."

"Thank you, it will be of help." Holmes uncoiled his thin frame from his chair to select one of his least foul pipes, which he began to stuff with the rank black shag that he favoured. I took my own pipe and pouch from the table, and out of consideration for our fair client went to open a window.

"Now, pray continue your story," said Holmes.

She nodded. "Last Tuesday evening, I had completed the reading of an especially tedious manuscript in the most atrocious handwriting. I decided to take a stroll through the woods to clear my head, as I often do. I must have been out for about half-an-hour or so, and dusk was falling as

171

I made my way home. Within a hundred yards of my gate, I was startled by some disturbance deep in the woods. It sounded for all the world as if a large animal was thrashing around. Then, as suddenly as it had begun, the noise ceased. I listened for a while, but there was nothing more."

"A fox?" I suggested.

Miss Winsett shook her head vigorously. "No fox could have made that amount of noise, Doctor," she said firmly. "At last I went on my way and, as I reached my gate, I met Sir Charles's gamekeeper, Harper. A surly, ill-mannered man with hardly a civil word for anyone," she added, her distaste apparent. "I told him what I had heard, thinking he would also have heard it, but he denied all knowledge and dismissed the matter most rudely, muttering about nervy women who saw danger in every shadow. I became angry and said if he had so little concern for his master's property, I would speak to Sir Charles myself. On that he grudgingly agreed to look around and walked way."

"You had no doubts?" asked Holmes.

"None. I am not given to imagining things."

"Of course not. Proceed."

"I was still angry when I awoke the next morning, so after breakfast I retraced my steps to where I had heard the noise. A short distance off the path I found the ground scuffed and the undergrowth flattened as if a heavy object had been dragged through the bushes into a denser part of the wood. I penetrated as far as I could, but found nothing. I gave up then, having ample work to do, and dismissed the matter from my mind."

"That was Wednesday," Holmes said musingly. "Something has since arisen to give you further concern?"

"Indeed it has, or I would not be troubling you," she said. "On that same night as I was preparing for bed, I looked out of the window and saw lights moving about in the wood. My immediate thought was of poachers, but they could hope for nothing more than a few rabbits, and that was Harper's business, not mine, so I went to bed."

"You heard nothing during the night?"

She shook her head. "In the morning – that was yesterday – I had to go into Bickstone village to the post office, and my curiosity getting the better of me, I again examined the site of Tuesday's disturbance, and this time I met up with Harper. He appeared agitated on seeing me, and in his usual uncouth way warned me against leaving the footpath, as he had set snares and also was liable to use his shotgun at any sudden movement. I did not deign to argue with him and continued on my way, angry rather than concerned – that is, until last night."

Miss Winsett paused, a frown creasing her forehead, while we waited in silence for her to resume.

172

"It was in the early hours of this morning," she went on. "Well before dawn, I was awakened by noises that convinced me that someone was trying to enter the cottage by the front door."

"Great Heavens!" I exclaimed. "You must have been terrified!"

"Frightened, Dr. Watson, yes, but not paralysed. I struck a match to light my bedside lamp and almost at once the noise stopped. My clock told me it was a few minutes to four, and of course, there was no prospect of further sleep, so I dressed and made a pot of tea. I examined the windows and both front and back doors but they were all secure. Then my eye caught something lying on the mat inside the front door. It was this." She reached for her bag and from its depths she produced a small ivory box and held it out. "Those marks are blood, Mr. Holmes," she said tremulously. "They were still sticky when I found it!"

"You have remarkable strength of character, Miss Winsett," said my colleague as she laid the box on his outstretched palm. "Have you opened this?"

"I could not bring myself to do so," she said with a shudder. "There and then I resolved to seek your advice, having heard accounts of your perspicacity from an old friend of mine, Alice Charpentier. As soon as was reasonable I put on my coat and set out for Bromley to get the first available train. Not without some trepidation," she added with a nervous laugh, "I opened my door and looked round carefully before going out, and there on the tiles of the porch was the print of a man's boot. It only strengthened my resolve, and here I am. What does it mean?"

Chapter II: An Ivory Box

Sherlock Holmes began to refill his pipe, his whole attitude suggesting that this was the most important task in the world. I watched him keenly, for even after more than two years of living in close proximity to him, I had learned never to anticipate the workings of his agile mind. He clamped the amber stem between his lips and struck a Vesta on the iron fender, and not until his head was wreathed in a haze of pungent smoke did he speak again.

"Tell me, Miss Winsett, why have you come to me rather than to your local police?"

"Local police?" She gave a short laugh. "In view of Harper's unhelpful manner, I had little hope that Constable Old would prove at all encouraging, especially as he and Harper are close friends."

"A not-unusual situation between gamekeeper and policeman," observed Holmes. "All the same, I take your point." He picked up the

173

small box from where he had laid it on the table and began to examine it carefully with his magnifying glass, muttering beneath his breath as he did so.

"Ivory," he proclaimed at last. "Beautifully made, but of a most peculiar design. A snuff-box, perhaps, but rather large for that." He raised it to his nose and sniffed. "No, it has never held snuff or tobacco, so what can it be? Those stains are indubitably blood, but whose?" He held it out to me. "Tell me what you make of it. Then see if you can open it,"

At first sight, it appeared to be not a box but a solid piece of ivory, and it wasn't until I inspected it under the glass that I perceived the faint lines that defined the lid. I turned it over and over, admiring the smooth symmetrical surfaces, but failing to see how it could be opened, I shook my head.

"As you remarked, a fine piece of workmanship," I said as I gave it back to him. "I have seen similar things in India, but nothing so meticulously made as this. Can it be opened, do you think?"

"It was intended to be, Watson, therefore it can be. The thing is to find the trick." He studied it for a few seconds then squeezed it lengthwise in his hand, but to no effect. Turning it through ninety degrees he repeated the action, with the same lack of result. Next his long fingers gripped it at either end and he went through the motions of breaking a biscuit, and this time he was rewarded with the faintest of clicks.

"Eureka!" he cried triumphantly.

Our visitor and I craned forward expectantly while Holmes, his puckish sense of humour showing in the curve of his thin lips, kept us waiting for interminable seconds. Relenting at last, he probed gently with his thumb-nail until the lid was fully raised. I could not see the inside of the box, but the sharp intake of my friend's breath was enough to tell that whatever it contained it held some significance for him.

"Come on, Holmes!" I said impatiently. "Do not keep us in suspense. What is in there?"

He continued to stare into the interior of the box as it lay in the palm of his hand, the warmth from which caused a delicate musty fragrance to pervade our nostrils. His dark brows were drawn together in intense concentration. Then he looked up with a grim smile.

"A message," he said. "But for whom? Quickly, Watson – the paper-knife."

Containing my impatience I went over to fetch the thin stiletto that Holmes kept as a souvenir of one of his earlier cases. The name "*Ricoletti*" was engraved on the bone handle, but apart from a casual reference, he had never confided any of the details to me.

174

Taking the knife, he fished delicately in the mysterious box, and then with a sigh withdrew a small piece of paper, holding it gingerly by one corner between his acid-stained finger and thumb. It was perhaps two inches in length and half of that across, and from where I stood by his shoulder, I could just distinguish some faint writing.

"What is it, Mr. Holmes?" Miss Winsett's curiosity matched my own, and sensing it, Holmes relented and flashed her a quick smile. "Forgive me, Madam," he said contritely. "I'm afraid my courtesy has been overtaken by the problem with which you have presented me. Pray excuse me and tell me if this scrap means anything to you. Do not touch it, I beg of you."

He laid the oblong of paper on the small table at her elbow, and she twisted in her chair to look at it. I craned my neck for a better view and managed to discern the faint scrawl.

"'Tell C. Har'" I read aloud, my mystification reflected in my tone. "What the deuce does it mean?"

"Miss Winsett?" Holmes regarded her keenly.

"I do not understand," said she. "Is it some kind of a puzzle?"

"Indeed it is," Holmes replied. "However, I do not think it is so intentionally. It was delivered to you, so for the present and in the absence of other information, we will assume that it was intended to convey something to you. The bloodstains on the box and on its contents are significant."

"Is it human blood?" I inquired. "Miss Winsett has spoken of the likelihood of poachers in the Bickstone woods, so a rabbit – "

"I have considered it, Watson," Holmes interrupted somewhat acidly. "I shall apply such tests as may elucidate the matter, but I have little hope of a definitive result. At the same time, I think it very unlikely that whoever chose such a bizarre way of delivering a message to the lady would be concerned with the dissection of a harmless wild animal. The writing was done under stress on a piece torn from a newspaper. Most papers leave a part-column blank to accommodate late items that reach them after the page has been made up. It was written with a blunt hard-lead pencil – note the slight tear where the tip has penetrated – and by a semi-literate hand." My friend bent a keen look at me. "Come, Watson, you know my methods. What more can we deduce?"

"Very little, I fear," said I, shaking my head. "If your reasoning is correct, I would suggest that someone is hoping that Miss Winsett will understand the meaning and convey a warning to 'C. Har' whomever that may be. That someone is possibly injured and, unable to approach her in person, has chosen this strange way to contact her."

175

"Capital, my dear fellow!" chuckled Holmes. "You prove an apt pupil." His tone became more serious. "However, I fear that Miss Winsett could be in danger were it realised that our unknown messenger had been successful in having any kind of communication with her, and therefore she must be on her guard at all times."

The young lady's eyes flashed defiantly, and her words made it plain that her beauty was matched by her courage.

"Have no fear on my account, Mr. Holmes," she cried. "I am not one of your vapid misses to swoon at a hint of danger. As a young girl, I lived through the Siege of Paris and I am not easily intimidated. Tell me what I must do to get to the bottom of this business and I will do it."

I looked my admiration at this show of spirit, but my friend's demeanour was grave when he spoke.

"Be that as it may, Madam," he said. "I doubt not your resolution nor your bravery, but I pray you not to be foolhardy. There are several unexplained factors in this chain of events and I need time to disentangle them. For the present, my advice to you is to stay away from your cottage and from the immediate vicinity of Bickstone." He stopped her protests with a peremptory gesture before getting to his feet to walk over to the window. "I must think," he muttered.

For several minutes he stood motionless, apparently staring blankly at the window. Our visitor and I exchanged glances and waited in silence. Suddenly his spare frame stiffened and he spun round on his heel, his eyes sparkling.

"Miss Winsett," he said crisply, "have you any reason to believe that you were followed here this morning?"

She shook her head in bewilderment. "The thought never crossed my mind. Who would wish to do so?"

"Perhaps you can enlighten me," he replied. "Come to the window, please, but have a care not to show yourself." He steered her gently so that she could see through a chink in the curtains. "There – that man wearing a brown billy-cock who lurks in the doorway of the draper's shop opposite. Wait, he will look up shortly."

I followed to stand behind the lady and looked over her shoulder. At first I saw nothing. Then as two potential customers made to enter the shop, a bulky figure detached itself from the shadows and came into full view. Celia Winsett's hand flew to her mouth and she gave a little cry of astonishment.

"Why, that is Samuel Harper!" she gasped, "The gamekeeper of whom I spoke. What does it mean, Mr. .Holmes? Why should he follow me?"

"That is what we must find out." My companion led her back to her chair. "Meanwhile, my advice that you should stay away from your cottage is justified. Have you a friend who would welcome your unannounced company for a few days?"

"You seriously believe me to be in some peril?"

"I would be less than honest if I denied it," Holmes said gravely. "I beg you, Miss Winsett be guided by me."

She bit her lip before slowly nodding her agreement. "Very well, Mr. Holmes. As much as I resent hiding myself away, I must put myself in your hands. I have an old school friend living at Lewisham. She has recently married an officer of the Orient Steamship Line and, her husband being on a voyage, she will doubtless be glad of my company.

"Excellent. It now remains for us to remove our Mr. Harper whilst you make your exit unobserved." He cocked an eyebrow in my direction. "Watson, old fellow, if I can draw him off, will you escort Miss Winsett to her friend's address?"

I cast an appreciative look at our client and nodded vigorously. "It will give me the greatest pleasure," I replied. "How do you propose to fox him?"

Instead of answering he turned to the lady, his eyes glinting at the prospect of action. "Stand up, please," he said brusquely.

Clearly perplexed, she did as he commanded without demur. Holmes looked her up and down then gently turned her round, examining her as if she was an exhibit in a museum. His inspection complete, he gave a nod and, without further speech, he vanished into his bedroom, leaving the lady to stare at me with a flush of embarrassment staining her pretty cheeks.

"What is he doing, Dr. Watson?" she asked in a bewildered voice. "I felt like a slave on the auction block."

"He meant no discourtesy," I said pacifically. "I am afraid his brain works too quickly for we lesser mortals to stay with him. Once he gets his teeth into a problem, all else is forgotten. Rest assured that his every move has a good reason behind it."

She nodded and resumed her seat while I made my way to the window to look down into the street. Our watcher was still there, and I had the leisure to study the coarse brutal features that cast furtive looks at our door. He was well-built with an upright carriage and, following my friends precepts, I deduced that some part of his life had been spent in military service, although his present attire indicated a more rustic way of life. I was still assessing him when Holmes's voice drew my attention.

"Well, Watson, will it pass if not too closely scrutinised?"

I turned to find the figure of a woman standing in the doorway of my friend's bedroom, and it took me several seconds to realise that it was

177

Holmes in one of his incomparable disguises. He wore a grey costume very similar to that worn by Miss Winsett and a light brown wig was surmounted by a small hat with an attached veil that partially covered his beaky nose. Our client stared at him in dumbstruck amazement and half-rose from her chair.

"Great Heavens above, Holmes!" I chuckled. "I would not be averse to dining out with you myself."

"This is no time for flippancy," he said coldly. "I take it your answer is in the affirmative?" I nodded. "Good," he continued. "This is what we must do. Have Mrs. Hudson send for a cab – a four-wheeler. When it arrives, you will escort me down to it and instruct the driver to take me to London Bridge Station at a leisurely pace. Once you are satisfied that our man has taken the bait and followed me, you will secure another cab and take Miss Winsett to Lewisham with all despatch. I can rely on you to be certain you are not followed. Once there, Madam, you will not leave the house unless escorted by Dr. Watson or myself. By that, I mean you must ignore any letters or telegrams telling you otherwise. Is that clear?"

"Quite clear, Mr. Holmes," she replied. "But what am I to tell Emily – Mrs. Footer?"

Holmes considered this for a moment before speaking. "Is she a trustworthy and sensible person? Good, then tell her as much as you think is necessary, but impress on her the need for complete secrecy, even to the extent of denying your presence there. Should Watson or myself call for you, the name we will use is Verner, Ignore any other. Watson, the cab."

Five minutes later I escorted the disguised Holmes to the growler that stood at our door. Then, leaving the door open a fraction, I watched it drive slowly away. To my great satisfaction, I saw our sinister observer secure a passing hansom and set off in pursuit of the four-wheeler and disappear in the direction of Marylebone Road. I rushed upstairs and, grabbing my hat and stick, with scant ceremony hustled Miss Winsett down and into a hansom that had just discharged its fare close by. I kept a wary eye out, but by the time we had reached the City, I was confident that no one was on our trail, and then did my best to take my pretty companion's mind off of her troubles.

An hour later we stopped at a pleasant villa in a tree-lined avenue between Lewisham and Lee. Mrs. Footer was a blue-eyed fluffy-haired woman of similar age to her visitor, and expressed delight at the prospect of company while her husband was far from home.

She ushered us in, complaining that time hung heavily on her hands, although my professional eye told me that it would not be many months before she would have more than enough to keep her busy. I adjudged her to be sensible and level-headed, so staying only long enough to repeat in her presence the instructions issued by Holmes, I left the two old friends together. I made my way back to Baker Street, taking the train from Lewisham to Charing Cross, thence on by cab.

I arrived to find Holmes in his old blue dressing-gown, ensconced in his deep armchair, the air thick with smoke from the old and oily clay pipe that he favoured when mulling over a problem. On my entrance he glanced up, laying his pipe to one side.

"The lady is safely hidden?"

"As far as I can be sure," I nodded. "I saw no signs of us being followed, and Mrs. Footer seems a reliable woman with no overt curiosity. I seated myself opposite him. "How went it with you?"

He threw back his head and laughed aloud. "Oh, Watson, would that you had been with me! I led our man a fine dance, As soon as I was sure I had him on my tail, I told the driver I had changed my mind and wished to go to Waterloo. Once there I said I meant Charing Cross, so with much grumbling about women who did not know what they meant he crossed the river again. Fortunately the Strand was in its usual state of congestion, and I seized the chance to abandon the cab in the confusion. Giving the driver a sovereign, I told him to continue to Charing Cross Station and wait there five minutes before going about his business. Then, concealing myself in a doorway near the Savoy, I watched my pursuer go by. It only remained for me to return here where I have spent the past hour trying to make some sense of this business."

"Do you think Harper will make his way back here when he realises he has been fooled?"

My friend shrugged. "I care not so long as Miss Winsett is out of his reach. What do you make of it?"

All the way back from Lewisham I had been cudgelling my brains for an explanation, but to little avail. Now, with Holmes's keen eye transfixing me, I realised how fruitless had been my cogitations and I gave a sigh of exasperation.

"Well," I began cautiously, "I can only surmise that our pretty client is in possession of some information that is important enough for the fellow to trail her to our doorstep,"

"Or he thinks she has," Holmes put in.

"True," I agreed. "Is it possible that she has not told us everything? Is she concealing something?"

"I believe she has told us the truth in so far as she knows it, but we must not overlook the possibility that she has omitted some detail, the significance of which she is not aware. However, in my view it all revolves around this." He reached out to tap the ivory box left behind by the lady

179

and which still reposed on the table. "Find the reason for its being delivered to the cottage and we have one end of the thread."

"And how are we to do that?" I asked doubtfully.

"Why, the answer must lie at Bickstone, so it is to there we must go."

He broke off and turned his head, frowning at the sounds of loud voices followed by a heavy tread on the stairs. "Stand by, Watson," he growled.

"This may be our Mr. Harper."

I had but half-risen from my chair when the door burst open to reveal the figure of a youngish sun-tanned man thrusting his way past an outraged and protesting Mrs. Hudson. It was certainly not the villainous-looking Harper and I strode forward to confront him.

"Who the devil are you?" I demanded. "What is the meaning of this intrusion?"

The man stared wildly around the room. "Mr. Sherlock Holmes?" he cried. "Which of you is he?"

"I am Sherlock Holmes," said my friend sternly. He had not moved from his chair. "By what right do you burst in on me so rudely? Have a care, sir! I am not to be trifled with."

"Mr. Holmes, hear me, I beseech you!" said the man urgently. "I have come seven-thousand miles, and I believe only you can avert a terrible wrong and help to bring a vicious killer to his just punishment."

"I am a busy man," Holmes replied. "However, I will spare you five minutes to make your point, then I shall decide whether to hear more or advise you to take your problem elsewhere, Mr. – ?"

"Carmody. Miles Carmody. I have no friends in London, nor indeed in England, and knowing your reputation, I have come to plead with you. It is over four weeks since I left South Africa, and I may yet be too late."

At the mention of South Africa, Holmes showed a flicker of interest and he waved our importunate caller to a chair. "Very well, Mr. Miles Carmody," he said. "You have five minutes of my attention. Thank you, Mrs. Hudson, you are not to blame."

Muttering her indignation, our landlady retreated to the nether regions, leaving our agitated visitor facing Holmes across the hearth-rug.

I took my seat and studied him closely. I saw a well-set-up man of some thirty years with the deeply bronzed features of one who has spent decades in the tropics and whose clear eyes were accustomed to gazing out over vast distances. His clothes, although well-made and expensive, were obviously of colonial cut, and his accent had that peculiar twang that was some way between Cockney and North American.

"Well, sir," snapped Holmes. "Time passes, so please state your business."

180

Miles Carmody took a breath, then he plunged into his story, speaking rapidly as though afraid he would be dismissed before he had finished. I placed my notebook on my knee to make those notes which my friend averred were of so much value to him, but which in reality served me better when I came to chronicle his achievements.

Chapter III – Death in the Veld

"As I said, Mr. Holmes, my name is Miles Carmody," the man began. "Most of my life has been spent in South Africa, chiefly in Natal. I have been a hunter and a prospector, and Lady Luck has enabled me to acquire a not-inconsiderable fortune – this in association with a very close friend." He leaned forward, fastening his gaze firmly on Holmes. "Tell me, sir, does the name Listel mean anything to you?"

I watched my friend's face, but it remained impassive. "I have heard it mentioned," he replied. "Proceed, I pray you."

Carmody's expression darkened, then he recovered to go on with his story.

"My associate was Alistair Listel, the son of Sir Frederick Listel who, in addition to his own African interests, owned a modest estate not far from Bromley, which I believe is in Kent. Two years ago Alistair went up-country, having heard of a promising find of diamonds up in the Drakensberg. He never returned from that safari and has not been seen since."

"He went alone?" asked Holmes. "No guides or porters?"

"He intended to pick them up in Ladysmith. I had planned to accompany him but went down with a bout of malaria. Alistair decided to push on and assemble our party in Ladysmith, and I was to follow as soon as I was strong enough to do so. He took with him his servant, William Knowles, and an old Kaffir tracker named Ulombo. It was two weeks ere I was fit enough to travel, and then I set off with a party of settlers who were heading for the Orange Free State. It was a slow trek, as you may imagine, and I fully expected to find Listel waiting impatiently for me at Ladysmith. Imagine my consternation when told that he had never reached the town and nothing had been heard of him!"

By now Holmes was showing a keen interest in Carmody's story, and his former impatience had completely evaporated.

"You intrigue me, Mr. Miles Carmody," he said. "Forgive my earlier ill humour and continue at your own pace. Did you follow the same route as your partner would have done?"

"Almost, but with one deviation: Old Jan Pienaar, the trek master, wished to visit a relation some ten miles west of Colenso, so we made a loop across the veld. I follow your train of thought, Mr. Holmes, and my own reasoning was on the same lines: Had any misfortune befallen Listel, we might have come across him on the way, unless it was on the stretch we had by-passed. We left the trail about seven miles short of Colenso and rejoined it some nine miles above."

"So you decided to search that section?"

"That was my intention," Carmody said in a sombre tone. "I set out at first light the next morning with a spare pony, and had covered but five miles when my attention was attracted to a horde of vultures circling the sky off to my right. Fearing the worst, I galloped off and, about a furlong into the scrub, I came upon Listel's servant Knowles lying under a thorn bush. He was near to death and indeed, would have expired within hours had I not chanced upon him. He was in a parlous state, having been beaten and stabbed several times, and his right leg was broken. From his appearance, I knew he had been without food or water for several days. I did what I could for him, and by some miracle the brave fellow recovered sufficiently to give me the gist of what had happened. It was a ghastly story, even the little he was able to tell before lapsing into delirium, and as soon as the heat had gone from the day, I slung across my spare mount and got him back to Ladysmith where he could be cared for properly. Two days later he was able to tell me the full story, and when I heard it my blood boiled." He stopped and clenched his fists, too affected to go on.

"A brandy, Mr. Carmody?" asked Holmes. "Or perhaps a cup of tea?"

"Tea will be fine. I am not a day-time drinker, despite what you may have heard about we rough Colonials."

I summoned Mrs. Hudson and requested a tray. Then, while we waited, we all charged our pipes, allowing our visitor to compose himself.

"I'm afraid I have been remiss, sir," said Holmes from behind a blue haze. "This gentleman is my good friend Dr. Watson, without whom I would be lost. He serves to keep my feet firmly on the ground."

Carmody and I exchanged nods while I poured the tea, and once settled my companion urged our caller to resume his narrative.

"It transpired," said the latter, "that soon after leaving Colenso, Listel's small party had been set upon by a marauding band of Basutos. The Kaffir guide had been killed and Listel and Knowles carried off, for what reason never became clear. After three days travelling the band split into two parties, Knowles being taken by one half and his master by the other. That party that had Knowles used him as a slave, meting out vicious punishments for no reason and giving him barely enough food to keep body and soul together."

"But he escaped?" I put in eagerly. "Or was he just turned loose?"

"He escaped," said Carmody, a note of respect in his voice. "In spite of his wretched state, he retained enough strength to creep away when the gang of ruffians were all drunk on that beastly beer they brew, He had no idea where he was or how long had elapsed since his capture, his sole aim being to get away. Some instinct must have led him in the right direction, but by ill-luck he fell into a gully, thus breaking his leg. He had resigned himself to death when I came upon him, and but for that chance would not have survived another night. What made the whole business more terrible was the fact that Knowles was of the firm belief that one of the raiding party was a white man."

"Great Heavens above!" I cried. "Was it true?"

"True enough," said the South African bitterly. "My inquiries turned up the fact that a renegade soldier who had been dishonourably discharged for looting and ill-treatment of the Kaffirs had taken to the bush and assembled a group of natives to prey on travellers who were weaker than themselves. However, once Knowles was out of danger, I organized patrols to search for Listel and bring these brutes to justice. Although we did catch some of the gang, it was not those who had taken my partner. Knowles' evidence was enough to hang those we caught, but nothing could be got from them about the remainder, except that the renegade white man had abandoned them. He was never heard of again, and it was the general belief that he had either perished in the bush or had got away from the country undetected. Gentlemen, I swear to you that should I ever meet up with Samuel Harper, I shall strangle him with my bare hands!"

For once I saw Sherlock Holmes caught off balance. His dark eyebrows shot up and his mouth dropped open while I nearly fell from my chair in amazement. I was rendered speechless, but before I could order my whirling brain Holmes had recovered and resumed his habitual expression of austere attention.

"This matter becomes more interesting by the minute," he murmured. "I think I am ahead of you, Mr. Miles Carmody. You are here in pursuit of this despicable renegade whom you know as Samuel Harper. I am right, am I not?"

"Indeed you are, sir, but you have not heard what put me on his trail."

"Then I beg of you, tell me more."

Carmody continued, his voice hard and bitter as he took up his story again. "Once I had done all that could be done, I returned to Durban, having lost all enthusiasm for my original project. Knowles, fully recovered, willingly entered my service and it was our unhappy duty to tell Sir Frederick the details of events leading up to the sad fate of his only child. He took it hard and aged ten years in as many weeks. I gave him what comfort I could, but from then on he was a broken man."

"He lived in Natal, then?" Holmes interjected.

"Not exactly. He had divided his time equally between his estate in England and his business interests in South Africa, but fallowing the death of Alistair, he had no inclination to return to the old country. In the ensuing months he and I became very close, so much so that I believed he came to look on me as a substitute for his dead son, and I learned a lot about his family circumstances. With Alistair's death, the heir to the baronetcy was Sir Frederick's younger brother Charles. They had been estranged for upwards of thirty years, having quarrelled bitterly over the woman who became Alistair's mother. They had both paid her court, but Frederick had won her, and from then on they had neither met nor communicated in any way. All Alistair's adult life had been spent in Natal, and I am not even sure that he knew that his uncle existed.

"I hinted to Sir Frederick that in the circumstances it seemed absurd that this feud should continue, and one day he confided to me that he would instruct his solicitors to attempt a reconciliation." He paused dramatically. "Mr. Holmes, that was never to be, for within days of this news, he was foully done to death in an alley-way in Durban."

"Good God!" I cried. "What a terrible coincidence. Father and son both murdered within months of each other!"

Miles Carmody's mouth was set in a grim line. "Coincidence, Doctor? So I believed then, but I no longer think so, and neither will you when you hear of the subsequent events."

Holmes rubbed his hands. "This is interesting indeed," he said. "I pray you, sir, do not keep us in suspense."

"As I related," our visitor went on, "I had retained Knowles in my service, and a week after Sir Frederick's murder he came to me in a state of extreme agitation. He had been shopping in town and stopping for a drink in a bar. He had seen a man with a hunting rifle that Knowles swore was Alistair's. The man had vanished before Knowles could accost him, and he had hurried to me with the story. I questioned him closely but he was adamant, saying he had handled the weapon often enough to know its every line and contour. There was no trace of the man in town, but we did find out from the bar owner that his name was Hartley and he came in from time to time. I used every means at my disposal and a lot of money besides to get a line on him, but to no avail."

"How long ago was this?" Holmes asked.

"A year or more, and as time passed my hopes diminished. Then last February I was in Pietermaritzburg on business when Hartley's name cropped up. It seemed he had been disposing of an inordinate amount of gold and diamonds, to an extent that forced the close circle of dealers to buy them for fear of the market collapsing. I need not tell you, gentlemen, that when my inquiries indicated he had headed back to Durban, I dropped everything and set off in hot pursuit. Alas, once more I lost him, and although he was known to have been in the town, to all intents and purposes he had dropped out of sight."

"So you have never actually set eyes on him?" said Holmes. "You could have passed him by in the street without recognizing him?"

"That is so, although I have had some very good descriptions of him, and Knowles certainly knows him."

"Then what brought you to England and to me?"

"That came about by a flash of inspiration on the part of Knowles. He had scraped an acquaintance with a clerk in the Union Steamship office, and by a little judicious bribery, Knowles had been able to get a sight of the passages booked over the last month."

"And Hartley's name was there!" I cried, but Carmody shook his head.

"No, Dr. Watson, it was not, but another name was. There was a cabin booked on the *Trojan* in the name of *Sir Alistair Listel!*"

Our visitor paused to see the effect of his announcement on us. On my part, for the second time in the space of half-an-hour I was dumbfounded.

I looked desperately at Holmes, but he had his head laid back and his eyes closed, a faint smile playing around the corners of his mouth.

"Do you not see?" said Carmody eagerly. "An impostor on his way to England to claim the Listel estates and title!"

"Possibly," murmured my colleague. "On the other hand, could it be that Alistair Listel had not perished as you believed?"

"Balderdash, and you know it!" exploded the South African, "Why would he conceal himself from both his father and me if he were still alive? Even had he escaped his captors after his father's murder, why not proclaim himself?"

"I could advance several reasons," Holmes said. "However, your theory of an impostor is the most tenable, so we will proceed on those lines. I assume you set off hot-foot after this putative Sir Alistair?"

"Not immediately," Carmody admitted. "I was obliged to settle my affairs and could obtain no passage to England until the Natal liner *Limpopo* sailed twelve days later. In the meantime Knowles – bright fellow that he is – had continued his perusal of the sailing lists and by mistake had picked up one for 1881, and whose name do you think he came across?"

"Samuel Harper's," Holmes replied instantly.

185

"You are right, sir." Carmody sounded disappointed that his bombshell had proved a damp squib. "August '81 – an open berth for Samuel Harper, seven guineas. I was convinced that there was a connection between Harper and the man calling himself Alistair Listel whom I believed to be Hartley, and by Jove, I was right!" Holmes remained silent and presently our visitor continued.

"Knowles and I left Durban on the *Limpopo*, but we were nearly two weeks behind our quarry when we landed, and I at once despatched Knowles to this Bickstone Place to get the lie of the land. Remember, it was he who could identify Hartley positively, and I deemed it wiser to ascertain that he in fact meant to go ahead with the imposture. I took rooms in the Brecon Hotel, just off Chancery Lane, receiving daily reports from Knowles proving that both Harper and Hartley were in the vicinity of Bickstone, Harper in fact being employed as a gamekeeper by Sir Charles."

Holmes gave a puzzled frown. "Why have you come to me if you know this much?" he said. "Surely you are in a position to refute any claim by Hartley to be Sir Frederick's son and heir? Knowles was Listel's personal servant and can identify Harper as the renegade who attacked him and Listel, so what do you want of me?"

"The situation has changed," Carmody replied. "Knowles has been sending me daily intelligence of his observations, and even when there was nothing to report he would still telegraph. Now I am worried, for I have had no word from him since Tuesday and I fear for his safety. I hesitate to reveal my presence for obvious reasons. Therefore I seek your aid and advice. Help me, Mr. Holmes, I beg of you. You may set your fee and I will gladly meet it twice over. See?" He took from his pocket a leather purse and poured a shower of bright new sovereigns on to the low table beside him. Despite my friend's austere nature he had a healthy respect for money, having in the past known the want of it. At the same time, it would not influence him to engage in a case that held no interest for him, although he had no reservations about accepting what he regarded as his just dues.

"My charges, Mr. Carmody, are determined by the intricacies and dangers of any matter to which I apply myself," he said. "Put your money away and we will come to an equitable arrangement on the successful resolution of your problem." He spoke to me over his shoulder. "Be a good chap, Watson, and see if our watchdog has returned." I went to the window and squinted through the crack in the curtains to scan the street below.

"All clear, Holmes," I reported, resuming my seat. "He must have given up for the time being."

"Good." Holmes turned back to the South African. "Your case, sir, is a complex one, not least because it impinges on another matter that has been brought to my attention. I must ask you one or two questions and I expect straight answers."

"I have nothing to hide, Mr. Sherlock Holmes. I have been open with you thus far and shall continue to be so. Ask away and I will answer frankly."

"Then tell me, Mr. Carmody," said my companion, fixing his sharp eyes on the other's face, "do you know or have you heard of a Miss Celia Winsett?"

Miles Carmody shook his head blankly. "No. The name means nothing to me whatsoever. Should it? Who is she?"

"She is a very attractive young person in her middle-twenties with brown hair, grey eyes, and a forceful personality."

"She sounds most delightful, Mr. Holmes, but no, I have no acquaintances at all in England. I am sure I would recall such a charming young lady had I the good fortune to meet her."

Holmes got to his feet and went over to the dining table where, from under the tea-cosy, he produced the ivory box left by Kiss Winsett. He whipped round with it in the palm of his hand and thrust it under the eyes of the startled Carmody.

"And this, sir: Does this mean anything to you?"

Chapter IV – Bickstone Lodge

Miles Carmody's features took on an ashen hue and his eyes bulged from his head. He stared at the object lying in Holmes's palm as though mesmerised. After some seconds he looked up at the thin face looming over him and his expression changed to one of furious anger. He would have stood up, but Holmes restrained him with a sinewy hand planted firmly in the middle of the chest. Carmody struggled vainly for a few seconds, then he spoke in a harsh grating voice.

"How came you by that?" he almost snarled. "What is it doing in your possession? I demand to know what game you're playing!"

"Then you do recognize it?" said Holmes quietly. "Fear not, I shall conceal nothing from you if you will but tell me what it is and from whence it came. Trust me, sir, I beg you."

For a time Carmody's eyes alternated between the ivory box and my friend's face. Then his anger died away to be replaced by an expression of sadness.

"It seems that for the moment I must trust you, Mr. Holmes," he said in a jerky voice. "I believe you to be an honourable man – but I warn you, I am a bad man to cross."

"I do not take kindly to threats," replied Holmes, a hint of steel in his voice. "However, I will make allowances for the shock I have sprung on you and assure you of my continued good will. Come now, tell me about this curious artefact and why it gives you so much concern."

Still retaining the box in his hand, he sat down and waited for the other man to speak, watching him closely the while.

"That box," said Carmody in a low strained voice, "I last saw two years ago in the possession of Alistair Listel. It was given to him by an old Zulu whom Listel had saved from slavers. It still goes on, you know," he added, and Holmes nodded for him to continue.

"I believe the native used it to carry a magic charm," went on the South African. "Of course, it was only the box he gave to Listel, not the charm. There is quite a trick in getting it open."

"So I discovered," said Holmes with a smile.

"Was there anything inside it?"

Without comment Holmes passed him the scrap of stained paper.

"Well, Mr. Carmody?" he said after a few seconds.

"I think this may have been written by Knowles," said Carmody, his face set in grim lines. "How the box came into his hands I can only surmise, for I am certain he did not have it before." His voice grew animated. "Then my friend and partner may still be alive!"

"Do not pin your hopes on it," said Holmes bleakly. "It could have been taken from him at the time of his kidnapping and Knowles recovered it from – " He stopped and raised an eyebrow.

"Harper!" cried the other. "Knowles has found Harper! By God, I have him at last!" He sprang to his feet to stride wildly around the room, his eyes blazing. "He must be at Bickstone, so there is no time to be lost if we are to apprehend him." He came to a halt in front of Holmes, frowning darkly. "You have still not explained how the box came into your possession, Mr. Holmes. Has Knowles been in touch with you?"

"No. I had not heard the name until it came from your lips. If you will but calm yourself and sit down, I'll redeem my promise to tell you as much as I'm able. Ah, that's better," Holmes took three cigars from the coal scuttle and handed one each to Carmody and me before settling back in his chair with a contemplative expression.

"I find that your business runs parallel to that of another client," he began. "Averse as I am to discussing the confidential matters of another, I feel that in this case I'm justified in doing so in the interests of you both." He blew a smoke ring from his cigar and watched it dissolve above his

188

head. Then, choosing his words carefully, he outlined the story told earlier by Miss Celia Winsett and the steps we had taken to ensure her continued safety. Carmody looked grim when he heard Samuel Harper's name and his involvement, but he remained silent until Holmes had completed his story.

"Where is this courageous lady now?" he asked, but Holmes shook his head.

"Only the good Doctor and myself know that, and for the present it must remain so. As for Knowles, I believe he may by now be beyond human aid."

"You mean – ?"

"I fear such to be the case. By your account, we're dealing with desperate and ruthless men, and with at least two murders to their credit, they wouldn't stop at one more to achieve their ends. All the same, Watson and I will proceed immediately to Bickstone, for that is where it all pivots."

"I shall come with you," said Carmody. "I can identify Harper, and most probably Hartley also."

"No, that will not be wise." Holmes shook his head. "As you can recognize them, so can they you. Both Watson and I know Harper, but it remains to be established if he and John Hartley are actually in league. My advice to you, Mr. Miles Carmody, is that you go back to your hotel and await the outcome of our investigations at Bickstone."

"You want me to sit around in idleness, not knowing what's going on?"

"For the moment, yes," Holmes replied firmly. You have sought my help, and I must be allowed to follow my own methods. Should your presence be necessary, I need to know where I may find without undue delay."

Our client's mouth was set in rebellious lines. Then, with a deep sigh, he spread his hands in resignation. "As you say, Mr. Holmes, I have come to you for aid and I would be foolish not to abide by your advice, When may I expect to hear from you?"

"I shall telegraph you twice daily," said Holmes. "At ten o'clock in the morning and at three in the afternoon. Any instructions from me must be obeyed to the letter, and should you not hear from Watson or myself on two successive occasions, you will then contact Scotland Yard and tell them the whole story, My name will ensure the attention of one of the leading inspectors – Gregson, Lestrade, or Peter Jones, Now, Dr. Watson and I will set off for Bickstone, but you, Mr. Carmody, will wait here until darkness falls before leaving as unobtrusively as possible. With luck your visit here isn't known, and we will hope to keep it so. Come, Watson – the game's afoot!"

189

Within twenty minutes we were on our way to catch our train to Bromley, the nearest station to Bickstone. From my association with Holmes, I had become used to these sudden journeys and always kept a Gladstone bag ready-packed for any such eventuality. The evening was mild, but I wore my ulster and was comforted by the drag of my old service revolver tugging against my right-hand pocket. I knew that Holmes had his small pocket pistol, and we both had the weighted sticks that had served us so well on more than one occasion.

"Do you believe Knowles to be dead?" I asked as we rattled down the City road.

"I fear so," replied my companion, rousing himself from his reverie. "If he had come on the trail of Hartley and had been recognized, I would not give a pinch of snuff for his chances. I would like to be proved wrong, but it would be against all reason."

"But what is Miss Winsett's part in it? I see no connection between her and the deaths of the Listels. And why was the box left with her?"

"That was purely fortuitous," said Holmes. "My present theory is that Harper stole it from the younger Listel at the time of his capture and presumed murder. By some means Knowles obtained possession of it but, being unable to get away undetected and being at his last gasp, he thrust it through the letter-box of the cottage."

"What would that achieve?" I objected. "The lady could know nothing of its significance and may well have retained it as an amusing ornament."

"Knowles was determined that anything was better than letting Harper recover it. The fact that Miss Winsett brought it to us was sheer chance that stemmed from her frightening experiences and Harper's aggressive and surly attitude towards her."

I pondered on this for the rest of our journey to London Bridge, referring to the notes I had made of our interviews with Miss Winsett and Miles Carmody. Once installed in our carriage, Holmes rested his back against the cushion, the fingers of his right hand drumming idly on his tweed-clad knee and a curved cherry-wood pipe drooping from his mouth. We had passed through the sooty cramped dwellings and reeking factories of Bermondsey before he spoke, breaking into my train of thought as though I uttered them aloud.

"Of course I distrust coincidences, Watson" he said. "All the same, I have never denied their existence, and the fact that Miss Winsett and Mr. Carmody should appear in our rooms within a few hours of one another is surely coincidence."

"You believe their stories, then?"

190

"Until I hear anything to change my opinion. The fact that Harper should trail the lady to London points to his having at least a suspicion that Knowles could have communicated with her in some way."

"But he wasn't certain enough to make a direct approach to her."

Holmes gave an impatient grunt, "If all we have been told is true, he is probably under orders from Hartley to draw the minimum of attention to themselves – especially if they are unaware that Carmody is in the country."

"'If all we have been told is true'?" I echoed, but Holmes had withdrawn into himself, and not another word did I have from him until the train deposited us at Bromley.

"What now?" I asked as we stood on the station forecourt.

"Firstly we take rooms at yonder inn." He pointed with his stick at a modest building almost facing the station. "Then we will seek out Sir Charles Listel. I fancy a direct approach will best serve our ends. I think it too soon for any impostor to have made a move, bearing in mind the uncertainty surrounding Knowles's actions."

"To be quite honest, I fail to see that such a ploy succeeding," I said dubiously. "Sir Charles is not going to accept such a proposition without the most exhaustive inquiries. Carmody can vouch that Hartley is an impostor, and even had Carmody not come to England, investigations in Natal would reveal the truth."

Holmes shot me a keen glance. "Your perspicacity does you credit, my dear Watson!" he said. "If your reasoning is correct, and I have no quarrel with it, then we must fish in deeper waters." He pushed open the door of the inn and we found ourselves in a clean but unpretentious bar lounge.

"Good evening, gentlemen. What is your pleasure?"

The speaker was a huge ruddy-faced man who looked up from the newspaper spread before him. Well over six feet in height, he had shoulders as wide as the proverbial barn door, and though now running to fat, I saw him as the archetypal front row forward, barging his way to the try line and shrugging off the opposition by sheer weight and speed.

"A glass of beer each for my friend and myself." Holmes leaned against the bar. "Also rooms for us both, if you have them."

"No problem there, sir." Two tankards of nut-brown ale were placed before us. "Will you be staying long?"

"It depends on how long our business takes," said my companion, his tone carefully non-committal.

"You'll be down from London about this here, then?" A massive forefinger stabbed at the newspaper. "Terrible thing, to be sure."

191

He turned the paper towards us and we both stared at the place indicated. It was a bare report in the stop press column of a man's body found partly concealed in a copse on the outskirts of Bickstone Village. The item was but half-a-dozen lines long and gave no other details, other than it had been found by a man walking his dog.

"How long since you had this paper?" Holmes demanded sharply of the landlord, for such I presumed him to be.

"Why, sir, not above three minutes afore you gents walked in," the man replied. "Old Joe Collins, him as collects 'em off the train, he always drops one in for me afore he takes 'em round the town." He leaned forward conspiratorially. "I see, sir," he whispered huskily. "No need to say more, and Bert Davis knows how to keep mum. Have to in this trade. Now, gents, your rooms."

The accommodation was simple but clean, and no sooner had Davis's footsteps taken him back to the bar than Holmes slipped into my room, shutting the door behind him.

"What do you make of it?"

"That the unknown victim is probably Knowles." My colleague nodded and I went on thoughtfully. "That newspaper must have come on the same train as did we. By the smudging of the print, I deduce that it was a very late item and the papers were bundled up hot from the press. We must have been on the train before the news was on the streets."

"My own reasoning precisely, but does it aid us?"

"Only by confirming your theory that Knowles has been done away with, if indeed it is he."

Holmes nodded and gave a wry smile. "I know what you're thinking, old chap. I'm ignoring my own precepts and speculating without solid facts, and by Jove, you are right! All the same, I'm keeping an open mind until I have a firmer foundation on which to work." He became his usual brisk self. "Come, let us introduce ourselves to Sir Charles Listel and see what transpires."

A word with Davis procured for us the use of a mud-stained trap and a bored-looking nag. Holmes took the reins and we trotted steadily through the lanes in the direction indicated by the landlord. With the trees now in full leaf and the angle of the sun casting dappled shadows across our path, a more tranquil scene would be hard to imagine, yet my companion, his teeth clamped firmly on the stem of his pipe, seemed oblivious to his surroundings. It wasn't until we had passed through the stone pillars marking the entrance to the Bickstone Lodge estate that he spoke.

"A more pleasing aspect than the Manor House at Stoke Moran, Watson?" he remarked as the building came into our view, and indeed, his comment had my heartfelt agreement.

The house was a square solid edifice, severely functional yet clean-lined with none of the extravagant ornamentation seen in so many of our country houses, the builder having resisted any temptation to add towers and turrets or any other flamboyant features. The main entrance was centrally placed with four large windows on either side, while the two upper storeys were geometric in their precision under a slated roof with dormer windows, giving on to what I took to be the servants' quarters.

With its mellow brickwork and freshly painted woodwork, the place had a look of permanence and stability that seemed timeless.

We approached the door by a broad flight of steps and Holmes applied himself to the bell-pull, being rewarded by a faint peal from within. The door was shortly opened by an elderly butler to whom Holmes presented his card and asked to see Sir Charles Listel on urgent and confidential business. We were shown into a spacious hall hung with pictures and trophies from Africa, but were not left long to admire them.

"Sir Charles will see you in the smoking room," announced the aged retainer. "This way please, gentlemen."

In the smoking room, a well set-up man was standing in front of a screened fireplace, and he advanced to greet us with hand outstretched.

"Mr. Sherlock Holmes, you are indeed welcome!" he said warmly. "And this can only be Dr. Watson – I've seen you mentioned in the newspapers in connection with Mr. Holmes's investigations. Again welcome!"

His grip was firm and dry, and I found myself looking into a strong-featured face that met my gaze frankly and openly. His hair was thick and dark with a sprinkling of grey, as was the small neatly trimmed beard and moustache. His eyes were on a level with my own, and when he smiled, it was to reveal a set of strong white teeth.

"Be seated, gentlemen." He waved us to deep leather armchairs. "I know of you by repute, but little thought I should have the privilege of meeting you. How may I be of assistance?" He came forward with a box of Havana's, and Holmes directed his whole attention to ensuring that his cigar was burning evenly before he spoke.

"Sir Charles, this is a delicate matter, and I fear that what I have to say may prove painful to you. For that I apologise in advance. However, certain information has been laid before me which cannot be ignored and which it is my duty to pass on to you."

"A moment, Mr. Holmes," the baronet interjected. "Is this likely to take long? Ah, I see by your expression that it will. I am about to dine and would take as a favour if you would join me. My housekeeper is liable to take umbrage if her routine is disturbed."

I was gratified that Holmes accepted the offer. We had eaten only cold meats during the day, and although I had known my colleague to go days on end with no more than a few sips of water, my own constitution demanded regular sustenance if it was to function properly.

Our host rang for the butler and gave the necessary instructions, then took his place in a chair facing us while he waited for an explanation of our presence.

"Do you know a Miss Celia Winsett?" Holmes asked abruptly.

Sir Charles was taken aback by this sudden question and gave a puzzled frown.

"I am acquainted with the lady," he replied. "It would be an exaggeration to claim that I know her. She is the tenant of one of my cottages, but that was arranged through a business friend. I understand she is in the employment of a well-known publishing house and she has impeccable references. I have never met her formally, although we exchange civilities should we pass in the village. I trust I have given her no offence or cause for complaint."

"On the contrary, sir, she speaks most highly of you. Unfortunately she has recently had some disturbing experiences and was driven to me for advice." Holmes went on to relate the story told by Miss Winsett, omitting to say that the man Harper had apparently followed her to London that very morning and making no reference to the steps we had taken to protect her. As he finished Sir Charles gave an exclamation of annoyance.

"This is monstrous!" he cried, "I shall convey my personal apologies to the young lady and rest assured that Harper will account for his attitude."

"Miss Winsett has decided to remain in London for the present," said Holmes. "I take it you have no clue as to what lies behind these strange events?"

The baronet shook his head, but before he could speak the butler came in to announce that dinner was served and we were conducted to a small dining room in which the lamps were already lit.

No more was said until we were seated at a circular dining table and the first course had been place before us by a pretty maid, and we were left to ourselves.

"Now, Mr. Holmes, you asked if I could account for the strange events that have befallen Miss Winsett, and I can truthfully answer no."

"This ivory box means nothing to you?"

"Could it be a token from a bashful suitor?"

"Bloodstained and with a cryptic message enclosed?" Holmes asked ironically. "Pardon me if I do not treat your suggestion seriously, but I believe the lady's problems arise from a matter much closer to you."

"To me?" Sir Charles looked incredulous. "You are surely mistaken in that. I have already told you that my acquaintance with her is of the slightest."

"Nevertheless, it is so and brings me to my previous statement that what I have to say may be painful to you."

The maid entered to remove our dishes and replace them with others. Holmes resumed when the door closed on her.

"It concerns your late brother and his son."

Our host blanched and his knife and fork fell on to his plate with a clatter. For several seconds he seemed paralysed with shock. Then he recovered to give Holmes a perplexed and angry look.

"Mr. Holmes," he said slowly, "I trust I am a tolerant and reasonable man, but I find your manner in the worst possible taste. Are you hinting that there was some connection between my poor dead brother and this lady? Confound you, sir, I demand an immediate explanation!"

My friend sighed. "And you shall have it, Sir Charles. I have already apologised and I have no wish to reopen old wounds. I hold the view that crime should not be allowed to go unpunished, and as both of your kinsmen were apparently murdered. I am sure you feel the same way."

"Indeed I do!" cried the baronet. "But surely the answer must lie in Africa and not here?"

"We shall see. May I go on? I understand there was a coolness between yourself and the late Sir Frederick. Is that not so?"

"It is, and God forgive me the fault was mine alone." Sir Charles plucked at his beard in considerable agitation, his eyes sad.

"Would it grieve you to speak of it?"

"Can you suppose otherwise?" said the other bitterly. "What good can come of it now?"

"It may lead to the murderers being brought to justice," said Holmes sternly. "I am on their trail, and I believe I already have one of them under my hand. I need more facts, and only I can judge what is relevant and what is not. Will you speak, sir?"

Sir Charles appeared to ruminate, and when the maid came to change our dishes, he dismissed he curtly with orders that he was not to be disturbed until he rang.

"Yes, Mr. Holmes, if it will serve to bring those brutal miscreants to retribution I will speak, much as it pains me to do so. Come, gentlemen. Let us repair to the smoking room. It is a long story." He threw down his napkin and opened the door for us to pass through.

Chapter V – A Family Feud

We were settled in the deep chairs, a decanter of brandy and a box of the finest Havana cigars on a table within our reach, when Sir Charles Listel commenced to talk of the events that led up to the quarrel with his brother. At first his voice was low and hesitant, but soon it seemed that he was finding some relief in speaking of it and he rapidly gained confidence.

"It all began more than thirty-two years ago," he said reflectively. "I was little more than a boy at the time, some months short of my twentieth birthday. We were a happy family consisting of my father, my older brother Frederick, and myself. The only cloud had been the death of my mother some three years before these lamentable events occurred, although I knew it to be a happy release from her suffering."

"Was this your home?" my colleague interjected.

"Yes. It was built by my grandfather during the Regency and, as you may imagine, it was even more rural than it is now. During my boyhood and youth I saw it grow, but now I fear that ere long it will become no more than a suburb of the octopus London." He sighed. "But to continue . . . ."

"A frequent guest under our roof was a Mr. McNeil and his only daughter Agnes. She was about my age and when we were children, we were as brother and sister. Frederick, four years my senior, treated us with an amused tolerance, but with the passing years I found myself regarding her in a rather different light, and by the time of which I speak I was hopelessly in love with her.

"One weekend Agnes and I were left alone, our fathers and Frederick being closeted together in the study. I found the courage to declare my feelings for her in the hope that they would be reciprocated." He paused and reached out for the decanter to recharge his glass before going on.

"Gentlemen, she laughed at me," he said with intensity. "Oh, not unkindly, but rather as a parent or nurse humouring a child. I began to plead my cause, but she stopped me quickly and took my hand. 'Dear Charles,' said she, 'I beg of you, say no more. I love you dearly, but only as a brother.' And with that she ran from the room, leaving me hurt and bewildered, not able to understand that I had been rejected.

"I went into the garden, miserable and wretched, but soon, with the capacity for self-delusion so often possessed by the young, I told myself that I had been over-hasty, frightening her with my sudden declaration, and decided that all was not lost and that I must proceed more gently. It was at that point that Frederick came upon me and seized my hands to spin me around in a crazy dance.

"'Congratulate me, Brother!' he cried. 'I am the happiest man in the whole world! Agnes and I are to be married!'

"I was thunderstruck, unable speak to from shock. It was though I had been stabbed in the heart, and I could only stare helplessly at Frederick as he prattled on joyously, oblivious to my hurt. 'I have been with our father and Mr. McNeil to discuss the arrangements, and you, dear Charles, are the first to know. Oh, what a party we shall have to announce it to the world!'

"It was then that he saw the expression on my face and looked at me askance. 'Surely you had not entertained hopes in that direction?' he gasped. 'Oh, Charles, Agnes and I have had an understanding this twelve months past, and have but waited until now to make it official. You must have seen it.' He placed his hand on my shoulder but I threw it off, beside myself with rage. I found my voice at last, ranting and raving like a madman. I called him the foulest of names and would not be silenced, until at length he was stung to reply. How long the quarrel went on I do not know, but eventually our father came upon us and I turned my bile upon him. I will not go into details of what I said, but it culminated with my father banishing me from the house. Next morning I went away, never to see my father or brother again."

"Good Lord!" I gasped. "What a tragic story!"

The baronet nodded grimly. "All the Listels suffer from a stiff-necked pride, and none of us would attempt to heal the breach. In spite of all, my father made me a generous allowance, and when he died five years later, he had made provision for me in his will."

"Your pride did not preclude you from accepting his bounty," Holmes observed somewhat maliciously.

"I regarded it as no more than my due," Sir Charles replied, ignoring my colleague's aspersion. "By then I was making my name in the City as a stockbroker, but so bitter was I still that I did not attend my father's funeral. I had heard that Agnes had died in giving birth to a son in South Africa, and that further fuelled my resentment of Frederick. I knew a lot about his affairs, several of my clients having shares in his many companies, and I knew that he spent as much time in Natal as he did here at Bickstone. Over the last ten years, his son had taken an increasing part in their business interests, but Frederick seemed content to stay in Africa for long periods."

"You never met your nephew?" Holmes inquired.

"Never. To the best of my knowledge he was only in England as a child, and that but briefly. However, four or five years ago, at the time of the Zulu Wars, I found my thoughts dwelling for long periods on my brother and his son. Age mellows one, Mr. Holmes, and I saw the futility of bearing a grudge all those years, but fearful of a rebuff, I was reluctant to take the first step," His voice broke. "Now it is too late."

Holmes and I exchanged glances and he gave me a quick nod.

"If it is any consolation to you, Sir Charles," I said gently, "your brother had the same thoughts, but, alas, his murder intervened before he could translate his intentions into deeds."

The baronet bowed his head. "God bless you for telling me that, Dr. Watson. How futile are the words 'It might have been' when it is too late." He suddenly looked up, suspicion lurking behind his eyes. "How came you by such knowledge?" he demanded. "I have been patient over-long with your personal probing into my intimate affairs, and I think I am due an explanation."

"And you shall have one, sir!" cried Holmes. "Answer me but one more question and I shall reveal the purpose of my interest in your affairs."

Sir Charles studied my friend's face, then gave a tight-lipped nod of assent. "Ask away, Mr. Sherlock Holmes," he said. "I know of your high standing in official quarters, and I doubt that this is impertinence on your part."

Holmes inclined his head at the compliment and leaned forward.

"Then tell me this, Sir Charles: Have you any reason to suppose that your nephew did *not* perish at the time of his kidnapping? That he is still alive and consequently the rightful holder of your title and estates?"

Sir Charles Listel stared at us open-mouthed, his face white as chalk. He struggled to rise from his chair before the effort proved too much for him. Then he slumped back as though he had received a mortal blow. At last he found the strength to speak in a cracked and choking voice.

"What say you, sir?" he stuttered, "Who has conceived such a fantastic tale? Have you heard this with your own ears? By God, Mr. Holmes, if I thought it to be so, I would be the first to rejoice that, though my poor brother is no more, his son has somehow survived. I beg of you, if you know such to be the case, tell me now!"

His distress was such that my medical instincts came to the surface and I hurried forward with a glass of brandy which I held to his lips. The glass rattled against his teeth as he took a gulp, but presently the colour returned to his cheeks and he sat upright in his chair.

"Well, sir," he demanded, "what have you to say?"

"Very little for your comfort, Sir Charles," replied my companion quietly. "I know little more of your nephew's fate than has been reported. However, I have received intelligence that a man purporting to be Alistair Listel has arrived in this country from South Africa, but regrettably I have had no opportunity to verify the report. I deemed it advisable to apprise you of events thus far. Crimes have been committed, and I fear that murder has taken place very close to here within the past few hours – and maybe you yourself could be at risk."

Our host had recovered himself and he stood up to look down at us with a steely look in his eyes which was returned by Holmes.

"No more of this circumlocution, Mr. Holmes," he said brusquely. "The time has come for plain speaking, and for you to enlighten me as to the meaning of all this."

"Willingly, Sir Charles." Holmes began to fill his pipe, speaking with great deliberation as he did so. "Much of what I have to say has been told to me by others and does not arise from my own observations. Therefore I cannot yet vouch for its truth. Some three hours after Miss Celia Winsett had brought me her strange story this morning, I had another visitor who told me an equally bizarre tale that seemed to have some connection with the lady's narrative." He applied a light to his pipe and went on, "Tell me, sir, do you know a Mr. Miles Carmody?"

"No, the name means nothing to me."

"What of John Hartley? No? William Knowles?"

"I have heard none of these names," the baronet said curtly. "For the love of Heaven man, can you not string two sentences together without a lot of questions and queries?"

"Questions are the tools of my trade," replied Holmes. "However, I recognize your impatience and will ask no more for the moment." With that he went on to relate clearly and concisely the story we had heard from Carmody, interrupted now and then by exclamations of shock and anger from Sir Charles as the tale unfolded. As my friend finished, our host's complexion had taken on a choleric hue and he was almost incoherent in his rage.

"Are you asking me to believe that my man Harper is responsible for the abduction and death of my nephew?" he stuttered. "That he had the cold-blooded effrontery to come to this country and shelter under my roof with that on his conscience?"

"I am merely repeating what I was told," said Holmes. "I am inclined to wait until my investigations bear some fruit before I take any precipitate steps,"

"Precipitate steps indeed! I will have Harper apprehended this very instant." He looked up sharply. "You spoke of a murder having taken place recently near here. Is that to be laid to Harper's account also? Good God, why are we sitting here while that fiend is at large?"

"He will keep," said Holmes tersely as the furious man paced back and forth. "He will not abscond having ventured so much, and I do not believe he is a principal. Do you know of his movements today?"

"He asked for the day off to attend to some private business. Where he went I do not know, but I assume he has returned by now."

"He was in London this morning – that I do know – and he was very interested in Miss Winsett's movements until Watson and I muddied the trail. More immediately, there is the danger to yourself of which I spoke. Remember the ivory box delivered to Miss Winsett? If Carmody's account is to be accepted, it formerly belonged to your nephew and was last in the possession of his man Knowles. The latter, in fear of his life, passed it on to the lady to prevent it falling into hands of his pursuers, and in the hope that it would foil their plans. If Harper knew that, he would attempt to recover it from her – hence his observation of her."

The baronet ceased his pacing. "If what you say is true, Mr. Holmes, I see little danger to myself. Surely it is in the interests of these villains for me to remain unharmed? Another death in the Listel family must certainly attract comment if nothing more, and that would not be to their advantage."

"That is so, Sir Charles, as far as it goes, but I repeat, all I have related is hearsay, and until I ascertain and sift the facts, I would prefer that you remain on your guard at all times."

"Forewarned is forearmed," the baronet said stoutly. "What do you propose?"

"First of all, I should be interested to hear how it was you came to employ Samuel Harper in the first place," said Holmes, "By all accounts he is a most unsavoury character, even if we believe only Miss Winsett's story of her experiences, which I have no reason to doubt,"

Our host frowned. "I admit I have never found the man particularly attractive, but I have nothing against the way he performs his duties. Never did I suspect him to be as depraved as you say he is. He turned up here about a year back, apparently down and out and begging of the chance to earn a few shillings. This was soon after I had been told of the deaths of my brother and nephew and the fact of my inheritance, which brought me no joy whatsoever. I was in the lowest of spirits and had just come here at the insistence of the estate's solicitors to take possession, although my heart was sad with futile regrets for the past."

He hesitated, then braced himself to continue. "Harper told me he was an old soldier down on his luck and, although he was evasive about his antecedents, I gave him a few odd jobs which he carried out in a satisfactory if sullen manner. Remember, my brother spent an increasingly large part of his time in South Africa and retained few permanent staff here. As I came to terms with my situation, I began to take my responsibilities more seriously and organize the estate to the best advantage."

Once again he paused and fixed us with a stern eye. "Let it be understood, gentlemen, I had become a very wealthy man through my own efforts, and although my succession to the title and estates almost doubled my financial holdings, a very large sum was needed to restore Bickstone to what it had been in my father's time. I think I can boast that I have almost achieved that ambition," he added with satisfaction.

"So you allowed Harper to assume the position he now holds?" Holmes interjected.

"I needed a gamekeeper and he seemed to fill the bill, so why not?"

"Excuse my intrusion, Sir Charles," I put in. "What happens to the estate after you pass on? Have you no heirs?"

"An interesting point, Dr. Watson. My personal fortune is mine to dispose of as I will, but the Bickstone Estate is another matter. Let me explain, but I beg you to respect certain confidences that may not meet with your approval."

"We need only to know of matters affecting this present inquiry," Holmes replied. "Anything else you choose to say will be treated with the utmost discretion by the doctor and myself."

"I wish to make my position quite clear," Sir Charles said. "The Bickstone Estate is entailed and may not be broken up or sold without recourse to complicated legal proceedings, which I do not doubt would only benefit the vultures of the law. The attorneys for the estate believe there to be a distant cousin in line of succession, but have so far been unable to trace him. I understand that should that remain the case, then on my death the title lapses and the estate goes to the Crown. Therefore, great care has been taken to separate my personal fortune from that which has descended to me through recent unhappy events, I have never married but, not having lived the life of a monk, I do have reason to make certain financial provisions for the future. You are both men of the world, so need I say more?"

"I am sure we understand," Holmes nodded.

"Thank you, Mr. Holmes. Now how will you proceed?"

"Nothing more is to be achieved tonight, so Watson and I will return to Bromley. You, Sir Charles, must give no hint that you have been made aware of anything untoward. We are staying at The Green Dragon by Bromley Station, and tomorrow I shall seek information of the man whose body was found today. I shall also attempt to learn what I can of this fellow Hartley whose name has cropped up. On no account must you allow Harper to know that you are in any way suspicious of him, Can you avoid him?"

Sir Charles considered this carefully before answering. "It will be difficult if I am here, but I think I have a solution," he said at last. "I frequently go up to London and spend a couple of nights at my club, so if I depart early in the morning, there is little chance of my running into him. He has a small cottage on the far side of the grounds and seldom approaches the house. He is not liked by the indoor servants, and if I have any instructions for him I usually seek him out. In all honesty, he needs little supervision in his duties."

"Then let that be your course," nodded Holmes. "I shall be in touch with you at your club, which is – ?"

"The New Lyceum, just off Pall Mall."

"I know it," said my companion. He rose to his feet. "Speak to no one of the matter and wait to hear from me. I give my word that your confidences are safe with both Watson and myself."

The baronet himself saw us to the door and out to where our nag was chomping patiently in the nose-bag that I had slipped over his head on our arrival.

It was well past ten o'clock when we reached The Green Dragon. A buzz of conversation came from the tap room, but Bert Davis came through to the lounge at once, leaving a young woman to see to the needs of the bar.

"Back again, gents?" greeted the landlord. "Can I get you anything?"

"Not for me, thank you," said Holmes. "I shall retire immediately, but we would appreciate an early breakfast."

"As early as you like, sir. Will seven o'clock suit?"

"Admirably. Goodnight, Mr. Davis. Coming up?" This last to me.

"I think I shall have a nightcap first and see you in the morning," I replied. "A large Scotch, please landlord, and one for yourself."

Davis lingered over the drinks, obviously willing himself to say something. Eventually he leaned over the bar and spoke in a hoarse whisper.

"Begging your pardon, sir, but I don't think I have your names. Not that I'm curious, mind you, but – "

I moved my head closer to his. "For the moment, Mr. Davis, we must remain *incognito*," I said meaningly, and his brow furrowed. "It is better that no mention is made of our identities or the reason for our presence here. One word in the wrong ear could hamper our investigations, as I am sure you will understand – not that we think you untrustworthy, but for the time being that is how it must be." He nodded and winked but seemed satisfied with my confidence, and twenty minutes later I climbed the stairs, pausing outside Holmes's room. No sound came from within so I took myself off to my much needed rest, falling asleep the moment my head touched the pillow.

Chapter VI – Inspector Arnold

I was awakened by a persistent hammering on my door, and my blurred senses took some little while to remind me where I was.

"Yes, what is it?" I called, sitting up to knuckle the sleep from my eyes.

"Half-past-six, sir." It was the landlord's gruff tones. "Hot water outside and breakfast in half-an-hour." I heard him deliver the same message at the adjacent door, then the creak of the stairs as his bulk returned to the nether regions. I went to collect my jug and on impulse knocked on my friend's door, being answered by a querulous invitation to enter. The room was thick with tobacco smoke and Holmes was sitting on the bed, his knees drawn up under his chin and his oily old clay pipe in his mouth. His coat had been thrown carelessly on to the floor, but otherwise he was fully dressed, even down to his boots, and it was evident that he had spent the night in this attitude.

"Come along!" I cried, flinging open the window to dispel the foul atmosphere. "It was you who demanded an early breakfast, and your shaving water is cooling rapidly."

He stared vacantly at me for several seconds before swinging his legs on to the floor. Then with that sudden change of mood peculiar to him, he gave me a broad grin.

"Then move yourself, man!" he cried. "Let us not keep mine host waiting. Pass me the jug, there's a good fellow,"

I had barely completed my toilet when Holmes came bounding into my room looking as fresh as if he had slept the clock round. As I finished dressing, I told him of the landlord's curiosity regarding our identities and the steps I had taken to avoid a direct answer.

"Capital," he said approvingly. "Nevertheless, I fear our names have become too familiar to the masses to be hidden for long."

"I would point out that our appearances in the press have gone a long way to enhancing your reputation," I reminded him tartly. "You will concede that your services have been much in demand since the Jefferson Hope case was brought to the public's attention. Why, only two years ago you were virtually living from hand-to-mouth, while now – "

"Fair comment, my friend," he laughed. "I'll not deny the truth of it. Come, I find the aroma of frying bacon irresistible, and I would not have the estimable Davis offended by our tardiness."

The morning sun was already warming the streets of the little country town as we made our way towards the police station, Holmes twirling his stick and whistling blithely as though a walk in the spring sunshine was his only concern. Our objective lay at the top of the hill close by the market-place, and I saved my breath to allow me to keep up with my companion's lengthy stride. Inside the station, which was decorated in institutional brown and green, we were confronted by a stolid-looking sergeant seated behind a desk. He looked up from the ledger in which he was writing, his eyes keen as he tried to gauge our relative importance and status. He decided that we merited his respectful attention.

"Good morning, gentlemen," he said in a deep bass voice. "May I be of help?"

"Good morning, Sergeant." Holmes was at his most suave. "We would like to speak to the senior officer in charge."

The sergeant bit the end of his pencil then scratched his head with it. "That'll be Inspector Arnold, sir, what with Chief Inspector Lewis being laid up with a busted leg. Mr. Arnold not being in yet, perhaps you could tell me all about it."

"With all due respect, Sergeant, I can only speak to your inspector," said Holmes firmly. "I am sure you're an excellent officer, but this is a matter of prime importance."

The man behind the desk frowned. "Wait if you will, sir, but Inspector Arnold is a busy man and won't be best pleased if his time is wasted."

"I do not waste anyone's time," retorted Holmes icily. "I need to see your inspector, and see him I will."

"As you wish, sir." The sergeant remained respectful, but his voice held an aggrieved note. "It's just that he likes me to sort the wheat from the chaff, if you take my meaning." Once again he scrutinised us carefully as if to confirm his first assessment of us. "There's a waiting room through here, gents, so you can make yourselves comfortable until the Guv'nor arrives."

We were led along a passage into an austere room furnished with a scrubbed wooden table and several hard wooden chairs.

"What names shall I give, sirs?"

"That too is for the inspectors ears alone," replied Holmes. "I would remind you that it is urgent that we see him at the first opportunity, and I'm sure he will forgive any failure on your part to protect him from a couple of importunate strangers. What's your name, Sergeant? I should like Mr. Arnold to be aware that you did your duty in a polite and respectful manner."

"Mower, sir. Sergeant George Mower. I'll tell him you're here the moment he arrives." He gave us one last look before shutting the door and clumping back to his desk.

We lit our pipes and made the best of the uncomfortable chairs, but a bare five minutes elapsed before the door was again opened by a stocky man in the uniform of an inspector. He paused on the threshold and eyed us curiously. He was beardless but sported a fine flowing moustache and side-whiskers, with sharp intelligent eyes beneath thick bushy brows.

"Good morning, gentlemen," he said presently. "I'm Inspector Arnold. Mower tells me you will speak to no one but myself and refused to give your names or any indication of your business."

"Close the door, please, Inspector," said Holmes in a low voice. "No blame attaches to the sergeant. He acted most properly and, I might add, sensibly"

Arnold stepped into the room, kicking the door to with his heel. He removed his cap and laid it carefully on the table, frowning slightly as he did so.

"Have we met?" he asked in a puzzled tone. "Your face seems familiar, yet I cannot place it."

"You may have seen us in the company of Gregson or Lestrade of Scotland Yard," replied Holmes. "Do you know either of them?"

"Gregson I know slightly, and Lestrade is an old colleague of mine. We served together in 'M' Division more than ten years back." Arnold's face cleared and he snapped his fingers. "I have it! You are Mr. Sher – " He broke off as my companion raised a warning finger to his lips.

"Yes, Inspector," said the latter quietly. "I am Sherlock Holmes, and this is my close friend and confidant, Dr. Watson. For the moment, I want our presence here to be known to as few people as possible, although it might later suit my purpose to be recognized."

"It must be a matter of some import that brings you here." Inspector Arnold picked up his cap. "Come to my room where we may be more comfortable and private." We followed him to an office containing two desks and he took the one nearer the door, signalling us to draw up a couple of chairs facing him.

"Sergeant Mower tells me that the Chief Inspector is absent with some injury," Holmes remarked conversationally.

Arnold looked up with an ironic gleam in his eye and gave a tight smile. "Yes, he came a cropper with the local hounds some weeks ago and seems to taking a while to recover." His tone hinted that little love was lost between the two senior officers and Arnold would not be unduly concerned if his superior took a year to return to duty. "Without being rude, gentlemen," he went on, "I must ask you to be brief. I have to attend an inquest at ten-fifteen, and our respected coroner is not noted for his patience with delays."

"I understand, Inspector," smiled Holmes. "May I assume that the inquest is on the body found yesterday near Bickstone?"

"That is so. Do you have some knowledge of the matter? Do you know who he is?"

"Not with certainty, but I have reason to think he may be one William Knowles, recently arrived in this country from South Africa."

"You can identify him?" the inspector said hopefully.

Holmes shook his head. "To the best of my belief, we have never set eyes on the man. However," he said swiftly as Arnold's face fell, "I would be interested in seeing the body. There may be more to this than a simple murder, but I must beg you not to press me for any more specific details at present. You have my promise that I will tell you more when the time is ripe."

Inspector Arnold stroked his moustache thoughtfully before giving a slow nod. "I have heard you do nothing without good cause, Mr. Holmes. What do you want of me?"

"I would like Watson and myself to view the body before the inquest. Is that possible?"

"The mortuary is but a short step from here."

"Good. Will the coroner adjourn the inquest if you ask him to?"

"I can find a reason, and Mr. Noakes and I work well together."

"Good," said Holmes, rubbing his hands, "That will give you more freedom to carry out your investigations. Now, Inspector, can you tell me anything about a Samuel Harper? He is employed by Sir Charles Listel as a gamekeeper on the Bickstone Estate."

"I know the fellow." The inspector tugged at his side-whiskers. "He came close to being charged with the assault of an innocent walker who was on a public footpath running through the Bickstone lands. Sir Charles managed to smooth things over, but I distrust the man. I've had occasion to speak to the local constable about his over-familiarity with Harper. I say, you don't suppose that he is concerned in this murder?"

Holmes ignored the question and the gleam of hope died in the other's eye. "Have you come across the name John Hartley in the past week or so?" he asked.

"Not I, but Sergeant Mower may know it. Not much gets past him."

"What of Miss Celia Winsett? She leases a cottage on the Listel land."

"A most charming young lady." Arnold brushed his moustache with the back of his forefinger and his eyes sparkled. "Were I but ten years younger, I – " He pulled himself up short and flushed with embarrassment.

"Forgive me, gentlemen. I was carried away by thoughts improper to an old married man. Yes, I have a nodding acquaintance with the lady. I have travelled from London with her on two or three occasions after she discovered my identity. She said she preferred to travel in company rather than in a ladies-only compartment with what she described as a lot of old frumps." He grinned as he recalled it. "She professed to enjoy the smell of tobacco smoke, and I suspect she is not averse to the occasional cigarette herself in the privacy of her cottage. A very modern and independent young woman, if I may say so – but surely she cannot be involved in this fellow's death?"

Holmes shook his head vigorously. "There is a connection, but there are no grounds for assuming she had any part whatsoever in it other than the proximity of her dwelling. In fact, it's possible that she's in danger from the same source."

The inspector sat bolt upright in his chair and looked sternly at us.

"I must remind you, gentlemen, that if you have knowledge of this or any other crime, it is your duty to reveal it to the authorities. I know you have been of help to Inspector Lestrade in the past, but I'm also aware that he has been made to look a fool at times, and I have no intention of being held up to ridicule in my own district."

"Whenever Lestrade has made a fool of himself, he has required no assistance from me," Holmes replied with some irony. "Be easy, Inspector. When I have hard facts I will tell you, but what I suspect is not evidence and is of no use to you. Dr. Watson will confirm that I work in collaboration with the official force, not as a rival, but I must be permitted to proceed in my own fashion. Do I make myself clear?"

The policeman took this in with narrowed eyes. Then he suddenly relaxed and gave a rueful chuckle. Leaning across the desk, he held out his hand to Holmes who took it with a thin smile,

"It seems I have little choice in the matter unless I clap you both in a cell," said Arnold, "and that will get us nowhere. Take your own steps, and I wish you luck."

"I make my own luck," replied Holmes briefly. "Tell me, Inspector: Is Sir Charles Listel well regarded in the area?"

"Very highly esteemed in the short while he has been here. We see far more of him than of Sir Frederick, who preceded him. A tragic business, all the same. Are you familiar with the details?"

"We spoke to Sir Charles yesterday and he told us the whole story. I know Sir Frederick was murdered in South Africa, but was there ever any doubt about the fate of his son, Sir Charles's nephew, who would have inherited?"

"None that I ever heard," said Arnold, frowning. "I understand his death was accepted by the Natal authorities and by his father."

"A somewhat hasty acceptance, surely," said Holmes. "His body was never found, was it?"

"They probably have their own ideas of doing things in the colonies." The inspector dismissed the subject airily. "Now, sirs, if you want to go to

207

the mortuary, we must go now, but if you cannot positively identify the man, our cause is not advanced."

"We shall see. Lead on, Inspector."

Before we left the station, Holmes delayed to speak to Sergeant Mower, who still sat at the front desk with his pencil and ledger.

"The inspector tells me you are a pretty sharp sort of fellow, Sergeant," said Holmes with a note of flattery in his tone. "You miss very little of what goes on around here, I gather."

"That's my job, sir," rumbled the sergeant. "I like to show myself when I can get away from this desk. There's nothing like the sight of a uniform to make the bad lads think twice before getting up to mischief."

"Quite so, and you will know of any strangers who come on the scene without any apparent reason?" Mower nodded smugly and my companion went on. "Have seen or heard of a man calling himself John Hartley in the past week?"

"No sir, I have not. The only stranger around here is a man staying at The Limes. That's a small private hotel just down the London Road on two beat."

"Have you spoken to him?"

"Seen him the once, sir, but only to wish him a good morning as he came out of The Limes last Tuesday."

"Then you had a good look at him? Describe him."

"Youngish, about your age, sir. Clean-shaven and walking with a slight limp. Darkish features, as if he'd spent a lot of time outdoors, but at a guess I'd say he had a beard at one time." The sergeant wrinkled his brow as he thought back. "I know this sounds queer, sir, but I know I have never set eyes on him before, yet somehow he seemed familiar, although for the life of me I can't say why."

"But you do not know his name?"

"No, but I can soon find out if you want, sir." Our reception by Inspector Arnold had evidently impressed Sergeant Mower.

"No," said Holmes quickly. "Make no inquiries, I beg of you. I would rather find out who he is in my own time. You are remarkably observant, Sergeant Mower and should go far. Come, gentlemen – time presses."

We turned to the door and from the corner of my eye I observed Holmes to unobtrusively slip a half-sovereign on to the desk.

"A good man, Inspector," my colleague remarked as we made our way to the mortuary. "You are lucky to have him."

"Indeed I am," Arnold agreed warmly. "I sometimes think the station would fall apart if we lost him. Unfortunately for us, his pension is due in another two years."

We reached the mortuary in less than five minutes. It was a drab brick building flanked on one side by a derelict chapel and on the other by a cab-yard. The wicket door was opened by a rotund red-faced man of indeterminate years who looked completely misplaced in his macabre surroundings.

"Good morning, Jolly," said Arnold, "We want to have a peep at that poor fellow who was brought in yesterday."

"He ain't moved," replied the incongruously named attendant, a note of ghoulish humour in his voice. "Found out who he is, Inspector?"

"Not yet, but another examination may give us something we have overlooked. These gentlemen are here to give an opinion."

Chapter VII – The Inquest is Adjourned

The smell of disinfectant inside the mortuary took me back to my days as a student in the dissecting rooms at Barts, although this was somewhat primitive by the standards of the great London teaching hospitals. Arnold must have sensed my thoughts and gave me a wry smile. "I fear our town is outgrowing its needs," he remarked apologetically. "Both the government and the local authorities are reluctant to put money into any project that does not give visible prominence to their devotion to civic pride. Why, even my own service is starved of anything more than the bare essentials to enable us to function at a minimum level."

He broke off and clamped his mouth firmly shut, as though fearful of allowing his feelings to run away with him.

"You speak truly," said Holmes. "A police constable's pay is a mere pittance, yet he must be seen to be an honest and upright citizen setting an example to the community he serves – as indeed most of them are, We must look at our system of policing to get away from the old notion of mere thief-takers and watchmen to make it a profession that carries status. That will only come about by engaging educated and intelligent men who are attracted by a career that offers scope and advancement and with pay commensurate with their abilities."

The inspector shot my friend a sideways glance and shrugged. "Would that it were so, Mr. Holmes, but I fear that it will be many years before that comes about. Meanwhile, an educated policeman is an embarrassment to his colleagues and superiors alike."

I detected an underlying bitterness in his words and gauged that he was speaking from experience. On the other hand, I knew that education and intelligence did not always go hand-in-hand, a view that was strongly shared by Sherlock Holmes.

We came to a halt by one of the pitiful heaps that lay covered by a coarse sheet, and on a muttered word from Holmes the inspector bade the attendant leave us, which he did so with a barely concealed air of resentment.

"Do the honours, please, Watson," my friend said tonelessly. "This is your province."

I uncovered the still form and we looked down on the naked corpse of a man of middle years with greying short-cropped hair and features that had long been exposed to a fierce tropical sun. The body was lean but well-nourished and strong, with whip-cord muscles and no surplus flesh.

I ran my eye slowly over him, noting the unmistakable marks of two old bullet wounds, one on the right shoulder, the second on the upper part of the left thigh. Both had been the subject of the roughest of surgery, such as had been called upon to provide in the heat of battle. The left leg had at one time been broken at the shin and had been badly set, from which I deduced he would have carried a marked limp. The hands showed signs of recent lacerations, and two of the fingers on the right were broken and stuck out at an awkward angle.

On turning him over, I saw that the back of the skull was a pulpy mess that could only have been caused by a number of savage and vicious blows, any one of which would have proved fatal. His right shoulder showed the exit wound of the bullet that had entered from the front, and his back was a mass of striations such as might come from the claws of a large and savage animal.

"Well, Doctor, what do we have?" asked Holmes when I straightened up. "Just the facts, please."

I recounted my findings as succinctly as possible, with Holmes nodding slowly as I spoke.

"Age?" he said when I had finished.

"Between forty and forty-five, not more. Without a full examination, I estimate the time of death at not less than twenty-four and not more than thirty-six hours ago."

"He was found just before half-past seven yesterday morning," put in Inspector Arnold. "The blood was still sticky then, so you are well within those limits."

"The cause of death is obvious," I said. "Those blows to the head were given with unbelievable ferocity, and the skull is too badly shattered to make any attempt at guessing at the weapon used."

As I was speaking, Holmes had begun his own inspection of the corpse, going over it inch by inch with his ubiquitous magnifying glass, every now and then muttering to himself, and once or twice giving vent to a muted cry of discovery. He paid close attention to the hands, whipping out his pocket-knife to scrape some fragments from under the nails, placing his finds in separate envelopes which he stowed carefully in his pocket.

Inspector Arnold watched him with eager eyes, and when Holmes had finished he looked at him expectantly.

"Well, Mr. Holmes, can you put a name to the unfortunate fellow?"

Holmes returned his look, "I have never seen him before now," he said evasively. "No doubt his clothes have been scrutinised to no avail? Good. Still, I should like to see them for myself,"

"If you think it will be of any use, but I can assure you there is nothing to be gleaned from them." The inspector sounded put-out that Holmes should cover the same ground as he had, but all the same he went to have a word with the mortuary-keeper, who very shortly came over with a paper sack.

Holmes extracted the garments one by one, subjecting each to a searching inspection under his glass. Beginning with the coarse serge trousers he turned the pockets inside out, paying particular attention to the seams before following the same procedure with the jacket. From each he shook out some dust into the little envelopes which he invariably carried about his person. The collar of the coat and of the flannel shirt were stiff with dried blood, and my friend's lips compressed into a thin line at this evidence of the savagery of the attack. The remainder of the clothing yielded nothing, although Holmes seemed to spend an inordinate amount of time over the shoes, albeit without further comment.

At last he signified that he had finished and we moved away to a small cubby-hole situated in a corner near the door. There was a grubby table littered with empty beer-bottles and scraps of food which Arnold viewed with fastidious disgust, and a solitary dirt-encrusted chair that we all ignored.

"Nothing has been removed, Inspector?" asked Holmes, his hands thrust deep into his pockets.

"Nothing but a few coins which I have locked away in my desk at the station. They amount to four-shillings-and-five-pence, along with a coin that I have not identified." The policeman stroked his moustache again, apparently a favourite gesture of his. "So your inspection has not been productive after all, Mr. Holmes?"

"Oh, I wouldn't say that," my friend replied cheerfully. "The poor fellow, obviously a stranger to this country, had probably arrived within the past couple of weeks with a companion, but they have been at some pains not to have been seen together. His killer is also from abroad but has been here longer. He is a powerful man, some six feet tall, now bearded, but most likely clean-shaven during his time in the army. A man of violent

211

temper, stupid, but possessing a modicum of low cunning. Beyond that I hesitate to go."

Inspector Arnold flushed a deep brick-red as he stared angrily at Holmes. "Are you laughing at me?" he demanded with suppressed fury. "That sounds like a lot of mumbo-jumbo to me, and I warn you, this is not a matter to be treated lightly. This is murder."

"Let me assure you, Mr. Arnold, I am not laughing at you, and I do not treat these matters lightly. There is yet much to be discovered, but I have taken you into my confidence thus far and, when I have ascertained the truth, you will be presented with all the facts necessary to clear up this dreadful affair." Holmes laid a placatory hand on the other's arm.

"Come, Inspector, surely my word is to be relied on?"

The policeman spread his hands in a helpless fashion, then straightened his shoulders. "Very well, sir," he said reluctantly. "I shall place my trust in you. Do still want the inquest to be adjourned?"

"It will be best. However, Watson and I will attend, as I think our presence here, if known, may cause our quarry to make an ill-judged move. Where are the proceedings to take place?"

"In the billiards room at The Golden Fleece." Arnold pulled out his watch. "It is but a step from the police station, and I have some papers to collect on the way. Will you accompany me?"

"I have a small matter to attend to," Holmes, replied. "We will meet you there, and if you can arrange that we have seats for us to one side where we may see and be seen it, will be of help."

We left the building and its gruesome inhabitants, the inspector to return to his office and Holmes and myself to walk in a leisurely manner down the road to the post office. My companion was humming quietly to himself, an air which I recognized as one he played frequently upon his fiddle when feeling particularly pleased with himself. I shot him an exasperated look.

"Really," I expostulated, "you are the most annoying of persons when the mood takes you!"

He paused in mid-stride to look quizzically at me.

"What offence have I been guilty of now, Watson?" he asked mockingly.

"Why, all that rubbish describing the killer to Arnold," I said. "We both know that you gave him an obvious description of Harper, yet you were vain enough to let the poor man believe that you had deduced it all from your inspection of the body. It was no more than the trick of a music-hall mind-reader."

"So it was, old chap," he agreed equably. "All the same, it will go some way to reinforcing my credibility when the facts are known. Come,

Doctor, you must allow me my little vanities, and you well know that I am no charlatan." He walked on and I hurried to catch up with him.

"Why not just denounce the villain and let Arnold gather in him and his accomplice?"

"What real evidence have we? None at all. And his accomplice. Who is he? Do we know?"

"Surely it is the stranger at the hotel of whom the sergeant spoke?"

"Ah, the mysterious stranger who is just waiting to present himself as the rightful heir to the Listel estates and the title." He turned into the post office, a small frown creasing his brow. "I wonder, Watson. I wonder. However, it is time to telegraph Mr. Miles Carmody to reassure him of our efforts on his behalf. Hold my stick, there's a good fellow."

He went to the counter where, taking a sheaf of telegraph forms, he wrote not one telegram but three. I watched in silence, somewhat put out by his refusal to confide in me, but aware from past experience that no question of mine would be answered when this airy mood was upon him.

"Now, Watson," he said as we came out into the sunlight, "I see a cosy little tearoom across the road, and we have just time to indulge before the inquest opens. I wish our arrival to be observed by as many people as possible. Incidentally, I shall be returning to London by the first available train after the proceedings, but I intend to be back some time in the afternoon." He handed me a telegraph form. "Should I be late, you will despatch this to Carmody at a quarter-to-three. Also, you could spend a profitable hour looking at the scene where the body was found. There will be little to find after all the feet that will have milled around, but you know my methods and may spot anything that has escaped the melee."

"You may count on me," I said confidently, gratified by this evidence of his trust in me. "I suppose you don't care to tell me why you find it necessary to go up to town?"

"Not at the present. It is something that I should have thought of before we left. I fear I have been remiss." He dabbed a spot of cream from his lips and grinned boyishly across the table at me. "I say, Watson, these cream buns are excellent. You must try one."

When we arrived at The Golden Fleece, we found Arnold waiting expectantly by the door of the billiard room, where he led us to a couple of wooden chairs placed close to the table from where the coroner would conduct his business.

"I think this will suit, Mr. Holmes," Arnold said in a low voice. "You can observe the whole room from here and cannot fail to be seen yourselves. I spoke to Mr. Noakes, the coroner, and he is happy to accede to my request for a week's adjournment."

"Thank you, Inspector." Holmes rubbed his hands together briskly. "By then you will have the culprit under your hand, unless I am much adrift."

While they were talking, I let my eyes wander around the assembly. Most of them were the usual run of sensation-seekers one encounters on these occasions, and whose hopes were doomed to disappointment this time.

Directly facing us was a mournful looking fellow with a notebook on his knee whom I took to be a reporter from the local newspaper. Facing the coroner's table sat a grey-haired man who appeared filled with a nervous self-importance, and next to him was a round-faced perspiring constable. Some way to the side was a bushy-whiskered man nursing a silk hat and a Gladstone bag, whom I at once identified as of my own calling.

Almost immediately the coroner entered. We all stood, then sat like so many puppets on a single string and the official waited for the shuffling to cease before opening the proceedings. He was a thin dry stick of a man, the most prominent and prosperous of the local solicitors as Arnold had confided to us, and he went about his task in a brisk and business-like manner.

The red-faced constable was the first witness to be called, identifying himself as James Old. He stated that at half-past-seven o'clock, he had been summoned by Mr. Henry Miskin to a hedgerow on the boundaries of the Bickstone Estate where a dead body lay in a shallow depression. He had remained at the scene, sending Mr. Miskin to fetch a doctor and Inspector Arnold. No, there were no signs of life, and the body had lain there for several hours.

Next to be called was the grey-haired man, Henry Miskin. He described how he had been walking his dog in the early hours of the morning when the animal had shown signs of excitement, dashing to-and-fro and barking loudly.

"Most unusual, sir," said Miskin, prepared to make the most of his moment. "Walks along beside me as good as gold with never a murmur. Why, only the other day – "

"Yes, yes," put in the coroner, somewhat testily. "Just keep to the point, please, Mr. Miskin,"

Somewhat affronted, Miskin told of running to fetch the constable, who was in the middle of his breakfast, and together they returned to the body. Old had then sent the witness to fetch Dr. Stephens and Inspector Arnold.

"Do you frequently take that path?" asked the coroner.

"Night and morning without fail, sir," replied Miskin. "Bruno likes to have a set routine."

214

"Had the body been there the previous night, you would have expected the dog to be attracted to it?"

"Most certainly, sir."

"Thank you Mr. Miskin." The coroner dismissed him and called Dr. James Stephens.

The doctor was brief and to the point. He had been called to view the deceased at twenty-past-eight on Friday morning. He judged death to have taken place seven to ten hours previously, and it was due to multiple fractures to the back of the skull. He was not qualified to give an opinion as to whether the death had taken place there or elsewhere, but the corpse had lain there for at least five hours,

"Hypostasis," I whispered to Holmes, who nodded impatiently.

Dr. Stephens was saying that there was no other apparent cause of death other than that stated, but without a *post-mortem* examination he could not swear to it. "Thank you, Dr. Stephens." The coroner made a note. "You are a busy man and I will detain you no longer." He looked over his spectacles.

"Inspector Arnold, I believe you wish to make a statement?"

"Yes, sir." The inspector got to his feet. "This is a case of willful murder, and I request an adjournment of one week to allow further inquiries to be made. You may feel, sir, that should my request be granted, that on resumption it will be necessary to sit with a jury."

"You expect to name a suspect then, Mr. Arnold?"

"I have every hope of so doing, sir."

"Very well. This inquest is adjourned for seven days from now."

As we stood to allow the coroner to leave, I was aware that Holmes's attention was fixed on the exit. I followed his gaze but saw nothing unusual, and before I could speak, Inspector Arnold bustled up to us.

"Well, Mr. Holmes, I've done as you asked, but why put things off for another week? That description you gave me fits Samuel Harper like a glove, so why not pull him in now?"

"Proof, Inspector, proof," Holmes replied. "Why was the man killed? With whom did he struggle before he was killed? Who held him captive and allowed him to escape? No, there are many questions to be answered, not least who is the killer's accomplice?"

While my friend was speaking, Arnold's face mirrored his perplexity and he was left shaking his head doubtfully.

"I have a deep suspicion that you are not telling me all you know, sir. No mention has been made of the unhappy victim being held prisoner or of an accomplice." Arnold's expression hardened. "I think you are creating mysteries where none exist. Why not see it as the sordid crime that it is and which unfortunately occurs only too often?"

215

"If that were all, do you think I would be concerning myself with it?" snapped Holmes. "I assure you, Inspector, there are many more calls upon me than a mere wayside killing that a village constable could solve between breakfast and lunch."

The policeman flushed angrily and Holmes relented.

"Forgive me, Inspector," he said contritely. "That was discourteous of me, but take my word that there are more important issues at stake than you may imagine. Yes, I have held back certain matters from you, but only in the interests of the confidentiality that my clients have a right to demand. The outcome will bring you credit, although the full facts may never be made public for some years, if ever. Now, I have much to do, as has the good Watson, but remember I am working with you and not against you."

Somewhat mollified, the inspector pursed his lips and, although he was plainly still dissatisfied at being kept in the dark by my colleague, he took his leave of us affably enough.

Holmes and I walked briskly down the hill to the railway station and I waited in the booking hall while he purchased a ticket.

"Wait for me at The Green Dragon," he said, tucking the ticket into his watch-pocket. "I hope to be back late afternoon or early evening, depending on how quickly I can find the people I want. Take good care of yourself while at the murder scene, and make sure our names are known to our good landlord. The more people hear of us, the more likely it is that things will happen" His head went up like a gun-dog's. "By Jove, Watson, I do believe I hear a train approaching." With a wave of his stick he sprinted onto the platform, leaving me with several unasked questions on the tip of my tongue. Giving a mental shrug, I crossed the road to The Green Dragon, thankful that Holmes's restless nature was not urging me to my task on an empty stomach.

Chapter VIII – In Bickstone Woods

As I stepped out of The Green Dragon, I heard the chimes of a distant church clock signalling midday. Over my cheese and beer, the landlord had made a rough sketch of the route I should take to the place where Knowles' body – for I was convinced that it was he – had been found, and I had also discovered that the same path would lead me to Miss Celia Winsett's cottage.

"The other gentleman off on his own, sir?" Bert Davis had asked diffidently, thus giving me a chance to reveal our true identities.

216

"That is so," I said. "Mr. Holmes and I each have our own inquiries to pursue. He found it necessary to return to Baker Street, but I expect him back later this afternoon."

"Mr. Holmes? Baker Street?" The landlord's jaw dropped and his eyes widened. "Not *the* Mr. Holmes? Mr. *Sherlock* Holmes?" I nodded and he went on. "Then you'll be Dr. Watson that has been in the newspapers!" Again I nodded and he gave a broad grin. "You played for Blackheath if I remember right."

"You do," I replied, "but that was a while back. However, it seems useless to hide it now, as we have already been recognized by several people in the town."

"Well, all I can say is I'm flummoxed and proud to have you under my roof." Davis wagged his head and went to attend to the other bar, leaving me in no doubt that our presence would soon be common knowledge, exactly as Holmes wished.

The weather remained fine with the scent of hawthorn blossom in the air. My pipe was drawing sweetly and I strode out blithely, swinging my stick and humming softly to myself. It was hard to contemplate that so sordid a crime had been committed in this lovely countryside, yet the fact remained, proving once more how truly Holmes had spoken on several occasions when he declared that the rural scene often held more hidden evil than the worst slums of our great cities.

The sun was warm on my back, and I slowed my pace to an easy stroll, breathing deeply of the fragrant air. In less than half-an-hour, I reached the point where I had to leave the road and climb a low stile on to a path that led through the Bickstone woods. Now I proceeded more slowly still, my eyes searching for the shallow ditch or depression where the body had been found. Presently I came to a small break beside the track that gave evidence of the passage of many boots. The ferns were trampled and broken and the grass flattened. I stopped to survey the scene before leaving the path, telling myself that this was what Holmes would have done. Two or three minutes of silent contemplation yielded nothing and I stepped gingerly from the path. The ditch, such as it was, was about three yards in, more like a shallow gully, but so many feet had milled around that I was convinced that even my hawk-eyed colleague would have found little to encourage him.

I began to cast about in a wider circle, probing amongst the bushes with my stick, but all to no avail. I started to lose all hope of finding anything and was about to give up when my sleeve snagged on a bramble bush. With a muttered curse, I laid down my stick and knelt to free myself. Carefully lifting the offending branch, I began to withdraw my arm when my eye lit upon a small brown object lying on the dead leaves beneath the bush. Had I not been kneeling I would have missed it, for it was almost the same colour as the mould on which it lay. I reached out to retrieve it, but inadvertently allowed a thorn to rasp across the back of my hand, leaving a long red laceration. In my excitement I took little heed of the sharp pain and squatted on my haunches to examine my find.

It was a pouch of soft leather, some six or seven inches in length, rolled and secured by a thong of the same material. I undid the tie to unroll the pouch, my eyes lighting up in triumph on perceiving the initials "*W.K.*" on the inner flap, obviously burnt on with a hot iron in the same fashion that American ranchers brand their cattle. The inside held a few crumbs of tobacco that gave off a distinctive aroma when I sniffed at them. Confident that Holmes, with his encyclopaedic knowledge of the weed would quickly place its origin, I rerolled the pouch. Wrapping it in my handkerchief, I tucked it away in an inside pocket.

Much heartened by my discovery, I licked the few droplets of blood from the back of my hand and renewed my search, finding nothing more but a scrap of paper already yellowing from exposure. I looked at it for a moment, then recalling Holmes's dictum that the insignificant trifles often yielded vital information, I slipped it into my pocket book and straightened my aching back.

I resumed my walk with the feeling that my time had not been wasted and that I had justified my friend's faith in me. I was now in no doubt at all that the dead man was William Knowles, and his proximity to Miss Winsett's cottage gave substance to the idea that it was he who had put the ivory box through her door in a final despairing effort to keep it from the hands of his enemies.

But who were his enemies? Miles Carmody? His story was plausible enough, yet Holmes had hinted at one stage that he was not completely ready to accept it at face value. Miss Winsett? Unthinkable. She was merely an innocent bystander who happened to be living near the centre of these events, and her credentials could easily be checked. I remembered Holmes's precept that by eliminating the impossible, whatever remained, however improbable, must be the truth. I smiled to myself. That young lady was certainly eliminated from our inquiries.

There remained Samuel Harper and John Hartley. The latter might be the stranger at The Limes of whom Sergeant Mower had spoken, but who was John Hartley? The name had fallen glibly enough from Carmody's lips, but no one else to whom we had spoken admitted knowing of him, and only the South African's account assigned to Harper the villainous role he was reputed to be playing. That Harper was an uncouth oaf, surly and aggressive, there seemed to be a general agreement. My own glimpse of him lurking in Baker Street had not predisposed me in his favour, but did his spying on Celia Winsett make him a murderer?

I stopped and leaned against a tree to jot down my deductions in my notebook:

(1) On the evidence of the tobacco pouch, the dead man was William Knowles.

(2) He had put the ivory box through Miss Winsett's letter box.

(3) Harper had followed the lady to London hoping to recover the box.

(4) Ergo, Harper had killed Knowles, but not finding the box on him, had reasoned that Miss Winsett had obtained possession of it without being aware of its significance.

At that point I gave up and continued on my way. I still had no answer to the question of John Hartley's identity or whereabouts, and neither had I any real confirmation of the truth of what Carmody had told us, even though his distress on seeing the ivory box had been real enough.

Perhaps Holmes would be able to supply the answers on his return from whatever errand had taken him to London.

Thus cogitating, my steps brought me to a fork in the path. I knew from the rough map drawn by Davis that to the left the track continued on to join the main road that ran from Bromley towards Sevenoaks, while the right branch led to Miss Winsett's cottage and thence on to Bickstone Lodge. I took the way to the right, my thoughts still revolving in my head. The trees were now more closely set and I was thankful for their shade to keep the sun from my back. It was a lovely setting if one hankered for the quiet country scene, but I was a confirmed town dweller, happiest in the hustle-and-bustle, smells, and cries that made London with all its drawbacks the most fascinating city in the world.

I paused, reaching for my handkerchief to wipe my perspiring brow, and then recalled using it to wrap the pouch I had retrieved from the bushes. I resorted to flicking away the beads with my forefinger before going on at a slower pace, my stick sloped over my shoulder.

I was brought up short by a figure stepping from behind a tree to stand squarely in my path. I recognized him at once as Harper, and at close quarters he looked even more unprepossessing and brutal than when I had seen him from a distance in Baker Street.

"Where do you think you're going?" he growled threateningly. He held a single-barrelled shotgun across his arm, its muzzle a black menacing ring that seemed to peer at me like a malevolent eye. I am not by nature of a timid or cowardly nature, but I am not ashamed to admit to a certain amount of trepidation in the situation that presented itself at that moment. Nevertheless, I put a brave face on it and glared back at him in what I hoped was righteous indignation.

"What the deuce is it to you?" I snapped back, pleased to hear my voice firm and strong. "Lower that gun immediately before you have an accident with it!"

He leered at me, revealing a set of broken and discoloured teeth.

"Accident?" He gave what might pass as a laugh. "There'll be no accidents if you go back the way you came. You're on Listel land and I'm Sir Charles's keeper. You're trespassing, so get yourself gone!" The gun waved jerkily and, despite my inner qualms, I had time to note that although his finger was on the trigger the hammer was not cocked.

"You are talking rubbish, my man," I said, taking heart that I was not likely to be shot by accident. "This path is a right of way to the cottage of a friend of mine and I intend to go there. Step aside at once or Sir Charles shall hear of your conduct before this night is out."

"Sir Charles ain't at home, cully," he sneered. "No more is your lady friend at the cottage, so you might as well be off." His eyes narrowed in a scowl. "I know you," he went on. "You're the lackey of that interfering know-all, Sherlock Holmes. Watson, ain't it?"

I bristled with anger at his contemptuous tone and set my jaw pugnaciously. "I am Dr. Watson," I said through gritted teeth. "I also have the honour to be the friend and colleague of Mr. Sherlock Holmes, who proved too clever for you yesterday. Now, once more I say, stand aside and let me proceed. It is none of your business if Miss Winsett is at home or not."

I took a pace forward, one eye on his right thumb as it hovered over the trigger of the shotgun. Harper's face suffused with rage and I saw his knuckle whiten as he prepared to cock the piece. The barrel swung towards me and my own anger overlaid any fear that I might have.

My stick still lay across my shoulder and with a sudden violent movement I slashed it down heavily on the fingers of his left hand where they grasped the weapon.

He gave a howl of agony and the gun fell to the ground where I placed my foot firmly on it, while Harper nursed his bruised fingers and uttered a string of foul obscenities. For some seconds we faced each other, mutual hatred flowing between us like an electric spark. Then, with astonishing speed for one of his bulk, he swooped to pick up the gun. By now my blood had reached boiling point and, with equal rapidity, I brought my knee up to catch him fairly on the side of the jaw. Like a released spring he came upright, then his eyes glazed over and he toppled slowly backwards like a felled tree to lay unconscious on his back.

I stared down at him, amazed at my primitive response and finding myself shaking with the reaction. As I grew calmer my medical instincts prevailed, and I knelt down to assure myself that he had sustained no serious injury. A quick examination put my mind at rest, he being in no worse case than I had often found myself when I had played for Blackheath in my student days. His jaw would be a tender reminder of me for a couple of days, and the fingers of his left hand were bruised and bleeding from my blow with the stick. I felt no pity for him nor regret for my actions, telling myself that it was quite likely that before long he would receive his just deserts at the hands of the public hangman.

I rolled him on to his side so that he would not swallow his tongue and then turned my attention to the fowling-piece. Breaking it open, I extracted the cartridge and threw it into the undergrowth before taking the gun by the barrel and smashing it against a convenient tree until the mechanism was beyond repair by even the most expert gunsmith. Finally I hurled the now useless weapon as far as I could into the trees and, with a last glance at the still torpid Harper, I went jauntily on my way.

Five minutes brought me to a point where the trees had been cut back and the cottage stood before me. It was a low, graceful stone edifice, no mere labourer's dwelling, but a place that had probably been intended as a summer retreat for the family at the Lodge. It had a small paved area surrounding it, with miniature flower-beds and rockeries set in, and the whole was enclosed by a white paling fence. In all a pretty and charming sight, enhanced in no small degree by the gay chintz curtains that hung at the square windows on either side of the brightly painted green door.

Miss Winsett, I decided, was a young woman of considerable good taste.

Moderating my pace, I began a slow circling of the building, staying outside the fence and casting the occasional wary eye over my shoulder against the chance that Harper had recovered quickly enough to follow me.

The fence continued unbroken until I came to a gate that led up to the back door, beside which stood a large water-butt painted the same pleasing shade as front and back doors. The path I had followed to the cottage continued beyond the rear. It was overgrown and little used, eventually disappearing into a rough meadow or paddock which sloped gently away into the distant woods, above which I could glimpse the chimneys of Bickstone Lodge. Charming as the place was, I decided it was too isolated and lonely for my gregarious nature, but Celia Winsett obviously thought otherwise or she would not live here.

Completing my patrol, I found myself once more at the front of the cottage. Lifting the gate-latch with my stick, I went cautiously up the flagged path towards the door. My eyes swivelled from side to side, looking for signs of recent intrusion, but all seemed well. I tested the front door and found it secure, as was the back, and the windows showed no indication of attempted forced entry. I reluctantly came to the conclusion that I would find nothing of any use to our investigation and turned back to the gate.

I was about to pass through when my eye caught something that pulled me up in my tracks. There on the white gate-post, some eighteen inches above the lower hinge, was a darker patch. I knelt to get a closer view and found it to be a bloody palm-print, extending round the wood to become four fingers, as though the owner had tried to pull himself along. I studied the marks intently. Then, without touching them, I set my hand at the same angle and came to the conclusion that whoever had made the print had been trying to drag himself out through the gate.

222

I took out my notebook to make a careful sketch of the print. Remembering Celia Winsett's account of how the box had come into her possession, I had no doubt that the marks had been left by the man who now reposed in the Bromley Mortuary and whom I was now certain was the unfortunate Knowles.

Getting stiffly to my feet, I scanned the scene again, anxious to miss nothing that might be of help, but look as I might I saw nothing – or observed nothing, as my colleague would have it.

Setting off at last, I looked at my watch and realised that I would have to step out smartly in order to get off the telegram to Carmody by a quarter-to-three. I felt well pleased with my afternoon's achievements, not least by the encounter with Harper and its' satisfying outcome. On coming to the scene of the fracas he had gone, no doubt to lick his wounds and call down all kinds of curses on my head.

When I reached the town, it was crowded with Saturday afternoon shoppers, and I realised that Sir Charles Listel's prognosis for its future was well on the way to being fulfilled. It was but a half-hour by the excellent train service from central London, and with the streets of the capital becomingly increasingly clogged with traffic, it was as easy for a business man to travel here as it was to go by cab or omnibus to Islington or Holloway, with a finer prospect at the end of the journey.

I despatched the wire and then strolled slowly back down the hill towards the station and The Green Dragon. I went up to my room to ruminate on the results of my excursion. The encounter with Harper was entirely unforeseen and, although it had done little to advance our inquiries, it at least confirmed that he had some reason for not desiring our presence near the scene of the murder, and by extension Miss Winsett's cottage.

At the same time, if he was but a hired thug, his reaction might force his principle into the open, whomever he was. Was he the mysterious John Hartley of whom no one had heard except for Miles Carmody? Time would tell, I said to myself, and turned my attention to my finds.

I took my handkerchief from my pocket and, laying it on the dressing table, undid it carefully to expose the leather pouch. For some minutes I stared at it, but in the end I was no farther forward than before. I was chary of handling it overmuch before Holmes could see it, having experienced his wrath when my blundering had destroyed evidence that was only apparent to him. I extracted the scrap of paper from my pocket-book and set it beside the pouch. It was no bigger than the piece that had been in the ivory box and of the same texture. I felt sure that one had been torn from the other, but as Holmes had the original, I had no way of comparing them. I tore the sketch of the handprint from my book and added it to my other trophies. Then, with a sense of achievement, I removed my boots and lay down on the bed. The old wound in my shoulder, a relic of the battle of Maiwand, was playing up and I closed my eyes in an effort to ignore it.

I must have succeeded, for my next recollection was of being shaken by the arm, and I opened my eyes to find Holmes looking down at me.

"Oh, you're back," I mumbled blearily and he nodded gravely,

"Your deductive powers grow apace, Watson. Yes, here I am, and while I have been chasing over half of London, here are you plunged in swinish slumber,"

"Here, steady on," I protested as I struggled into a sitting position. "I have been far from idle, as you shall hear."

"Then you must tell me all about it," he said, resting his hand on my shoulder. "Apart from the fact that you have been on your hands and knees in the Bickstone woods, found a particularly spiteful bramble, and collected some memorabilia to show me, I can only hazard a guess at your activities." I looked at the scratch on my hand, the blood now congealed, and the stains of leaf-mould on my knees and nodded sagely.

"However," he was saying, "as the good Mrs. Davis has laid out an inviting tea for us, your story must wait. I shall relate my part as we eat."

I got to my feet and followed him down the stairs to the parlour where a table was spread with a tempting selection of jam and fresh-baked scones that set my mouth watering.

For a quarter-of-an-hour, he spoke of anything but the matter in hand, waxing lyrical over the efficient running of the South-Eastern Railway, and going on to expound on the great social changes wrought by the harnessing of steam locomotion.

"Reflect, Watson," he said, helping himself to a spoonful of jam. "In our parents' youth, it would have taken days – sometimes weeks – to make a journey that we accomplish in a few hours. If that is so in our small island, think of the benefits it has brought to the vast spaces of the American continent,"

"That may be true as far as it goes," I replied. "Consider the less-beneficial effects. Think of the pollution of the air we breathe from all those reeking funnels, and the scars on the countryside where the iron road has sliced through once-green fields."

"Your argument is a sound one, but all progress demands a price, and if we are not prepared to pay it, then we stand still." Holmes drained his cup and sat back, clearly in no mood for a lengthy debate. "Now to business." From his pocket he brought out a pipe and held it up. "I bought this in Bradley's this afternoon. It cost me half-a-guinea, but I could not resist it and I shall begin to break it in as I talk."

Chapter IX – The Mystery Deepens

Very soon the room was filled with a blue haze, the pungent fumes of Holmes's black shag, leavened to some small extent by the sweeter aroma from the Arcadia mixture which had replaced the "Ships" that I had once favoured. I waited patiently for my friend to begin his story.

"When I left the train at London Bridge," he said, having ensured that his pipe was burning evenly, "I went directly to Baker Street where, despite my protests, Mrs. Hudson insisted that I put myself outside a good plate of cold beef. To keep the good lady happy, I made short work of it before setting out to find Wiggins and his motley crew."

He referred to the band of street Arabs whom he called his "Baker Street Irregulars", and whose services he commissioned when he required fast and accurate information from the darker recesses of the underworld.

"They can go anywhere and hear everything when the mere sight of an official looking person seals people's lips," he had once said. "All they need is organizing."

"I found Wiggins in his usual haunts behind Euston Station," Holmes went on. "I sent him to the Brecon Hotel off Chancery Lane, where Miles Carmody is lodged, I myself following in a hansom. I cudgelled my brains for a means of giving Wiggins a sight of Carmody, but soon after arriving at the hotel the problem resolved itself. My man came out of the hotel and took a passing four-wheeler, and I clearly heard him tell the jarvey to take him to Trafalgar Square. Wiggins had my orders, and from now on our South African friend will not make a move unremarked by Wiggins or one of his minions."

"You hold doubts about Carmody, then?" I asked. "I thought such might be the case from your earlier comments."

"I admit to some perplexity," said my companion. "His story hangs together, yet for the life of me I cannot fathom why he should bring it to us, unless he wants some chestnuts pulled from the fire without burning his own fingers."

I nodded my comprehension and Holmes continued.

"My next move was to call on Sir Charles Listel at his club. I thought it politic to keep him informed of such events as could be disclosed, but he is an impatient man and insists that come what may he will return to Bickstone Lodge by Monday afternoon at the latest. I made no attempt to dissuade him, but I obtained his written permission that we should be allowed to make free of his grounds as I saw fit." He waved a sheet of paper. "Our passport to the Bickstone Estate should our presence be called into question." He shot me a keen look. "Watson, you are smirking. What is so amusing, pray?"

"All in good time," I said. "Carry on with your story."

He studied me for some seconds then continued. "I returned to Baker Street for a few items that I might need and, as an afterthought, I took the liberty of bringing you a change of linen and another suit, which is just as well, having seen the state of your clothing."

"Which is hardly surprising in the circumstances," I pointed out, but he was already going on with his narrative.

"I then went on to Lewisham to assure myself of Miss Winsett's welfare – not that I think her to be in any danger now that she has told us all she knows. She is quite content to remain with her friend Mrs. Footer for a few days more, but she has given me her keys and permission to enter the cottage, the latter again in writing." Another sheet of notepaper joined the first. "In return, I promised to forward to her any correspondence to her friend's address in order that her work does not fall behind. By now the afternoon was well advanced, so I made my way to Catford, from where I caught a slow train, arriving here to find you lazing your time away on the bed."

"Which was well deserved, as you shall shortly hear," I retorted. "It seems that my time has been spent more productively than yours."

"We shall see." He knocked the ashes from his pipe and inspected it judicially. "You know, I believe this is going to turn into a fine smoke

226

eventually." A rap on the door preceded the entrance of the landlord, an envelope held in his hand and a look of concern on his battered features.

"A telegram for you, Mr. Holmes," he said awkwardly. "The girl took it in shortly after the doctor went out. She put it on a shelf and I didn't hear of it until a few minutes ago, or you'd have had it when you came in. Fact is, sir, she didn't know your name."

Holmes took the envelope and tore it open, scanning the contents quickly. "No harm done this time," he said. "In future, make sure that any messages are given to me or to Dr. Watson at the earliest possible moment. Now, Mr. Davis, about dinner tonight: Can you feed us, or would you prefer us to seek sustenance elsewhere?"

Davis rubbed his chin thoughtfully before answering. "Well, sir," he said, "we usually only have commercials and the like here. I reckon you'd feel more at home at The Golden Fleece. Not that my missus ain't a good plain cook," he added defensively.

"I am sure your good lady has no shortcomings in the kitchen, Mr. Davis, as your own well-nourished frame testifies. Nevertheless, we shall take your advice and see if our presence causes any stir in the town."

He stopped the man on the threshold. "Tell me, do you have many strangers in your house?"

"Quite a few, sir. Being opposite the station is pretty good for business. Folks tend to come in after a journey, or to while away a few minutes before their train goes. Then there's the commercial gents who I might see once a month or once in six months, according to their line."

"No one who has seemed out of the ordinary? You must be able to pick out the odd ones in your trade."

The landlord's face brightened. "Well, now you come to mention it, Mr. Holmes, there was one queer cove nine or ten days back. Let me see. It wasn't the Thursday, as that's market day and you get all sorts in here then and don't take much notice. No, must have been Wednesday. At first I thought he might be a gypsy or tinker with his dark skin and funny way of talking, but he was civil enough, so I served him."

"He asked no questions?"

"He ordered his drink – whisky, if I remember a'right – then asked where he could buy a map of the district. I sent him to Traylors, that big stationer's halfway up the High Street, so he drinks up and goes."

"I see." Holmes gave the landlord a nod of dismissal and got to his feet. "Come, Watson, I am agog to hear your story and you are impatient to tell it, and while you do so, you can change out of those disreputable clothes into something more in keeping with the class of establishment in which we shall be dining."

227

We ascended the stairs and Holmes went to his own room to return with the old carpet-bag he utilised to carry around the clothing and materials he used when adopting any of his many disguises. He opened it to lay out the apparel he had brought for me. Then pulling up the bedside chair, he straddled it to lean on the back with his chin on his fists.

"Now, Doctor, come clean, as our American cousins would have it, and leave nothing untold."

His aquiline features were turned towards me as I began my narration, and taking him at his word I went into minute detail, even to the extent of describing each twist and turn of the path I had followed until I had found the place where the body had been discovered.

"You were correct in assuming that it had had many feet over it," I said. "I doubt if even you could have found much indication of the sequence of events. However, I persevered, and it was while I was grubbing about in the brambles that I found that." I pointed to the soft leather pouch on my dressing table. "I handled it as little as possible, knowing your methods, and beyond finding those burnt-on initials and a few crumbs of tobacco inside, I have left it to you."

He gave me an appreciative look and went over to stare down at the pouch, his whole body still except for the flickering of his eyes as he scanned the innocent looking object. Presently he produced his lens and began a more intense scrutiny, still not putting out his hand to touch it.

His lips moved silently and an occasional grunt was his only audible reaction, and to hide my impatience I began to remove my boots before divesting myself of my coat and collar.

Holmes pulled the chair up to the dressing table. Then, with his silver pencil-case, he turned over the pouch and began his examination anew. Finally he picked it up, rubbing it between thumb and forefinger before holding it to his nose. He tipped the few grains of tobacco onto the dressing table top and, with his pencil-case, he carefully heaped them together into a small pile.

"Well, Watson, what have you made of it?" He raised his eyes to look at my reflection in the mirror. "You must have had some thoughts on the thing."

"Of course I have," I said peevishly. "I am not a gun-dog to fetch and carry a stick for his master, but as I said, I left the detailed examination to you."

"I meant no offence," he replied pacifically, turning to face me. "I sometimes feel you have too little faith in your own acumen and I'm honestly interested in your opinion. Let me hear it, I pray you."

"Very well," I smiled at his genuine regret at having ruffled my feelings, but so often had his brilliant mind made my own plodding efforts appear puerile that I had become over-sensitive to his remarks. "The way I see it is this," I went on. "The position of the pouch in the bushes tells us that it could not have been kicked there by accident. *Ergo*, it was meant to be concealed – either as a clue, or to keep it from the hands of the killer, and perhaps both. When we examined the body at the mortuary, I observed that among the other injuries, the back of one hand bore scratches such as I sustained when I retrieved the pouch." I held my hand out. "Therefore we may assume that the dead man put it there."

"Bravo! Excellent reasoning, Watson. Proceed."

"The initials, '*W.K.*' fit the man that Carmody called 'William Knowles'. For the lack anyone else to hang the initials on, we can take the risk of ascribing the ownership to Knowles and that name to the corpse – that is, until we learn otherwise," I added hastily, knowing my friend's abhorrence of guesswork unsupported by hard facts.

"A reasonable hypothesis. Go on."

"The pouch is hand-made from a single piece of leather, with the side seams closely stitched and treated with some resinous substance to inhibit the ingress of air and the consequent drying out of the tobacco. That is all I deduced. The tobacco crumbs I leave to your more specialized knowledge."

Holmes beamed at me and clapped me on the shoulder. "Admirable," he chuckled. "You excel yourself, Watson. You have left little unobserved, and have put the correct interpretation on your observations." He picked up the pouch again. "The leather is exceptionally soft and supple, so I suggest it comes from the skin of some species of antelope in which South Africa abounds. As for the tobacco, that is my special province, as you so rightly say." He bent over the little heap and sniffed delicately.

"A pity we have so little to work on, but I detect the distinctive aroma of the weed cultivated in the north of the Transvaal and favoured by the Dutch settlers. It is beginning to find its way on to the European market, but I fear it will never pose a threat to the Virginia plantations. However, let us make the ultimate test."

Pulling out his new pipe he scooped the small pile into the bowl. Then, tamping it down carefully, he struck a match. Dry as it was, the tobacco was gone in a couple of puffs, leaving a slightly sweetish odour hanging in the air. Holmes tapped the ash on to the marble top of the washstand to study it with his glass before sweeping it into his hand and disposing of it through the open window without comment.

He turned back to me with raised eyebrows and I pointed to the scrap of paper with a brief explanation.

"How close to the pouch was it?"

"Within four feet, but it appeared to have been discarded rather than concealed. It may have been torn from the same piece that was in the box, but you can compare them."

This he was already doing, nodding absently to himself. "They match perfectly and there is a small trace of blood where it was held to be torn. It tells us little, but you did well to bring it. I take it you then went on to Miss Winsett's abode?"

"Indeed I did, but not without incident," I chuckled. I went on to tell of my meeting with Harper and its outcome, erring not at all on the side of modesty. If the truth be told, I found the recollection a satisfying leg-up, and I went into every detail with relish so that by the end of the story, Holmes was laughing immoderately.

"My dear fellow!" he gasped, wiping his eyes. "I constantly find myself amazed by your unexpected limits. I have never doubted your courage, but to find in you the talents of a street brawler is a fresh facet of your nature."

I grinned back at him. "Oh, there is little difference between a street brawl and what goes on in a loose ruck on the rugby field. Of course," I said in a more serious vein, "I suppose you realise that we have come out into the open and nailed our colours to the mast?"

"As I intended, although I did not see it so picturesquely as you put it. Carry on, but do restrain your sense of the dramatic or we will never get our dinner."

The remainder of my afternoon's activities was quickly told, with Holmes displaying a keen interest in my sketch of the blood-stained palm print, measuring with his pocket ruler and questioning me closely on its precise position and angle.

"It seems I must congratulate you, Doctor," he said as he straightened up. "Not only on the results of your labours, but on the inferences drawn by you. You are more valuable than a whole troop of Lestrades and Gregsons, and if I sometimes chaff you, it is only because of the deep respect and affection I have formed for you over the past two years."

I experienced a warm glow at this spontaneous tribute, for it was seldom that Holmes's austere nature allowed him to express any emotion. At times he seemed nothing more than a disembodied brain, and it was indeed a rare occasion that he revealed his more human side.

"I think I know your moods by now," I said in an attempt to hide my embarrassment. "How are we to proceed?"

"Our immediate objective is dinner," he replied, "Tomorrow we will retrace your steps, and as I have Miss Winsett's keys and her permission to enter her cottage, we will see if, in her agitation, she overlooked any

230

small matter that may assist us. Oh, by the way – this telegram is from the Union Steamship Company's office in London." He smoothed out the form he had crumpled in his pocket. "I asked if the name of Alistair Listel appeared on the passenger list of the *Trojan* sailing from Durban on the relevant date. It did, but curiously the berth was never taken."

I plucked at my moustache as I absorbed this. "So if Carmody was being truthful, he came on a wild goose chase. Even had Hartley been the one to make the reservation, he had a change of heart before the time came for him to sail."

"That could be one explanation, but if so why was Knowles killed? If Hartley decided not to go ahead with the imposture, why should Harper take a hand?"

"Because Knowles recognised him and might expose him to Sir Charles?"

"A possibility, but I think there is more to it. Giving Carmody any benefit of the doubts I have expressed puts a different aspect on the whole matter. But make no mistake, Watson – the truth will be uncovered one way or another." He smiled grimly. "That was guaranteed the moment I interested myself in the case."

He left me to marvel at his supreme belief in his own powers, a belief that owed not a little to a streak of vanity that made him singularly reticent about the few cases where he had been at fault or where the official force had beaten him to a solution. It was that same vanity which professed distaste for my own attempts to bring his genius to the attention of a wider public. "Melodramatic scribblings that would not be out of place in the yellow press," he had once described my wishes, averring that I would be better employed in showing his work as an exercise in observation and logic.

Half-an-hour later, we descended the stairs and made our way out through the lounge. A group of four men looking like well-to-do farmers fell silent as we passed, and eight curious eyes followed our progress until the door closed behind us. It was evident that our identities were now known to the patrons of The Green Dragon, and it would not be long ere the news spread farther afield.

I observed as much to Holmes and he signified his agreement.

"As I hope it will. There is nothing like putting a ferret down a hole to bring a rabbit into the open."

"Maybe," I retorted. "I also recall that in India they tied a kid in the open to tempt a tiger. I hope we get the rabbit and not the tiger."

"I think Harper caught his tiger this afternoon," he chuckled, and I could not help but join in his merriment. It being Saturday night, the dining room of The Golden Fleece was busy with the more prosperous citizens of

Bromley and their comfortable wives as they enjoyed a brief respite from the business of making money. When asked if we had reserved a table, Holmes assumed his most authoritative manner, which resulted in a table being quickly available, the head waiter snapping his fingers to bring us immediate attention. My companion looked over the menu and treated me to a sardonic wink,

We had not reached the point of making our choice when I glanced up in time to see Inspector Arnold come through the door. He was alone and out of uniform, and when I drew him to Holmes's notice, the latter caught Arnold's eye and waved a hand.

"By yourself, Mr. Arnold? Then why not join us? Your company will be most welcome."

"Why, thank you, gentlemen," the inspector accepted with alacrity. "My wife and daughter are on a visit to my mother-in-law in Essex and I was not relishing a solitary meal."

A chair was brought and he took his seat, his presence creating even more attention from the waiter. Through the soup and main course the talk was of the weather and the current political situation, but it was over an excellent sherry trifle that Arnold turned to me with a note of mock reproof on his voice.

"Well, Doctor, what is it I hear of you engaging in fisticuffs with our local worthies?"

"You have long ears, Inspector," I said cautiously.

He waved a deprecatory hand. "Please, not Inspector tonight," he said. "I merely made an observation – but yes, I do make it my business to know what goes on in the district. It would astound you to know how quickly news reaches me."

"What have you heard, Mr. Arnold?" Holmes was deceptively casual.

"Only that a certain gamekeeper was, and probably still is, swearing to have revenge on the good Doctor. He is said to have a nasty bruise on the jaw and a bandage on the fingers of one hand. Do you wish to comment, Dr. Watson? Just across this table."

I shrugged. "It was a minor incident," I replied. "I took exception to being threatened with a shotgun while on a public footpath and I fear I acted instinctively."

Arnold chuckled. "I think my instincts would have erred more on the side of caution. Do you intend to press charges?"

I shot a quick glance at Holmes, thinking it might suit his purpose to have Harper removed from circulation for a while. He gave an almost imperceptible shake of the head and answered for me.

"No," he said grimly. "When Harper is charged, it will have to be for something more serious. Watson is well able to take care of himself, as I

232

have good reason to know." He signalled the waiter, and soon we repaired to the smoking room with coffee, brandy, and three excellent cigars. "Are you on duty tomorrow?" he asked as we sat down.

"Yes. With Chief Inspector Lewis incapacitated, I have a lot on my shoulders. Do you have something in mind?"

My companion drew on his cigar before replying. "I take it you keep some sort of eye on the hotels and boarding establishments in the area? Occasional visits to ensure they keep within the law and are not harbouring undesirable characters?"

"As I said, I make it my business to be fully informed, and either Sergeant Mower or I make irregular calls at such places."

Holmes leaned forward. "Would it excite comment if you were to make such a visit on a Sunday?"

Arnold fingered his moustache. "Probably, but I could put forward a plausible reason for so doing. What have you up your sleeve?"

"A look at The Limes where Mower observed the stranger, but we will discuss it tomorrow." Holmes changed the subject and the talk became general.

The rest of the evening passed in convivial fashion, Arnold plainly thankful to delay his return to an empty house. He proved an entertaining companion and an excellent raconteur as he reminisced on his twenty and more years in the police service. One particular case in which he had been involved provoked lively discussion between him and Holmes, It had become known as the Penge Starvation Case and had received a lot of publicity some six years earlier, and Arnold's account proved of great interest to Holmes and myself. The whole case had hinged on conflicting medical evidence which the judge had ignored in his address to the Jury. The prisoners, although sentenced to hang, had been reprieved and were now serving life sentences.

"In my view, they were lucky to escape the rope," Arnold asserted. "It was one of the most callous and deliberate crimes in my experience. One can understand without condoning a murder committed in the heat of the moment, but to systematically starve a helpless woman to death needs a special kind of inhumanity."

"Did not the defence suggest that death was primarily due to chronic consumption?" Holmes put in and our guest reluctantly agreed.

"A problem that we increasingly face is the advance of medical knowledge," went on my colleague. "We must ask ourselves if it is now in the realm of reason to expect twelve ordinary men chosen at random to listen to and comprehend all the medical and scientific jargon currently produced in our courts. How can they agree when the experts cannot?"

The discussion swung back and forth and a bottle of very fine port circulated until a discreet cough from the smoking room waiter hinted to us that our departure would not be unwelcome and, on looking 'round, we saw that we were the last patrons of the public rooms, We arranged to meet Arnold at the police station after lunch, and with expressions of mutual regard we went our respective ways.

Chapter X – A Close Shave

"You know, Watson," said Holmes as we sat at breakfast on the Sunday morning, "I do believe Inspector Arnold is wasted in this quiet backwater." He speared the last sausage in the dish and transferred it to his plate. "With the right mentor, he could be a leading light of the Scotland Yard Detective Branch."

"Gregson and Lestrade would not like to hear you say so," I replied, securing a rasher of bacon for myself, "Neither would Peter Jones."

"Good men, all within their limits – but with little imagination and too set in their ways. Arnold has a lively mind and is not afraid to use it."

"Perhaps he is content to remain where he is and wait to fill Chief Inspector Lewis's shoes," I said. "I gathered from our talk over dinner that Lewis is contemplating retirement, and Arnold will not be too unhappy if he goes."

Holmes wiped his lips with his napkin and got to his feet. "You are probably right, but it is none of our concern. Come along, there's a good chap. The sun is shining, and I look forward to a little gentle exercise in the Bickstone woods. You have your pistol?"

I patted my pocket. "After yesterday's little incident, I shall not venture in that direction without it." I wolfed down the last of my breakfast and followed my colleague out to the front of The Green Dragon, where we paused to get our pipes going.

"What do you intend?" I asked as we set off.

"To retrace your steps of yesterday. We now have *carte blanche* to enter any part of the Listel preserves, as well as Miss Winsett's abode." He gave a thin-lipped smile. "It will be interesting to find out if friend Harper is prepared for another joust, or whether he is still licking his wounds after your assault."

"Have a care," I admonished him. "He is a dangerous and unpredictable character, and I'm convinced that it is he who is responsible for the deaths of Knowles and the two Listels."

"Knowles almost certainly, but the Listels? We have only Carmody's word on that, and I have yet to make up my mind about that gentleman."

234

"Speaking of Carmody," I asked, "will he not be expecting to hear from you? Ten o'clock and three was the arrangement."

"And so he will. That was taken care of while I was in London. I am not without acquaintances who can produce and deliver a telegram from any point of the compass I require."

"Society must be thankful you are on the side of the law," I reflected. "Heaven help us all should you ever turn to crime."

We walked in silence until we came to the point where we had to leave the road and cross the stile onto the woodland path. As the trees closed in, I kept a wary eye open for any sign of a vengeful Harper lurking in the shadows, but we came to our first objective without incident.

I pointed out the place and Holmes nodded. As I expected, he stood to survey the scene before entering the brush, humming tunelessly under his breath. After a while he walked a few steps along the path before, to my surprise, he crossed to the other side. Again his eyes swept back and forth. Then, with a muffled cry, he dropped on to all fours to examine the ground at close quarters. Pulling out his lens, he began to crawl slowly into the bushes, muttering incomprehensively all the while. When I made to follow him he spoke irritably over his shoulder.

"Remain where you are. I take it you did not look over here on your previous visit?"

"Of course not," I said huffily. "The body was over there."

"I am aware of that," he replied, looking up at me. "Think back, man. Dr. Stephens estimated death as having occurred seven to ten hours before he examined the body. He also guessed that it had lain there for some five hours, but would not commit himself to saying that death had taken place at that spot."

"You should not blame him for being cautious," I protested, rising to the defence of my profession. "Many a doctor has been criticised for making a perfectly reasonable diagnosis that has, by some freak, turned out to be wrong."

"I am not blaming him," said Holmes testily. "Had he said differently, I would have distrusted him at once. As it is, we can build a theory with no preconceived notions. Now, remain as you are until I call you."

He turned his back on me and began a crouching shuffle into the undergrowth until he was lost to my view. For upwards of five minutes I remained fretting at the spot where he had vanished, becoming more and more baffled as the seconds ticked by. At last I could contain myself no longer and called to him softly.

"Holmes, what are you up to?" There was no response so I tried again, this time raising my voice. "Holmes, for Heaven's sake!"

"What is it?"

235

His voice came from behind me, and, spinning around, I found him almost at my shoulder, rumpled and dishevelled with traces of twigs and leaves adhering to his clothing. His face had a grin of gleeful triumph spread across it.

"Really," I said angrily, "this is no time to be playing games. What the deuce have you been up to?"

"Looking for the truth, and finding it."

"You mean – ?"

"Yes, the place where the murder took place." His wiry fingers dug into my upper arm. "Follow me, but with care, if you please."

He took me back some twenty yards, then with another word of caution he pushed his way into the bushes, I followed silently, taking pains to place my feet in his own steps, until we reached a less-overgrown area.

He stopped abruptly so that I almost cannoned into him.

"Now, what do you see?" he asked, pointing to a spot six or seven feet to his left.

I looked to where he pointed, and after half-a-minute I could see a discernable flattening of the undergrowth, the broken branches already beginning to wither.

"Now continue," my colleague was saying. "From this point we can see that some sort of struggle has taken place. And look, beneath that bush, is a dark stain that can only be blood. I have taken a specimen." He patted his pocket. "However, there is no doubt in my mind that this is the spot where the man we believe to be Knowles had his final encounter."

He took me by the sleeve and moved on, treading as delicately as a cat, and I could see clearly that a heavy and bulky abject had been dragged through the gorse and ferns. The trail took us to where Holmes had first wormed his way in, and we emerged on to the path somewhat the worse for wear,

"Well, are you convinced?" He straightened up and brushed the leaves and bracken from his clothes,

"It seems probable," I agreed slowly. "I may appear dense, but if Knowles was attacked there, why drag him over to where he was found? That was a far better place of concealment than that shallow gully."

"A valid point," Holmes admitted. "I think I have a plausible explanation, all the same. Look, here is where he was pulled out of the brush, and here," he crossed to the other side, "is where he was dragged to his final resting place. Despite all the boots that have milled around, it is still possible to see the flattening of the grass."

"That could have happened when the police removed the body," I demurred .

"Rubbish." Holmes sounded impatient. "See where the blades lie close to the bushes where few feet have trodden? My reasoning is that Knowles had concealed himself on the other side, but had been tracked down by his killer."

"Harper," I interjected.

"If you like. The killer, in a fit of ungovernable rage, savagely bludgeoned his victim, but bear in mind it was dark. He needed to find the ivory box that might be an incriminating clue as to what was going on, so the body was dragged into the open."

"And when the search was fruitless, rather than return the body to the thicker brush, Harper took him over here to where there was an easier ingress."

"Precisely."

"It could be so. When he failed to find the box, Harper followed Miss Winsett to London in the belief that it had been passed on to her."

"That is my reasoning, but I'm willing to listen to any constructive objections you may have." Holmes raised an interrogative eyebrow. I turned it over in my mind, then snapped my fingers as a thought came to me. "Why should Harper think that Miss Winsett had the box?"

"You examined the body. What did you make of the injuries other than those that proved fatal?"

I thought back to the scene in the mortuary.

"The broken fingers could have come about by his trying to protect his head," I said slowly. "Some of the other abrasions may have been caused when he was dragged through the bushes, but there were some that had been inflicted at least twenty-four hours before death. Where does that lead us?"

"It leads us to the theory that he had been held under duress in an effort to make him reveal the whereabouts of the box. Suppose he had escaped but, being so hotly pursued, he had but little time to recover it from where it was concealed. He saw the cottage and pushed the box through the letter slit before making a last desperate bid for freedom, but was caught and met his end there." Holmes pointed with his stick.

"If you are correct, the next thing is to find where he was held," I said, but Holmes shook his head dismissively.

"I think I know that, but one thing at a time. Do you wait here while I see if there is any more to be learnt at the spot where the body was found. Not that I don't trust your diligence, old chap, but you know my methods. Check and double check."

I knew my friend to well to take no umbrage at his going over the same ground as I already had, admitting that his perception was far keener than mine. Meanwhile I waited and pondered, slowly piecing together that

237

which he had so swiftly comprehended. In our early association I had regarded him as something of an egotist demonstrating his superiority over more pedestrian intellects, but gradually I had come to recognize the near infallability of his keenly-honed mind.

"My congratulations, Watson." He reappeared, a look of approval on his usually austere features. "You missed very little, and that little is of no great moment."

"What was the little?" I asked good-humouredly, too pleased with my own deductions to feel any chagrin at having overlooked what my friend considered a trifle.

He extended his hand, palm up, to show a small brass button bearing an embossed crest. It was obviously from a military uniform, but the design was unfamiliar to me and I shook my head.

Holmes took out his magnifying glass and handed it to me together with the button. Under the lens I could make out the crude representation of an animal that I took to be some species of antelope, while around the circumference was the legend "*Natal M.R.*"

"Little enough in itself," my colleague was saying. "It merely goes to reinforce the South African connection if we need it. Now, my dear fellow, I can see you have been chewing over the situation. What conclusions have you drawn?"

I returned the glass and button to him and began to fill my pipe, wondering if I was going to bring forward objections that Holmes would quickly demolish. I decided to begin on what I considered safer ground.

"First of all," I began, "I think if Knowles was held captive, it is reasonable to assume it was by Harper. Therefore, it was probably in the latter's cottage. Bear in mind Sir Charles told us he lives on the far side of the estate and is shunned by the other servants. Sir Charles also said that on the few occasions he needs to speak to Harper, he searches him out in the woods or waits until he comes up to the Lodge."

"Well reasoned, Watson. Continue."

Thus encouraged I went on with more confidence.

"What we need to do is to get Harper safely out of the way, and then search his cottage for more evidence."

"Breaking and entering," said Holmes slyly. "Have you no respect for the law?" He gave a thin smile. "I have been pursuing the same idea, but we shall see. However, you have something to add, have you not?"

"Yes. If, as you maintain, Knowles was killed on the other side of the path and his body dragged over to this side, how do you account for the tobacco pouch being hidden under the bushes? Surely Harper would not have put it there?"

"Most unlikely, but think back: Did I ever say that Knowles was killed over there?"

My mouth fell open in astonishment. "You certainly implied so," I said, trying to recall his actual words. "You led me to believe that you had found the spot where the assault took place before the body was removed to where that fellow Miskin found it."

"Just so, but you examined the body. Are you positive that the wounds to the head must have been immediately fatal?"

Holmes took out his pipe and began thumbing tobacco into the bowl as he looked quizzically at me. "Come, Watson," he urged. "Your considered professional opinion."

I opened my mouth to speak, and then changed my mind. I gnawed at my moustache and thought back to yesterday's scene in the mortuary. Again I saw the pitiable remains of what had once been a live human being and the terrible injuries that had brought that life to an end. I recalled my hospital days when the victims of accident or assault had been brought to in comparable condition, some to expire under the surgeon's knife and others to by some miracle to survive. How many remained alive because of, or in spite of, our attentions was problematical, but it was my firm belief that the will to live played a great part in the cases of those who lived.

I met Holmes's eye squarely and shook my head.

"No, I cannot say with complete certainty that he could not have clung to life for a short while if some great need had driven him. The human animal is seldom prepared to accept defeat in the struggle for survival, however inevitable it is in the end."

"Thank you," Holmes said quietly. "I think as you do, but it is good to have your experience to back my views."

"Then you think that Knowles may have regained consciousness long enough to conceal the pouch as a pointer to his identity? Why was it left on his person?"

"Because Harper, if he was the assailant, was looking for the ivory box and ignored all else. Let us go. There is nothing more for us here."

We walked on to where the path branched off, and had taken but a few paces along the right-hand fork when a loud voice hailed us from behind.

"One moment, gentleman. May I have a word?"

We turned to see a figure in blue approaching us, and I recognized him as the Constable Old who had given evidence at the previous day's inquest. He was breathing heavily, and when he reached us he removed his helmet to mop the perspiration from his face with a large spotted handkerchief.

"Good morning, Constable," said Holmes. "P.C. Old, is it not?"

"That's right, sir." Old replaced his helmet. "You'll be Mr. Sherlock Holmes, and this gent is Dr. Watson. I saw you at the inquest yesterday."

Holmes nodded and we waited for the constable to go on.

"May I ask your business here?" inquired the latter.

"Why?" Holmes's tone was cold and forbidding.

"Well, sir, I suppose you know you are on Sir Charles Listel's land, and that is trespassing."

"Nonsense," snapped my colleague. "This footpath is a public right of way and may be used by anyone."

The constable's face went a deeper red. "That's as may be, sir, but you wasn't on the path a hundred yards back. I saw you coming out of the bushes."

"Quite so, and if you keep watch you may well see us do so again," said Holmes. "Dr. Watson and I have written permission from Sir Charles to come and go as we please on any part of his land."

Old looked nonplussed but went on doggedly. "In that case, why didn't this gentleman say so yesterday instead of assaulting Sir Charles's keeper who was only doing his job?"

"For the same reason that I would resist anyone who threatened me with a gun in a public place," I declared. "Has Harper made an official complaint to you?"

"Well, not exactly, sir, but I heard all about it." The policeman began to shuffle his feet and his eyes wavered. "A savage attack, as I understand."

"Then let him bring charges," said Holmes contemptuously. "For your information, Old, we are now going on to the cottage leased by Miss Winsett, who has also given us permission to enter. If you have any further doubts, I recommend that you consult Inspector Arnold and obtain his views." He stepped forward and tapped Old on the chest. "A word of advice, Constable: Be very careful with whom you make friends. Your career could be in jeopardy should you choose the wrong people. Now if there is nothing more, we will be on our way, and should you see Harper before we do, which I don't doubt you will, you may tell him of the situation. Come, Watson, time presses and we have much to do."

We left the discomfited P.C. Old to stare after us as we continued until we turned a bend in the path when Holmes gave vent to a bark of laughter.

"I wonder what Harper makes of that?" he chuckled. "He was lurking in the bushes and could hear every word."

"Do you think he has Old in his pocket?" I asked.

"Not exactly. I think they could be on friendly terms and our not-too-bright constable is inclined to believe any yarn that Harper may concoct, but I cannot see him conniving at any illegal or felonious acts. No, Watson, Old is honest enough, and unless he does something particularly stupid, he will remain a village constable for the rest of his time."

The cottage came into view and Holmes approached to within twenty yards before pausing to take in the general scene. I repeated the details of my previous day's actions, my companion nodding absently as I spoke.

"Apart from the gate-post, you saw no signs of blood elsewhere? The door or letter-flap, for example?"

"None apparent, but Miss Winsett may have well removed any that were there."

"Or someone else did?" Holmes knelt to examine the post through his lens. "Yes, Watson, it was as you deduced." He straightened up. "You are an excellent draughtsman. Your sketch is well-nigh perfect."

"I spent many a long hour in the dissecting rooms and at anatomy classes," I reminded-him, as I followed him to the door which he examined, together with the step. Next he took a key-ring from his pocket and inserted one of the three keys into the lock, pushing the door open just sufficiently for us to squeeze through. His sensitive nostrils flared and he stooped to retrieve the few items of mail lying on the mat.

"It seems the inspector assessed the young lady accurately," he remarked as he shuffled through the letters. "I detect the faint smell of tobacco smoke in the air – a mixture of Turkish and Egyptian, if I am not at fault. I cannot conceive that she is in the habit of entertaining gentlemen friends. Therefore, it is she herself who enjoys a cigarette. A small enough vice in an independent young woman."

"What do you hope to find here?" I asked curiously.

"Probably nothing, but I shall look, just the same."

The first door he opened turned out to be the bedroom and I felt distinctly uncomfortable at such an intrusion. Holmes must have felt the same, for after a cursory glance he shut the door and went on to the kitchen with its gleaming pots and pans and black-leaded stove.

Nothing there attracted his interest, and we crossed the passage to find ourselves in a surprisingly spacious drawing room which ran from front to back of the house. A solid oak writing desk was placed under the south-facing rear window with ink-stand, pens and blotting-paper set neatly on the leather top. None of the five drawers was locked and Holmes opened each in turn. Three were empty, while the others held only items of stationery which he took out, replacing them in the same order after confirming that there was nothing of importance among them. There was little else to be seen, apart from a half-dozen books in English and French that were obviously connected with the lady's work as a publisher's reader. Holmes took them all down, shaking them to see if anything was

241

hidden in the pages, again drawing a blank. The grate was empty except for some crumpled sheets of crepe paper which Holmes, with his usual attention to detail, rummaged through. On a small table by a high-backed chair sat a sandalwood box, and on lifting the lid I found it to hold both Turkish and Egyptian cigarettes, thus confirming my companion's surmise.

"No more than I expected," he said as he replaced the crepe paper and gave the room a final sweeping glance before heading for the door. "Still, it pays to explore all avenues."

He stood in the passage-way while I looked round to see that all was left as we had found it. As I turned to the desk, I looked out of the window to the expanse of rough meadow beyond. To the right was a small copse or spinney, and my eye was attracted by a single flash of light, as though the sun's rays had been reflected from a bright object. For some seconds I concentrated my gaze, but the flash wasn't repeated and I told myself I had been mistaken. Closing the door behind me I went to join my colleague, whom I found fitting a key into the lock of the back door.

"If we hasten, we shall be in time for a bite to eat before we meet Arnold." He swung the door open. "You are never at your best on an empty stomach."

I was looking over his shoulder with the spinney directly in my line of vision, and again I caught the glint of reflected light, but this time accompanied by a blurred movement. For a split second I was paralysed. Then with a warning yell, I launched myself at Holmes to seize him by the waist and hurl him to the floor. Almost simultaneously there was a dull thud above us, followed by a sharp report that I knew could only be a rifle shot, a familiar sound during my time on the North-West Frontier.

We sprawled in an untidy heap on the floor, my heart going like a trip-hammer. Then Holmes disentangled himself to crawl a few feet along the passage with me close behind him. Levering himself to one elbow, he took a couple of deep breaths.

"I hope you treat your patients with more respect than you do your friends," he said whimsically. Then in a more sober tone: "I find myself in your debt once more, Watson. You are not harmed, old chap?"

I flexed my muscles and found that, apart from a slight stiffness from the old wound in my shoulder, I was sound in wind and limb.

"Nothing to cry over, but do not give me too much credit. I acted wholly from instinct." I stretched out a leg to push the door shut with my foot, and then we both climbed to our feet.

"Harper?" I hazarded, only to find I was addressing Holmes's back.

He was looking along the passage, his head moving from side to side, and I guessed him to be searching for signs of what could only be the bullet that had so nearly found its mark in one of us. He looked over his shoulder at me, his brow furrowed in concentration.

"Harper? No, I think not. He would not take such a risk after hearing our talk with Old. Even that obtuse fellow would be capable of adding two and two together should one of us be found dead or wounded."

"Then whom do you suspect?"

"The elusive John Hartley is a name that springs readily to mind."

"If he exists," I replied doubtfully. Then, struck by a sudden thought, I went on eagerly: "I say – could not he and Carmody could be the same person?"

"It has crossed my mind, but do you think he would have pointed us towards Hartley were they one and the same? Mark my words, Watson, there is someone behind this who thinks we are getting too close and wants us out of the way. I shall find him, whatever name he is hiding under. Now, tell me what caused your sudden flurry of activity."

"Little enough." I described what I had seen, indicating the position of the copse in relation to the cottage. "What I saw must have registered subconsciously, for I have no clear picture in my mind."

"So if the shot was fired from the trees, it would have passed at an angle from right to left, ending up on the right-hand side of the passage as we face the front door. Fired by an expert marksman it would have found a billet about – " He spun round and pointed. "There!"

He took a couple of paces and stabbed a finger at the frame of the bedroom door, and sure enough there was a white scar on the woodwork at head height. Closer inspection revealed a hole in the angle where the door frame met the plaster of the wall. Holmes took out his pocket-knife and began probing and after a minute he withdrew the blade gently, and with it a misshapen lump of metal which dropped into his hand.

"One of us had a narrow escape, Watson," he said sombrely. "It is too badly damaged to tell us much, but I think it came from a high-powered hunting rifle with an optical sight. As heavy as an elephant gun, but lethal to a smaller animal. The bullet is nickel-jacketed, with more penetration than a conventional one." He dropped it into his pocket.

"Now to keep our appointment with Inspector Arnold. I doubt that our unknown friend is lying in ambush. He will be long gone, and if as I suspect he is a skilled hunter, he will have left no tracks for us to follow. Coming, Watson?"

Chapter XI – A Stroke of Luck

At the police station, we were met with awed respect by Sergeant Mower, he clearly having been apprised of my companion's identity, and suitably impressed. The inspector greeted us with a smile.

"A most entertaining evening, gentlemen," he enthused. "I cannot recall when I last enjoyed myself so much."

"We were glad of your company," Holmes replied. "It refreshes the mind to banish all immediate problems and bend it solely to pleasure."

"But the problems remain, Mr. Holmes. Sergeant Mower has told me things that may prove of interest to you. Will you hear him?"

At my friend's acquiescence Mower was sent for, and after a slight delay while he deputised a constable to take his place at the desk, he came into the office to stand woodenly before us with his eyes fixed on a point somewhere above our heads.

Arnold set the ball rolling. "Sergeant, repeat to these gentlemen what you told me earlier."

Mower gave a cough and began to speak in stilted tones. "Following on our conversation of yesterday," he said in a monotone, "I instituted inquiries regarding the gentleman of what we spoke who has been residing at The Limes for the past week or so. I remembered your injunction not to make formal investigations and therefore – "

"Oh, come now, Sergeant," Holmes cut in. "You are not in court now. Just relax and say what you have to say in your own words."

Mower's eyes slid sideways to his superior who gave a nod of encouragement. Something like a smile showed briefly on the sergeant's broad features and he leant forward confidentially.

"Well, Mr. Holmes, sir, I know you didn't want no proper inquiries made, but there's a lot to be picked up over a pint of beer and a game of dominoes, if you take my meaning."

"Such as stories of respectable medical practitioners who involve themselves in brawls in the countryside," said Holmes solemnly.

"I heard that from Jim Old," Mower said with a sheepish grin. "I had to pass it on to the inspector just in case there was a formal complaint."

He drew his brows down and frowned at me. "Take my tip, Doctor, and keep away from them there woods when you're alone."

"No cause for worry," said Holmes lightly. "Watson and I have been that way this morning and cleared things up with P.C. Old. If we find the good doctor's body peppered with duck-shot, we shall know where to look for the culprit."

"Thank you, Holmes," I grunted. "A great consolation to me, I'm sure. Please go on, Sergeant."

"Well, sirs, I happened to hear that the party you are interested in turned up at The Limes a week last Friday and asked for a room. He had next to no baggage, but pulls out a purse-full of gold and pays for two weeks in advance. Mr. Curnow, him what owns the place, ain't the sort to turn away good money, if you know what I mean, so he lets him have a room. It seems he's no trouble – keeps to his room, and only goes out on the odd occasion, usually after dinner."

"How the deuce did you learn all this without making inquiries?" asked Holmes with an air of amusement.

"Well, sir, Sid Friar, him as works as gardener at The Limes, he comes into The Crown for his pint and a yarn. Then old Ma Brown what does the rough work there, she's chummy with my missus, and her tongue flaps like a flag in a gale."

"Mrs. Brown's or your wife's?" Holmes put in facetiously.

"Both of 'em," the sergeant replied gloomily. "Anyway, there's Sid's eldest girl, her what got into trouble with a soldier from Woolwich – she's a kind of chamber-maid up there, so it's only a matter of keeping your ears open and your mouth shut to pick up things. Anyhow, that's the sum of it, gentlemen, for what it's worth."

Holmes gave a dry chuckle. "A veritable network of secret agents, and all of them ignorant of their functions."

"Local knowledge, Mr. Holmes," Arnold said smugly. "That is what makes for good policing. Now, if you are ready, shall we go?"

Our steps took us about half-a-mile out of town towards London, past the Beckenham turn until Bromley Hill began its descent to Catford and the outer fringes of the metropolis. The Limes, when we reached it, was on our left, a large house shielded from casual eyes by a row of the trees from which it derived its name. A freshly painted board had been erected at the entrance to the carriage drive, proclaiming the name in large gilt letters and the legend "*A.J. Curnow, Prop.*" in smaller script below. The drive was clean and freshly raked, and the whole aspect spoke of a warm but dignified establishment.

Inside the entrance was a small reception area, and Arnold's ringing of the bell on the desk brought forth a short stout man from behind a glass-panelled door. His bright button eyes widened as they fell on the inspector and his smile was more one of query than of welcome.

"Why, Inspector Arnold," he said tentatively. "What brings you here on a Sunday afternoon? Not trouble, I hope?"

"Not for you, Mr. Curnow, and I apologise for disturbing you at this time, but with Mr. Lewis absent, I must fit my in duties as best I may. As

Mr. W.S. Gilbert so recently reminded us, a policeman's lot is not a happy one." He became confidential. "You will have heard of the dreadful affair in Bickstone Woods, no doubt?"

"Who has not?" replied Curnow. "But what has it to do with me? This is a most respectable establishment and – "

"Of course, sir," Arnold interjected smoothly. "It is not suggested otherwise, but inquiries must be made. My problem lies in that we have been unable to identify the victim or find from whence he came."

"Very sad, I'm sure, Inspector, but how does it concern me?" Curnow looked puzzled as he put the question.

"Well, sir, I have to ask if any of your residents are unaccounted for, or have left suddenly within the past two or three days?"

The little man puffed up like a turkey-cock and spoke pompously.

"Most certainly not! This is a genteel establishment and I do not have the kind of clientele who would choose to behave so."

"I do not suppose the victim chose to have himself murdered," Holmes put in drily, and received a frown from Curnow.

"I do not know who you are, sir," said the latter firmly, "but I do not believe that respectable people go around getting themselves murdered, least of all in a lonely wood."

"Then we must pray that you are not set upon by footpads one of these dark nights," said Holmes icily. "That would surely impair your reputation for respectability. As for who I am, my name is Sherlock Holmes and this other gentleman is Dr. John Watson. Inspector Arnold will vouch for our respectability."

Curnow's plump features sagged and his eyes turned helplessly towards Arnold, who hid his amusement at the foregoing exchange.

"Mr. Holmes has an interest in the matter, sir," said the inspector in a tone intended to soothe the hotelier's ruffled feelings. "As he is unfamiliar with the district, I invited him to accompany me on my routine inquiries."

"We merely wish to ascertain if anyone is missing, or if any strangers have recently sought your hospitality," added Holmes.

Curnow bit his lip and spoke with some diffidence. "As Inspector Arnold knows, most of my guests are long term residents. It is seldom that casual travellers seek accommodation here. Two or three over the past six months, if that."

"But is it not a fact that one such visitor came to you recently and is still here?" Holmes insisted.

It was like drawing teeth, but Curnow at length nodded reluctantly. "A Mr. Martin took a room last Friday week. He is still here, so he cannot be the unidentified man of whom you speak. He is of impeccable behaviour, gentlemen, I assure you, despite being from foreign parts."

"A foreigner, say you?" Arnold seized on the word eagerly. "What kind of foreigner?"

"You misunderstand me, Inspector. I did not mean a foreigner in that sense, but he is some sort of Colonial who has lived abroad and has a desire to see the old country. That much he confided to me."

"He is here now?" asked Holmes. "On the premises?"

"Indeed. He came down to breakfast at nine o'clock, then retired to the smoking room with the Sunday papers until lunch. I believe he is now in the sun-lounge."

"Then he has not set foot outside all day?" said my colleague.

"Most certainly not. I served him coffee with my own hands at eleven and he lunched with Colonel Milton, discussing the respective merits of the Mauser and Martini-Henry rifles – not a subject I regard as suitable for the Sabbath," Curnow concluded primly.

"Well, that's that," said Inspector Arnold. "I hope we haven't put you to too much inconvenience, sir, but we now know that our body is not that of your Mr. Martin."

"Am I being discussed?"

We turned to find a broad-shouldered man standing in an open doorway.

He was around thirty years of age with tanned features and penetrating blue eyes that held us in an unwavering stare. Curnow gave us a look of reproach and made to speak, but Holmes stepped forward to take charge of the situation.

"Mr. Martin?" My friend gave one of the charming smiles he could produce on occasion, but the other seemed impervious to it.

"That's my name," he said coldly. "Henry Martin. Who are you?"

"I am Sherlock Holmes, and I'm trying to help Inspector Arnold put a name to an unfortunate fellow who has been fouly done to death near here on Friday. Finding you to be safe and well, it seems we must look elsewhere."

"Why should you think it was me?" asked Martin.

"Well, sir," Arnold put in, "I have had no missing person reported to me, so must therefore assume that the victim was a stranger to the area. As Mr. Curnow has assured us of your well-being, we need trouble him nor you further." He turned to the exit. "Good day to you, sir, and to you, Mr. Curnow. Are you coming, Mr. Holmes? Doctor?"

"A moment, please." Martin stepped forward. "Should you not identify your man, what will become of him?"

"Why, sir, a pauper's grave, and quickly, seeing as how warm the weather is," replied Arnold. "What else?"

247

"What else indeed?" muttered Martin. Then with a violent movement, he swung away through the door behind him.

Holmes was in an uncommunicative mood as we retraced our steps, giving monosyllabic responses to any attempt by Arnold to engage him in conversation. It wasn't until the inspector had bidden us a subdued farewell and turned into the police station that my companion showed any sign of animation.

"Well, Doctor, what do you make of our Mr. Martin?" he asked as we made our way down the hill.

I shook my head. "I don't think it can be coincidence that another Colonial could appear on the scene," I said. "Nevertheless, if Curnow is to be believed, it wasn't Martin who used us as target practice earlier."

"Quite so. Therefore we must look farther afield. But make no mistake, Watson: Friend Martin is deeply involved. Did you observe him at the inquest yesterday? No? He was there, and not out of idle curiosity. He also displayed an inordinate interest in the final destination of the man we have called Knowles. I wonder why?"

"Look here," I said. "Surely the simplest way of settling if it is Knowles or not is by having Carmody down to take a look at him. After all, it was he who sent the man down here."

"I have considered that, but I still admit to some perplexity about the part Carmody is playing in the whole scheme of things."

We had come within sight of our hostelry and Holmes took me by the elbow to steer me cross the road towards the station. A solitary four-wheeler stood on the forecourt, the cabbie leaning against the wheel and puffing at a short clay pipe. He straightened up at our approach and set his billy-cock firmly on his head.

"Sorry, Guv'nor," he said. "Can't take you nowhere until after the Lunnon train's been and gorn."

"We can wait," Holmes said carelessly, "Meanwhile, perhaps you can answer a couple of questions." A coin changed hands, "Is this your regular stand?"

"More or less. Weekdays there's three or four of us, but Sundays is diff'rent. Not so many trains, see, so me and the others take it in turn to hang about."

"Last Wednesday week, can you remember that far back?"

"All depends, dunnit, Guv? What are you after?"

"A man came off a train and went over the road for a drink. He was a dark-featured, gypsy type of fellow. Did you see him?"

The cabbie knocked out his pipe on the palm of his hand and nodded.

"I seed him, Mister. He come out and stood looking about, and I was going to ask if he wanted a cab when he goes across to Bert Davis's. I wouldn't've taken no notice, but ten minutes later he comes out and hails me. Ah, that's mighty civil of you, sir." He took the tobacco pouch that Holmes held out and began to fill his pipe.

"Where did he want to go?" asked my colleague.

"He didn't seem to know. First off he made me stop at Traylor's up the High Street. Then he kept me hanging about while he looked at a map he'd bought. Next he tells me to take him to Shortlands where he got out, and that's the last I see of him."

"Did he have any luggage?"

"One case plastered all over with labels what he'd left in the station when he went over the road. He sent me in for it when he picked me up, and mighty heavy it was, I can tell yer." The cabbie scratched his ear. "He had a funny way of talking, but I couldn't place where he come from."

He cocked his head to one side in a listening attitude. "That'll be the train now. Don't suppose there'll be anyone on it for me, but I dursn't not be here.

As it happened there was only one passenger who alighted, and he a guard coming off duty.

"Wasting your time, Jack," he said to the cabbie. "No one's travelling today," He strode off swinging his lantern, his red and green flags tucked under his arm.

"All right for him. He gets his money if the train's empty," The driver spat on the cobbles and looked hopefully at Holmes and me. "Was you wanting to go somewhere, gents?"

"You can take us to Shortlands and show us where you set down this man." Holmes paused with a foot on the step of the cab. "What kind of place is it?"

"Nothing special. A few folk have moved there from Lunnon, and there's some talk of a railway station."

"Hotels?"

"Depends what you call hotels. Couple of pubs, but they ain't much cop. You don't want to stay there, Guv."

Holmes climbed in and I took my place facing him. The cushions were old and cracked but the interior of the cab was clean and well-swept, the owner evidently taking great pride in what gave him his uncertain living. The horse, although somewhat elderly, was well-fed and groomed, with the harness brightly polished.

During the fifteen minute journey, my companion withdrew into himself, his stick supporting his chin on his hands, I knew better than to break his train of thought and gazed idly out of the window as we descended a steep hill, the dwellings becoming more scattered as we left the town behind. We came to a halt beside a railway embankment.

249

"This is it, gents," said the jarvey as he opened the door. "I dunno what the bloke did. He just stood there with his case until I went."

"Then we shall do likewise." Holmes handed the man a half-sovereign.

"You'll have to shanks it back, sir," the man warned us. "You ain't likely to get a cab from here."

"That's all right," Holmes replied cheerfully. "My friend can do with the exercise. He carries overmuch weight."

"Thank you," I said peevishly as the four-wheeler retreated towards the town. "That was quite slanderous and uncalled for."

I found myself addressing his back, for already he was crossing the road to a small cottage that seemed to perform the functions of general store and postoffice. As was to be expected on a Sunday, the door was firmly locked, but Holmes made his way round the side of the building with me at his heels. We came upon a small, neatly kept garden where an elderly rosy-cheeked woman looked up sharply from her chair as we came into her view.

"Good afternoon, Madam." Holmes removed his hat.

"If you want anything from the shop, you must wait until tomorrow," the woman said uncompromisingly. "This is the Lord's Day, and I'll not break it for you nor anyone else." She folded her hands on her lap, clearly not prepared to argue the point.

"Neither would we ask you to," Holmes replied with warmth. "I merely wish to inquire if there is an hotel or boarding establishment nearby. I understand an acquaintance of ours has come to stay in the district, but we are unable to trace him."

"Nothing of the sort round here," said the woman, shaking her head. "Only two beer-houses, and they don't take visitors." She fixed us with bright, intelligent eyes. "There was a stranger come in a few days back asking the same thing, but where he went I can't say."

"Dark featured, with an outlandish way of speaking?"

The woman nodded, "That's right, but I've not seen him since. Reckon he must have gone on to Bromley or Beckenham."

"Then we must look elsewhere," said Holmes in a disappointed voice. "I apologise for intruding on you, Madam."

We retraced our steps to the road, where my colleague stood frowning in deep concentration.

"What now?" I asked after some minutes had passed. "We seem to have drawn a blank here."

"The trail has gone cold, I fear," he said despondently. "How do we proceed? Is it likely we should be more successful in Beckenham, or shall we enlist Inspector Arnold in our search? If only Wiggins and his cohorts were here! They would root out our man in no time."

"But they are in London and we are here," I pointed out. "Either we go on to Beckenham, where I doubt we will find much, or we return to Bromley and set Arnold to work. Unless," I added with heavy-handed irony, "you intend to camp out here for the night."

Holmes stared at me, his eyes gleaming, then his shoulders began to shake with silent laughter.

"Oh, Watson!" He clapped me on the back. "You are priceless, a veritable jewel! Where would I be without you?"

I looked at him in bewilderment, quite at a loss to comprehend his sudden change of mood,

"What have I said now?" I asked. "Really, you are the most infuriating of fellows at times."

"What have you said? Why, my dear chap, you have gone straight to the nub of the whole problem." He seized my arm and literally dragged me to the side of the road. "Reason it out," he said excitedly. "For whom are we looking?"

"Why, John Hartley, if he exists."

"And what do we know of him?"

"Only what we have heard from Carmody, if we credit all he told us."

"Give him the benefit of the doubt for the time being. Well?"

I thought back and assembled my thoughts in sequence. "Let me see," I said slowly. "Hartley is from Natal, alleged to have some connection with the deaths of the two Listels, and has journeyed to England to pose as the younger Listel. He is probably in league with Harper, and one or both is responsible for murdering Knowles."

"Excellent, Watson, excellent. Now – "

"Wait a minute," I interjected. "Surely Hartley will be unable to proceed with the imposture while Carmody is here to denounce him? Unless the latter is also in league with him."

"Would Carmody have come to us in that case? No, that hare won't run. Go back to what you said at the beginning: Hartley is from South Africa and has probably led the same sort of life as Listel, Carmody, Knowles, and Harper."

"Where does that get us?" I asked, mystified.

Holmes made no direct answer, but looked up at the sky appraisingly.

"This weather is really most delightful," he mused. "Do you know we have had no rain for over two weeks and still the glass remains high." My exasperation began to show, but Holmes ignored it and gave me a keen look.

"I imagine that in your campaigning days," he remarked, "you spent many a night in the open with only the stars for cover."

"Frequently," I replied tersely. "Some less comfortable than others," My mouth fell open as I began to get the drift of his apparently inconsequential chatter. "By Jove, are you suggesting that our man is sleeping rough?" I gasped.

"Why not? A man likely to be skilled in bush-craft would have little difficulty in remaining unobserved, should he so wish."

"He would need food," I pointed out. "Unless he had an accomplice – Of course! Harper!"

"Quite so."

"You are not proposing to ask Harper where we should look? It would take as long to scour the open countryside as it would to investigate the hotels in the neighbourhood."

Holmes nodded absently, then his head jerked up and a low whistle escaped his lips.

"Watson, I do believe the gods smile on us! Behold, a rustic Wiggins, as I live and breathe!"

I followed the direction of his gaze, and trudging along the dusty road I saw a boy of some eleven or twelve years, attired in a coat several sizes too large and a pair of out-at-knees knickerbockers. One hand was tucked inside the coat with the other holding it firmly together, and as he drew nearer it was obvious that beneath the coat he had something concealed.

He saw us standing by the roadside and his steps slowed, but he still, came on, eying us warily as he did. Holmes crossed the road to intercept him and he made to dodge, but Holmes grasped him firmly by the scruff of the neck.

"Steady on, boy. We mean you no harm, and that rabbit beneath your coat is no concern of ours."

The lad wriggled vainly for a few seconds before succumbing sullenly to the inevitable. He looked up suspiciously at my colleague, but something in Holmes's voice seemed to reassure him.

"I ain't done nuffing," he said truculently. "I come across it lying in the road, see."

"I'm sure you did, and I said it's of no interest me." With his free hand Holmes dipped into his pocket and brought out a shilling. "Here, take it," he urged. "There will be a couple more if you answer a few questions."

The boy reached out a grubby hand and snatched the coin, his eyes now alert and confident. "Wotcher want to know?" he said.

Holmes released his hold and smiled thinly. "You live around here? Good. Then I expect you know all the woods here."

252

The urchin nodded. "It's nearly all Listel land – him up at the big house."

"You mean Sir Charles? He hasn't been here long, has he?"

"'Bout a year. Old Sir Frederick, he didn't mind us taking the odd rabbit or hare, but he weren't here much. Since the new bloke came, he's put in that there 'Arper, so we dursn't get seen. Shoot you as soon as look at you, he would."

"But you chance your arm now and then, I bet."

The lad gave a broad wink, and Holmes chuckled as he went on casually.

"Have you seen anyone strange in the woods? Someone who should not be there?"

"There's been a bloke lurking there this past week gorn, but I dunno if he shouldn't be there seeing as how 'Arper's pretty thick with him." The boy's eyes filled with new suspicions. "'Ere, you ain't crushers, are you?"

Holmes relieved his fears by taking out a florin which immediately vanished into the ragged garments.

"Anyfing else you want to know, Guv?"

"Would you show us where this man is hiding?"

"Come orf it, mate. Take you two old blokes in there in daylight? Why, you'd be like a couple of bulls charging about. 'Arper'd be on to us in five minutes. I'll tell you how to find it, if you like."

"Well," sighed Holmes, "I suppose that must do." He pulled a map from his pocket and opened it out, "We are here." He jabbed his finger at the spot. "Now where is this fellow hiding?"

The expression on the grubby face told us that the map meant nothing to the boy, but on being pressed he gave clear directions which Holmes followed on the map, marking the key points with a pencil.

"That seems plain enough." The map was refolded, "Now, you will say nothing to anyone about speaking to us. Do you understand?"

"Trust me, Squire. I 'ope you does that 'Arper good and proper."

Another florin appeared and followed its predecessor in the blink of an eye. "Thanks, Guv. You're a toff."

Holmes watched the ragged figure out of sight before turning back to me. "A well-spent five shillings," he said. "I do believe we are nearing a solution to this tangled affair."

"Are we going after them now?" I asked eagerly.

"Not immediately. I must give the matter careful thought before finally proceeding. I wouldn't want to blunder at this stage. In any case, we need the cover of darkness for our movements."

253

I gave a sigh of resignation. "Once again, you have lost me. I thought that if we found Hartley and connected him with Harper and the murder of Knowles, we would be home and dried. It seems you have other ideas."

"You are right, up to a point, but there are wider matters to be taken into consideration. I must be certain of my facts." He took my arm and smiled. "Now, old friend, are you prepared for the climb back to town?"

Chapter XII – Death in the Night

On our return to The Green Dragon, Holmes shut himself in his room, ignoring all my entreaties to come down for the dinner prepared for us by Mrs. Davis. I gave up at last and, excusing his absence to the good lady, made the most of an excellent meal. Later I took a solitary walk, racking my brains for a clue to the workings of my colleague's mind, but all to no avail. Apart from his brief visit to London, of which he had given a full account, I had seen and heard all that he had, yet I was still floundering when he seemed to have most of the threads in his grasp.

I reviewed the present extent of my knowledge. It was almost certain that Harper or Hartley, perhaps both, had disposed of Knowles. Holmes had apparently dismissed his earlier reservations over the story told by Carmody, while Celia Winsett entered into it not at all. If, as Holmes appeared to think, the mysterious man in the woods was Hartley, then who was Martin, the latest guest at The Limes? His whole appearance and mode of speech marked him as from the Colonies, and it was surely more than coincidence that so many of the protagonists in our drama were from the far-flung outposts of Empire.

Harper and Hartley were both branded as miscreants by Carmody, but unless one or the other could be made to talk, no proof existed. Not that the lack of legal proof would deter Holmes if he was convinced of their guilt. He was not beyond manufacturing evidence if the occasion demanded it, or even of taking the law into his own hands.

I turned back to our lodgings, determined to tackle Holmes at once. On the landing, my hand was raised to rap on his door when it was flung open violently and my colleague faced me with a scowl on his face.

"Where the deuce have you been?" he demanded. "I've been waiting these twenty minutes for you to show up."

"Really – " I said in an injured tone, but he cut in impatiently.

"Not now. Get your hat and stick and come back here. It might be wise to slip your revolver into your pocket."

I was back in under a minute. His room was thick with tobacco smoke, a sure sign that he had spent the intervening hours in concentrated thought. He was in a state of nervous tension, and from my familiarity with his moods, I guessed that he had not only found all his answers, but had a clear plan of action designed to bring about what he would regard as a final result.

He had his map spread open on the bed, and he beckoned me across to look over his shoulder.

"See, we are here." He pointed with the stem of his pipe. "This is the path we took to Miss Winsett's cottage, and here is Bickstone Lodge."

I followed the direction of his pipe-stem and nodded.

"Here is the spot where the putative Hartley is skulking, so if we cut across here, we can be there within half-an-hour. Do you follow?"

I studied carefully the route he had traced. "You think we can trust that boy? Suppose we encounter Harper on our way?"

"The boy I believe," said Holmes. "As for Harper, I imagine we can deal with him between us. In fact, I would welcome a passage of arms with that scoundrel."

"Then we go now?"

"At once. The moon will be up shortly, and sufficient to light our way without leaving us unduly exposed. Take those two out of the game and I'm confident that tomorrow will see the whole matter resolved."

"I would have thought that if they are taken," I observed, "the matter will be ended tonight."

"We shall see," Holmes said enigmatically. "Are you ready?"

We made our way quietly down the stairs and let ourselves out of the back door, unseen by the landlord or his wife. Holmes stepped out confidently in the direction he had memorised from the map, and soon we were following a faint but definite path through the woods, the silence disturbed only by the rustlings of nocturnal creatures in the undergrowth and the occasional cry as one fell victim to a predator.

Not a word passed between us until, after what I judged to be twenty minutes, Holmes stopped suddenly and gave a warning hiss. He raised his arm and pointed. Following his finger I discerned a faint yellow glow some two-hundred yards ahead, and my companion's teeth gleamed in the nascent moonlight as he gave a triumphant grin.

"Wait," he breathed. "Be prepared for anything."

His injunction was superfluous. I already had my hand in my pocket, the walnut butt of my old service revolver nestling reassuringly in my palm. I edged my way forward behind Holmes, each step being carefully tested before I dared to trust my full weight on it. The time seemed interminable before we were in a position to make out any details, but at last we were able to crouch in the shadow of a large beech tree to take stock of the situation.

I saw that the yellow glow came from what looked like a dark-lantern set on the ground by the glowing embers of a small fire, the smoke from which drifted down-wind to us. I could see a figure moving back and forth between us and the light, seemingly watching and pacing with some impatience. Long minutes crept by. Then, from the darkness of the woods, a man appeared. I had no difficulty in recognizing the burly form of Harper as he came into the circle of light and came to a halt facing the other slighter figure.

They immediately began what looked to be some kind of altercation, their words coming to us as a dull indistinguishable murmur. The voices rose and fell, and a sign from Holmes took us closer by another ten yards, now creeping along on our hands and knees like hunters stalking their prey.

Now we could hear what was being said and it was Harper who was leading forth belligerently, a shotgun held loosely by his side.

"No, Mr. Hartley," he was saying angrily. "You listen to me. For near on two years, I've danced to your tune and done all you've said. What have I had out of it? Nowt but a few mouldy quid you've thrown my way when it suited you. I was me what spotted Knowles and put him away, and it's my neck what'll feel the rope if we come unstuck."

"We will not come unstuck if you keep your head," came the lighter tones of the man we now knew was Hartley. "As soon as I get my hands on Bickstone, we will both be on Easy Street, but don't get too greedy. You are the one that did for young Listel, and there are still questions being asked about that in Natal."

"With Knowles shut up," Harper sneered, "who knows anything?"

"I do, and you will do well to remember it."

"Who did for the old man? That wasn't me, I was out of the country at the time. Don't you threaten me, Mr. Clever Hartley."

Both men had raised their voices, and now Harper took a step back and raised his arm to level the shotgun at the other.

"Stop being a fool, Harper." There was a note of steel Hartley's voice, but no hint of fear. "We're both in this together, but you'll do well to remember Frederick Listel. I can well do without you, but what are you without me? Nothing! If I put you away now, it would not make the slightest difference to my plans."

He half-turned and I felt Holmes's hand grip my forearm as he began to rise to his feet, but events overtook any move that we could make.

I saw Hartley spin round, a pistol in his hand painting directly at Harper. There was an explosion of noise, and the sharper crack of the pistol sounding above the double boom of the shotgun. There was a commotion in the undergrowth and trees as the sleeping wild-life of the woods registered its protest at the invasion of its domain. Then I had my revolver out and was stumbling after Holmes who was already halfway to the scene. A terrible sight greeted our eyes. Harper had fallen into the fire, but even as Holmes dragged him clear, the black hole in the centre of his forehead was enough to tell me he was already dead. I turned quickly to where Hartley lay, uttering a cry of horror as the faceless apparition swam into view. He had caught the full blast of both barrels full in the face and, with all my medical training and my experiences in Afghanistan, I still felt sickened by what I now saw. All that remained was a bloody mask, and my hand, still clutching my revolver, hung limply at my side.

Even Holmes was shaken and momentarily lost for words as his eyes took it all in.

For about thirty seconds he remained frozen, then he recovered to turn a bleak look in my direction.

"There is work to be done," he said through gritted teeth. "Pull yourself together." He took out his watch and studied it. "It wants ten minutes to midnight. Make a note of the time. No, wait. Call it midnight – that will give us a little leeway to arrange matters. There is no doubt that these two are dead, but please pronounce it officially."

I came out of my trance and did his bidding, but it was a perfunctory task that needed no medical skill. I stood up and grunted confirmation.

Holmes picked up the dark lantern and with cold deliberation began to search through Hartley's pockets, returning some items and putting others to one side. He turned to Harper and repeated the procedure, this time retaining but one small piece of paper. He rose to his feet and looked down at the still forms, the faint silvery moonlight that penetrated the trees adding a dimension of unreality to the ghastly scene.

"They died as they lived," said Holmes as he turned away. "Violently and sordidly, and I cannot feel any pity for them. However, it's left to us to see they have left nothing that will embarrass innocent parties."

He swept the beam of the lantern around and it wavered before coming to rest on a dark opening in the thickest of the bushes. My straining eyes picked out a natural arbour formed by the hawthorns and, ducking my head, I followed my colleague inside.

There was a bed of dry bracken with a ragged blanket lying in an untidy heap on it, while on the floor was a tin plate with the remains of a meal and a stub of candle in a chipped saucer. My eye was drawn to a tapered green canvas case leaning against the back of the shelter.

Holmes had already seen it and he picked it up, unlacing it to reveal a superbly made hunting rifle. It was similar to those I had seen in the possession of regular army officers in India who, in between spells of active duty, enjoyed the thrills and pleasures of the chase.

"But for your quickness, this might well have done for one of us this morning," my companion remarked, now back to his normal self. "I take it you feel no sense of bereavement over the demise of this pair?"

"Only in so much that I would have preferred to see them dangling on the end of a rope," I retorted. "The way they went was too clean."

"But final, and with less chance of unwanted facts becoming public."

In the dim light of the lantern my expression told Holmes that I was lost, and he patted my shoulder gently.

"Bear with me. I promise I shall place the whole business in its proper perspective tomorrow. There is no more for us here, so we had better inform the police without delay, like good citizens."

We moved out into the open, and after a look around him he continued.

"Do you think you can find your way to the police station? I doubt that Arnold will be on duty, but whomever is will know where to find him,"

"It will take the better part of two hours to rouse out Arnold and get back here," I pointed out. "Will you be all right alone?"

"Of course," he said impatiently. "It will give me time to ensure that all is as it should be. Off you go, there's a good chap."

"One of these days you will go too far," I said over my shoulder as I set off, his chuckle following me into the gloom.

The moon was obscured by the time I reached the police station. The sergeant at the desk was unknown to me, but on my giving my name, it was obvious that the news of Holmes's and my involvement in local affairs had been relayed to him.

"Mr. Arnold has left instructions that you and Mr. Holmes be given any help you need, sir, but I don't know what I can do at this time of the morning." He glance significantly at the clock which stood at a quarter-to-one. "There's only me and one constable in the station."

"Then you can send him to fetch Inspector Arnold," I retorted. "You'll be in hot water if you delay, that I promise." The sergeant bent a resentful look on me, but at length he turned to the door behind him and called out. A sleepy looking constable stuck his head through, yawning and scratching his head.

"Straighten yourself up, Miller," the sergeant growled. "Get round to Inspector Arnold's house and tell him Dr. Watson wants him urgent. And get a move on," he added.

"What, at this time of the morning?" said the astonished constable. "He'll bite my head off."

"He'll do more than that if you waste time!" I snapped. "You can tell him that Mr. Holmes is waiting with two dead men in Bickstone Woods, and I'm here to show him the place."

Both policemen stared open-mouthed at me, and I felt myself struggling with my already frayed temper. Then the constable vanished like a startled rabbit, fumbling to fasten the neck of his tunic as he went. He was soon back, helmeted and flushed of face as he scuttled out of the station.

My mood was not such that I could remain still, and I went out into the night air where I paced to-and-fro, puffing furiously at my pipe.

Arnold arrived much quicker than I anticipated, his bearing as alert as ever despite the lateness of the hour.

"What the devil is going on, Doctor?" he snapped as soon as we met. "What's all this about dead bodies in the woods?"

I gave him the bare facts, thankful that he didn't ask any questions whose answers might conflict with any version that Holmes might have to give him. When I had finished he gave a curt nod, and I thought I caught a sardonic gleam in his eye.

"I sent Miller for Sergeant Mower," he said. "As soon as he arrives we can go. I'll get a couple of lanterns to take with us."

He vanished into the station. His back was barely turned before the sergeant came puffing up, his tunic not yet buttoned and his night-shirt stuffed into his trousers.

"What's the panic, Doctor?" he panted. "Miller gave me some story about dead bodies in the woods and me being wanted here."

"True enough, Sergeant, but Inspector Arnold is here to tell you all about it." As I spoke the inspector came down the steps and we set off on our errand, Arnold telling Sergeant Mower even less than I had thought fit to impart.

We entered the woods, now completely shrouded in darkness with the disappearance of the moon, our only light the bobbing rays of the bullseye lanterns carried by the two policemen. There being no need for caution now, we made rapid progress traversing the same ground as Holmes and I had covered earlier. I was relieved that my sense of direction hadn't failed me, and we came upon Holmes seated on a tree-stump puffing contentedly at his pipe.

"A pretty kettle of fish," the inspector said as soon as we were within earshot of my companion. "How did this come about?"

He stopped to survey the scene, his expression thunderous in the glow of the lanterns.

"None of our doing, Inspector," replied Holmes as he stood up. "No doubt Watson has sketched in the outlines?"

259

"Only in so far as you arrived to find these two quarrelling, but I want to know how it was you were so conveniently here."

"Let us say on information received," Holmes said easily. "Of course, you recognize Harper," he indicated his body. "This other character goes by the name of John Hartley."

"Confound it all, Mr. Holmes!" cried the inspector. "I know of your reputation and I have a lot of respect for you, but if you had knowledge of criminal activities, it was your plain duty to inform the police."

"Is it a crime for a man to camp out at night?" asked Holmes with a touch of sarcasm. "After all, he may have had permission from the land owner or his agent. I heard that a man that I believed to be Hartley was here, and Watson and I came along to find out if it was so."

"Why?" Arnold asked bluntly.

"Because I had this Hartley connected with Harper in your murder case. What we overheard tonight confirmed it, but this happened before either of us could intervene."

"You had better tell me all about it," sighed the inspector.

"It's a long story, but I shall make it as brief as possible," said Holmes. "I also have the interests of my client to consider. As you will have gathered, I came here in connection with the Listel family. A client of mine was uneasy about the death of Sir Frederick and the abduction and presumed death of his son and heir Alistair Listel. This fellow Harper had been named as one of the kidnappers of the younger Listel, and by a strange quirk of fate I learned from another client that he was employed by Sir Charles."

"The other client being Miss Winsett," put in Arnold.

Holmes continued without denying or confirming this. "By various means, I have ascertained that your murder victim is one William Knowles, the former servant of Alistair Listel. Knowles came to England in pursuit of Harper."

"With the intention of taking the law into his own hands?" hazarded Arnold. "Why was this Hartley on the scene?"

"That is where it becomes complicated. He was the brains behind the events in Natal, and came to team up with Harper. With Harper established on the estate, I think they were waiting for the opportunity to enter the Lodge and loot it for all it was worth."

Even to me this sounded feeble enough, and Inspector Arnold narrowed his eyes suspiciously, but already Holmes was pressing on.

"When Knowles turned up thirsting for vengeance, this unsavoury pair had to silence him or be exposed for what they were."

"But why did Knowles not go to the police?" asked the inspector.

"As you rightly guessed, he intended to deal with them himself, and anyway, how much credence would you have given his story?"

"It might have saved his life. We would have investigated and alerted Sir Charles to the possibility. It would depend on how convincing Knowles was."

"Knowles didn't think that way. He had suffered at the hands of Harper and Hartley and believed they had killed both Listels. Bear in mind his Colonial background, where justice tends to be of a more rough and ready kind than we're accustomed to."

Holmes went on to relate how we had come upon the two men engaged in what was their fatal altercation, carefully avoiding any mention of what had brought us here in the dead of night.

To me the whole story was a flimsy fabrication, and I could tell that Arnold was not overly impressed. To his credit, he outwardly accepted Holmes's version, no doubt happy to be in a position to close the files on three violent killings in as many days.

No mention was made of the rifle, and it was no longer in Hartley's lair when Arnold and Kower gave it their attention. The first signs of dawn were appearing before the latter was sent off to fetch reinforcements, and five minutes later Holmes suggested that our presence was unnecessary.

"You may go, gentlemen," the policeman nodded. "Dr. Watson is ready to certify that these two are dead, I take it?"

"Yes, of course," I said. "Even to placing the time of death as a minute or two either side of midnight."

"Then I shall ask you to call at the station later to make formal statements. Shall we say noon? There is also the matter of identification. Harper presents no problems – he is well known – but we still have nothing definite on those you have supposed to be Knowles and Hartley."

"That will all become clear later," said Holmes firmly. He turned away before any more questions could be posed. "Come, Watson. Breakfast is calling."

He made off in a direction different from that by which we had come, and as soon as Arnold was lost to view he darted into the scrub to come out clutching the green canvas rifle-case.

"Holmes!" I protested. "What are you up to now?"

He unlaced the case and brought out the weapon, holding it out to me stock first.

"What do you see, Watson?" he asked softly.

I looked at the weapon and in the growing light I could distinguish on the butt a circular brass plate. Looking more closely, I made out the initials 'A.L.' stamped on it, and I stared up at Holmes's grim face.

"'A.L.'" I muttered. "Alistair Listel?"

"Undoubtedly. This is probably what put Knowles on to Hartley in Durban, if you recall Carmody's account of things. It must be returned to its rightful owner."

"Who – oh, I see. You intend to give it to Sir Charles, as he was the heir to the title. It will be a fine gesture and much appreciated." Holmes replaced the rifle in its case. Then, with a rare display of affection, he put his arm around my shoulders.

"Watson, my friend, we have had a long night. Do you feel up to carrying on for a little longer? I want to go through Harper's cottage to make sure he has nothing that could give rise to awkward questions."

I couldn't refuse and followed gamely in his footsteps. He seemed to know exactly where he was heading, and less than fifteen minutes later we came in sight of a low stone building. The door was locked, but burst open when Holmes applied a shoulder to it to admit us to the single room.

There was little in the way of furniture. A narrow bed in one corner, a plain wooden table and chair, and a minimum of cutlery and crockery. A thorough search, which included stripping the bed to its bare frame and lifting the coarse matting on the floor, produced nothing more than a pair of pistols with ammunition for them, along with a box of shotgun cartridges. Holmes went through the pockets of the clothing hanging behind the door, coming up with a leather purse that held half-a-dozen sovereigns. This he returned, and then stood in the centre of the room for one final scrutiny.

"Nothing," he said in a satisfied tone. "I think we can now go ahead to finish this intricate matter. Forgive me if I remain reticent for the next few hours, but you know my methods."

"I know you love mystifying me, but I really cannot see what else remains. I'm still puzzled by your remark to Arnold regarding the identification of Hartley and Knowles. Don't underestimate that officer. He has a fine brain and a lot of common-sense to go with it."

"I quite agree, but he also wants to have his door-step clear of any unsolved crimes. Now come along – there are still things to be done and breakfast to be eaten."

He ushered me out of the cottage and wedged the door shut, and then struck an unerring path that eventually brought us to the road leading to the town. Despite my importunings he refused to say another word on the matter, and at last I gave up and retreated into an offended silence.

Chapter XIII – The Mist Clears

When we reached The Green Dragon, a bleary-eyed Davis was rolling empty casks into the yard for collection by the brewer's dray-man. He looked his surprise at our dishevelled appearance, but diplomatically made no comment beyond asking if we wanted breakfast at once.

"Give us time to clean up, Landlord," said Holmes as we made for the stairs. "Then you may dish up the biggest meal you can put together."

"Twenty minutes, sir," grinned Davis, "The missus has the stove going, and the girl has just come in with a trug of morning mushrooms."

Shaved and with fresh linen, I felt a lot better, and the laden plates set before us were quickly wiped clean. My companion still avoided any mention of the events of the night and I held my impatience in check, well aware that any questions of mine would be met with silence or evasions. Holmes would speak when he was ready, and not before.

We took our pipes to the benches in the front porch, where Holmes sat with a vacant look on his face, only the curling puffs of smoke from his pipe giving any hint of life. Somewhere in the distance a clock struck eight. I stood up to look down at my colleague.

"If you don't want to talk," I said, "I shall stretch out on the bed for a couple of hours."

He looked up absently and gave a jerk of his head. "You carry on. I have a few arrangements to make before we see Arnold."

He too rose to his feet and without another word set off towards the town, leaving me to stare at his retreating back. I shook my head in frustration and went up to my room. The sleepless night followed by the hearty breakfast induced a feeling of lassitude and, removing my boots, I settled down on the bed.

The next thing I knew was being shaken awake by Holmes, and I opened my eyes to see him looking down at me with a sardonic grin.

"Half-past-eleven o'clock," he was saying. "Straighten yourself up, and I'll meet you below,"

I splashed water on my face. Then, collecting my hat and stick, I went down to where Holmes awaited me. I expected that we would go straight to meet Inspector Arnold, but instead Holmes took me by the arm to steer me across the road to the railway station where he purchased platform tickets for us.

"What are we doing here?" I asked patiently. "We are due at the police station at midday."

"Plenty of time," he replied. "There is a train from London at eleven forty-four, and if Mr. Miles Carmody has heeded me, he will be on it.

When he arrives, please back me up in all I say, and for goodness' sake, do not add anything to my story."

"Have I lost your trust?" I said bitterly. "You revel in keeping me in the dark, yet expect me to blindly follow your every whim."

"I'm sorry." He sounded genuinely regretful. "Had you been awake mid-morning, I could have told you more. As it is, time is short."

"As you say," I said resignedly. "No doubt you will condescend to explain in your own good time."

A whistle and a plume of smoke in the distance heralded the train's imminent arrival and it clanked to a halt within seconds of its appointed time. A bare handful of passengers alighted, Carmody among them.

"Go and secure a cab before they are all taken." Holmes went forward to greet the South African while I went resentfully to do his bidding.

The first cab on the rank was driven by our old friend of the previous day. He acknowledged me with a finger to the brim of his hat.

"'Morning, Guv. Where to this time?"

"Probably the police station," I said shortly, unable to hide my chagrin at my friend's cavalier treatment of me. "My colleague is meeting someone from the train. He will tell you."

Presently Holmes and Carmody came out, the former talking animatedly and the other listening with an angry frown. They remained on the forecourt for another minute, and then Holmes ushered Carmody into the cab.

"Police station, Driver, but slowly please." Holmes waved me in ahead of him and took his place next to me facing our client, who gave me a brief nod of recognition before turning his attention back to Holmes.

"So Knowles is definitely dead." Carmody's voice was angry and bitter.

"I'm afraid so. He was dead even before you approached me about the matter. If it is any consolation to you, sir, his killer has already paid the price, along with his accomplice."

"Harper? Hartley? You have accounted for them?"

"Not I, Mr. Carmody. They disagreed and shot one another twelve hours since."

"Then my friend and his father too are avenged. Would that I had not involved poor Knowles in this and brought him to his end." Carmody stared blankly into space for a while. "One thing I would like to know, Mr. Holmes," he said. "Why have you brought me here so urgently?"

"Three reasons. First, Inspector Arnold, the senior police officer, has two bodies that need identifying officially. Knowles, of course, presents no problem, as you were close to him. The other man is Hartley, whom no one seems to know. That is where your help is needed."

"I fail to see what I can do." Carmody frowned, "Surely you haven't forgotten that I stated categorically that I would not recognize the man if he passed me in the street."

"Quite so, but Arnold does not know that, does he? Believe me, sir, it would save a lot of unwelcome questions if you could swear to his identity."

"Unwelcome questions? Unwelcome to whom?"

"That will become clear when we have crossed this bridge," replied Holmes. "I told you there were three reasons for bringing you here, and I ask you to trust me as we move on one step at a time. Will you do so?"

As he finished speaking, our conveyance pulled up at the police station and he fixed Carmody with compelling eyes.

The latter returned the look, then jerked his head in assent.

"Very well, Mr. Holmes," he said curtly. "You must have some valid reason for asking me to perjure myself, but I shall expect a full and convincing explanation before very long."

"You shall have it. Harper can be sworn to by any number of people here, so do not concern yourself with him. Just identify Knowles and Hartley and we can make the next step. Now, I'm sure Inspector Arnold is waiting with some impatience, so let us attend him."

We were taken at once to the inspector's office, where Arnold looked curiously at Carmody.

Holmes performed the introductions. "Inspector Arnold, this is my client, Mr. Miles Carmody, a former associate of Sir Frederick and Alistair Listel. He has come at my behest to identify the bodies of William Knowles and John Hartley, both of whom he knew in South Africa."

"That is most gratifying, Mr. Carmody. May I ask your relationship to the two deceased?"

"Knowles was formerly the servant of my friend, Alistair Listel. I took him into my service following the disappearance of my partner. I'm fully convinced that the other man, Hartley, was the murderer of Sir Frederick."

"Convinced?" said Arnold, "You had no proof?"

"I was getting close to the truth. That was my reason for engaging Mr. Sherlock Holmes."

I caught a smile on my friend's face at this plausible half-truth, which the inspector accepted at its face value.

"Well, sir, that will certainly tidy things up for me. First, though, I must take a statement from Mr. Holmes regarding the events of last night. You will bear with me? Paperwork is the bane of official policing." We disposed ourselves around the room and Holmes repeated his version of what he had said in the woods. Arnold took it down in a flowing hand and at the end he read it back. Holmes, agreeing to its correctness, affixed his signature to the pages. Then Arnold turned his attention to me.

"Do you have anything to add, Doctor?"

"Nothing," I replied. "Holmes and I were together the whole time and I saw all that he did."

Inspector Arnold, ignoring the ambiguity of my words, gathered his papers together. "Then the one statement will be enough," he said. "Mr. Carmody, I must now ask you to accompany me to the mortuary to perform your sad task. Are you prepared?"

"That's why I am here. Shall we proceed?"

Holmes and I waited outside as Carmody and Arnold went into the drab building, and as soon as we were alone I rounded angrily on my companion.

"How much longer am I to be kept dangling?" I demanded. "This secrecy is becoming intolerable. I might just as well return to London if you do not see fit to confide in me."

"And leave the final outcome to your imagination?" he retorted mockingly. "No, Watson, I want you with me when the last act is played out, if only to see my downfall should I be wrong."

"Last act? Wrong in what?"

"We shall see. Not another word, I beg you. Here is the inspector."

The other two joined us on the pavement, Carmody wearing a look of savage anger, while Arnold looked both satisfied and relieved.

"Well, gentlemen, that is enough for me to complete my report," said the latter. "I must warn you, Mr. Holmes, and you, Doctor, that I shall require you to give evidence at the inquest on Hartley and Harper tomorrow morning." He turned to Carmody. "You, sir, I need to attend the resumed inquest on William Knowles, which is set for next Saturday."

For a moment Carmody looked rebellious, then he nodded slowly.

"If it must be, Inspector. I shall be staying to see that poor Knowles has a proper funeral. That is the least I can do for a man for whose death I must bear a great responsibility."

"Then I will bid you good day, gentlemen. Eleven o'clock at The Golden Fleece, Mr. Holmes, and for you Mr. Carmody, the same time and venue on Saturday. Do not hesitate to call on me if I can help you in any way."

Arnold touched his cap and turned away, leaving us to our own devices.

Carmody watched him out of sight before speaking.

"Well, Mr. Holmes, as I must remain here, I should be thinking of accommodation. What do you suggest?"

"It can be arranged," Holmes replied. "First, I must enlighten you as to the other two reasons for bringing you here. Will you consent to a meeting with the heir to the Bickstone Estates?"

Carmody nodded. "I think I owe it to him. As you know, Sir Frederick had intended to effect a reconciliation with his brother, but fate decreed otherwise. Sir Charles is a worthy successor?"

"Sir Charles is a fine, upright gentleman," Holmes said gravely. "He too was anxious to heal the breach and was devastated by the deaths of his brother and nephew. He did not seek the title, but has put his heart and soul into the well-being of Bickstone. He has become highly regarded in the short while he has been here, and without wishing to give offence, I believe he pays more attention to the estate than did his predecessor."

"He is here now?"

"No. In the light of what you told me on Friday, I advised him to spend the week-end at his club. With Harper on the scene and Hartley somewhere in the background, I deemed it prudent. However, I believe he returns today, but before seeing him I would introduce you to someone else. Do you know a Henry Martin?"

"I am acquainted with no one in this country. Why?"

"I think Mr. Martin may be of interest to you, and you may find it instructive to meet him, even though the name is unfamiliar."

Carmody looked unenthusiastic, then gave a careless shrug.

"Very well. Having sought your advice, I should be foolish not to accept it. Where is this Martin?"

"Ten minutes' brisk walk will see us to where he lodges."

"Then lead on."

We bent our steps in the direction of The Limes. During our walk, my brain had been churning over and over, and I began to get a glimmering of what Holmes intended. The whole notion, if true, was so fantastic that I stopped in my tracks.

"Good God!" I cried.

Holmes swung round to direct a minatory glare at me as I remained frozen to the spot, getting to grips with what I suspected.

"Come along, Watson," he snapped. "This is no time for one of your flashes of inspiration."

I returned his glare and forced myself to fall in step with them, my mind in a whirl as I thought out the implications of what would happen if what I guessed proved to be right. For the remainder of the walk, Holmes kept up a constant flow of small-talk, presumably to preclude any further comment from me.

We found the pompous Curnow shepherding the first guests into lunch, and at our entrance he came forward with an inquisitive look.

"I gave Mr. Martin your message and he is expecting you, Mr. Holmes," he said. He was obviously curious as to what was happening, but received no satisfaction from my companion.

"Thank you, Mr. Curnow," replied the latter. "If you tell us the number of his room, we will announce ourselves. We are not to be disturbed under any pretext whatsoever. Is that clear?"

The little man pursed his lips, giving a reluctant nod. "Very well. I'll see to it. Mr. Martin's room is Number Seven, first floor rear." He turned away and forced a smile for the benefit of an elderly lady who had appeared at his elbow, leaving us to ascend the stairs ahead.

We found the room and, at a sign from Holmes, I rapped smartly on the panel of the door.

"Come in. It is unlocked." The voice was muffled by the woodwork.

Holmes threw open the door and preceded us in.

"A visitor for you, Mr. Martin."

Over my friend's shoulder, I could see Martin standing beside the window, his hands thrust deep into his trouser pockets. He looked up at us carelessly. Then, as I advanced into the room with Carmody at my heels, his jaw dropped.

Carmody had stopped abruptly, and I saw Holmes's face relax into an expression of triumph mixed with relief as Martin bounded forward with arms outstretched.

"Miles, by all that's wonderful!" he cried. "However did you find me here?"

Carmody stood paralysed, his features showing disbelief and shock as Martin came towards him. His lips worked soundlessly as he attempted to speak, and when the words came in was in a hoarse croak.

"Alistair! Oh, my God! It's impossible!" He literally choked on the words and reached out to grasp my shoulder for support. "Can this be true?"

Chapter XIV – The Long Pursuit

I gently eased Carmody into the room and shut the door. It was during our walk from the mortuary to The Limes that it had begun to dawn on me that Martin was not all that he seemed, and Holmes's mysterious and reticent behaviour had implanted the idea that Henry Martin might be the supposedly dead Alistair Listel. The sheer audacity of such an imposture was well-nigh incredible, for surely there was someone in the small community would have recognized him. The idea had buzzed around in

268

my head, but we had reached The Limes before I could put my theories into any coherent order.

My amazement was tempered by a sense of gratification that I had gone some way towards untangling the strands, albeit somewhat late in the day, and I had no doubt that Holmes would explain his chain of reasoning in his own good time. Meanwhile our attention was on the two South Africans.

Carmody pulled himself together and reached out to take the other by both hands, and for the best part of a minute they contemplated each other in silence. Both had been unprepared for the meeting, but whereas Martin, as I continued to think of him, was surprised and delighted to see his erstwhile partner, the latter was dazed and uncomprehending.

"Yes, it is I, Miles. Not a ghost." The words were accompanied by a wry smile. "But I do not understand your presence here, or even in this country."

"I could say the same." Carmody's voice was unsteady, but he was regaining control of himself. "What does it mean, Alistair? Why have you led everyone, even your closest friends, to believe you dead? What was the object?"

"A long and involved story, Miles, and in some respects I have let my thirst for revenge bring sorrow and tragedy to those closest to me. One thing I must make absolutely plain, both to you and to these gentlemen: Alistair Listel is dead, and subject to any reasons for him being restored to life, will remain so. I am Henry Martin, a diamond merchant and prospector from the Transvaal – or South African Republic, as it is becoming known.

"But why? Surely you have come here to claim your rightful title and place in society?"

"Title? Society? Bah! What is there here that I do not have already? Could you, Miles, live in this cramped and confined country, beset by artificial laws and conventions? No, I see by your expression you could not even contemplate it."

"Then what brought you here if not for that purpose?"

"I think I have an inkling," Holmes interpolated, pushing himself away from the door-jamb against which he had been leaning. "If Mr. – er – Martin is willing to talk before strangers, it will be instructive to hear how far my deductions were accurate."

"And how it was you could live here without being recognized," I added.

"Your question is easily answered, Dr. Watson," said the man who was now Martin with a laugh. "I spent very little of my life at Bickstone, and none at all since reaching adulthood. In fact, this is the first occasion

I have been in England for upwards of sixteen years. As a further precaution, I have kept out of the public gaze as much as possible without appearing furtive, although I think Mr. Holmes spotted me at the inquest on poor Knowles last Saturday."

"I saw you, but I confess to being uncertain as to who you were. My first thoughts inclined me to the idea that you might be Hartley, but I discarded that very early on." Holmes gave a short laugh. "At first, both Watson and I had doubts about Mr. Carmody's account, even to wondering if Hartley really existed. But I digress. Pray continue, Mr. Martin."

"I think you all deserve an explanation," said Martin, as I will call him henceforth. "I make one stipulation. Not a word of this will go beyond these four walls. You will see why when I have finished. Is that understood?"

"I can give that assurance on behalf of Watson and myself, with one proviso," replied Holmes. "Watson shall be allowed to make a record of events for our archives, with all names and places changed so that no outsider can correlate them to actual people. Refuse this and I reserve the right to speculate and to encourage Watson to someday publish the results of my speculations."

Martin scowled, but after a moment's thought he gave his grudging assent.

"So be it. I am in your hands and must accept your word."

He settled back in his chair and produced a case of black cheroots to offer around. Carmody took one, but Holmes and I took out our pipes, and soon the room was filled with the fumes of the differing tobaccos.

I took out my notebook and rested it on my knee, pencil poised to take down the story that Martin was about to tell.

He began slowly, choosing his words with care.

"As I gather Miles has told you, Knowles and I were abducted some two years ago, and when our captors split into separate parties, Knowles very quickly contrived his escape. I was taken to a Kaffir kraal in the Drakensberg and, although closely confined, I was not mistreated physically. Hartley, as I discovered him to be, put in an occasional appearance, probably to pay the natives to keep me there. After a few weeks I tried offering them bribes to release me, but whether for fear of Hartley or of official retribution, I remained a prisoner.

"It was during one of Hartley's early visits that Harper turned up and the pair of them became involved in a violent argument. I gathered that Harper had brought the news of Knowles' escape and his reappearance in Durban. I also overheard that one of them intended to bring about the death of my father so that Hartley could come to England posing as me and claim the Listel estates. With Knowles free they were in a dilemma, and I suspect

I was only allowed to stay alive until such time as Knowles and my father were out of the way. I reasoned too that Miles, as my close friend and partner, was also a marked man. Remember, gentlemen, all this took place over a period of several months and I could keep only a vague track of time."

"Why were you not killed at once?" asked Holmes. "That would have been the obvious way forward for the conspirators."

"That is true, but let me tell this in my own way," Martin replied. "Hartley's visits became less and less frequent, and I began to find that the natives bore me no real animosity. In fact, they began to allow me a measure of freedom to wander around the kraal, although closely watching me at all times. Bhoteslana, the chief, spoke some Taal, and he began to hint that he would be glad to have me off his hands but for the fear of punishment if I returned to my own people."

He broke off to take a corn-cob pipe from his pocket and began to fill it. The rest of us followed suit and I went to throw wide the window to allow some of the fumes to disperse. Eventually Martin took up his tale again.

"The time came when Hartley had failed to show up for some considerable period," he went on. "By now I had established a degree of trust between myself and Bhoteslana and made a final plea to be released. I promised them complete immunity from pursuit, but pointed out that I knew my servant was free and likely to stir up a hornet's nest in his search for me. I also planted the idea that Hartley had deserted them and they would see no more of him.

"Came the day when the chief agreed to hold a meeting of his council to decide my fate. I tell you, I was on thorns during their deliberations. The way I saw it, there were four possible outcomes: They could kill me, keep me prisoner, let me go, or the fourth being that Hartley would turn up and persuade them to take one of the first two choices – certainly not the third! Three days dragged by. Then, late at night, Bhoteslana came to me with the news for which I had prayed. I was to be escorted as far as the plains, from whence I could make my way to Ladysmith or wherever suited me. I reiterated my promises of good faith and, at first light, I was taken on my way. I bear old Bhoteslana no ill-will, for on the whole I was not badly treated, and the Kaffirs have little conception of right and wrong as we know it."

Martin stopped talking to relight his pipe, then sat in silent contemplation as we waited for him to go on.

"But why did you let everyone remain ignorant of your survival?" cried Carmody. "Surely your father and I deserved better than that!"

"You did," replied Martin. "Especially my father, but I was in no state of mind to think of that. My period of captivity had exceeded eight months, and I was left with only a burning resentment and an overwhelming desire for vengeance that consumed me above all else. To my eternal shame and regret, I did not even warn my father of his peril. I knew he was still alive, but my sole aim was to lay my hands on Hartley and Harper and make them pay for those lost months. During my time as a prisoner I had grown a full set of whiskers, which left untrimmed gave me the appearance of a Boer farmer, and I found I could move about with no fear of recognition except by those who knew me best.

"I soon got on to Harper's trail and then I lost him, but Hartley was another matter. As soon as I thought myself near him he would turn up fifty or more miles away. I must have scoured half of South Africa to find myself frustrated time and time again – and then the blow fell. The news of my father's murder reached me in Pretoria, some three weeks after the event, together with a rumour that Harper had left the country. I was stricken with grief and remorse, blaming myself for not giving my father the warning that could have saved his life, and for letting him die in the belief that I was lost to him.

"Soon my grief was supplanted by a fierce rage and an obsessive determination to hunt down these inhuman fiends and deal out my own justice, irrespective of the consequences. To the title and estate I gave little thought, the first being of little moment, and as for the estate – well, Miles will tell you that I already have more money at my disposal than I can ever spend."

"How did you trace Hartley to England?" Carmody put in.

"Bush telegraph. You, know, the rumours and stories that circulate amongst the hunters and trekkers. Hartley was a figure who flitted about the country, dealing, prospecting, and with a finger in several pies, yet difficult to pin down. No one really knew him, but a lot of people knew of him, and I heard that he had been in Pietermaritzburg realising his assets."

"Just as I did," said Carmody, "and a fine old stir he caused in the market."

Martin nodded. "I headed back to Durban and made some judicious inquiries from which I learned that a passage had been booked in the name of Sir Alistair Listel on the *S.S. Trojan*, which had sailed a day or two earlier. I took the first available ship to England, not knowing then that Miles and Knowles, staunch friends that they proved to be, had been working on the same lines. I reasoned that if the plot was to go forward, the centre of it would be at Bickstone, so I came here to observe events.

"I quickly identified Harper, but his accomplice was as elusive as ever. I was content to wait, believing Miles and Knowles to be in South

Africa and knowing there was a breathing space until they had been disposed of.

"I had taken to wandering the woods at night in the hope of catching the two scoundrels together, and had I done so I assure you their lives would not have been worth a moment's purchase. You can imagine my astonishment when last Tuesday night I ran into Knowles during my search. I had no idea that he and Miles were in the country, and he, convinced of my demise, came near to having a seizure. When I at last persuaded him I was not a ghost, we each told our stories, and he justifiably reproaching me for my secrecy. We arranged to meet the next night and I agreed to his informing Miles of my presence. Alas, I never saw him again, and when I read of a murdered man being found in Bickstone Woods, I knew instinctively that it was he. I was stunned. Should I break my cover and play a lone hand? That was the question I asked myself, and there seemed to be just one answer. On Saturday I attended the opening of the inquest and found that a police inspector, Arnold as he was named, had his head screwed on right and with the resources at his disposal might well discover what I had so far failed to do.

"I noticed that I was being closely observed by a total stranger. That was you, Mr. Holmes, although I didn't know that until you came here yesterday with Inspector Arnold." Martin gave a faint smile. "Even in South Africa your reputation is not unknown. Nevertheless, I was in the dark as to your interest, and the thought of Knowles being buried in an unmarked grave caused me considerable anguish. I brooded on the matter, unwilling to reveal my true identity. Then this morning, I received your message asking me to wait in my room for you to call. As you stressed the importance of the meeting I did so, with never a thought as to this outcome. I had been on the point of trying to establish contact with you, Miles, but it seems Mr. Holmes has been one step ahead of me."

Holmes gave a deprecating wave of his hand. "Would that I had been consulted earlier," he said. "Your man Knowles might still be alive had it been so."

"That was something I did not foresee," Carmody said defensively. "I wanted to get on the track of Hartley, and as Knowles could recognize him and I could not, it seemed the best line to take."

"No blame attaches to you, Miles," Martin consoled him, "Had I but trusted my two old friends, both he and my father would have been preserved. However, I have still to hear your account of things. Then I must consider my future position."

"What is there to consider?" asked Carmody. "It seems plain to me."

273

Martin shook his head. "Anything but plain," he said, "but tell me your story first. Our paths must have crossed several times during our separate pursuits of Hartley. Are those two villains still at large?"

"They are both dead," said Holmes. "Mr. Carmody has been told all the details and he will bring you up to date." He rose to his feet and signalled with his eyes for me to do likewise.

"Watson and I will leave you for the time being. You must have much to discuss." He looked at his watch. "It is approaching the hour of two, so if we return at four o'clock, any remaining matters can be cleared up then. Is that agreeable to you?"

Martin looked across at his friend before nodding. "Four o'clock will be fine. I'm anxious to know how you came to the correct solution, and I shall positively gloat to hear of the end of the murderers of my father and my old servant. I shall also ask some very serious questions of you before I make a final decision, and I believe you to be well-qualified to advise me. Four o'clock it is, then."

As we passed through the entrance hall, Mr. Curnow looked up from his desk.

"Is Mr. Martin remaining upstairs?" he asked anxiously. "The other gentleman is still with him? What of lunch?"

"Mr. Martin and the other gentleman have discovered they have some common interests," Holmes replied mendaciously. "No doubt they will send for anything they need, but wait upon a summons."

The little man shrugged as if washing his hands of the matter, then returned to his ledger as the door closed behind us.

"What now?" I asked. "I would remind you that it is now several hours since we breakfasted, and I for one have quite an appetite. I would also think I deserve some kind of explanation."

"There is little that you don't already know," answered my colleague. "You seemed to have grasped the fact that Martin was in reality the Alistair Listel who was presumed by everyone to be dead. In fact, I was afraid you were about to blurt it out as we approached The Limes."

"It had only just occurred to me," I confessed. "You knew much earlier."

"Not so much. I admit my thoughts had been tending to that theory, but it wasn't until we found Hartley that I had any degree of certainty."

"What led you to it in the first place?"

Before he could answer, the clip-clop of hooves and the jingle of harness made us look round to see our old friend the cabbie heading towards us. Holmes waved his stick and the driver looked down at us with a grin.

"Again, gents? Where to this time?"

"Only The Green Dragon."

"Hop aboard. I was going back to the station." He was pleased enough to pick up a few extra coppers for a journey he was making anyway.

Despite my impatience, Holmes refused to say any more of the reasoning that had led him to the revelation of Martin's true identity, and twenty minutes later we had made significant inroads into a succulent steak pie provided by Mrs. Davis.

"Now then," I said, pushing my plate aside and determined not to be put off any longer. "Can we continue?"

Alas, my hopes were in vain, for at that moment the landlord put his head around the door with an apologetic cough.

"Sorry to intrude on your meal, sirs, but Sir Charles Listel is here and asking for you, Mr. Holmes. I explained you were having a late lunch, but he said he'll be happy to wait."

"That's all right, Davis," said Holmes. "We've finished. Let Mrs. D. clear away, and then you may show him in,"

The baronet, as I still thought of him, came in with a genial smile on his face. "I arrived back an hour ago and Inspector Arnold told me the sorry tale – at least, that part of it he finds it politic to believe – but I suspect there is more to it than you chose to divulge."

"More than I intend to divulge, Sir Charles," replied Holmes. "All the same, there are certain facts that you should know, and there is another who has first-hand knowledge of the events in Natal. Cast your mind back to our first meeting last Friday when I spoke of a Miles Carmody who had brought me into the case."

"Yes, I remember well."

"Mr. Carmody has travelled down to here and desires to tell you all he can of your relatives. He was on intimate terms with both your brother and your nephew, and feels it would be a courtesy to seek you out."

"Inspector Arnold told me he was in the town. Is he under this roof?"

"No, he has business of his own to conduct, but with your permission I shall bring him to Bickstone Lodge this evening that he may talk to you with some degree of privacy."

"Of course you must bring him!" cried Sir Charles. "Come to dinner, all of you. I shall send my carriage to fetch you at seven-thirty, if that is convenient." He gave a shuddering sigh. "To think that I harboured that murderer for almost a year and yet had no inkling of his real character until you spoke to me on Friday."

"Perhaps it was as well," said my colleague. "Had you shown any signs of suspicion, you may have gone the same way as others who stood in the path of that precious pair. Arnold told you that he and his accomplice killed each other during a quarrel last night?"

"Indeed he did, but not how you managed to get on the trail of that other villain."

"I have my methods, and it doesn't do to explain them all. As my good friend the doctor knows, if a conjurer reveals his secrets, he receives little credit for his skill,"

Sir Charles looked from one to the other of us before turning away with a rueful laugh.

"Then I must perforce be content with that, sir," he said. "I wish you a good afternoon and shall look forward to your company tonight."

Holmes escorted him to the door, and on returning met my scowl with a display of bland innocence.

"Good grief!" I expostulated. "How can you continue to play cat-and-mouse with that gentleman when his whole future may be turned upside down within hours?"

"You think so? We shall see. Meanwhile we must apprise Mr. Carmody of tonight's arrangements, and before you explode, I assure you all will become clear very soon."

Fuming with annoyance at his attitude, I followed him out to secure a cab – not our old acquaintance this time – to take us to The Limes, and on the way Holmes gave me a swift resume of his deductions.

"As you already know," he said, speaking rapidly. "I – or we – quickly agreed that the man murdered on Friday was William Knowles, and his killer was Harper, although we had no firm evidence. I also toyed with the idea that the man calling himself Martin could be Hartley. However, after the attack on us yesterday morning, we had it from Mr. Curnow that Martin had been under his eye almost constantly during the relevant time, so it could not be he. Harper we had already discounted for obvious reasons, so that left Hartley still in the game. Thanks to a chance remark from you and the encounter with the boy we picked up his trail.

"Now we have four South Africans in the picture: Knowles who is dead, Carmody in London, and Harper and Hartley on the loose – so who is Martin? We placed him as being from the colonies, but Carmody did not speak of anyone else being involved, and it was too much to accept him as a casual visitor to the centre of action, so at the expense of a couple of ounces of shag, I decided that he could only be Alistair Listel who, for reasons known only to himself, wished to remain dead."

"Unbeknown to any of the other participants?" I said doubtfully.

"Certainly until he and Knowles crossed paths that night in the woods. Martin had kept very much to himself without seeming to be furtive, and it was soon after that encounter that Knowles was recognized and taken by one of the plotters, probably Harper. You saw his body, Watson, and know that he had been subjected to inhuman treatment,

276

probably in an attempt to find out what he knew and who else threatened the two villains."

"Most likely he was kept prisoner in Harper's cottage," I put in quickly.

Holmes nodded. "On Thursday night, he contrived to get away, but weakened by his ill-treatment, he stood little chance. With Harper closing in on him, he reached Miss Winsett's cottage hoping for succour, but too late!"

I envisaged the awful scene in those dark and forbidding woods as Holmes paused dramatically before continuing.

"He could literally feel his hunter breathing down his neck and, in a despairing effort, scribbled that cryptic message on a fragment of paper – 'Tell C Har' – 'Tell Carmody Harper' – and slipped the box through the letter-slit before making one final attempt to elude his pursuer, but all in vain. Harper caught up with him, and the final outcome we know."

As I digested this, the cab turned into the driveway of The Limes, and as it crunched to a halt, I sat motionless to contemplate what Holmes had said. There were of necessity several gaps in his reading of events, but I had little doubt that it was reasonably accurate.

"Was Miss Winsett ever in danger?" I asked,

"Only if Harper guessed that Knowles had communicated with her. He may have tried to find out had she remained at Bickstone, but that we shall never know." He descended from the cab and, throwing a coin to the driver, told him to wait for us.

Curnow was not in evidence and we went straight up to Martin's room, finding the reunited friends engaged in a mild dispute. It was apparent that Martin was making a point that Carmody found hard to accept, and on our appearance the farmer turned to us immediately.

"Your arrival is opportune, gentlemen," he said. "Perhaps you can persuade Miles that I know what I am about."

"If we knew your intentions, we would be better placed to comment," said Holmes with a faint smile. "Enlighten us, I pray you,"

Carmody stirred restlessly in his chair. "The whole thing is preposterous!" he muttered. "It would suit me very well, but I am sure it is in some way illegal."

"Nonsense!" cried Martin. "All I am doing is preserving the *status quo*, and at the same time following my own inclinations. Miles admits that it is a solution that would please him, yet he quibbles over the matter of legality."

"There are other considerations," Carmody muttered, but he was silenced by an impatient gesture from my companion.

"Please let me hear Mr. Martin's proposals," he said. "I have a fair notion of what he sees as the right course in the interests of all, but I wish to hear it from his own lips." He sat down uninvited, his long legs stretched out before him and his fingers laced across his waistcoat. "I beg you, sir, proceed." He laid his head back and, with half-closed eyes, waited for Martin to speak.

The latter waved me to a chair and then took his stance by the window to face all three of us.

"My decision is this," he stated firmly. "I have made it after much thought and observation and it is irrevocable. No argument shall deflect me from my purpose. Alistair Listel is no more, lost and presumed dead somewhere abroad. The title and estates of Bickstone remain with the rightful holder, Charles Listel, Who loses by it?"

Chapter XV – The Curtain Falls

Henry Martin's jaw was set in stubborn determination as he glared across the room, ready to defy any attempt to deflect him from his purpose. Carmody, for his part, looked helplessly at Holmes, who sat calmly watching from beneath hooded eyes.

"Well, Mr. Holmes, have you nothing to say?" snapped Martin, breaking the silence that hung in the air.

"What is there to say?" queried my colleague. "If you are set on this course, who am I to dissuade you? Wait – " he added when Carmody made to protest. "Three points occur to me: What brought you to this decision? Can you rely on Mr. Carmody to dissemble convincingly when he meets Sir Charles, as he almost certainly must? Thirdly, how will you account for yourself on your return to South Africa, which you no doubt intend?" Martin appeared to relax slightly and propped himself against the window-sill, his arms folded on his chest.

"Let me answer those points in the order you asked them," he said. "I did not go into this lightly, and during the short while I have been here, I have learnt much. I have listened more than I have talked – a word here, a word there has been sufficient to set people off, and a large part of my knowledge has come from Mr. Curnow and Colonel Milton. The latter has been resident here since his retirement from the army some five years ago.

"It was not difficult to introduce my uncle's name into a conversation, and I gained the impression that he has become a highly respected figure during the year or so he has been at the Lodge. It appears that a number of the older people still remember my grandfather and deplored the fact that my father was more attentive to his African interests than to the Bickstone

Estate. Of course, my uncle had spent his youth here, but had been away for upwards of thirty years when he inherited, and was an unknown quantity." He paused briefly to light a cheroot. "Miles tells me that you gentlemen regard him in a favourable light," he said. "Is that so?"

Holmes answered for us both. "We have met him only twice, but his reputation in the City and locally is that of a man of probity, as well as being a shrewd business man."

"And his stewardship of the estate has been to its advantage?"

"In every way." Holmes picked his words carefully. "At the risk of being disrespectful to the late Sir Frederick, I hear that the estate is now better managed than at any time during the past quarter-century."

"That I can believe," said Martin with a wry smile. "My father was ever more the man of affairs than the country squire. He was content to let an agent run the estate with but the occasional visit from him. It was not mismanaged, but it lacked dedicated attention."

"And you have a similar outlook as did Sir Frederick," Holmes put in quickly.

"I cannot deny it. Miles and I have been more-than-successful in our many ventures, and I have little or no desire to vegetate in this cramped environment. Of course, on the death of Alistair Listel, all his assets reverted to his partner, but I have sufficient capital at my disposal to buy my way in, should he so desire."

"That is ridiculous!" cried Carmody. "Why, our capital has appreciated by some twelve-per-cent since your disappearance, and we could resume on the old footing."

"That is for discussion between you and Harry Martin," said the latter with a look that showed he thought he had carried the day. "But to get back to what I was saying: I have given my reasons for remaining dead, and as I cannot think that Hartley and Harper will suffer by having my murder charged to their account, neither do I care."

We all laughed, relieving some of the tension that had built up. Then Martin continued his exposition.

"There is then no doubt that Bickstone will benefit from my uncle's attentions, and as I indicated, I am wealthy enough not to covet what I have never had. To move on to your second point, Mr. Holmes, I hope and believe that Miles can carry it off. It would have been preferable if he had met my uncle before I was discovered, but we must take the hand we are dealt. I shall depend on you, Miles. Surely you can see that Bickstone will prosper under my uncle's hand, and I would be miserable were I tied down here. Unless," he added slowly, "you wish to play a lone hand back in Natal?"

279

"Never think that!" replied Carmody indignantly. "That was a most unjust thing to say. Nothing would please me more than to resume our old footing, but consider my position. I am not accustomed to falsehood and dissimulation, and I would be fearful of revealing the extent of my knowledge by some slip of the tongue."

"Nevertheless, you will do it," Martin said confidently. "That brings us to your third question. On our return to South Africa, I shall not appear in Natal. During my wanderings in pursuit of Hartley, I picked up rumours of rich pickings to be had in Cape Colony to the north of Kimberley. Once Miles has been persuaded to go along with my suggestion of the new partnership, I think we could head that way and do pretty well for ourselves."

Carmody's face had taken on a look of resignation as his friend's confident enthusiasm made itself felt, and I could see his doubts fading away as he saw the prospect of a return to the old familiar life.

"What do you think, Mr. Holmes?" he asked. "Do you believe it to be the right course, and if so, can it really succeed?"

Holmes stroked his sharp nose thoughtfully as he considered his reply.

"I see no objections to Mr. Martin's scheme in principle," he said. "Of course, you must understand that yours will be the most difficult role to play. We are bidden to dine at Bickstone Lodge tonight, and it would not surprise me if Sir Charles offers you his hospitality for the remainder of your time here. If you think you can sustain your part then yes, I see no reason why it should not work out." He turned to Martin. "You are resolved?"

"Indeed I am. Miles will come up trumps, never fear."

"What is the position in law?" Carmody frowned. "What of the succession after Sir Charles? He is unmarried, with no heirs, and he is no longer a young man."

"Neither is he old," Holmes pointed out to nod of agreement from Martin. "It is always possible that his known commitment to Bickstone may well prompt him to seek a suitable wife. That, of course, is speculation pure and simple. If Alistair Listel is to be presumed dead and remains so, the legal position does not arise."

"Confound you all," muttered Carmody. "You are driving me willy-nilly into a corner. I would ask nothing better than to be free on the veldt with my old friend and partner, but it goes against the grain to practise this deception." He looked morosely at Martin and sighed deeply. "Yet if I refuse, it will cause us both grief and possibly future regrets."

"Then you'll do it, Miles?" There was urgency in Martin's tone. "For my sake, and for the good of Bickstone?"

"For your sake and for my own selfish reasons," replied Carmody. "For Bickstone I really could not give a hang. Yes, I'll do it for you, Harry Martin, and for our partnership."

"Stout fellow!" chuckled Martin. "You see, it will not take long for you to adjust to a new companion."

He went over to clap his friend on the shoulder and wring his hand fervently before turning to Holmes.

"Well, sir, it seems everyone is to be satisfied, but you spoke of dining with Sir Charles this evening?"

"That is so. He is sending his carriage at half-past-seven for Mr. Carmody, together with Watson and myself. Stick to the story you told me on Friday and all will be well. I foresee no problems."

"Rehearse your story well," I put in. "Holmes and I will be on hand to field any loose balls."

"Must I accept his invitation to remain at Bickstone should it be extended?" asked Carmody doubtfully.

"It would be a much appreciated kindness," said Holmes. "He will want to hear of your life in Africa with his brother and nephew. It is only of today's events that you need guard your tongue. Meet us at The Green Dragon at seven-thirty. It is directly opposite the railway station."

"Then it is settled," said Martin. "Miles, I must trust you to see that Knowles has a proper burial. I shall leave here in the morning."

"You will not stay for the funeral?" Carmody showed surprise.

"As much as I want to, I think that the circumstances being what they are I should remove myself from the scene. Knowles would understand and approve, I feel sure."

"Mr. Martin is right," Holmes interjected. "Despite his long absence, there is always the possibility of someone recognizing him."

"Then I shall see to it," said Carmody. "We were well served by the poor fellow, and he suffered much. Leave it to me."

Holmes and I prepared to depart and Martin came forward to shake us both warmly by the hand.

"Mr. Holmes, Doctor," he said diffidently. "I can never thank you enough for your help and discretion, but is there some more tangible way of showing my gratitude without causing offence or embarrassment?"

Holmes gave a rich chuckle. "My dear sir, I am a professional in every sense of the word. Call on me at Baker Street before you leave the country and I will present our account. I have in my possession a fine hunting rifle bearing the initials '*A.L.*' on the stock which I found in Hartley's hide-out. I am sure it will be of more use where you are going than in this relatively civilized country. It will be easy for me to take it with me tomorrow for you to collect later."

281

Despite a limited wardrobe, we made ourselves reasonably presentable for our dinner engagement. Sir Charles Listel was visibly affected on meeting Miles Carmody and was eager to hear all that could be told of the life led by his brother and nephew in Africa.

We dined well that night, with Holmes first giving his account of the affair in an untypically modest manner, Carmody followed with his version, which was virtually the story told to us at our first meeting.

It left the baronet in no doubt that both his relatives had perished in the manner described and Carmody, his course now set, gave no hint of the deception that was being practised.

As forecast, Sir Charles invited Carmody to remain under his roof for the duration of his stay in the area, an invitation which was accepted without demur. On the plea of tiredness, which for my part was genuine enough, Holmes and I were returned to the town well before midnight and I fell into our beds in a state of exhaustion.

The inquests on Tuesday went smoothly, Inspector Arnold no doubt having primed the coroner beforehand, and soon after midday we were seated in a first-class railway carriage on our way back to London and the familiar sights and sounds, not to mention smells, of the Metropolis.

It was the following Monday when Martin and Carmody called on us to announce their imminent return to the Dark Continent. Martin was overjoyed to recover his hunting rifle, stroking the weapon affectionately.

"I must remove those initials," he said with a laugh. "It could prove awkward if Harry Martin had to explain those away." He became brisk.

"Now, gentlemen, the reckoning." Holmes laid a piece of paper before him and the partners studied it for a few seconds before Martin produced a purse of coins.

"I assume that Dr. Watson's bill will be near enough the same," he said as he tipped the gold on to the table and began counting. "If I double this, there will be no shortfall?"

I opened my mouth to protest, but a warning glance from Holmes turned my objections into a spluttering cough.

"I do not think Watson and I are likely to fall out over any small items of expenditure," said my companion with a genial smile. "It has been a pleasure to apply ourselves to your problems, and I know I speak for Watson when I extend our warm wishes for your future ventures."

I nodded my agreement and soon afterwards the two South Africans left, to vanish forever from our lives.

That same day Miss Celia Winsett put in an appearance. Having read a newspaper account of the shootings at Bickstone, she was anxious to know if it was safe for her to resume the residence of her cottage, her friend's husband having returned from his latest voyage. She was assured

282

her that there was no reason for her to absent herself any longer, and showed evident relief at the prospect of going back to Bickstone.

"That is good news indeed, Mr. Holmes," she said with a smile. "As fond as I am of Emily I find her preoccupation with her forthcoming happy event a trifle wearing. Now she has her husband home until that occurrence, and I shall be pleased to have my rustic retreat back. Now, I believe I am in your debt, so if you will tell me the sum I shall settle it at once."

"My dear young lady, your problem was incidental to the matter," said Holmes. "I have been well recompensed for my efforts, and both Dr. Watson and I are happy that you can revert to your chosen way of life. There is one point I must mention: You will find a small chip in the frame of your bedroom door and a hole in the plaster beside it. I am sure that a word to Sir Charles will see it put to rights."

The following months were busy ones, and it was mid-September when I realised that the evenings were drawing in and summer was nearly over.

I was breakfasting alone one Monday morning, Holmes still lying abed. I shuffled through the letters by my plate, laying the obvious bills to one side, which left but one missive that seemed worthy of attention. It was a large, square envelope of good quality, postmarked at Bromley. I didn't recognize the writing and I turned it over in my hands as if willing it to reveal its contents.

It failed to do so, and at last I reached out for a knife to slit open the envelope and extract a single embossed card. I stared blankly at it, allowing the words to register on my bemused brain. As they did so I was aware of a broad smile spreading across my face and I hastily sifted through the pile of mail beside Holmes's plate, coming up with an identical envelope addressed to him.

Carrying both, I blundered into my colleague's room with but the most perfunctory of knocks. He was at his wash-stand in his old blue dressing-gown, his face lathered as a preliminary to shaving, and on my precipitate entry he turned with razor poised in mid-air.

"Holmes!" I blurted. "Look here – this is astounding! You will never guess what we have here!"

"Quite so, Watson. I never guess, I deduce." He turned back to the mirror to continue his interrupted task.

"Then deduce this," I snorted, nettled by his apparent lack of interest and brandishing the envelopes behind him.

He looked at my reflection in the mirror and drew the razor along the side of his face before turning to me.

283

"You have not read *The Times* this morning?" He threw an arm at the pages strewn in disorder beside his bed.

"Only the cricketing column in *The Telegraph*," I replied. "What the deuce has that to do with these and your confounded deductions?" I again waved the envelopes at him.

He wiped his razor and plunged his face into the bowl of water before answering, by which time I was almost dancing with impatience.

"My deductions lead me to the conclusion that we are invited to attend the wedding of Sir Charles Listel and Miss Celia Winsett." He buried his face in a towel. "Had you read *The Times* this morning, you could not fail to notice the announcement of their engagement – unless of course you had eyes only for the cricket. Those envelopes in your hand are of the kind used for the conveyance of such social messages."

He patted my shoulder. "Do not look so crestfallen, old fellow. The event and the invitations are just as much a surprise to me. In truth, the whole affair of Bickstone Lodge had quite slipped my memory."

"We shall go, of course?" I said.

"Unless something turns up to divert us." He raised an eyebrow. "An interesting thought, Watson, all the same. Perhaps there will be an heir to the title and estate after all, eh?"

The Adventure of the
Lonely Soldier

Looking through my notes of the various cases in which I have been associated with my friend Sherlock Holmes over the years, I feel that I have done myself less than justice in my accounts of a number of them. Of course, Holmes himself deprecates what he describes as the lurid sensationalism of my literary efforts and the undeniable fact that I have often selected the more dramatic incidents of his career to lay before the public. Therefore when I came across an affair in which I played a major part and which contained no element of that so-called "lurid sensationalism", or even a blood-curdling crime, I decided it was time to refute my friend's charge of cheap dramatics and at the same time give myself a little of the credit I consider my due.

It was a beautiful June morning in 1886 when Holmes and I were lingering over a belated breakfast. He was reading *The Daily Telegraph* while I perused my morning mail and found little enough to please me. He at length discarded the newspaper with an exaggerated sigh of boredom, and for a full five minutes sat staring into space with a pensive expression on his sharp features. When he suddenly spoke, it was to break into my train of thought in the way that so annoyed me, yet never failed to draw my grudging admiration.

"If I were in your position, Watson," he said, "I would take the *locum*'s post that you are offered. It would only be for a short while and is unlikely to be too onerous. Also, it would go some way towards alleviating your present problem."

I looked up in exasperation.

"Really," I said with some asperity. "It's too bad of you. You expect me to ask you how you divined my mental processes and, having explained it to me, you will became annoyed when I agree how simple it all is, saying you would receive more credit if you left your reasoning shrouded in mystery."

He waved a negligent hand and chuckled.

"Very well," said he. "I shall explain and allow you to tell me how obvious it all is, and I promise I shall take no offence – this time."

I fell in with his mood. "Good enough. Tell me how you arrived at your conclusion – which, by the way is correct in every detail – and I will guarantee to be properly amazed and say nothing to hurt your feelings."

He pushed his chair away from the table to stretch his long legs out before him, surveying me with a quizzical expression.

"On your plate this morning there were four letters," he began as he commenced to fill his oily old clay pipe. "The first that you opened was most certainly a statement from your bank – the envelopes are unmistakable – and I gathered it did not make the most pleasant reading. The next two were obviously bills, as I saw when you laid them down, at which point I surmised that this fine June morning was spoiled for you. However, after reading the final letter, you turned your attention back to the others and began to chew your moustache as is your wont when trying to arrive at a decision. I therefore deduced that the last letter was an offer of some financially gainful employment, and as your only qualifications are medical, I was certain it was from a professional colleague requiring a stand-in for a short period and asked if you would be willing to oblige. At that juncture I offered my uninvited opinion and advised you to accept. After all, old chap, it would only be for a short while, and not only does it have some pecuniary advantages, but with the whole world submerged in a sea of banality, you could at least keep your mind occupied until your pension arrives at the end of the month."

I could not resist laughing.

"As usual, Holmes, you are right on target. This letter is from a mutual friend of ours. No doubt you will remember young Stamford, the fellow who first introduced us at Barts?"

"By Jove, I do!" Holmes exclaimed. "He will always have my gratitude on account of that happy introduction."

"Well," I continued, "he's now in practice out Finchley way and feels himself in need of a break. Consequently, he has asked me if I'd be willing to take over his practice for a couple of weeks, starting ten days from now.

"There you are, then. As I pointed out, it kills two birds with one stone, so why hesitate?"

I looked away before answering. "My only reservation is over leaving you to your own devices for that length of time."

"Pray do not concern yourself about me, my dear fellow," he replied with a faint smile. "I see no prospect of any dramatic case arising where I should need your invaluable assistance."

"That isn't what I meant, and well you know it," said I as my eyes drifted to the mantelpiece where his blue-leather hypodermic syringes case lay gathering dust.

He shook his head. "Have no fear. Even the prospect of artificial stimulation could not raise my spirits just now."

My mood lightened. Heaven knows how hard I had worked to wean him from his abominable seven-per-cent solution, even at the risk of incurring his wrath at times.

"Very well," I said after a moment's thought. "I shall give the matter some thought and perhaps take a ride out to Finchley this evening to let Stamford know of my decision. Perhaps it will be no bad thing to get away from the smoke and grime of the town for a week or two."

At this moment our attention was drawn to the sound of a cab stopping outside our chamber, and on its heels the jangle of our doorbell. A few moments elapsed before the page-boy put his head 'round the door to ask if Mr. Holmes would see a Miss Ruth Medwin.

"Indeed I will," replied my friend, a spark of life coming to his eyes. "This may be of some interest, but if not nothing is lost."

The lady who entered was tall and slim, dressed in black and with a small veil partly covering her face. Holmes waved her to the basket chair, apologising for the fact that we were still at breakfast. He rang for Mrs. Hudson to clear the table and stuffed the discarded newspapers into the coal-scuttle beside the grate.

Our visitor sat, removing her gloves and raising her veil. I observed with pleasure that she was a handsome woman, about the same age as ourselves, and it crossed my mind that it was a great waste for one with her attributes to be unmarried. Holmes sat facing her, his back to the window, and I took a seat on the sofa, trying to look inconspicuous and alert at the same time.

"So, Madam," said Holmes when Mrs. Hudson had completed her task and departed, "pray tell me how I may be of assistance to you."

The lady hesitated for a moment before speaking in a low and pleasant voice.

"I am afraid, Mr. Holmes, my story does me little credit, and I would be more at ease if no third party was present to hear it."

I made to rise from the sofa but Holmes motioned me back with an imperious wave of his hand and looked coldly at our visitor.

"Dr. Watson has my complete trust and is privy to all my cases," he said. "You may have the utmost confidence in his discretion, I assure you."

Miss Medwin inclined her head in acquiescence. "So be it, then. I accept your word. My story properly begins about nineteen years ago when I was seventeen. My father, who died last year, was a very successful cabinet-maker in business on his own account in Bromley. At that time, my mother was ailing, and for some months had been in a private sanatorium in Hampshire. I was employed as a book-keeper at an hotel near Chislehurst, not from financial necessity, but my father had always

287

encouraged me to be independent, and I in turn welcomed the opportunity to be so.

"Towards the end of the year there came to stay at the hotel a young army officer who let it be known that he was awaiting orders to rejoin his regiment. I gathered that he had no close relatives or friends, and that was his reason for staying with us, although this was never stated in as many words. We found pleasure in each other's company, and most of my free time was spent with him until shortly before Christmas, when his orders arrived to embark for foreign service. I never saw him or heard from him again."

Here she paused to look down into her lap, obviously in the grip of some strong emotion. I went over and poured a glass of water, which she sipped gratefully before continuing her story in a barely audible voice.

"Imagine my horror, gentlemen, when early in the New Year I became aware that I was to have a child. For days – nay, weeks – my mind was in turmoil, and I came near to doing away with myself but lacked the courage. Eventually I gave in my notice and returned home to relate my sorry tale to my poor father, throwing myself on his mercy. He was shocked and distressed, more so because I would not reveal the name of the man responsible, and added to the worry of my mother's illness must have laid a grievous burden on him.

Here Holmes interposed a question. "Did you make no attempt to communicate with your lover?"

She shook her head. "No. Whether from pride or shame I know not, but I could not bring myself to do so."

"Pray proceed."

"My father gave me his support, arranging for me to stay with the widow of an old friend of his in the country, close to the nursing home in which my mother was living. It was given out that I had gone away to be near my mother and was accepted as natural in the circumstances. My mother, rest her soul, never learned of my disgrace and passed away in the August of 1868, just a week before my child was born. When I eventually returned home, the story was spread that the baby was my mother's, and that she had died at his birth. That child was brought up as my younger brother. Imagine if you can, gentlemen, how I suffered, stifling my natural expressions of maternal love in order that my secret should be kept. For over seventeen years that fiction was maintained, and then at the end of last year my father died and I was left to sort out his affairs. Among his papers were documents relating to my son's birth, and although I thought I had them in a safe place, by some mischance they came into Rupert's hands."

"Rupert being your son, I presume?" asked Holmes.

"Forgive me. I thought I had mentioned his name, but yes, that is so. That was about six weeks ago, and he was stunned and angry, reproaching me bitterly and forcing me to tell him the whole truth. He demanded that I name his father, and after several painful scenes I gave way and told him. He must have been brooding on the matter for weeks, and then yesterday I found that he had disappeared from home, leaving behind a letter telling me that he was going to trace his father to confront him and demand reparation, or extract revenge for both of us. I spent a sleepless night wondering what to do for the best, and at last came to the conclusion that you, Mr. Holmes, are the person most likely to be able to help me. Please, I beg of you, find Rupert and restore him to me before he takes any irrevocable step."

Holmes studied her intently for a long minute, his brows drawn together in a frown of concentration. Suddenly he appeared to arrive at a decision, rising to his feet to stand looking down at her.

"What was the name of your lover?" he asked abruptly.

The lady raised her eyes to meet his.

"Is that necessary?" she asked.

"Come, Madam," said my friend impatiently. "You ask me to find your son and expect me to guess in what direction he may go. I am not a bloodhound or a mind-reader. If you desire my assistance, you must be perfectly frank with me."

Her eyes dropped and her reply was barely audible to me.

"He was Lieutenant James Harwood of the 66th Foot."

I sat bolt upright on the sofa, amazed beyond belief.

"Why, Holmes – " I began, but was silenced by a frown and a wave of his hand.

"Tell me, Miss Medwin," he inquired of our client, "What are your circumstances?"

Her head jerked up and she showed more animation than at any time since her arrival at our rooms. "My financial situation is very comfortable. Perhaps I should explain that since my father's death, I have been determined that his business should continue, to be passed to Rupert on his coming of age. I can manage the accounts and other book work, while the workshop is in the capable hands of a foreman who has served my father these past fifteen years, and he has the assistance of a carpenter and an apprentice with an odd-job boy for labouring work. I have an income of some eight-hundred pounds a year from the business, and another two-hundred from my father's investments."

Holmes raised his eyebrows while I gave vent to a silent whistle. "A thriving business indeed, and a credit to your father's industry."

The lady gave a small nod of acknowledgement and went on. "As you say, Mr. Holmes, and therefore you may be certain that any fees that you ask will be fully and properly met."

A frown passed over my friend's brow to be replaced by a look of sardonic amusement. He began pacing the floor, his chin sunk in his chest and his long thin fingers tapping nervously together. At length he seemed to make up his mind and swung around to face the lady.

"Very well, Miss Medwin, I will see what can be done. Leave me your address, and I will communicate with you if I have news or need further information."

He led her to the door and escorted her downstairs where I heard him hail a cab. When he re-entered our sitting room, there was a broad smile on his face.

"Come along, Watson," he chuckled. "I can see you are bursting to tell me. I didn't miss the significance of the lady's allusion to the 66th Foot. I know you were attached to them in Afghanistan, although I believe in recent years they have been renamed the Berkshires – 2nd Battalion, if my memory is not at fault. I also deduce that you have some knowledge of our Mr. Harwood."

I nodded eagerly, pleased for once that I could be the one to give my friend information that would help him.

"Indeed I have. I attended him professionally when he contracted malaria not long before the Battle of Maiwand."

"How closely were you acquainted with the gentleman?"

I considered this for a moment before replying. "He wasn't a man with whom one could get on close terms," I said. "He was very withdrawn with no real friends, although not disliked. In those days he was a captain, a good and conscientious regimental officer who was very careful of the welfare of the men under him – but as I have inferred, not a clubbable man. I must say that I was surprised to hear his name come up in the context of Miss Medwin's story, for he had no sort of reputation as a womaniser."

"Have you heard of him recently? Any idea of his whereabouts at the present time?"

I shook my head. "No, I've heard nothing of him since I returned home in '80. I don't even know if he is still serving."

Holmes went over to the bookshelf and, taking down the *Army Lists* for the previous five years, flicked rapidly through the pages before shaking his head. "He isn't listed for the last few years – not since '82 in fact – so it would be reasonable assume that he has either left the service or is no longer in the land of the living, which makes our task that much more difficult. Tell me, old chap, as an expert on the fair sex: What where your impressions of our Miss Medwin?

I automatically brushed my moustache and squared my shoulders. "A most intelligent and capable woman and still paying the price of her youthful indiscretion. Deuced attractive, too. I hope we can be of assistance to her."

He smiled faintly. "Ever the knight errant, Watson, as I might have expected. But more to the point, what did you make of her story? Was she being entirely frank with us?"

"Good Lord!" I expostulated, "Why should she not be? Her story seemed quite consistent to me, although I was a trifle surprised that you accepted the case. It seems so ordinary that even Gregson or Lestrade could not go wrong."

"You may be right, but I have a feeling there is more to this than there appears on the face of it."

He filled his pipe with the foul black shag that he favoured and for several minutes remained lost in thought, his head wreathed in the noxious fumes. I charged and lit my own pipe in self-defence. All at once the memory of those days in Afghanistan lit a spark in my mind and I smacked my fist into the palm of my hand, bringing a frown of annoyance from Holmes.

"By Jove, Holmes!" I cried, ignoring his scowl, "I believe I can be of real help here. A week or so back, I heard from an old Army friend whom I met in Afghanistan. He is now retired and living near Reigate in Surrey. He seemed to know Harwood better than most, and it may be that they have kept in touch."

Holmes reacted enthusiastically and sprang to his feet to clap me on the shoulder. "Bravo, Watson! I can always expect the unexpected from you. Are you willing to forgo your lunch? It would be of immense help to me if you would see your old comrade and make the necessary inquiries yourself. I know I can rely on your tact and discretion. I presume, of course, that your old friend will not take it amiss if you arrive unannounced?"

I felt a glow of gratification that my friend was putting his trust in me, and I jumped up eagerly. "Of course. I'll do as you wish and Colonel Hayter – that is the old soldier's name – will no doubt provide me with a sandwich. In his letter he bade me call on him any time without ceremony, so I'll do just that."

"Right, Watson. Off you go, as soon as you may. Meanwhile, I have another avenue to explore. Telegraph me if anything of urgency comes up."

At London Bridge I was fortunate enough to walk straight on to a train for Redhill, from whence it was but a short drive in the station trap to Colonel Hayter's residence on the road to Reigate. Any fears I may have

291

had regarding my unheralded appearance were at once dispelled by the warmth of the old soldier's welcome.

"Watson, my dear fellow!" he cried. "You are a sight for sore eyes." Hayter pumped my hand vigorously and almost dragged me into his comfortable study where we were soon toasting our renewed acquaintance with a glass of most excellent whisky.

"I see civilian life suits you, judging by your straining waistcoat buttons," he chuckled.

"I must admit that I find it a lot less hectic than it was in the service," I laughed. "And I'll be bound you agree." He gave a wry smile and neither agreed nor disagreed, but I gained the impression that after forty years in uniform, he was finding it a mite difficult to adjust.

We chatted of this and that and presently the Colonel said, "I take it you are not in general practice?"

"No, not at present. I just about scrape by on my pension and the few pounds that my medical work brings in. I manage to keep well occupied with other interests, all the same."

He nodded. "I'm sure you do. I've read the newspaper accounts of your association with Mr. Sherlock Holmes and that must be quite demanding. He seems a bright character, from all accounts."

"He is a great man," I said simply and took advantage of the turn of the conversation to place my problem before the Colonel. "He is one of my reasons for being here, as well as the pleasure of seeing you again."

Out of deference to the old chap's feelings I bent the truth slightly. "I was coming to see you and when Holmes knew your background, he suggested that you might provide just the information we needed to clear up a little matter that has been occupying us since this morning."

My host raised his bushy eyebrows and nodded for me to continue.

"The matter is quite delicate and it depends very much on getting in touch with James Harwood, who, no doubt, you will remember.

"Jimmy Harwood? Good Lord! Whatever can you want with him?"

"As I said it is very, very delicate," I replied. "A young man is looking for Harwood and may do him some physical harm if we cannot head him off."

The Colonel looked quizzically at me.

"You say it is a delicate matter. Can you say more on the subject? You know I can be trusted not to gossip."

I knew this to be true, so after a moment of consideration, I decided to take him into my confidence.

"Well, Colonel, the facts are these. This young man's mother has named Harwood as the boy's father, and he is now searching for Harwood to take revenge on behalf of himself and his mother."

The Colonel stared at me, incredulity and consternation written on every line of his features. It was a full minute before he spoke.

"I don't believe it! Oh, I'm not doubting your good faith, Doctor. I am sure you are telling me the facts as you know them, but I will not believe that of Jimmy Harwood!"

"That's not the point, Colonel. It does not signify whether he did this thing or not, but that young man *thinks* he did and may do him some injury unless we can reach him first and put him on his guard." He looked at me thoughtfully and brushed his moustache with his fingers.

"Now look here, Watson – What you have told me has come as quite a shock. Before I can agree to give you any information about Harwood, I must have time to think. Why not stay to dinner and give me a chance to get things straight in my head?"

I realised that if I was to secure the information I would have to accede to the Colonel's request, so I agreed, arranging for the Colonel's groom to take a telegram to the post office to tell Holmes of my quandary. For the life of me, I couldn't see why such an issue was being made of my simple request, but I had too much respect for my host to object. I pointed out that not having anticipated an overnight stay, I had no change of linen or even a toothbrush about me, but he waved this aside, saying he could provide me with a nightshirt and the necessary toiletries, and as we would be dining alone we could dispense with dressing.

We did not allude to the matter of Harwood immediately, spending the time until dinner chatting inconsequentially of this and that – old friends, old times on the frontier – and over the meal he regaled me with amusing anecdotes garnered during his long army career in various parts of the world. Afterwards we repaired to the library, where we sat over cigars and with a decanter of the Colonel's most excellent brandy on a table between us. Presently the conversation flagged, and for a quarter-of-an-hour we sat in companionable silence until suddenly he broached the subject that was uppermost in my mind.

"Look here, Watson, I know you would not be making this inquiry unless it was of some importance, but if I am to help you, I must know more about it. Do you feel free to tell me the whole story?"

I pondered this and tried to imagine the line Holmes would take in a situation like this, but having no way of receiving his guidance, I was left to make my own decision. I knew Hayter well enough to be sure he was not asking out of idle curiosity and must have a very good reason for his caginess, and unless I could persuade him that my need for the information was valid, my errand would be fruitless. I made up my mind to be frank.

"Very well then, Colonel," I said. "I will tell you the story as it was told to Holmes and myself, with the proviso that I am not pressed to reveal

293

the client's name. If you then consider that I haven't told you enough, then I shall have to think again."

"That sounds reasonable enough," he nodded. "Pour yourself another drink and let me see what I make of it." With a freshly charged glass before me, I related the events from the time that our client entered our rooms until I arrived at Reigate. He listened without interruption, a frown of deep concentration creasing his forehead while his cigar burned unheeded in the ashtray. When I had finished he rose to his feet, took a few paces back and forth, and then came to a halt directly in front of me, a grim smile on his lips. He was silent for a few seconds, but when he at last spoke, it was with barely concealed anger in his voice.

"Watson, your client is either a very simple woman, or a cunning and scheming vixen who should be thrown into gaol!"

"I say, old chap, that's pitching it a bit strongly!" I expostulated. "That's not how it appeared to me!"

He stemmed my protestations impatiently.

"If you and Holmes swallowed that pack of lies, then the wool has been well and truly pulled over your eyes. I see no help for it but to give my reasons for saying so if I am to clear the name of a gallant and honourable gentleman. What I shall tell you was confided to me under a solemn pledge of secrecy, but in the circumstances I feel justified in breaking that pledge in the interests of all concerned."

He returned to his chair and took another cigar. When it was burning to his satisfaction, he told me a story so incredible that I shall set it down in his own words as far as I can recall.

"When I first met James Harwood," he began "I was stationed in the Punjab, at Rawalpindi – let me see, that would have been 1875. He was a lieutenant at the time, a little over thirty years of age, I suppose. He was a solitary man with no close friends and apparently no social life as we knew it out there. He performed his regimental duties well and was always willing to swap duties with his fellow subalterns, but his character made it difficult for anyone to form any kind of close friendship with him.

"He was promoted to captain in 1877 and became my adjutant, and I came to know him as well as he would allow me to. I think I can say that our relationship matured remarkably well over the following months. One evening – I recall it being just before you joined us – I was sitting alone in the mess over a drink when Harwood came in and joined me. We chatted a while on regimental matters and speculated on the possibility of moving through the Khyber into Afghanistan where the natives were making trouble. After a while, I noticed that he was consuming rather more brandy than usual. Not that he was over the top, but he was an abstemious man and one or two was his usual limit.

"After a while the talk turned to more general matters, and I remarked that I was not looking forward to a lonely retirement which I knew was not very far off. As you know, Watson, my wife had succumbed to the Indian climate, as so many European women do, and then Harwood said he had no reason to contemplate leaving the service, as he had no ties of any kind with England. I observed that he was still a young man and there was nothing to stop him marrying and making a life in the Old Country, and this seemingly innocent remark provoked a most astounding reaction. He flushed under his tan and his eyes became angry. He half-rose from his chair as if to attack me, but then he slumped back and drank the rest of his brandy at a gulp. For a short space he was silent, and then he leaned forward with a look of anguish in his eyes.

"'Colonel,' he said hoarsely, 'you have been a good friend to me in the months we have worked together. Will you permit me to unburden my troubles on to you in the strictest confidence? I assure you that you will hear nothing dishonourable, but if my story should become generally known, the humiliation would be more than I could bear, and I vow I would make away with myself.'

"I was quite taken aback by the intensity of his utterance and to me it sounded somewhat overdramatic, but it was evident that he was in need of a confidante, so I promised that if he wished to talk, I would listen and repeat nothing of what was said. He began by telling me of his early life as an orphan in the care of an uncle who had died when he, Harwood, was almost twenty-one. At the age of eighteen he had suffered a serious illness, the nature of which he did not specify, and on the death of his uncle he took a commission in the army. He served in England and Ireland until 1867, when he was sent to the Regimental Depot at Reading. Towards the end of the year he took some leave and, having no home of his own, he went to a small hotel in Kent. There he met a young lady and found immense pleasure in her company, but when he realised that the warmth of his feelings was being returned, he decided that the only honourable course was for him to disappear from her life."

My host took a sip from his glass and watched for my reaction.

"But why?" asked I, a note of puzzlement in my voice. "Surely if they were both attracted to one another, there was no impediment to it taking its natural course?"

"Exactly my reaction," said Colonel Hayter. "I made that very point to him and was rewarded by a bitter laugh as he reminded me of the illness he had spoken of earlier.

"'That illness, Colonel, left me impotent! Emotionally I can have the same feelings as any other man but physically I am but half a man – a eunuch! What right have I to consider marriage or any close relationship with the opposite sex?'

"While I was digesting this astonishing statement, Harwood continued with his story. His orders came to embark for foreign service and he was able to disappear from the lady's life with no embarrassing or indelicate explanations, and he had spent the last few years ensuring that he did not again find himself in a like situation. Of course, this went a long way towards explaining the lonely and unsociable way of life he had chosen to lead, and I was deeply moved by his astounding story. I reiterated my pledge of secrecy and, until this evening, not a word of it has passed my lips, but your visit here and its purpose puts an entirely different complexion on the matter. Naturally, neither you nor Holmes must divulge what has passed here, unless Harwood himself gives direct permission."

The Colonel sat back after pushing the decanter and cigars towards me while I tried to put my thoughts into some sort of order. My first reaction was one of deep compassion for the young man whose life was thus blighted. I am a great admirer of the fair sex myself and am not averse to a little light dalliance with an agreeable partner, so I could feel for any man placed in situation such as Harwood found himself. My next feeling was one of anger that any woman could stoop so low as to try to fool Holmes and myself in such a base manner, but I knew that Holmes would want unassailable proof that we were being thus manipulated.

"One question, Colonel," I said grimly. "This hotel in Kent where Harwood stayed: Did he say precisely where it was?"

He pondered this before answering then nodded "Yes, I recall he specifically mentioned Chislehurst as the nearest railway station."

That settled it for me, and shortly, with the Colonel refusing to say anything further on the subject, we retired for the night, where under the benign influence of Colonel Hayter's brandy I slept like a top. In spite of that, I was up and about early.

"Well, Doctor," said my host as we applied ourselves to the bacon and eggs, "what is your next move?"

"I rather think that is up to Holmes," I replied. "We seem to have been inveigled into a false position, and if I know Holmes, he will not rest until the situation has been rectified. He won't take kindly to having such a deception played on him."

"In that case, all that remains is for me to give you Harwood's address – but remember, it must not go beyond the two of you."

"You have my word, sir."

With the address stowed safely in my pocketbook, I caught the first available train to London Bridge, from whence a cab deposited me at our Baker Street rooms shortly after nine o'clock. To my astonishment, my friend was nowhere to be seen, and my telegram of the previous day lay unopened on the table beside a note in Holmes's angular scrawl which gave me no more information than that he was expecting to return by mid-morning.

He walked in within the hour, his face set in a stony mask, but he would say nothing of his own movements until I had given my account of my visit to Reigate. At the conclusion of my narrative he was predictably angry.

"This is infamous, Watson!" he snapped. "Does the woman take me for a complete fool? My own inquiries only go to confirm an impression that I had from the outset. After you departed for Reigate yesterday, I went down to the hotel at Chislehurst where Miss Medwin was employed at the time of her alleged seduction. I had no difficulty finding it, as it is the only one of any size in the area. I took a room for the night posing as an amateur historian, so no comment was aroused when I began to ask questions. I was soon on good terms with the proprietor and such of the locals who frequented the bar. The place has changed hands now, but it was easy to get people to talk, and several of the regular patrons remembered the previous owner – not with any degree of respect or affection, I might add. He had a thoroughly unsavoury reputation and had to leave the district rather hurriedly after a big scandal concerning the wife of a local tradesman. I also had it on good authority that he has since died of a loathsome disease caused by his own excesses." He lapsed into silence, his fingers drumming nervously on the arm of his chair. When he next spoke it was with a note of urgency in his voice.

"I believe that time is of the utmost importance. Are you willing to miss your lunch again that we may resolve this matter before more harm is done?"

"If you deem it necessary, but I fail to see what we can do now."

"Think, man, think! You know my methods. What have we achieved so far? What is my guiding principle?"

I pondered for a few seconds before it dawned on me. "Why, of course! We have eliminated the impossible, so whatever remains – "

" – However improbable, must be the truth. Stout fellow! Now I want you to make all haste to Harwood's address in Bayswater, and under no circumstances must you leave him alone until I arrive. Do you think you can manage that?"

Without replying I picked up my hat and stick and was about to depart when he stopped me.

"On your way stop at the first telegraph office and send this for me."

He thrust a piece of paper into my hand which I saw was addressed to Ruth Medwin, enjoining her immediate attendance at Baker Street on a matter of extreme urgency. "Let us hope that our man is at home and we are in time to avert a catastrophe," were his parting words to me.

I took a four-wheeler to Harwood's lodgings, which were situated in a quiet little backwater near Kensington Gardens, stopping only to send the telegram to Miss Medwin at her address in Bromley. My knock was answered by a comfortable-looking body who might have come from the same mould as Mrs. Hudson. Taking my card, she quickly returned to announce that Captain Harwood would be delighted to see me, as he himself showed when I was shown into his sitting room. He seized my hand in both of his and pumped it vigorously.

"My dear Doctor!" he exclaimed. "This is indeed an unexpected pleasure! Remove your coat and make yourself comfortable in that chair. I hope this is not a flying visit?"

He had aged somewhat in comparison with my last memory of him, and his complexion revealed that the malaria in his system had not yet burned itself out.

I felt justified in a half-truth, remembering the need for discretion, and hoping that the Colonel had not been in touch with him.

"I happened to visit Colonel Hayter yesterday," I began. "He told me you had left the service and passed on your address to me."

He smiled fondly at the mention of the old soldier and nodded. "He is the only one from the old days with whom I have kept in touch. How is he?"

I assured him of the Colonel's continuing good health and cast around for an opening to broach the real purpose of my visit. It was he who provided it by asking if I was in practice and if so, where.

"No, not at present," I replied. "My pension keeps my head above water, although I am kept pretty busy in other directions. Perhaps you have heard mention of Mr. Sherlock Holmes?"

"Who has not? I have read in the press of his cases with the utmost interest."

"Then you will not be surprised if I tell you that we are at present engaged on a case. What may astound you is the fact that you are part of that case – a part I hasten to add that is none of your doing."

"I, Doctor?" He indeed looked astounded. "Whatever connection could I have in any case of Mr. Sherlock Holmes?"

"I'm sorry, old man. I am not at liberty to reveal any details at this precise moment. Will you take me on trust and answer me but one question?"

He hesitated briefly before acceding to my request. "Why, yes, Doctor, I will trust you and answer whatever is in my power, but I must confess to some bewilderment."

"Thank you. Have you in the last day or two received an unexpected visitor?"

"Is that all?" he laughed. "I can answer that with a straight 'No'. If I sat here all day waiting for callers, I would have a long and lonely vigil. I can guarantee that no one has asked for me in the past three weeks until you turned up."

I breathed a sigh of relief and relaxed in my chair. "In that case, all there is to do is to wait until Holmes arrives here in person, when he will give you an explanation of this strange affair."

He stared at me in amazement tinged with irritation. "Good Lord, Doctor, I have every respect for you both as a medical man and as a person, but it seems that you are presuming on both my respect and my tolerance. Why should Holmes want to come here? What business can he have with me?"

I hastened to placate him. "Please, old man, bear with me. It is most important that we await him, and I am in the awkward position of having my lips sealed until he gets here in person. Continue to trust me and hear what he has to say. It will, I hope, prevent sorrow and embarrassment to more than one person."

He gave an amused chuckle and appeared to be mollified. "Very well, Doctor. I know you well enough to appreciate that you are no practical joker, so I will go along with what you ask. But I'm neglecting my duties as a host – put it down to lack of practise. Can I get you a drink?"

"Thank you, and if it is not too presumptuous a couple of biscuits would not come amiss. I overlooked lunch in my haste to reach you."

As he handed me my drink, he eyed me keenly. "You are convinced that it is important for me to remain here until your colleague arrives?"

"Believe me, Captain, it is vital. I only regret that I cannot be more explicit, but I must not anticipate any action that Holmes may wish to take. He has all the strings in his hands."

He gave a resigned shrug and leaned back in his chair. "Tell me, Doctor, what is Holmes really like? Is he as brilliant as he is portrayed?"

I smiled faintly at the question but went on to give some examples of the workings of that quicksilver mind. Harwood seemed genuinely interested, and the time passed pleasantly enough and we began to reminisce over our days in India. He was evidently pleased to have someone to talk to. I gathered he had been invalided out with recurrent malaria, and since his return to civilian life had done very little with himself. I presently glanced at the clock on his mantelpiece and saw that I had been with Harwood for more than two hours, I began to speculate on what might be delaying Holmes when the sound of wheels and a knock on the door allowed me to relax.

The door opened to admit the lean figure of my friend, followed closely by a heavily veiled woman who I had no difficulty in recognising as our client. With no word of greeting he stood to one side and the lady gave went to a choking sob as her eyes fell on the man facing her.

"James!" The name was dragged from her lips and came from the very depths of her soul. With trembling hands she raised her veil to regard Harwood with a look of shocked despair, although she did not allow her eyes to leave his startled face.

For long seconds he stared at her, too dumb-struck to rise from his seat, and a kaleidoscope of emotions pursuing themselves across his face. Then recognition dawned and her monosyllable was answered by his own.

"Ruth!"

How Holmes had staged this dramatic confrontation he afterwards told me, when we had returned to Baker Street to demolish one of Mrs. Hudson's excellent steak-and-kidney puddings.

After I had left on my errand to Harwood's lodgings and sent the telegram to Miss Medwin, he had remained to await her arrival. She must have departed from Bromley on the instant, for little more than an hour had elapsed ere she was at the door, under the assumption that Holmes's quest had been successful. Her eagerness faded as Holmes faced her, a cold expression on his austere features.

"No, Miss Medwin," he said in a frosty voice, "I have not located your son, although I can fairly say that I am hot on the trail. I have summoned you here because I do not take kindly to being the victim of an attempted deception, and the only reason that I have not disengaged from the case is to save an innocent man from grievous hurt from the slander and calumny that you instigated. Are you now prepared to be frank with me, that we may more readily avert the results of your deception?"

She flushed a deep red. "I do not understand you, Mr. Holmes – " But he interrupted before she could say more.

"Pray, do not fence with me, Miss. I have incontrovertible evidence that the gentleman so glibly named by you as your seducer is completely blameless, and furthermore I warn you that I have a very good idea of the truth. If you can confirm my theory, then I may be able to salvage something from this sorry mess." She stared at him, her face chalk white, then burst into a fit of uncontrollable sobbing as she collapsed into the nearest chair. Holmes stood looking down at her, his face an implacable mask until at last she regained some semblance of calm and raised her head to stare at him with red-rimmed eyes.

"So be it," she said resignedly. "The story I told you was in part true, but the gentleman I so basely impugned was, as you said, in no way to blame. We did have a brief friendship, but his behaviour towards me was always perfectly correct." She moistened her dry lips. "It was soon after he had returned to his military duties that one dreadful night after the hotel was closed – we had no guests at the time – my employer came to my room and forced himself upon me. Remember, I was so very young then, and at first did not realise what was happening. By the time I recovered myself, it was too late, and he had accomplished his foul purpose. Frightened and ashamed, I quit that terrible place at the first light of dawn and returned home, telling my father only that I no longer found the work congenial. When I became aware of the result of that dastardly assault, I refused to talk about it, and the remainder of what I told you was nothing but the truth."

Holmes had listened to her in silence but now interposed a question. "But why bring the officer's name into it at all?"

"When Rupert found those papers that told him I was his mother and not his sister, I became distraught and uttered the first name that came into my head. Indeed, it was a name that had been with me all those years," she added. "Consequently when I came to you for help, it was natural that I should hold to the story I had told Rupert, hoping that you would find him and return him to me with no further complications. I can only beg your forgiveness for my deception."

"It is not I of whom you should ask forgiveness," Holmes said. "I already had some inkling of the true state of affairs through my own inquiries and merely needed to hear your confirmation of what I had suspected. I have some sympathy with you in the plight in which you found yourself, but I cannot condone your wild accusations against an innocent man."

"How – how did you find out that my story was untrue?"

"That is a point on which I cannot speak. Suffice it to say that I have my methods," Holmes replied before turning away to answer a knock that came on the door. He was handed a telegram which was addressed to Holmes or Watson. He tore it open and gave a cry of triumph. "Ah! The ends begin to come together. Come, Miss Medwin, we have a short journey to make."

The telegram was from Colonel Hayter and read:

> *Young man wild appearance inquiring of J.H. Have directed him to your address. Discretion paramount.*

> *Hayter*

Holmes sat down to scribble a short note which he sealed in an envelope. As he and Ruth Medwin descended the stairs he called Mrs.

301

Hudson, and taking her to one side, he whispered a few words into her ear. Then, hailing a cab, he with the lady made all speed to Bayswater, where the amazing confrontation between Harwood and Miss Medwin.

As they stared at each other the atmosphere became charged and tense, while Holmes looked on with the smug expression of a cat who has come upon a dish of cream.

"I believe you two have met before," he observed casually as he advanced into the room. Harwood dragged his eyes away from the pale visage of Kiss Medwin to look first at Holmes and then at me, his face darkening in anger.

"What is the meaning of this?" he demanded. "Is this some kind of plot?"

Even I felt moved to expostulate. "Really, Holmes, what is going on?"

He ignored me and addressed himself to Harwood, who had risen to his feet to face Holmes with clenched fists, as if about to launch himself in an attack on my friend.

"Captain, I realise that this has been a tremendous shock to you, and you are entitled to a full and frank explanation. However, that explanation will not come from me. This lady is far more able to provide you with all the answers to which you are entitled, and I believe she has the courage and strength of character to do so."

Ruth Medwin raised her head, and looked Harwood straight in the eyes.

"Yes, indeed," said she firmly. "It is my duty and mine alone, and however humiliating and demeaning it is, I must face up to it. Will you permit me to be alone with Captain Harwood that I may retain some small amount of pride and dignity?"

Harwood had recovered sufficiently from the shock of Miss Medwin's appearance to mount a further protest.

"What can this lady have to say that is so important? It is almost twenty years since we met, and I have heard nothing of her since then."

"Be advised by me, sir," said Holmes quietly. "Do the lady the courtesy of hearing her. It will benefit all concerned.

A moment of indecision, then Harwood jerked his head in agreement.

"Very well. I've nothing better to do," he said ungraciously.

"Then, Captain, perhaps your landlady will provide us with some corner where Watson and I may wait. I should say that I am expecting another visitor who I wish to greet on your behalf."

Harwood looked bewildered and then threw up his arms in resignation. "Do as you will. Take whatever steps you wish, just so long as we may have this bizarre affair cleared up."

Brusquely bidding Miss Medwin to be seated, he conducted us downstairs, where he handed us over to Mrs. Latimer, the good lady who attended to his domestic comforts. We were made comfortable in her own front parlour and she even provided us with a most welcome pot of tea.

Holmes sat quietly looking out of the window, ignoring my questions in a most annoying manner. What passed between Ruth Medwin and James Harwood we never knew, and forty minutes passed with no sign that their *tete-a-tete* was terminating.

Presently there came a loud insistent hammering on the front door knocker. Mrs. Latimer went to answer it and Holmes, moving like a cat, opened the parlour door. From where I stood I saw on the doorstep a young man in the grip of a fever of angry excitement, his voice hoarse as he demanded to be taken to Captain James Harwood.

Holmes stepped swiftly forward and interposed himself between the landlady and the youth, for he was little more than that.

"Thank you, Mrs. Latimer, I will attend to this."

The caller glared at him with blazing eyes, his face suffused with rage and hate. After several futile attempts he at last managed to speak.

"Are you the vile seducer Harwood?" he blurted out.

"No, I am not Captain Harwood," Holmes replied. "Neither am I a vile seducer, and nor for that matter is Captain Harwood. My name is Sherlock Holmes, and you I know to be Rupert Medwin. I am engaged by Miss Medwin to intercept you before you take any rash action that will hurt her and another entirely blameless person. Will you allow me to elucidate?" Rupert Medwin's expression was one of amazement and disbelief, but before he could answer, Holmes took him by the arm and drew him into the parlour where bade him be seated. Such was the force of Holmes's personality that the young man submitted quietly and my friend stood looking down on him with compassionate eyes.

"You are Rupert Medwin, as I know," Holmes began. "You were directed to this address by a letter left for you at 221b Baker Street, after pursuing a trail that led you to a Colonel Hayter, living near Reigate. Am I correct so far?"

The youth nodded and Holmes continued.

"What I am about to tell you now will undoubtedly be a further shock to you, but I believe you to be man enough to understand the stress that your – er – *mother* was under when she uttered the words that sent you on a quest to avenge a wrong that has been attributed to a completely innocent person. When she named Captain Harwood as your father, she knew that this was not so. If she wishes to give her reasons, then that is between yourselves, but at this very moment she is with the Captain, hoping to obtain his pardon for the slander on his honour. It is not an easy interview for her, and she needs your trust and support. Can that be relied upon?"

Rupert Medwin stared at Holmes uncomprehendingly and spoke in an uncertain tone,

"Why should she lie to me? Why lay blame where none exists? Is this some trick to save the man's skin?

Holmes towered over him with a steely glint in his eye. "All I have said is true. If you insist on making a scene, not only will you give sorrow and embarrassment to your mother, but take my word, Captain Harwood is just the man to take a horse-whip to you for your impertinence. Be guided by me and you may see your mother at once. Hear what she has to say. You will not regret it."

Young Medwin's shoulders sagged, all the aggression gone from him, and he shook his head forlornly.

"It seems there is no longer anyone left in the world who can be trusted," he said bitterly. "Very well, let me see her, and perhaps this time I shall hear the truth."

Holmes gave him a penetrating look before leading the way up the stairs, with myself bringing up in the rear. He tapped on the door of Harwood's room, and on being bidden to enter, threw open the door and announced dramatically, "Mr. Rupert Medwin!"

Ruth Medwin gasped as Holmes thrust the young man forward, then ran to fling her arms around him. "Rupert, darling!" she sobbed.

"Ruth!" he exclaimed and then burst into a nervous laugh. "Oh, hang it – I'll never be able to call you 'Mother' after all these years"

Ruth herself began to laugh with a touch of hysteria not far off. Then, as if caught by the infection, Harwood also joined in.

Holmes closed the door softly and smiled at me.

"Come, Watson, our part in this is finished, and unless my instincts are very much at fault, we have achieved far more than we set out to do. I must say that your part in this has been magnificent, and without your diligence, we may well have been floundering."

I brushed aside the compliment, although inwardly I had a feeling of deep satisfaction that for once my efforts had received recognition. Any praise from Holmes was genuine and sincere.

There is an epilogue to this unusual affair which gave us both cause to be content with our efforts. It was on another beautiful morning some weeks later, and I was looking forward to hearing the smack of leather on willow at Lords. Holmes, still in his dressing gown, was working his way through *The Times*, the floor around him littered with the sheets as he discarded them. I never cease to be amazed that a man with Holmes's orderly mind is unable to read a newspaper without it disintegrating under his touch. I had my hat and stick in my hand and was about to bid him good morning when he stopped with a cry of triumph.

"By Jove! What have we done? Just look at this!"

I peered over his shoulder at the item indicated by his pointing finger and read with astonishment the announcement of an engagement between Captain James Harwood, late of the Royal Berkshire Regiment, and Miss Ruth Medwin, only daughter of the late Daniel and Martha Medwin of Bromley, Kent.

I whistled through my teeth while Holmes chuckled and threw the page down on the floor amongst its fellows.

"I must say, we are the most unlikely agents of Cupid one could be expected to come across in a long day's march. Well, it's a happy outcome to what could have been a very unpleasant affair."

As he spoke the jangle of the doorbell was heard, and I looked at Holmes suspiciously.

"Are you expecting someone?" I asked. "Have you something in hand that you are keeping from me?"

"Not a thing," he replied with a shake of the head, "if this is a new client, I can promise you will be in from the start."

A knock on the door and the boy in buttons announced: "Captain Harwood and Miss Medwin."

The couple entered, both looking shyly happy, and received our congratulations. Then Harwood explained the reason for their visit. "Firstly, we wish to tender our thanks for manner in which you both acted in the late muddle. You have brought happiness to two lonely people that neither expected. How you arrived at the truth I do not know, and I shall not ask."

At this point he directed a keen look in my direction while I became busy getting my pipe to draw.

"Whatever your methods," continued the Captain, "it led to Ruth and I having a long and frank talk, concealing nothing from each other, and I she is content to have me as I am. I feel sure you take my meaning?"

We both nodded gravely, knowing that he was aware that we were privy to his tragic handicap.

"We intend to marry in the autumn," he went on. "Ruth wants to carry on her father's business until Rupert is of age and can take it over – which, incidentally, he is quite capable of doing even now. After that we will emigrate to the colonies. I am not much over forty and have years ahead to make something of myself, and with Ruth beside me, I have every incentive to do so. I only hope her faith in me is justified."

We expressed our heartfelt wishes for their future success, and as they were about to leave, Harwood took an envelope from his pocket and laid it tentatively on the table.

"I hope you will regard this as adequate remuneration, Mr. Holmes," said he. "I know you are a professional man, so if I have miscalculated your fees, do not hesitate to inform me and it will be put right without quibble."

With that they took their leave and Holmes returned to his chair where he tapped the envelope against his fingers. "You know, Watson," he remarked whimsically, "I find it most gratifying to be able to perform a service that not only brings comfort to others, but also gives the same comfort to my bank account."

So saying, he slit open the envelope to withdraw a cheque, the sight of which caused him to raise his eyebrows. He passed it to me without a word and I saw it was for a very substantial sum indeed. I returned it to him, and as I rose to make my belated way to Lords, he detained me with a gesture.

"I hope, Doctor, you will not take offence if I suggest that as it was you who carried a large part of the burden in this affair, you are entitled to an equal share of the rewards."

Before I could respond, he rose and walked quickly to his own room, shutting the door firmly behind him.

We never saw the Harwoods again, but some years later, after Holmes had returned from his perilous adventure at the Reichenbach Falls, he received a letter from Australia which told of their continued happiness and the success they enjoyed in rearing sheep on several thousands of acres. I wish them well, for they deserve it.

The Riverfront Affair

It was a glorious day in mid-July, and having been virtually driven from our rooms by my friend Sherlock Holmes's restless mood, I had spent the morning strolling aimlessly over Hampstead Heath. I had been endeavouring to record the events of the case of the lonely soldier, but with Holmes peering over my shoulder with a flow of carping criticism I had finally lost patience.

"Confound it, Holmes!" I had snapped, "I am merely rounding the facts in order to pay tribute to your perspicacity, not writing a text-book on the art of detection! Allow me my methods as I allow you yours, I beg you." With that I had seized my hat and stick to storm from the room. My return at noon coincided with the advent of a cab from which alighted a petite, slim young lady attired in what appeared to be deep mourning.

As I inserted my key, I was aware that the lady had followed on my heels.

"I beg your pardon, sir," she said in a low, musical voice. "Is this where I may find Mr. Sherlock Holmes?"

I turned and raised my boater. "Indeed it is, Madam. Have you an appointment with him?"

"No, but I'm praying that he will see me. I believe him to be the only man in London who can help me."

I examined the pale features beneath the light veil and saw strain and anxiety. "I'm sure he will see you," I replied stoutly. "I'm his colleague, Dr. John Watson. Follow me and I will announce you."

"I am grateful, sir. I'm Miss Caroline Masters, but the name will mean nothing to either of you." Her relief was most pitiful to see.

When we entered the sitting room, Holmes was standing squarely before the empty grate, his eyes glinting and his hands clasped behind his back.

"Welcome back, Watson!" he cried heartily. "And welcome to you. I trust you have brought me a problem to dispel my *ennui*. Pray be seated."

Miss Masters took the chair indicated facing the window. She raised her veil to reveal a beauty that even the pallor of grief could not mar. Beneath her bonnet strands of brown hair escaped, and large luminous eyes of the same colour with dark smudges below looked out at us hopefully. Her lips, under a *retroussé* nose, were full and red, while the small rounded chin was indicative of great determination. She was little more than five-feet-four in height, and I gauged her to be in her mid-twenties.

Holmes acknowledged my introduction briefly and looked keenly at her. "So, Miss Masters, tell me in what way we may serve you." He rubbed his hands together in anticipation.

"It concerns the death of my sister, Mrs. Jonas Prentiss," she began, her voice trembling slightly. "My half-sister, in reality, but Alice and I were so close as to regard ourselves as sisters."

Holmes stroked his chin thoughtfully. "Ah, I recall the name from a report in *The Evening News*. Did she not suffer an unfortunate accident close by St. Katharine's Dock?"

"It was no accident!" she said vehemently. "Nothing will persuade me otherwise. Neither was it suicide, as was suggested in some quarters."

"Then we are left only with natural causes or – murder." My companion met the lady's eyes. "Natural causes wouldn't bring you to me."

Miss Masters returned his look squarely. "Then you understand why I'm here, sir. I truly believe that Alice was murdered, yet no one will listen to me. Will you do so, Mr. Sherlock Holmes?"

He nodded gravely. "Indeed I shall, and with an open mind. Give me your story, omitting no detail however small. The good Dr. Watson, who has my complete confidence, will make notes. But first, may I offer you some refreshment?"

She expressed a wish for a cup of tea and a biscuit, but nothing more. I summoned Mrs. Hudson, and a tray arrived within minutes.

"Now, Madam," said Holmes when we were settled, "I'm at your disposal. Pray commence."

Our client folded her hands on her lap before starting to speak calmly and rationally. "My name you already know. Alice was the daughter of our father's first marriage, her mother having died in giving her birth. When my father remarried, Alice was five years of age. I was born a year later, but at no time did my mother treat Alice other than as her own. Thus in all respects we were really sisters, sharing a happy home life until my parents died so tragically in the *Princess Alice* disaster. I was sixteen then." Here her voice faltered but she recovered swiftly. "It had been a special treat for my mother to revive memories of an earlier time. You see, gentlemen, Father began life as a jobbing builder, but by dint of hard work and honest dealing, established a thriving business. He died a fairly wealthy man, yet he never lost the common touch, nor did he forget his roots. If only he had lived to retire and enjoy the fruits of his labours!"

"You said you were sixteen when you were orphaned," Holmes put in quickly as tears sprang to her eyes. "Your half-sister would have been what – twenty-two? She was unattached at that time?"

308

"Oh, yes. We resided at Brockley then, and she took charge of the household and became both mother and sister to me. It was three years later when she met Mr. Prentiss, whom she married within a year."

"I see." My colleague steepled his fingers to his lips. "There are questions I must ask if I'm to have a clear picture. Will you answer me frankly in all respects?"

"Of course. I place myself entirely in your hands." She managed a weak smile. "Please feel free to smoke if you so wish. Father was an inveterate smoker, and I love the smell of tobacco."

There was an interval while we charged our pipes. Presently Holmes studied the client over the flame of his match. "You say your late father was wealthy. How was his fortune distributed?"

"After a few bequests to loyal servants, the whole of it came equally and unconditionally to Alice and me. We shared more than fourteen-thousand pounds between us. Alice took her portion to her marriage, enabling Mr. Prentiss to begin his business as a sugar importer. After the marriage, the house at Brockley was sold and I purchased a small villa at Tulse Hill. I don't have an extravagant mode of life, finding myself well able to exist comfortably on the interest from the capital."

She looked at Holmes who was lying back with closed eyes, tendrils of smoke curling up from the pipe clenched between his teeth. "Am I boring you, sir?" she asked with some asperity.

"Far from it," he responded. "I find the background to your problem most informative." He sat up suddenly, "Tell me, why do you dislike your brother-in-law?"

"Is it so obvious?" she said, colour touching the pale cheeks. "But yes, you are right. I loathe and detest Jonas Prentiss with all my heart, and with good cause, for soon after his marriage he made improper and unwelcome suggestions to me. Since then, I have avoided him as far as I can without giving Alice cause to inquire the reason."

"So your prejudice leads you to doubt the nature of your sister's death, is that not so?" He held up a placatory hand as she bridled. "Please, do not take offence. I'm sure you have reasons as yet unvoiced. Tell me more of Mr. Jonas Prentiss, I beg you."

There was a short silence, broken only by the sounds from the street below. Eventually Miss Masters continued. "He is a petty-natured man who is arrogant with those dependent on him, but fawning and obsequious with those whose good-will he desires. In all honesty, I have no reason to suspect that my sister was other than happy, but I do know he spends much of his time away from their home at Balham."

"I take it you didn't visit on a regular basis?"

"Very seldom, and then only when Jonas was sure to be absent."

"I see. Proceed now to the circumstances of your sister's death, as if I have no previous knowledge."

There was a tremor in her voice that betrayed her emotion, but she began bravely enough. "Shortly before midnight on Thursday of last week, a patrolling constable found Alice's body at the foot of an iron staircase by her husband's warehouse at Bobbin's Wharf, which is below The Tower at St. Katherine Dock. Her skull was fractured and her neck broken. Everything suggested that she had fallen or jumped from the landing at the top of the stairway. The inquest decided she had fallen."

"But you aren't satisfied," stated Holmes. "Why?"

"For several reasons. Why was she at that place? She had never concerned herself with anything to do with her husband's business. How could she fall from that balcony, which I hear has a four-foot high guard rail round it? It was said she leaned over too far and overbalanced, but she and I are of a height and I cannot envisage that happening. As for suicide – that I discount entirely. She was in high spirits that very morning when she called on me, and moreover, it would have been against her very nature to do such a terrible thing. In any case, would you attempt suicide by plunging over a mere fifteen foot drop?"

"I see, Miss Masters," said my friend, watching her keenly. "An accident carries no such stigma as suicide, but you will not let the matter lie and wish me to upset the verdict. You understand that I search only for the truth, however unpalatable that may be? Are you prepared for that?"

"It is the truth that I want, sir. I have no fear of it."

"Then so be it." He pondered. "Go home now, and then meet me at four o'clock at your solicitor's office. Who is that?"

"Mr. Popkin, of Kells, Popkin, and Kells in Chancery Lane."

"I know of them. I must have your permission to ask and receive answers to any questions I deem necessary to my investigation. Do I have that?"

She nodded. "Ask what you will. There is nothing to conceal."

Holmes stood up. "Then until later. Whistle up a cab for the lady, Watson, and one for us. We have much to do in the time remaining to us today. Good afternoon, Madam."

Half-an-hour later we were sitting on hard chairs in the dismal office at Scotland Yard that Inspector Gregson shared with Lestrade and others. Today he had the place to himself, and across his scarred and ink-stained desk he surveyed us sourly.

"The Prentiss affair," he said in reply to my companion's direct approach. "Yes, I remember it, but it had little to do with me, being on the City Force's patch. I did make some inquiries on their behalf and conveyed the sad news to the lady's half-sister, a Miss Caroline Masters. What is your interest in it, Mr. Holmes?"

"Miss Masters isn't satisfied that her sister's death was an accident. I have been asked to set her mind at rest, one way or another."

Gregson threw up his hands. "You are wasting your time. The coroner found for accidental death and that is the end of it."

Holmes ignored his dismissal of the matter and went on as if the inspector hadn't spoken. "What inquiries did you make, Gregson, and with what result?"

"That is police business, Mr. Holmes." He wavered under my friend's penetrating look. "Well, if you must know, I merely ascertained the whereabouts of Mr. Jonas Prentiss at the time of his wife's death. You of all people should realize that in the case of an unexpected death, the deceased's spouse and near relatives are the first to be examined."

"And Mr. Jonas Prentiss satisfied you of his movements? He produced credible witnesses, I presume?"

"Indeed he did, albeit reluctantly. Don't take me for a fool, sir."

"Who were they?" Holmes's voice crackled.

"Oh, come now, you are surely aware that I cannot reveal that." Gregson ran his fingers through his flaxen hair. "If you must know, he was at a less-than-respectable club from seven o'clock until past midnight." He dropped his eyes, and drawing a sheet of paper to him scrawled something on it and slid it across the desk. "These are two of the gentlemen who vouched for him. Both are unmarried, so less likely to be embarrassed. You will remember that the information didn't come from this office."

"Trust me, my dear Gregson." Holmes pocketed the slip of paper. Then retrieved his stick and hat to depart without another word.

"What now?" I asked as we emerged into the sunlight of Whitehall.

"We have an hour in hand before we meet Miss Masterson again. I don't know about you, but I think that as we missed lunch, a dish of chops wouldn't come amiss, and I know the very place just off Holborn."

I agreed most heartily, but despite my curiosity Holmes remained close-lipped regarding the names he had inveigled from Gregson, We reached the dusty offices of Kells, Popkin, and Kells, Attorneys at Law, in Chancery Lane to find our client had preceded us and was waiting to introduce us to Mr. Martin Popkin, who was now the senior partner,

"I know of you by repute, Mr, Holmes," said he, "And Dr. Watson. Be seated, please."

The plump little man disposed himself behind his desk, his shrewd blue eyes watching us from behind his gold *pince-nez*. Folding his hands before him, he opened the conversation. "Miss Masters has requested that

I be entirely frank with you in respect of her affairs. However, beyond that I don't think I can go.

"In short, sir, anything that touches on matters peculiar to Mr. and Mrs. Prentiss I may not ask." Holmes did not appear discomposed. "What was the position on the death of Mr. and Mrs. Masters? What were the provisions for the daughters' future?"

"I shall strip away all jargon," replied Popkin. "In brief, as Miss Alice was of age she had charge of her own portion. Miss Caroline, on the other hand, was a minor, and I, along with Miss Alice, were her trustees. When she reached her majority our duties ended, although both ladies honoured me by seeking my advice in all matters." He paused to examine his hands. "Until Miss Alice married, when her husband assumed control of her affairs."

"You didn't approve of the match?" my colleague murmured.

"It wasn't my place to approve or disapprove. She made her choice,"

"Oh, come, Mr. Popkin," cried the lady. "You know very well you begged me to urge caution on my sister before she committed herself!"

The lawyer shifted uneasily in his seat. "We are a cautious profession, my dear. Nevertheless, the lady went ahead, but she did persuade her husband to allow me to continue as legal advisor to them both, although I believe Mr. Prentiss also seeks counsel in other quarters regarding his business."

"As a sugar importer, I understand," said Holmes casually. "Does his business prosper?"

"Come, sir, you know that is an improper question." Mr, Popkin looked out of the small window. "A small, newly established venture must always struggle when faced by competition from the large combinations."

"I see." Holmes looked pleased. "Miss Masters is comfortably situated?"

"Indeed. When her half-sister married, the house at Brockley was sold and her part of the proceeds more than paid for her present residence. She lives well within her income, and her capital has appreciated considerably over the years." He looked at the lady. "You enjoined frankness, my dear. I hope I haven't exceeded my duty."

"In no measure, sir. It is as I wished."

"You have been most helpful, Mr. Hopkin," said Holmes. "Tell me, did Mrs. Prentiss ever bring up the subject of life insurance?"

This time the solicitor visibly squirmed in his chair, but it was Miss Masters who answered.

"Alice and I had a reciprocal arrangement up until the time she married. Since then, my policy remains in her favour, but as was to be

312

expected hers now falls to her husband, as she predeceased him. It provided for a sum of ten-thousand pounds, if it hasn't been changed."

"A tempting sum," said my companion ambiguously. "Thank you for your time, Mr. Popkin. May we drop you anywhere, Miss Masters?"

"I thank you, sir, but no. I still have business with Mr. Popkin."

The sunlight seemed very bright when we came out of the fusty office. We made our way to a small tea-rooms, Holmes averring that we had a couple of hours to kill.

"You sailed a bit near the wind with the questions you asked," I observed. "I was surprised you gleaned so much."

"Mr. Popkin has neither love nor trust for Jonas Prentiss. He went as far as he could without actually saying so. We move apace, Watson."

"Tell me, what did Gregson write on that piece of paper which you keep hidden in your pocket?"

"Here, see for yourself. It is only the names of two gentlemen who confirmed Prentiss's movements on the night in question. And," he added , "the name of the premises where they were: The Sugar and Spice Club."

I looked at Gregson's scrawl, then gave a gasp. "Why, Holmes, I know one of these names: Major John Cradley, of all people, at that den of vice!"

For once my friend shoved himself capable of surprise at one of my pronouncements. "You know him? By Jove! Can you lay hands on him?"

I thought back over the years, recalling the handsome, carefree officer of Horse Artillery with whom I had struck up an acquaintance on the long voyage back from the sub-continent. I had met him a couple of times afterwards, but in my straitened circumstances was unable to move in the circles that an officer of independent means could do and the friendship lapsed. I realized that Holmes was waiting impatiently for my reply.

"If my memory doesn't fail me," I began, "I seem to remember that he was a member of the Artillery Club in Pall Mall. Whether that is still so, I cannot say."

"I leave the matter in your hands. Tomorrow you must make every effort to trace the gallant major and get his story. You know my methods. Every detail, however insignificant, can provide us with valuable data. I rely on you, my dear fellow."

"I shall do all within my power," I promised, hiding my delight at being entrusted with something my colleague deemed important. "But what will you be doing?"

"I shall have my hands full, have no fear." He glanced at his watch. "I think another pot of tea and more of those excellent cream buns, then we shall proceed to St. Katherine's Docks."

313

He seemed in no hurry, lingering inordinately over the tea. By the time we had secured a hansom, the sun was low in the vest. Even then he bade the cabbie to take his time while he sat back apparently lost in thought.

My attempts to draw him out were ignored until I finally lost patience. "Am I to be told nothing?" I asked fractiously.

"Not at this moment, Doctor. I wish you to view the location of the crime with no preconceived ideas in that honest head of yours."

"You are convinced a crime has been committed?"

"Indubitably."

"And the culprit? Surely Mr. Jonas Prentiss has had his movements verified by Gregson. The inspector, for all his faults, is a thorough man."

"Gregson?" My companion snorted. "Diligent he may be, but he lacks that vital spark of imagination to see beyond the end of his nose." He fell back into silence, only coming to life when we reached the seedy run-down area of the docks. The huge warehouses, stuffed with merchandise from all corners of the earth, looked down on the forest of masts in The Pool, while The Tower of London, untouched by its blood-soaked past, kept a paternal watch over the whole.

"The hub of the greatest empire the world has seen," said Holmes sombrely as we alighted. "How long will it survive? Wait here, cabbie." He tossed a coin to the driver who caught it deftly.

"Not too long, Guv'nor," growled the latter. "This ain't no place to be 'anging around after dark."

His throaty voice faded away behind us as we stepped out smartly, Holmes leading the way through the alleys betwixt the tall buildings as though familiar with every twist and turn. He stopped so abruptly that I almost cannoned into him. We were at the riverside, the oily water of an ebbing tide sucking greedily at the piles of a wooden jetty as if reluctant to return to the sea from whence it came.

"There, Watson: '*J. Prentiss – Sugar Importer*'." He pointed with his stick at the legend above a large set of double doors. "And there is the fatal staircase."

The iron structure ran up the side of the building, terminating at a small door some fifteen feet above. There was a landing at the top, and in the fading light I could just discern a guard rail such as our client had described. Holmes moved to stand directly beneath the balcony, his eyes searching the cobbles before looking upwards.

"Have we had any rain recently?" he asked.

"A heavy shower two nights ago, as you well remember. You had been to Bradley's for tobacco and came back soaked."

"So I did. Then I fear we will find nothing of use here."

The words had barely left his mouth when a hoarse shout came from close by. "'Ere, what's your game?" A heavily built man in late middle-age was shuffling over the cobbles grasping a cudgel.

"Game?" Holmes's voice was devoid of guile. "Why, no game, my man. Are you the caretaker here?"

"Night watchman, that's wot I am." The fellow eyed us suspiciously. "You ain't no call to be 'ere."

"You are just the man we were looking for," my colleague said smoothly. "My friend and I are writing articles on Thames tragedies, and as this was lately the scene of one we thought you could tell us of it." A coin glinted in his hand and the watchman relaxed.

"Dunno about that, Mister. It weren't me wot found the poor lady. It were like this: I do my rounds reg'lar every hour, 'round the outside, then the inside, on all the floors an' back again." He stepped close enough for me to smell the beer on his breath and the coin vanished in a grimy hand.

"Well, I'd been round at eleven o'clock an' 'Arry Chalmers, the beat copper, makes 'is point wiv the sergeant at twelve. After the sergeant's gorn, me an' 'Arry 'as a vet in the warehouse. Well, this pertickler night I'm just goin' out when I 'ears 'Arry blowin' 'is whistle fit to bust, so I nips round an' there 'e is wiv the lady. I never knew it were the Guv'ner's missus, did I? Anyways, afore long the sergeant comes galloping back wiv anuvver peeler, so I figgers I orter to leave to them an' slopes orf."

"Mrs. Prentiss seemingly fell from the top of those stairs," Holmes mused. "Can we go up for a look?"

"As long as you don't fall likewise." The man chuckled wheezily and led the way to the foot of the steps. "I'd best come wiv yer."

We mounted the iron treads and found ourselves on the platform. There was indeed a four-foot-high guard rail, and also two other bars beneath it, the top rail resting below Holmes's ribs as he leant over to look down. He straightened up with a shake of his head.

"If, as Miss Masters says, her sister and she were much of a height, there is no way she could have fallen accidentally," he said just loudly enough to reach my ears. He rounded suddenly on the watchman. "Is there a way up from inside the warehouse?"

"There is, guv, but that door ain't never been opened in my mem'ry. It's allus locked, and Mr. P. is the only one wiv a key."

Whipping out his lens, Holmes knelt on the cold ironwork to make an intensive scrutiny of the platform. At length he stood up, his face showing satisfaction. "Capital, Watson, capital," he muttered. "Now, my good man," he went on, turning to the watchman, "who has access to the building during the hours of darkness?"

"Well, sir, I has a key to the wicket in the main doors, as 'as Fred 'Awkins, the foreman, but it's me wot lets 'im in at seven in the morning. 'Course, Mr. Prentiss 'as a full set of keys, but nobody else ain't."

"Thank you." Another coin went the way of the first. "Say nothing about our visit. We want to be first with the story."

"Trust me, Mister, and don't you go falling down these stairs." The man gave a gap-toothed grin and led the way down, leaving Holmes and me to make our way back to where our cabbie was showing signs of impatience with the approach of darkness.

The ride back to Baker Street was made in silence, with my companion sitting back with closed eyes and fingers tapping nervously on his knee. I knew from long experience that I would get nothing from him in his present mood, so I contented myself with my own speculations, such as they were.

"What next?" I ventured as we sat down to the cold meats left for us by Mrs. Hudson. "Have we made progress? You have the most annoying habit of keeping me in the dark."

"Bear with me, there's a good fellow." He laid down his knife and fork. "Tomorrow you will set about tracing your Major Cradley. You know exactly what is wanted, and I know your tenacity will bear fruit. I have other fish to fry."

The next morning he left as I was shaving, but conscious of the importance he attached to the mission with which he had entrusted me, I wasn't long behind him. In the event my task proved easier and more successful than I could have hoped, and it was late afternoon when I returned to our rooms with a feeling of well-being and satisfaction with a job well done. Holmes hadn't returned, and I lay back in a chair to sift through the information I had secured. It wasn't long before the fumes of the wine and brandy, on top of the generous lunch pressed on me by John Cradley, took over. The next thing I knew was being shaken roughly by the shoulder.

I opened my eyes to find Holmes standing over me. "I hope you have achieved something," he said acidly. "Is old age catching up with you?"

I scowled up at him as I collected my fuddled wits. "What time is it?"

"Approaching six o'clock. I have been on the go for nearly ten hours."

"I haven't been idle." I stood up to stretch my cramped limbs. "Do you wish to hear the results of my efforts?"

He smiled suddenly. "I'm sorry, old friend. I should have curbed my tongue. Mrs. Hudson is bringing tea and we can exchange news over it."

I wasn't hungry, but the strong tea was welcome and I gulped it down thirstily while Holmes made inroads into a veal-and-ham pie.

"You first," he said through a mouthful of pie. "I vow it's a long time since I was so sharp set."

"As you wish." I collected my thoughts. "I went to the Artillery Club and had the luck to find that Major Cradley was expected for lunch this very day. Despite the long interval since our last meeting, he gave me a most hearty welcome, and insisted on lunching me while we spoke of old times."

"Get on with it, man," said Holmes impatiently.

"You are the one who impressed on me the importance of detail," I pointed out. "We had reached the coffee and brandy stage before I mentioned The Sugar and Spice Club. He made no secret of his visits to the place, even offering to put me up for membership. I hedged, saying I had heard rumours of the police making inquiries recently about the place. It was then he told me of Gregson's questions regarding Jonas Prentiss's movements because of the death of that gentleman's wife. Affecting ignorance, I pressed him for details, learning that he, Cradley, had confirmed that Prentiss was present at the club throughout the whole evening in question."

Holmes looked up with a frown. "He was adamant? Confound the man!"

"Wait – there's more," I said smugly. "I asked if Prentiss was a clubbable man, and that's when Cradley seemed puzzled. It seems that in the ordinary way Prentiss is a good mixer, always ready for a game of cards or whatever else is on offer at such a place, but this particular evening he was unsociable to the point of rudeness. He was morose, refused to join in a hand of cards, and ignored men with whom he had been on close terms for several years. He also drank more heavily than was his wont and left with barely a good-night to the company."

"Oh, you are a gem!" Holmes rubbed his hands together. "Where would I be without you!"

"Thank you," I said drily. "It means something?"

"It means a lot. One more journey tonight and we are home and dry."

"Hang it all," I said in exasperation, "am I not to know what you have been doing all day?"

"I, my dear Doctor, have bounced from one side of London to another with never a bite to eat. I spent several hours in Somerset House, looked up an old friend in The City, and then made my way to Balham."

"Balham! To where Prentiss resides? To what purpose?"

"To speak with a butcher's boy and a milkman. If you want to know what happens in any street, they are the people to ask. Now, I shall smoke a pipe or three, then we may sally forth."

317

"You have told me where you have been, but nothing of the results," I complained in exasperation. "Neither have you said where we go tonight. Really, Holmes, you would try the patience of a saint!"

"You are no saint, Watson, just a good, honest fellow. Allow me my little quirks, I pray you. Now be good enough to remain silent for an hour or so while I search for flaws in my reasoning." With that he flung himself into the basket chair, laying out a selection of pipes beside him. It was approaching nine o'clock before he moved again, then he uncoiled himself like a steel spring to bounce to his feet. "Come, Watson!" he cried. "Time we were on our way!"

Shaken from a doze I blinked up at him. "Where to?" I asked.

"A brisk walk will do wonders for your sluggish system after your lunch time excesses. No questions yet, old fellow, but see what you can deduce from what I hope will transpire tonight."

We set off at a smart pace along Marylebone Road before turning into Great Portland Street and thence through various twists and turns, giving me the impression we were making for the Middlesex Hospital. In that I was proved wrong when my companion's steps slowed as he began scanning the buildings on the other side of the road before stopping to draw me into a darkened doorway.

"What are we doing,?" I asked as patiently as I could.

"Waiting and watching," he said. "On no account are you to move from here, nor show yourself until I give the word. Do you see that door opposite – the one with the discreet light burning so dimly?" He pointed with his stick. "That, my friend, is the notorious Sugar and Spice Club."

For one awful moment I thought Holmes was going to drag me into the disreputable place, but his voice held a chuckle when he next spoke.

"Have no fear. Your Calvinist conscience is safe with me. As I said, we merely watch and wait – for how long I cannot surmise."

"You expect to find Jonas Prentiss paying a visit tonight?" I ventured.

He shrugged. "It matters not either way. It isn't he I wish to see. I fear we may have a long wait without even the solace of a pipe. On the other hand, we may be fortunate enough . . . ." He broke off as a closed hackney carriage stopped before the narrow front of the building opposite. Two men in evening dress alighted, going up the steps where they were admitted almost immediately to the gloomy interior, and the door shutting firmly behind them.

"Don't move." Holmes hurried across the road and engaged the cab-driver in a brief conversation, I saw the man shake his head before mounting to drive away as my colleague returned to me.

"I suppose it was too much to hope to strike lucky at the first attempt," he said, but the words had barely passed his lips when another cab drew up and the pantomime was repeated. During the next three-quarters-of-an-hour, this happened a further three times. Then with my tolerance wearing thin, I saw Holmes signalling me to join him. The old wound in my leg had begun to protest at the long period of standing in the small doorway and I was glad to get my circulation moving, but no sooner had I crossed the road than Holmes was hustling me into the cab and we set off.

It was a short journey, however, and after doubling 'round some side streets, we halted beneath the yellow glow of a street lamp. The driver descended and my companion opened the door and beckoned the man to get in.

He did so, taking the seat facing us and eyeing us warily. "Now look here, Mister," he began aggressively, "I only take people where they want to go. As long they behave themselves I ask no questions, nor do I like having to answer them." He was a man in his early thirties, clean-shaven, tidy, and less coarsely spoken than many of his calling. "Unless you are police."

"No, we are not," said Holmes, offended by being mistaken for the official force. "We merely want a little information, and I promise that once we have it, we shall forget we ever spoke to you."

The cabbie nodded slowly. "Ask away. I'll decide how much I can tell you. You wanted to hear about Mr. Prentiss. All I can say about him is that the times I've had him aboard, he's never been any trouble."

"Where do you take him?"

"Balham, mostly. It's a good trot out there and pays well."

"You say mostly, but you have taken him elsewhere then?"

The man rubbed his chin thoughtfully. "Just the once. Last Thursday it was. I remember it well because it was the wife's birthday and she was a bit upset because I wouldn't have the night off to take her out. There's a young'un coming along and we need the money, see."

"What happened that night that was so different?"

"Well, the gentleman came out about midnight, and as I was there he got straight in without a word. That was queer because he usually remarked on the weather or suchlike. Not exactly friendly, like, but civil. He looked as if he had a drink too many as well and that wasn't like him. We hadn't gone above half-a-mile when he stopped me and asked if I knew where I was going. 'Why, Balham as usual, aren't we sir?' I said. 'No. drop me off at The Oval,' he said. I did as he asked, and he gave me two whole sovereigns, then off he went without as much as a good-night. Well, on the strength of that I packed it in for the night. The wife was surprised to see me, as I seldom get in before four o'clock."

"Have you seen him since then?" asked Holmes.

"Last night. Then he was his old self again." The cabbie lowered his voice. "I did hear his wife had died, but you'd never think it."

"Thank you, driver. I'd be grateful if you didn't mention our little chat." There was a clink of metal and a couple of gold coins gleamed in the lamplight before they vanished.

"Terrible memory I have, sir." The man grinned. "Can I take you gents somewhere?"

Much to my disgust, Holmes refused the offer, saying as it was a fine night the walk would do us good. He was in an ebullient mood on the way back to Baker Street, twirling his stick and blithely whistling a vulgar music-hall ditty, but despite my probing, it wasn't until we were indoors with a pot of fragrant coffee before us that he deigned to speak.

"Tomorrow will see the finish of this little problem, my dear Watson. A minor puzzle, but satisfying in its way."

"You are saying you have the solution?" I said.

"Why, it's perfectly clear. Come, Doctor, you have as much, if not more information, than I had when I set out this morning. To what use have you put it?"

"Steady on," I objected. "You told me where you had been, but not a word of the outcome of your inquiries."

"After what we have learnt this evening, I thought you would be capable of deducing the chain of events. Did nothing strike you as strange?"

I took a sip of coffee, then wiped my moustache as I gave myself time to think. "The behaviour of Jonas Prentiss on the fatal night? It was remarked upon by Major Cradley and again by the jarvey who picked him up at The Sugar and Spice." I snapped my fingers. "Oh, I think I understand. It was not Prentiss who killed his wife, but someone he had employed to do so. He wasn't his usual self because of worrying whether or not the murder had been carried out successfully. Am I right?"

My companion gave me a quizzical look. "Let me say you are on the right lines, but I fear you have been derailed on the way, if I may make use of a railway metaphor. Go to your bed now. I shall be abroad early tomorrow, but I will join you for breakfast at nine o'clock. Goodnight, and sleep well."

In spite of the thoughts jostling for space in my mind, I did indeed sleep soundly, waking to hear the front door slam when Holmes made his exit. Promptly on the stroke of nine he bounced back in, with Mrs. Hudson on his heels bearing our breakfast.

He tossed a copy of *The Morning Post* to me. "See, I think of you all the time. I know you like to read the cricket reports and scores – but don't linger, I beg you. The game's afoot and we must be out within the hour."

He rubbed his hands together before helping himself to a generous portion of ham and eggs. "By Jove, it's a beautiful morning!" I knew by his ill-concealed excitement that we were nearing the final act of the drama, but it wasn't until we were in a four-wheeler and threading our way through the traffic that I dared to ask where we were going.

"First we go to Tulse Hill to collect Miss Masters," he said. "I sent her a telegram asking her to join us, From there we proceed to Balham, where I hope the lady's presence may gain us admittance to the house of that evil and calculating murderer, Jonas Prentiss."

"You are convinced it was he who killed his wife?" I frowned. "You don't believe his alibi to be sound, then?"

"We shall see. I hope my other telegram will be taken seriously. We may find our hands full otherwise." We were crossing Vauxhall Bridge as he spoke, and looking out of the window he drew my attention to the river below. "Just think," he mused, "what stories that great waterway could tell if it had a tongue to speak, yet it flows on as unconcernedly as it has for two-thousand years and more." With that he closed his eyes and sat back, not speaking until we were in Brixton Road. "Do you remember?" he said, his acute perception telling him where we were.

"Could I forget?" I replied. "Our very first foray together."

"Which you fancifully called 'A Study in Scarlet'," he chuckled. "I only took you along to demonstrate that I wasn't the charlatan you thought me."

"Which you did so successfully," I confessed ruefully,

We both laughed, and the rest of the journey was spent in recalling past cases, some of which, for various reasons, will forever remain untold. Miss Masters lived a neat detached villa a short way from Brockwell Park. No sooner had our carriage stopped than the lady herself came to meet us at the gate, still dressed in black, but with her veil thrown back to show her cheeks to have more colour than at our previous meeting.

"Mr. Holmes! Dr. Watson!" she cried in greeting. "I received your telegram, but I own to some perplexity at its contents. I understand you wish me to accompany you, but that is all."

"Only if you feel strong enough to meet Mr. Prentiss face to face," said my companion, his tone grave but gentle. "I know your feelings towards him and realize the very thought must be repellent."

Her eyes blazed. "Will it serve to bring to book the murderer of my dear Alice? If so, I would face the Devil himself!"

"Your presence may assist us in the essential matter of gaining entry to the premises. Without you, we must resort to other methods."

"Then I will come, sir. Why do we dally?"

I handed her into the cab, not hiding my admiration for the courage of this young and beautiful lady. After a brief word to the driver, Holmes took his place beside me, facing Miss Masters.

"What must I do, Mr. Holmes?" asked the latter as we moved off.

"Describe to me the interior of the house. I have only seen it from without."

"Then you will know that it's of recent construction, built by a coal merchant who was bankrupted by the cost. Jonas bought it at the time of his marriage, doubtless with my sister's money." She spoke bitterly.

"But inside – the layout." Holmes allowed his impatience to show.

She continued unperturbed. "The outer door opens onto a small foyer. Then the main door gives on to a passage running the length of the house. A large drawing room is on the right, and then a staircase leading to the upper floors." She was speaking as calmly as an estate agent would of a desirable property. "On the left there is a library and a dining room. I should say that upstairs, only the first floor is used. There are three bedrooms, the one used by Alice and her husband being over the library. The second floor is unfurnished. Do you need more?"

"Servants?"

"Very few. A parlour maid living in, a cook, and a woman for the rough work, both of whom come daily. Oh, and an occasional gardener." She looked at her gloved hands. "The parlour maid has been there only a few months, the previous girl having left in unfortunate circumstances."

Holmes fingered his long nose thoughtfully. "That is most helpful. Can you devise a reason for calling on this man whom you have avoided so pointedly in the past?"

A small frown creased her smooth brow, then she nodded. "Alice owned a pearl brooch which had been her mother's. She often said that she would like me to have it should anything happen to her. Could I not ask Jonas to allow me to take it as a memento?"

"Excellent. It will be an opening." My colleague looked at me with a mocking twinkle in his eye before continuing. "This shall be our ploy. The good doctor will assume the role of your fiancé, Mr. James Weston." I gasped aloud at his outrageous plan but he continued unabashed. "My part will be that of his brother and business advisor. If that doesn't do the trick we must take more direct measures, but let us try that first." For the first time since we had met her, Miss Masters laughed in genuine delight while I strove to keep from showing my disapproval.

"Oh, my poor Dr. Watson!" laughed our client. "Does the idea of being engaged to me hold such terror for you? Am I so unattractive?"

"In no way," I stammered. "I am dull dog and fear only for your sensibilities. Holmes should display more delicacy, and in any case I hardly think we could be taken for brothers."

"You think not?" From his pocket he took a small leather case, then turned away to make one of those remarkable transformations to his appearance which had served him so well in the past. Miss Masters' eyes widened when he next looked at us, and even I was astonished at what he had achieved in so short a time and with so little. He sported a moustache similar to mine, his cheeks were filled out, and by some mysterious means he gave the illusion of being shorter and bulkier than he actually was.

"What is your opinion, Madam?" he asked, and even his voice had a different timbre.

"Why, it's incredible!" Her amazement was plain. "You resemble the doctor as closely as Alice resembled me!"

"I still think it chancy," I grumbled. "Will Prentiss believe in a fiancé suddenly materializing from nowhere?"

"Have you a better suggestion?" he asked frostily, and I had to admit I hadn't, staying silent until our cab came to a halt before a large double-fronted house.

"Play your parts," Holmes enjoined us as we alighted. "There may be eyes watching us. Are you prepared?"

"The last time I was here was to visit Alice ten days ago," she said sadly. "I shall bear up, Mr. Holmes." She slipped her arm through mine and met my eyes. "I shall lean on you if I may, James." Her voice was steady.

"That is well done," nodded Holmes. "Don't hesitate to show the grief you naturally feel. He let us to precede him along the gravelled drive, and I confess to a fluttering heart as the lovely creature held my arm closely.

I tugged at the bell-pull, hearing the muffled ring from within. There was no immediate response. I rang again and shortly we heard hesitant footsteps. Through the frosted glass, I saw the inner door open to reveal a blurred form. When the outer door eventually opened it was by a tall, sharp-featured man. His black hair was plastered over a narrow skull, and a thin, dark moustache and boot-button eyes gave him a sinister look.

"Caroline!" The reedy voice was lacking in warmth. "This is an unexpected visitation. I will not pretend it is a pleasure, for we were never friends, despite my efforts."

"It isn't right to air our differences, Jonas, while we both mourn Alice," she replied quietly. "I'm here to beg a favour of you."

"And these gentlemen?" His tone was cold.

"My fiancé, Mr. James Weston, and his brother."

"Septimus Weston, sir." Holmes sounded genial. "Miss Masters requested our company."

"Fiancé?" Prentiss raised his scanty eyebrows. "This is the first I have heard of such an attachment. Alice certainly didn't speak of it."

"The engagement is recent, sir," I said truthfully before improvising. "We have been long acquainted, but with the so tragic death of Mrs. Prentiss, she turned to me for solace. I was proud to offer myself."

Jonas Prentiss turned his attention back to the lady. "What favour do you seek from me, Caroline? It must hurt your pride to approach me."

"May we come in, sir?" Holmes put in. "It isn't usual to conduct family business on the doorstep. Unless you have company," he added.

Prentiss's eyes wavered. Then he looked over his shoulder before standing aside to allow us entry. "Come in, but you will be wasting your time," he said surlily. "And mine too, which is more important." With ill-grace, he ushered us into the drawing room to the right of the passage, shutting the door firmly once we were in and making no offer of a seat.

"Come to the point, Caroline. What do you want?"

"I will be brief, Jonas. Alice had a small pearl brooch, a legacy from her mother. She knew I admired it and promised it would be mine if anything befell her. Will you follow her wishes in that respect?"

"Do you have it in writing? No, of course not." An unpleasant smile was directed at our client. "Let me tell you once and for all, Miss High-and-Mighty: Nothing of my late wife's leaves my possession, least of all to you. We had little to say to each other in the past, and even less now, so I will bid you and your friends good day,"

"You are resolved in your spite, Jonas? You will not reconsider?" Miss Masters flushed with humiliation, and I was about to intervene on her behalf when I intercepted a warning glance from Holmes, who had wandered aimlessly to where a sideboard stood beneath the window.

"You live alone now, Mr. Prentiss?" he said idly,

"Yes, if it is any of your business. I have no need for servants now, except for a woman who comes in daily to clean and prepare a meal."

"I see." My colleague parted the curtains to look out, but Prentiss had already opened the door, impatient for us to be gone. "In that case, there is no more to be said. Come, James, Caroline, We aren't welcome," Both the lady and I were astounded by his attitude, but I knew better than to dispute his actions. I took my temporary fiancé's arm in a firm grip to lead her from the room. Prentiss shut the door behind us and went towards the main exit, but my colleague stopped in his tracks, his eyes sweeping the passageway like a gun-dog seeking a pick-up.

With no further warning he exploded into action. Before the owner of the house knew what was happening. Holmes had flung open a door

324

opposite and darted in. There was a loud cry, followed by the sounds of a scuffle. Then, within seconds and before any of us had gathered our wits, he emerged with a vainly-struggling figure in his steely grip.

Miss Masters and I stood speechless, unable to believe what we saw. "Meet Josiah Prentiss." Holmes, drawing himself up to his full height, spat the padding from his cheeks and with one swift movement tore off the false moustache. "Astounding, is it not?"

I stared from the man in Holmes's grasp to the ashen face of Jonas Prentiss. They were mirror images of one another, even to the clothes they wore. Miss Masters gripped my arm, trembling violently as she leant on me for support.

Jonas Prentiss was galvanised into action. With a terrible oath he made a dive for the front door, wrenching it open to be faced by a grim-faced Inspector Gregson with two stalwart constables at his back.

"Not leaving, sir?" he intoned. At his signal the constables advanced, one to clap handcuffs on Jonas Prentiss, and the other, at a nod from Holmes, doing the same for his double who offered no resistance. A low-voiced exchange took place between the inspector and Holmes. Then the former stepped forward.

"Jonas Prentiss," he said solemnly, "I arrest you for the murder of Alice Prentiss." He gave the usual caution and then turned the other man. "Josiah Prentiss, I arrest you as an accessory before, to, and after the murder of Alice Prentiss." He completed the formula, and the two prisoners were led away to a police van which had pulled up before the house as my colleague and Gregson exchanged looks.

Holmes opened the door of the drawing room. "I think it safe to release the lady now," he said lightly. "It will be more comfortable in here to make explanations."

We entered the room, bemused by the abrupt and amazing sequence of events. Holmes waved us to chairs, then went to lean negligently against the mantelpiece. He fished in his pocket to produce an amber-stemmed brier which he began to load in a leisurely fashion.

"For Heaven's sake, Mr. Holmes," said Gregson, "Will you get on with it?" Not until his pipe was drawing did my friend speak. "Of course, Gregson. You don't need me to tell you that that pair of scoundrels must be handed over to the City Police. However, a great deal of credit will accrue to you for your smart work in the case." There was a sardonic gleam in his eye, Gregson having the grace to look sheepish as Holmes continued.

"When Miss Masters appealed to me for help," he began, "I was impressed by her unshakeable conviction that her step-sister's death wasn't an accident, nor was it suicide. You, Inspector, quite rightly

325

maintained that it was outside your jurisdiction, although you had made peripheral inquiries on behalf of the City force. I began by asking myself who would benefit by the death of Mrs. Prentiss. Obviously not Miss Masters, which left only the dead woman's husband.

"Unfortunately, Jonas Prentiss had witnesses to his actions for the times during which his wife could have been killed, too many for all of them to be in collusion. The question was could they all have been genuinely mistaken? By means which I need not go into – " Here he exchanged a wink with Gregson. " – I obtained the names of two of those witnesses, and by a stroke of luck, one of them was an old army comrade of Watson's. He took it on his shoulders to follow up the matter. No reflection on you, Inspector, but a friendly chat often produces more than the official approach.

"Meanwhile I was chasing other hares, and when the doctor and I compared notes, I knew I was on the right lines, incredible as it seemed. You know my dictum: 'When you have eliminated the impossible, whatever remains, however improbable, must be the truth.'"

"That's all very well," Gregson put in. "You may come and go at will, whereas I'm bound by regulations."

"And rightly so," Holmes said primly. "Where would we be without the due form of law and order?"

Gregson looked to see if he was being teased, but Holmes ignored the look and continued.

"Previously Watson and I had visited the scene of the tragedy. Despite being assured that the door leading from the inside of the warehouse to the fatal landing had been locked for years, I found evidence to show that it had been opened very recently. The iron floor of the landing had a semicircular scrape proving it to be so. I began to form the theory that Mrs. Prentiss had been lured to the building, persuaded to mount the inside stairs, go onto the landing, and from there had been sent to her death.

"Now, with whom would she be most likely to visit the warehouse? Why, who else but her husband? Even though she had never shown a great interest in his business affairs, he could have taken her there under some pretext. I hardly think she would go there with a stranger."

"So you already had Jonas Prentiss in your sights," Gregson observed.

"Oh, yes. While Dr. Watson was engaged with his old comrade-in-arms, I was at Somerset House, where I discovered that Prentiss was one of twins. It was obvious that if he wasn't where he was said to be, then someone was impersonating him, a view that was reinforced when I heard the account Watson had had of his unusual behaviour at the club. That was confirmed last night by another source. It was a long shot, but it hit the target. To proceed: After leaving Somerset House, I looked up an old acquaintance in the City and found that Prentiss's business was on the point of collapse. Another inquiry revealed that he stood to collect ten-thousand pounds in insurance by his wife's death."

"Great Scott! Are no secrets safe from you?" asked Gregson. "Even I would have to obtain a court order to get that kind of information."

My colleague ignored him. "I also came to Balham, where I was able to trace the butcher's boy and the milkman who waited on Prentiss. From them I found that he had left home seldom since his wife's so-called accident, an understandable attitude, but both thought there was another occupant of the house when they made their deliveries, the milkman at six and the boy at eight or eight-thirty. The daily woman had been told the night before not to return, so who else would be there?"

"What, no servants for a place this size?" Gregson showed his surprise.

"They were discharged the morning after Mrs. Prentiss's body was found. Tell me, Inspector: When did you inform him of her death?"

"Shortly after ten-thirty. He had been expected at Bobbin's Wharf at his usual time of nine, but when he didn't appear, Sergeant Lane from the City put in a request for our lot to do it,"

"The servants had already been sent packing by then – a strange state of affairs, was it not?"

"You believe Josiah Prentiss was already in the house? But where?"

"Miss Masters told us that the top floor was unfurnished and never used. He could hide out there with impunity. Probably neither brother trusted the other, and Josiah wanted to be around to be sure of his share of the spoils. But you grow impatient, Gregson. In short, I decided to smoke him out. I sent you a telegram, collected Miss Masters, and bluffed our way in. As soon as we entered this room, I knew I had them. Two partly-empty whisky glasses stood on the sideboard, and I heard the creak of a floor board from across the hall. When I twitched the curtains as a signal, you came up trumps. You will have to pass what you know to your colleagues at Leman Street, but I think Josiah will be ready to turn Queen's Evidence with a little persuasion."

I noticed our client showing signs of distress. I decided to intervene.

"Look here, Holmes," I said, "As a doctor, I say Miss Masters has been subjected to too much strain. Can we not take her away from this place?"

He suddenly became solicitous. "I apologize. I have been remiss. The inspector and I have more to say, so the doctor will take you home and leave me to find my own way. Is that agreeable?"

She accepted gratefully, and I wasn't averse to such a pleasant task. "I shall call on you when I'm more composed to express my thanks, Mr. Holmes," she said, offering him her hand. "Come, Doctor, I will hear no more sordid details. My faith was justified, and that is enough,"

She spoke not a word on the journey to Tulse Hill, staring out of the window with blank eyes until we arrived and I escorted her to her door.

"You will be all right?" I asked anxiously. "Is there anything I can do for you professionally?"

"Thank you for the thought, Dr. Watson, but have no fear for me. I'm not one of your vapid females, and my natural grief will pass in time. Now I'm sure you will excuse me, as I would be alone with my memories." With that she vanished into the house, leaving me with a strange sense of loss.

There was a postscript to the case some three months later. I was at breakfast while Holmes was still abed, and for one I had the newspapers before he could reduce them to an untidy muddle. The main story was the execution of Jonas Prentiss at Pentonville Gaol, but another item made me sit up in shocked surprise. It was a short announcement of the engagement of Miss Caroline Masters to Major John Cradley, late of the Royal Horse Artillery. I dashed into my companion's room to thrust the paper at him.

"Look at this, Holmes!" I spluttered. "Does she know what she is doing?"

He read the paragraph and looked up at me. "I imagine so. Why not?"

"Good Lord, the fellow's a rake – a member of that disreputable club!"

"My dear Watson," he said, "are you such a paragon of virtue? Will your past stand such close scrutiny?" With that he pulled the bedclothes up to his chin and closed his eyes, leaving me to reflect uncomfortably that his words held no more than the truth.

About the Author
and Curator

Terry Golledge (according to his son Niel Golledge, who provided these stories to this collection) had a life-long love of all things Conan Doyle and in particular Sherlock Holmes. He was born in 1920 in the East End of London. He left school at fourteen, like so many back then. In 1939, he joined the army in the fight against the Germans in World War II. He left the Army in 1945 at the war's end, residing in Hastings. There he met his wife, and his life was a mish-mash of careers, including mining and bus and lorry driving. He owned a couple of book shops, selling them in the 1960's. He then worked for the Post office, (later to become British Telecom, equivalent to AT&T), ending his working life there as a training instructor for his retirement in 1980. His love of Sherlock Holmes was obviously inspired by the fact that his mother worked as a governess to Sir Arthur Conan Doyle when he lived in Windlesham, Crowborough in Sussex. She married Terry's father after leaving Sir Arthur's employment around 1918. Beginning in the mid-1980's, Terry Golledge wrote a number of Holmes stories, and they have never been previously published. A full collection of his Holmes works will be published in the near future. He passed away in 1996.

Niel Golledge was born in 1951 in Winchester, England. He retired some years ago and currently resides in Kent, UK. His last employment for over twenty years was with a large newsprint paper mill, located near his home. He is married to Trisha, a retired nurse, and they have a son and daughter who have carved out careers in mental health and physiotherapy. He is an avid football fan of West Ham and loves to play golf. He is also a keen reader – but that goes without saying.

More Sherlock Holmes in Support of Undershaw
The MX Book of New Sherlock Holmes Stories
Edited by David Marcum
(MX Publishing, 2015-   )

"This is the finest volume of Sherlockian fiction I have ever read, and I have read, literally, thousands." – Philip K. Jones

"Beyond Impressive . . . This is a splendid venture for a great cause!
– Roger Johnson, Editor, *The Sherlock Holmes Journal,*
The Sherlock Holmes Society of London

Part I: 1881-1889
Part II: 1890-1895
Part III: 1896-1929
Part IV: 2016 Annual
Part V: Christmas Adventures
Part VI: 2017 Annual
Part VII: Eliminate the Impossible (1880-1891)
Part VIII – Eliminate the Impossible (1892-1905)
Part IX – 2018 Annual (1879-1895)
Part X – 2018 Annual (1896-1916)
Part XI – Some Untold Cases (1880-1891)
Part XII – Some Untold Cases (1894-1902)
Part XIII – 2019 Annual (1881-1890)
Part XIV – 2019 Annual (1891-1897)
Part XV – 2019 Annual (1898-1917)
Part XVI – Whatever Remains . . . Must be the Truth (1881-1890)
Part XVII – Whatever Remains . . . Must be the Truth (1891-1898)
Part XVIII – Whatever Remains . . . Must be the Truth (1898-1925)
Part XIX – 2020 Annual (1882-1890)
Part XX – 2020 Annual (1891-1897)
Part XXI – 2020 Annual (1898-1923)
Part XXII – Some More Untold Cases (1877-1887)
Part XXIII – Some More Untold Cases (1888-1894)
Part XXIV – Some More Untold Cases (1895-1903)
Part XXV – 2021 Annual (1881-1888)
Part XXVI – 2021 Annual (1889-1897)
Part XXVII – 2021 Annual (1898-1928)
Part XXVIII – More Christmas Adventures (1869-1888)
Part XXIX – More Christmas Adventures (1889-1896)
Part XXX – More Christmas Adventures (1897-1928)
Part XXXI – 2022 Annual Part (1875-1887)
XXXII – 2022 Annual (1888-1895)
Part XXXIII – 2022 Annual (1896-1919)

In Preparation

Part XXXIV (and XXXV and XXXVI???) – "However Improbable . . . ."
. . . and more to come!

The MX Book of New Sherlock Holmes Stories
Edited by David Marcum
(MX Publishing, 2015-   )

Publishers Weekly says:

Part VI: *The traditional pastiche is alive and well . . . .*

Part VII: *Sherlockians eager for faithful-to-the-canon plots and characters will be delighted.*

Part VIII: *The imagination of the contributors in coming up with variations on the volume's theme is matched by their ingenious resolutions.*

Part IX: *The 18 stories . . . will satisfy fans of Conan Doyle's originals. Sherlockians will rejoice that more volumes are on the way.*

Part X: *. . . new Sherlock Holmes adventures of consistently high quality.*

Part XI: *. . . an essential volume for Sherlock Holmes fans.*

Part XII: *. . . continues to amaze with the number of high-quality pastiches.*

Part XIII: *. . . Amazingly, Marcum has found 22 superb pastiches . . . This is more catnip for fans of stories faithful to Conan Doyle's original*

Part XIV: *. . . this standout anthology of 21 short stories written in the spirit of Conan Doyle's originals.*

Part XV: *Stories pitting Sherlock Holmes against seemingly supernatural phenomena highlight Marcum's 15th anthology of superior short pastiches.*

Part XVI: *Marcum has once again done fans of Conan Doyle's originals a service.*

Part XVII: *This is yet another impressive array of new but traditional Holmes stories.*

Part XVIII: *Sherlockians will again be grateful to Marcum and MX for high-quality new Holmes tales.*

Part XIX: *Inventive plots and intriguing explorations of aspects of Dr. Watson's life and beliefs lift the 24 pastiches in Marcum's impressive 19th Sherlock Holmes anthology*

Part XX: *Marcum's reserve of high-quality new Holmes exploits seems endless.*

Part XXI: *This is another must-have for Sherlockians.*

Part XXII: *Marcum's superlative 22nd Sherlock Holmes pastiche anthology features 21 short stories that successfully emulate the spirit of Conan Doyle's originals while expanding on the canon's tantalizing references to mysteries Dr. Watson never got around to chronicling.*

Part XXIII: *Marcum's well of talented authors able to mimic the feel of The Canon seems bottomless.*

Part XXIV: *Marcum's expertise at selecting high-quality pastiches remains impressive.*

Part XXVIII: *All entries adhere to the spirit, language, and characterizations of Conan Doyle's originals, evincing the deep pool of talent Marcum has access to. Against the odds, this series remains strong, hundreds of stories in.*

Part XXXI: *. . . yet another stellar anthology of 21 short pastiches that effectively mimic the originals . . . Marcum's diligent searches for high-quality stories has again paid off for Sherlockians..*

The MX Book of New Sherlock Holmes Stories
Edited by David Marcum
(MX Publishing, 2015-)

MX Publishing

MX Publishing is the world's largest specialist Sherlock Holmes publisher, with over five-hundred titles and over two-hundred authors creating the latest in Sherlock Holmes fiction and non-fiction

The catalogue includes several award winning books, and over two-hundred-and-fifty have been converted into audio.

MX Publishing also has one of the largest communities of Holmes fans on Facebook, with regular contributions from dozens of authors.

www.mxpublishing.com

@mxpublishing on Facebook, Twitter and Instagram

CPSIA information can be obtained
at www.ICGtesting.com
Printed in the USA
BVHW040400090922
646633BV00005B/60/J

9 781804 240779